RIDE A LONE TRAIL AND MASSACRE CREEK

Two Full Length Western Novels

GORDON D. SHIRREFFS

**WOLFPACK
PUBLISHING**
— EST 2013 —

Ride a Lone Trail and Massacre Creek
Print Edition
© Copyright 2021 (As Revised) Gordon D. Shirreffs

Wolfpack Publishing
5130 S. Fort Apache Rd. 215-380
Las Vegas, NV 89148

wolfpackpublishing.com

Paperback ISBN 978-1-63977-068-7

RIDE A LONE TRAIL AND MASSACRE CREEK

RIDE A LONE TRAIL

LUDGÖÖK'S GIRAFFES

CHAPTER ONE

KEN MACKLIN had crossed the Conchas an hour before dusk; and as the sun tipped the western ranges, etching their sawteeth against a brilliant backwash of rose and gold, he turned again in his saddle and studied the low hills behind him. He had a feeling that he was being tailed ever since he had watered his claybank in the Conchas. But then this was Guthook land and Lon Naylor didn't allow anyone, leastways a man of Ken Macklin's stamp, to ride across *his* range without taking an interest in his business.

Ken drew out his sack of makings and rolled a quirly as he rode, glancing now and then to right and then to left. The ground was open and rolling, broken here and there by steep-banked arroyos and draws, hardly visible at a distance except by a faint tracing of shadow on the ground. Many a man or steer had walked clean off the edge of one of those traps before knowing they were there.

As the sun slid down behind the range, leaving behind it just enough light to confuse a man looking to the west, Ken slid from his mount, found a slanted ledge that led down into a deep arroyo, and led the horse down into it. He ground-reined the claybank, then drew his Winchester from the saddle scabbard and levered a .44—40 into the chamber.

He padded up the arroyo, a lean, muscular man, who walked like a lobo and even seemed to act like one as he warily turned his head from one side to the other and sniffed the dusky air suspiciously.

He rounded a clump of fallen earth and rock, then swiftly scaled the arroyo wall behind it, to drop flat at a place where the arroyo lip had collapsed, leaving a shallow fold in the hard ground. He shoved back his dusty black hat so that it fell onto his back to hang by the chin strap. A scrap of brush served to conceal the rounded shape of his bare head, and when he at last settled down and ground out the cigarette butt, there was nothing to show where he lay hidden except for the faint wisp of tobacco smoke that drifted off on the dry, evening wind.

Ken waited patiently. He hadn't really seen anyone following him, but his years in the wild places of the Southwest had honed his natural senses and had developed a sixth sense. Without that sixth sense he would probably have been buried long ago in a lonely and forgotten grave.

Minutes drifted past and it was getting colder. But there was an Apache-like fortitude and insensitiveness to pain and hardship in Ken Macklin. He'd lie there all night if he had to.

The claybank whinnied softly.

Ken eased the Winchester forward, then peered down into the arroyo, along it, and to where the horse stood. Something showed at the lip of the arroyo, and even as he watched, the something moved quickly out of sight. Minutes later he heard a soft dry pattering of gravel and he saw a man slide down into the arroyo and pad along it, pass the claybank, peering from side to side until he came to a spot almost directly beneath Ken.

Ken grinned sardonically. It would be so easy. He wet his lips and edged forward a little "You looking for someone, *hombre?*" he asked clearly. He slid back just as the man whirled and fired at the sound of the voice. The big slug whispered faintly right past the spot where Ken's head had been. The man was good.

Ken lay flat. "You shoot again, *hombre*," he said boldly, "and I'll put a forty-four through your shooting arm!"

There was nothing the man could see, but the sound of that dry, threatening voice was enough to hold him where he was. It was almost uncanny, as though the man he had been following for an hour had suddenly vanished and was speaking from an invisible body.

"Throw down that cutter," said Ken.

The Colt struck the ground. Ken slid back, padded quickly further down the edge of the arroyo, then stepped over the side and slid down on his heels in a rushing of gravel. The man turned his head a little but did not turn all the way around to look at Ken.

"You can turn," said Ken quietly.

The man turned slowly and studied the lean hard face of the man he had been following.

"You shoot fast," said Ken dryly. "Startle you, *hombre?*"

"No. I knew you was up there."

"You're a liar too. Why are you following me?"

"Yore on Lazy J land."

"You mean '*Guthook*' land."

"Same thing. The old man don't like strangers on his land, and he don't like it called 'Guthook' no more."

Ken grinned. "Getting kind of uppity in his old age, isn't he? Tell me, why do you work for him?"

The man spread out his hands, palms upwards. "Yuh know why. Better pay, better food and better quarters. Yuh either work for Lon Naylor around here or work for one of these run-down spreads he's always tryin' to run outa the Conchas country. Me, I like to eat. Besides, Old Lon never tried to take anything from *me.*"

"Almost leaves you in a class by yourself."

"Yuh talk awful nasty, mister. I seen more than one saddle tramp leave here two jumps and a holler ahead of

Lazy J boys on the prod because he didn't have no range manners."

"Guthook range manners you mean."

The man waved a hand. "There yuh go again."

Ken grounded his Winchester. "Pick up your cutter. What's the name?"

The man picked up his Colt and began to wipe it. "Clem Brace."

"They still looking for you in Texas, Brace?"

Brace stopped wiping and looked steadily at Ken as he pointed the Colt blackly at Ken's midriff. "What was that yuh said?" he asked coldly.

Ken's head leaned forward a little. "Put it away. Now you listen to me: I'm just passing through, *hombre*. I'm not a sticky looper and if I was, I'd know better than to try for any of Lon Naylor's steers. I'm not a horsethief. I aim to steer shy of old Lon, but I'll be double-damned if I'm going to ride twenty miles out of the way to get to the Rio Frio country."

It was dark enough now so that Ken could not see Brace's expression. Brace slowly slid his Colt into its sheath. "How come yore heading for Rio Frio?" he asked quietly.

"Business."

The man seemed to be studying Ken and he knew a certain type of man when he saw one. One handgun, in a worn leather sheath, tied down and hung low on the thigh. The stranger had caught him neatly with his drawers down in that gully, and Clem Brace was no tenderfoot. There were two kinds of gunmen in that country. Those that rode with the Guthook *corrida* and those who fought against it, and the Rio Frio was the disputed border line between the warring factions. No man rode across Guthook land unless he had business there, or was a damned fool. This man was neither type.

"Now you just climb out of here, Brace, and go home."

Clem Brace nodded. "Take my advice, *hombre*," he said quietly. "Yuh get on that claybank and head for the closest boundary line of the Lazy J and don't stop until yore ten miles beyond it."

"I'll go my own way to the Rio Frio."

Brace shrugged. He walked to the side of the arroyo. "Yuh might tell me who yuh are," he said.

"Ken Macklin."

Brace turned a little and half-closed his eyes. "Yuh sure take yore guts with yuh, Macklin," he said. "I've heard old Lon talk about yuh now and then."

"Fond memories no doubt."

Brace grinned. "Talks like he has a mouthful of tacks, Macklin. I don't know what yuh did to him, but he sure hates yore guts." Brace shook his head. "Then yuh got the all-fire nerve to ride across *his* range."

"I didn't know he was still having it patrolled."

Brace nodded. "All the time, Macklin, and particularly in the past months since old man Harker was killed along the Rio Frio." There was a long silence. Somewhere out on the darkening plain a coyote howled. "Mebbe that's why yuh come back? Because of Harker's killin'?"

"Mebbe."

Brace nodded. He scrambled up the side of the arroyo and stood there looking down at Ken. "I can make it to the line camp in twenty minutes at a full gallop," he said. "Steve Wascoe is there with half a dozen of the boys. If I tell Steve yore here he won't waste any time saddlin' up to come follow yuh, Macklin."

"I'll agree to that."

Brace looked to the north. "Shortest way to the boundary line is almost due north. Cross Skillet Crick and yore on Double H land. Take my advice: Keep going until yuh reach the hills, even if yuh have to ride all night."

Ken nodded. "*Gracias,* Brace."

"Forget it. I've heard of you, Macklin. Mebbe I got a reason for tellin' yuh to high-tail outa here."

"Such as?"

The man studied Ken. "I don't want to have to kill yuh some day, that's all. *Adios, hombre.*"

Then Brace was gone. Ken walked back to his horse and stood there in the darkness until he heard the rapid tattoo of hoofs on the hard-packed earth, fading away to the south. He led the claybank up onto the open ground and swung up on him. Some of Lon Naylor's hired gunslicks in the old days could almost thread a needle with a forty-four rifle slug, and Ken Macklin had a cold feeling that times hadn't changed much on the Conchas.

The moon was up when Ken Macklin splashed across Skillet Creek. He turned in the saddle and rested a hand on his cantle roll to look back across the creek and Guthook land. The best land in that part of New Mexico. Lon Naylor had figured that angle years ago. He had taken over the Conchas bottoms, then the Rio Frio eastern bottoms, and all the land in between, by fair means or foul; but in that respect he wasn't much different than some of his neighbors. Only Lon Naylor was just a little tougher and a little meaner.

A cold wind swept across the rolling Guthook land. Ken shivered. It had been a long day in the saddle. He had hardly stopped since he had left the Cimarron several days before. He turned and looked toward the distant hills now silvered by the moon. Now he was on Double H land—the spread of Jordan Harker—and the Lazy J *vaqueros* would probably stay on their own side of the creek as long as Ken didn't look for trouble. That was easy enough. Ken Macklin had come back for his inheritance after receiving a letter from his foster-brother, Wes Harker, who had taken over the Double H after the death of Jordan Harker. Ken would get his share and then drift on. He wanted no part of the Double H and the bad blood between it and the Lazy J.

He slid from his saddle and led the claybank to a stand of timber set in between a V-shaped ridge. There was a place where trees had fallen to form a sort of rude shelter close against a vertical rock face. Ken unsaddled and picketed the horse, then made his simple camp by hanging his worn tarp over an extending branch of one of the fallen trees not far from the rock face. A few minutes work made a slab rock reflector behind the fire he kindled. Heat would be reflected into the tarp shelter and warm the rock face behind it.

It had been three years since he had been along the Conchas. Jordan Harker had been failing even then, but he had talked a hotheaded, twenty-two-year-old named Kenneth Macklin into pulling foot for other parts. Jordan Harker was as tough a fighter as Lon Naylor, but not as unscrupulous. He didn't have the gunslinging *corrida* that Lon Naylor had either, but he had his natural son Wesley and his foster son Ken Macklin, backed by a few tough old timers who hated Lon Naylor's guts as much as they admired Jordan Harker's courage in standing up against the Lazy J *corrida*.

Ken could still remember the thoughtful look in Jordan Harker's eyes when he had called in Ken and Wes after the gunfight on the main street of Conchas Corners where the two young men had outfaced and outfought five Guthook men. Two of the five had died with their boots on, one had been wounded and another crippled for life by the loss of part of his right arm. One of the two of the sons he loved would have to leave. Separately they were all right. Together they were like fire and tinder, and they were both better than average with guns and fists. Jordan Harker had left it up to them. Wes had wanted to leave, but Ken was the foster son, the one of strange blood, and he had insisted upon leaving.

Now Jordan Harker was dead. A rifle bullet had smashed into the back of his head one moonlit summer night on the banks of the little river he had loved.

Ken made up his bed beneath the tarp. There was a cold bite in the late fall air. It would probably be the last night he would spend in the open for some time. When he and Wes got together once more it wouldn't be easy to leave the big rambling Double H ranch house on the Rio Frio.

He dragged squaw wood by the arm load from the trees and piled it near the fire. Then he walked toward the swift-running creek and rolled a cigarette while he looked across Lazy J land.

If Clem Brace had ridden to the line camp and had alerted Steve Wascoe, the little hardcase foreman might just take it into his one-track mind to ride north toward Skillet Creek to see what Ken Macklin was about. But Lon Naylor had kept his boys under a tighter rein since the street fight in Conchas Corners. Ken had heard that he no longer sent his long riders out after men who had crossed his will. More than once his hired guns had followed men clear to Mexico, or east to the Panhandle, north to Wyoming or west to Arizona Territory to get payment in blood. But that had been in the old days when Guthook guns had been kept as hot as Lon Naylor's blood. Ken would be safe enough on Double H land, unless he went looking for trouble, which wasn't likely. Ken Macklin had cooled down quite a bit himself in the past three years.

He walked back to his shelter and pulled off his boots and denim jacket, then unbuckled his gunbelt and hung it over a stub branch within easy reach. He crawled into the bedroll and rolled another cigarette, resting easily on one elbow as he smoked, watching the dancing figures in the flames of his fire; there was a vague face in the flames. It had been three years since he had seen Estelle Naylor in the flesh. But in those long years he had seen her face in camp-fires from the Rio Grande north to the Platte.

It had always puzzled him as to how an old raccoon like Lon Naylor had ever sired a girl like Estelle. But then people of the Conchas country still talked of the beauty of the first wife of Lon Naylor; the one who had walked out on him, leaving him with a baby girl and a heartful of bitter memories.

Ken ground out his smoke and lay back to rest his head

on his saddle. Just being within miles of Estelle Naylor was enough to make him restless. He'd make no attempt to see her. There was no need to open old wounds. After all, the fight in the streets of Conchas Corners had been about Estelle Naylor. Two good men had died and one had been crippled because of that fight. That was enough blood for any man.

CHAPTER TWO

"HE'S ALONE," the voice said quietly. "Clem was right."

Ken opened his eyes. Three men stood beside the fire, looking down on Ken, but he could not see their faces beneath the wide brimmed hats and the turned-up collars of their sheepskin coats.

"Wake him," a cold, thin voice said. It came from the shortest of the three men. There was something familiar about that voice.

"I'm awake," said Ken quietly.

"Get up then," said the man closest to Ken. "Keep away from that hogleg hangin' there."

Ken nodded. He hadn't had any intention of reaching for his Colt. He wormed out of the warm covers, shivering in the cold blast of the night wind. The moon was on the wane, casting sharply etched shadows of the trees on the bare earth. He pulled on his boots and reached for his jacket.

"Wait," said a cold voice.

Ken turned a little. "I haven't got a hide-out gun," he said.

"Let it alone, Macklin."

Ken shrugged. He looked from one man to the other;

their faces were indistinguishable. Yet it seemed to him that he knew one of them. The shortest of them—a small, solid chunk of a man. But there was something odd about him.

The tallest man rubbed his jaws. "What are yuh doin' here, Macklin?"

"Camping," said Ken dryly.

"We can see that! But what are yuh doin' on Lazy J land?"

Ken glanced at him. "This is Double H land," he said. "I made sure I crossed Skillet Crick before I camped."

"That so? Yuh *sure* that's Skillet Crick?"

"You know damned well it is, *hombre.*"

The three men glanced at each other. "Throw some wood on that fire," the short man said.

The embers flared up a little as the wood was dumped atop them, and in a short time the fire began to lick along the dry twigs and thinner branches.

Ken touched his dry lips with the tip of his tongue. He lowered his gaze to the right arm of the shortest man, and an icy feeling came over him as he saw that the man lacked the lower part of his right arm. The sleeve had been cut short to just below the elbow. "Jim Dana," said Ken.

Jim Dana nodded. He raised the abbreviated arm. "Yuh remember me, and *this* then?"

"I don't like to maim a man, Dana."

The cripple came a little closer to Ken. "I remember yuh too damned well, Macklin. But yuh don't have to worry about maiming me. I do all right with this stub, don't I, boys?"

The two heads bobbed up and down.

The fire crackled noisily and in the growing light of it Ken saw for the first time that night the hard green eyes of Jim Dana and the icy hell that was in them.

"Yuh was told to stay off Lazy J land some years ago, Macklin," said Dana.

"I'm not on it now, Dana. That's Skillet Crick back there and you know it well enough."

Dana turned. "Slim, that Skillet Crick back there?"

"Nope."

"Charley?"

"Nope, Jim."

"They're lying and so are you, Dana," said Ken.

Dana moved closer and the smell of his liquor breath sickened Ken. "Yuh callin' me a liar, Macklin?" demanded the cripple.

Ken looked over Dana's shoulder. Both Charley and Slim wore their gunbelts outside of their coats, and he knew well enough he'd never have a chance if he made a break. They'd kill him and drag his body across the creek, then say he had trespassed or had started trouble. It wouldn't be the first time a man had died that way in the Conchas country.

"Well?" said Dana coldly.

"That isn't any other creek but Skillet," said Ken.

Jim Dana moved quickly. His left fist sank into Ken's belly just above the waistband of his Levi's, and as his head involuntarily snapped down, Jim Dana brought up the thick stub of his right arm and threw a shoulder forward with all his weight behind it. The hard stub caught Ken flush in the middle of the forehead like a battering ram and drove him back, sprawling across his bed. A boot hooked hard into his ribs on the right side, and his breath rushed out of him. He rolled over, came up like a released spring and reached for his hanging gunbelt. The cripple was too fast for him, and the stub struck at the back of Ken's neck, driving him forward against a tree trunk with stunning force. He half turned to meet a left in the belly for the second time. Then the stub caught him on the mouth and he felt a tooth crack as his lips were smashed back against them, and blood filled his mouth.

He staggered back and fell across the fire, yelling in agony as the flames seared through his thin Levi's. He ran into Slim who turned and shoved him toward Jim Dana. Dana waited with a terrible, cold grin on his broad face. But there was enough strength and speed left in Ken to raise a knee into Jim's belly and swing a hard jolting right and left into the broad face as it came down as Ken's head had come down. Dana cursed and fell heavily. Ken turned and lowered head and shoulders to charge Slim, hitting him below the rib cage and smashing him back against Charley who fell awkwardly over a log.

Ken staggered sideways, spewing bloody froth from his battered mouth, in time to kick Jim Dana in the throat as he tried to get up. Then Ken dived for his gunbelt, freed his Colt and cocked it, swinging from the waist to get Jim Dana lined up for a killing chest shot before he turned loose on the two cursing Lazy J men who were trying to get to their feet.

A gun cracked flatly from the edge of the little clearing. Ken lowered his Colt and looked toward three more men standing there wreathed in thin gun smoke.

"That's enough, Macklin," a familiar voice said. "Drop that gun."

"You go to hell, Wascoe," snarled Ken bloodily.

There was a long silence, broken only by the harsh breathing of the three men who had roused Ken from his sleep as they staggered to their feet and stared coldly from Ken to Steve Wascoe and back again.

"I said: Put up that gun, Macklin. You haven't got a chance."

"I'll take that chance before I let these bastards beat me half to death, Wascoe."

Steve Wascoe walked forward, a lithe little gamecock of a man dressed all in black leather, even to the tight-fitting gloves on his slender hands. The moonlight made his face seem as pale as death. "Jim, Slim, Charley," he said quietly, "get out of here. Cross the crick and keep agoing."

"But, Steve," said Jim Dana, "he . . ." His voice died away as he saw the look on Wascoe's thin face. He wiped the blood from his face and looked at Ken with reptilian ferocity. Then the cripple walked past Wascoe and the two men with him, followed by Slim and Charley.

"Put up that gun, Macklin," said Wascoe.

"Not on your life."

"You're safe enough ... *now.*"

Clem Brace stood behind Wascoe. He raised his head and caught Ken's eye. He nodded.

"Don't try me, Macklin," said the little foreman.

The cold wind whispered through the trees and it seemed to whisper of fast death amongst the gaunt cottonwoods, for there was hardly a faster gun in New Mexico than Steve Wascoe.

"Macklin?" said Wascoe softly. His gloved hands opened and closed. "This is your last chance."

Clem Brace nodded again, then swiftly crossed his heart.

Ken lowered the gun and let down the hammer. He dropped the Colt onto his bedding.

"That's better," said Wascoe.

"You can shoot now," said Ken. "What chance have I got?"

Steve Wascoe walked forward. "Clem, make some coffee, courtesy of Mister Macklin here."

The third man piled more wood on the fire and his dark eyes studied Ken as he did so. He was a Mex. He looked almost familiar to Ken, but then he had known a lot of men in the Conchas country before taking the long trail out of there.

Ken shrugged into his denim jacket.

"Gettin' cold," said Clem Brace. "Geese flying south. Winter comin' on."

Steve Wascoe nodded. "Time for the birds to head south.

Birds like you, Macklin. What are you doing back here in the Conchas country?"

"Visiting," said Ken dryly. He touched his smashed mouth.

"Jim sure can use that damned stub of his," said Clem Brace. "Better'n most men can use a fist."

"Someday I'll ram it down his damned throat," said Ken.

"Maybe," said Wascoe. He squatted by the fire and rubbed his gloved hands together. "You shouldn't have riled him, Macklin."

"He came up on me while I was asleep. I didn't rile him, Wascoe."

The man's incredibly pale-blue eyes fixed themselves on Ken's gray ones. "No, not tonight you didn't rile him, Macklin. You did that three years ago when you blew off his lower right arm."

"He had a gun in his hand, Wascoe. That's something *you* might understand. You've done a little killing and maiming yourself as I recall."

The fire crackled. Clem Brace placed the coffee pot in the embers of the fire and glanced warningly at Ken.

"You crossed Lazy J land this afternoon," said Wascoe quietly, almost as though he had not heard Ken's last remarks. "You should have known better than that."

"I was heading for the Rio Frio."

"You still know better. At least *you* should have known better, Clem here could have put a rifle slug through you half a dozen times."

Ken couldn't help but grin. "I could have done the same for Clem."

The blue eyes were icy. "You kill a Lazy J man on his land and you die on it, Macklin."

"The old 'Guthook law', eh, Wascoe?"

"Just why *did* you come back, Macklin?" he asked.

"Visiting."

"Nothing to do with the death of Old Man Harker, eh, Macklin?"

The coffee was bubbling, filling the cold air with its pleasant and pungent aroma. Clem Brace filled cups and passed them out.

Ken eyed the little gunfighter. "In a way," he said.

"Revenge?"

"No." Ken sipped at the coffee. "Revenge for what, Wascoe? No one knows who killed the old man."

"That's so."

Their eyes met across the coffee cups. There was a challenge in Ken's but nothing other than a cold, blue facade in Wascoe's eyes.

Steve Wascoe lowered his cup and placed his cigarette between his thin lips. "Maybe the old man left you something?" he asked.

Ken nodded. "Memories, Wascoe. Memories of a big, bluff man who took in a scared, starving kid and raised him as though he was his own son, beside his own flesh and blood. He never made any difference between us, Wascoe. We were his boys and that's all that mattered to him."

"Still, he run you out of this country."

"No, I went willingly. It was Wes or me. Wes was his blood."

Wascoe smiled a little "Some people say he should of sent Wes away."

"What do you mean by that?"

The foreman emptied his cup and stood up. "You'll find out soon enough."

Ken stood up and flipped his cigarette butt into the fire.

There was no use in questioning Steve Wascoe. He had talked more in the past few minutes than he usually did in a day's time.

The foreman rubbed his gloved hands together. "Look, Macklin, I've got nothing against you, but I work for Lon Naylor. What he says goes. He tells me you're making trouble, and I come looking for you to make trouble for you. That clear?"

"Clear enough. You ever get any thoughts of your *own*, Wascoe? Or does Lon Naylor still think for you and tell you what to do?"

A nerve twitched in the right-hand corner of Wascoe's thin mouth. "I'll pass that remark," he said tonelessly. "Macklin, you get on to the Double H tomorrow and you take care of your business there. Stay as long as you like, but don't come looking for trouble, because you'll get a bellyful of it. More than you can handle."

The foreman turned on a heel and walked off. Then he stopped, just at the edge of the flickering pool of firelight. "I'm sorry about the beating you got, Macklin. That was none of my doing."

Ken nodded.

"You won't be bothered for the rest of the night."

"Gracias," said Ken dryly.

Wascoe was silent for a moment. "It's been three years since you saw Wes Harker?"

"Yes."

"What do you think of his wife, Macklin?"

Ken stared. "I didn't know he was married."

CHAPTER THREE

K EN MACKLIN topped the ridge just as the false dawn lightened the eastern sky. There had been no further use in trying to sleep after the crowded events of the night. Ken had saddled up, packed his gear, then had led the tired claybank on through the cold night.

The Rio Frio was a dull pewter trace winding along the bottom lands through a fringe of great cottonwoods and lacy willows. Ken stopped below the crest of the ridge to roll a cigarette and to view the Rio Frio Valley. A great deal of blood had been shed for that peaceful looking trough in the vast earth. The Rio Frio had seemed to draw killing and fighting as a beautiful, but unscrupulous woman does. Ken wondered idly if the valley was worth it. Yet it had a beauty of its own, and the air always seemed fresh and scented with the dry, faintly medicinal odor that he had grown to like in past years.

The Valley had a dark history of violence and blood. The Indians had fought over it in the days before the arrival of the rapacious Spaniards, who in turn had fought with each other over it until the arrival of the Americans after the Mexican War. But the Americans still fought, and their range vendettas flared up and died away with sporadic regularity, leaving bad blood and hatred.

Ken led the claybank down the ridge as the first rays of the sun tipped the eastern hills. The west and northern sides of the great curve of the Rio Frio were Double H land, a legacy given to Dolores Castaneda, who had married the hard-driving Texas Jordan Harker, and had given birth to five children for him. Only three of them had survived: Wesley, now the eldest, who had his father's reddish hair and his mother's dark eyes; Miriam, who had her mother's dark hair and lovely skin, and her father's blue eyes; and little Job Harker, a mixture of his mother's soft, sensitive nature and an almost exact copy of his father's features and color.

Dolores' half-sister Luz had married tough old Lon Naylor, who had loved her with a hard, possessive passion, as he did with everything that was Lon Naylor's goods or chattels. Luz had left Lon Naylor shortly after the birth of her one child, a lovely little thing christened Estelle, and she had left Lon Naylor three things: The baby girl, a warbag of hatred and bitter memories for herself, and a slightly cloudy deed to the Rio Frio Valley, as opposed to the deed that Dolores Castaneda had brought to Jordan Harker as her dowry. The two Castaneda sisters had loved each other well, but they had sowed hate behind them. The taste was that of blood in the mouths of Lon Naylor and Jordan Harker, and the men who were related to them and who worked for them. That was the way of those days.

The sun warmed his back as he left the water course and rode the claybank up another ridge, only to halt it there and to look down upon the ranch buildings of the Double H. They had been the only real home Ken Macklin had ever known. He had lived there since the age of two months after being taken in by Jordan Harker who had raised Ken Macklin as his son. All they knew about Ken was that his name was Macklin, for it had been carelessly stitched on the thick serape in which he had been wrapped when Jordan Harker had found him on the banks of the

Rio Frio. The name Kenneth had been given him by Jordan Harker in memory of a younger brother who had died at Shiloh.

"Kenneth Macklin," mused Ken as he rested an elbow on his saddlehorn and eyed the ranch buildings. "I wonder who I *really* am?"

The sun was filling the wide valley of the Rio Frio with its light and warmth. The big windmill behind the ranch buildings turned a little and began to whir steadily in the freshening breeze. A cock crowed clearly.

Ken grinned, wincing as he felt his stiffening cuts draw and pull. The cold journey that night had done little to help his aches and pains. The only consolation he had was that Jim Dana and his two partners wouldn't be feeling too much better.

As he rode down the ridge he thought again of Steve Wascoe. The little banty hadn't been frightened by the fact that Ken had been holding a cocked six-gun in his hand while Steve's six-gun had still been sheathed at his side. Was Steve Wascoe really *that* fast, thought Ken. He knew of Ken. That fight in the streets of Conchas Corners had been written into a local ballad that even today was creeping slowly over the Southwest, while most of the participants were still alive. The gunplay had been so fast and furious that Ken had never really been clear about the sequence after the last fighting words had been spat out between clenched teeth, leaving no alternative but the crackling, smoking talk of the guns.

Two men had died, one had been wounded, and one crippled for life in that fight, and all of them Guthook men, while the two Double H men, hardly more than boys, had not been scratched. Local credit had been that Wes Harker had been responsible for the wounding of Ben Powell, while Ken Macklin had dropped both of the men who had been killed and had almost shot off Jim Dana's right forearm. Fact was that Wes had been drinking and maybe he hadn't been so steady, for at the marks he could easily outshoot Ken

Macklin with the handgun, although he could never match Ken with the long gun.

That was the main reason, other than the fact that he was not really the son of Jordan Harker, for Ken leaving the Conchas country. He himself had been a little sick after the gunfight and had wanted to get out of that country for a long, long breath of fresh air.

He slid from the claybank and led it toward the huge stable that Jordan Harker had built and finished even before he had built his permanent house. The stable was empty except for horses, though there were many empty stalls. Jordan Harker had been more of a horse breeder than a cattleman. Ken had never seen so few horses in the stable.

He took care of the claybank and then took his warbag, Winchester and cantle roll with him as he left the stable. The place was extraordinarily quiet but a thread of smoke rose from the kitchen chimney to be instantly raveled out by the wind. Ken placed his gear and rifle on the rear porch and slapped the dust from his trail clothing with his hat. He opened the kitchen door and peered into the kitchen. "Hello, Tacos," he said to the busy cook.

The lean cook turned around and stared. "For the love of God!" he said. "Ken! Ken Macklin!" Tacos tugged at the ends of his handlebar mustache and blinked his watery blue eyes. "I heard you was due in, Ken, but we didn't expect you so soon."

Ken gripped the older man's hand. "I just kept riding, Tacos. Wasn't much pleasure sleeping out nights with the cold weather coming on."

"Yeh. I know what you mean."

"Still cooking I see, Tacos. How many years is it now?"

"Before you was born, son. But I ain't cooking in this kitchen no more."

"How so?"

Tacos looked away. "I was just making up the fire in here before I got my own fires started in the cookhouse."

Ken stared at him. Tacos Firmin had been cook at the

Double H for at least seven or eight years, after a bad fall from a horse had partially crippled him and made him a little better than useless on the range.

Tacos waved a hand. "Times has changed here abouts, Ken. Got a woman cook here now. Name of Kate. Comes from Santy Fee. A good cook and a fine woman. It was Miss Harker's idea, not Mister Harker's. Wes liked my cooking well enough. He oughta! He was practically raised on it."

"Times have changed," said Ken. "Wes getting married. He always played the field. Always said no woman was smart enough to rope him."

Tacos closed the firebox door and straightened up to wipe the sweat from his face. "Yeh," he said quietly. "Well he went and done it."

"Local girl?"

Tacos stopped wiping his lean face and then eyed Ken closely. "Yeh, sort of . . . why?"

"Just wondered who she was."

"Yeh. Well, I got work to do. Find time to see me later, Ken, for a talk. We kin play the coffee pot awhile. I want to hear about your good and bad times these past three years." Then the cook was gone.

Ken shrugged. He walked into the hallway that led to the front of the house and the great living room Jordan Harker had loved so well. The house was very quiet. He took off his hat as he entered the living room. A fire crackled on the great hearth. Ken looked about in wonderment. The room had been changed more than he had even anticipated. Gone were the heads and hides of game animals, the rifles and shotguns that had rested on deerhorn pegs driven into the thick logs that formed the walls of the house. Gone too were the heavy, leather covered chairs and the thick-topped, rough hewn tables, with a deep seated patina, and the thick, almost indestructible Navajo rugs that had covered the polished, puncheon floor, formed of planking of irregular widths, pegged and seated tightly together with a beauty of its own.

The walls had been plastered and covered with wallpaper of subdued pattern. The furniture was of the latest, spindly-legged, overstuffed style, hardly seeming sturdy enough to support the weight of a tired ranch owner when he dropped into it. The floor had been covered with carpeting from wall to wall. The great table placed in the center was covered with a fine cloth and held a thick stemmed candelabra, almost like some of those Ken had seen in churches in Mexico, and just as expensive.

The walls had been hung with paintings and etchings. The room seemed more like the sitting room in a first-class hotel than the living room of a rancher in the Conchas country. A big wing chair had been placed in front of the fireplace, and Ken noted the feet that protruded toward the blaze; trousers of fine broadcloth and boots of the finest Mexican carved leather, polished to a deep gloss. Ken looked down at his own dusty and cracked boots and then at the fine carpeting.

He walked over to the chair and peered around the side of it to see a tousled redhead bent low. The right hand of the man held an empty glass. Beyond the chair was a small table with an almost empty bottle on it, placed on a silvery tray. Ken bent lower. "Wes," he said.

Wes Harker did not move.

Ken placed a hand on his foster brother's shoulder. "Wes," he said a little louder.

Wes Harker raised his head and looked at Ken with half-closed eyes. "Tacos?" he said thickly.

"No, Wes. It's me! Ken Macklin."

Wes Harker wet his lips and tried to focus his eyes. "Oh, Ken," he said. He shook his head. "Early, aren't you?" He straightened up. "You'll stay for dinner, eh, Wes?"

Ken straightened up. He took the empty glass from Wes' hand, noting that some of the liquor had dribbled from it onto the fine broadcloth trousers and thence to the carpeting. Mrs. Harker, whoever she was, wouldn't care much for that.

Wes grinned weakly. "You look like you just got off a damned ol' cattle car, Ken. Well, we're of a size. You go ask Katie to show you my wardrobe. Wear anything you like except my wedding suit." He laughed. "I'm going to have *that* stuffed and placed in a glass case for the museum at Santa Fe."

Ken walked around the back of the chair and picked up the bottle. He sniffed at it. Brandy, and damned good stuff too. He raised it and drank down a good slug. He wiped his mouth and felt the liquor warm his gullet all the way down. He had needed a drink or two like that the night before. He placed the bottle on the table and looked around. There was a polished wood liquor cabinet with the doors hung open. He eyed the bottles ranked in it, row after row. Nothing but the best. Cognac brandy, liqueurs, Scotch, the whole being of the very finest. Few fine bars in the Southwest could boast of such a varied and exquisite selection. Time was when Double H men drank beer, bourbon or rye, with the emphasis on the last.

Wes had asked him to stay for dinner, and Ken knew that his foster brother had probably spent the whole evening, before last night's dinner, and after that sitting and drinking in a little vague world of his own.

Ken walked over to the closest window and pulled back the heavy drapes letting the good sunlight pour into the room.

Wes peered at him. "Daylight?" he asked thickly.

Ken heard someone rattling around in the kitchen and he suddenly realized he was half starved. "I'll get something to eat from the cook, Wes," he said.

Wes stood up and held onto the back of the chair. Ken saw the slight paunch of the man who had always been lean as a lobo. Wes looked almost thirty and he had never been one to show his age in the old days. He had always looked years younger than he really was. They had called him the "Rio Frio Kid" back then and Wes had liked it.

"You'd better wait," said Wes quietly. "Mrs. Harker will

want to dine with us. You won't get anything from Katie, Ken, until you set at the table and get served. That's the way it is around here."

"You never told me you were married, Wes."

The bloodshot, dark eyes flicked up. "I didn't think it mattered much, Ken."

"You know well enough that it would matter."

Wes Harker hesitated. "Well, this was a little different. After all, you left and I stayed. But I wanted to go. It might have been you as well as me. I won, or lost, as the case may be." Wes laughed dryly.

"What are you trying to tell me, Wes?"

A soft voice broke in on them. "He's trying to get up enough courage to tell you that he married me, Ken."

Ken looked up quickly toward the door to the hallway. She was standing there, dressed in a crisp frock, like a picture from a fashion magazine. Her thick light-brown hair piled atop her shapely head, and her lovely dark eyes studying Ken. Something seemed to stab deep into his heart. Christ, but she was lovelier than ever! His firelight pictures of her had never really done her justice.

"Aren't you going to say hello to me, Ken?" she said with a smile. She held out a slim hand to him.

"Hello, Estelle," he said. He walked to her and took her hand, and the loveliness of her, the warmth, the very scent of this beautiful young woman he had loved ever since he could remember seemed to hit him like a maul.

"You ride early, Ken," she said. She eyed his battered mouth. "Did you have a fall?"

He touched his mouth. "Not exactly."

She raised a hand and tenderly touched the mashed and bruised lips. "Let me take care of that now," she said solicitously.

"*Gracias,* Estelle."

Wes Harker bowed a little. "The Florence Nightingale of the Conchas country," he said dryly.

Ken turned quickly with a hard look in his eyes. The man was carrying a tank full of brandy.

"Forget it, Ken," she said softly.

She led the way into another room he did not recognize. Years ago there had been a bathtub in it, filled with odds and ends. It had been a cold and dark room, never used except as a catchall. Now it was a picture of modern plumbing in the best taste. "Like it?" she said over her shoulder.

He grinned. "The only bathtub we ever used on the Double H was the horse trough or the Rio Frio."

She nodded. "You can see how I've changed things here, Ken."

"Yes, in more ways than one."

She turned quickly. "You mean him?"

"Maybe."

"I couldn't help that, Ken."

"Are you sure, Estelle?"

She looked away. "He never was very strong."

"And you like men strong, don't you?"

She busied herself with her medicines.

"Well, Estelle?"

She held her soft lower lip between her even white teeth. "You were gone a long time, Ken."

"Wes knew where I was most of the time."

"What did you expect me to do? Come looking for you?"

"No, but one word would have brought me back."

"You forget my father."

He couldn't help but laugh. "*Him?* Who can forget 'Guthook' Naylor, the Terror of the Conchas? Besides, if you *had* sent word to me, I would have ridden up to 'Guthook' castle and taken his treasure from it, and to hell with him!" He looked down at her as she reached up to wash the crusted blood from his mouth. "You knew that, Estelle. Admit it!"

"You talk too much," she said.

"It's the truth."

She dabbed hard at the wound and he winced. For just a fleeting instant he saw the hard, cruel look in her lovely eyes, like a beast lurking behind a bank of lovely flowers. There had always been a streak of natural meanness in her, the probable legacy of her hard-bitten father.

When she had finished she turned to look up at him, with her hands behind her, holding on to the edge of the commode, and the look in her eyes was enough to make Ken Macklin forget that she was his brother's wife. All the hungry longing of three year's time swept over him. Then he looked away.

"Ken?" she asked.

He knew what she wanted. All *he* wanted to do was to get out of that room and away from her.

"Ken!"

He turned toward the door, but he hadn't reckoned on the daughter of Lon Naylor. She gripped his left arm and turned him toward her, then slid her left arm around his neck and pulled his head down so that his crushed lips met hers. He winced at the savage pain of it and drank in the pleasure of_ it, until at last she released her hold and stepped back. "You're bleeding again," she said matter-of-factly. There was blood on her lips too. She dabbled at them with a soft cloth, then used the same cloth to wipe his lips and all the while she held his eyes with her damnably lovely ones, and he wished to God he had stayed out of the Conchas country forever.

CHAPTER FOUR

TACOS FIRMIN refilled the empty coffee cups and waved a hand. "So you can see how it is now, Ken. This ain't no ranch anymore. The land is still here and some of the cattle and horses, but it ain't a working proposition. Jordan Harker usta have twenty, thirty men riding for him in the old days. Now, countin' me, an old crock, we got about ten men, and there ain't one of them left from the old Double H *corrida*."

Ken stood at the window of the cook house looking toward the big ranch house. It had been an unusual breakfast for Ken Macklin, and he had never seen one like it before on the Double H. Napery and silver, covered dishes, and a woman to wait on table, while Wes Harker dozed at his place and toyed with his food. Estelle Harker had chatted on and on about her plans for the Double H, and for a town house. She could back up her play too, for Lon Naylor had always given nothing but the very best to the only child he had.

Tacos spat into the wood box beside the stove. "Seems like the place started goin' to hell after Jordan was killed. Wes was hitting the bottle. Miriam, she tried to stop him, but they had a big fuss, and it just got worse. So Miriam pulled out, taking Jobie with her, and they went to live in town whilst Jobie finished school." Tacos laughed dryly. "Nothing could keep that little buggar in school, not even Miriam."

"How is she, Tacos?"

Tacos looked up. "The only damned thing worth anything on the Double H, Ken."

"And Jobie?"

Taco spat. "He's a little sonofabitch, he is. You think you and Wes were wild? Hellsfire, that boy is ringy all the time. Fancies himself another 'Billy the Kid' or something. Ain't it loco how a kid will ape a killer like that?"

Ken turned. "He was always such a quiet little kid."

"Well, he's quiet all right. Damned dangerous quiet, that's what he is."

"Carries a gun then?"

Tacos nodded. "Two, Ken. I told him once a man must be a pretty damned lousy shot with one gun to have to carry two of 'em: It didn't go over very well."

"Billy the Kid only carried one."

Tacos shrugged. "Jobie Harker carries two."

"Is he any good with them?"

Tacos looked up. "Better than Wes. Maybe better than you. I know one thing though."

"Yes?"

The blue eyes were troubled. "He ain't better than Steve Wascoe."

Ken emptied his cup and held it out to Tacos. "Who is around here," he said.

"I often wondered, Ken."

"What do you mean?"

Tacos filled the cup and then eyed Ken. "Steve Wascoe did a lot of thinking after that fight you and Wes had with the Guthook boys in Conchas Corners. I often think that was why Jordan sent you away instead of Wes."

"Meaning?"

Tacos tugged at his dragoon mustache. "There would have to be a showdown some day, Ken, and it would have been between you and Wascoe. I wouldn't have taken any bets on it."

"Wes was faster than me, Tacos, and more accurate."

"That ain't the way it was that day at Conchas Corners."

"Wes had been drinking, Tacos."

Tacos nodded. "Drunk or sober it wouldn't have made any difference. Wes *is* faster and a better shot, but Wes can't stand up and look death in the eye and still shoot to kill like you can, Ken."

"Crap!"

"No, I'm right."

Ken sat down and sipped at his coffee. "What about the old man, Tacos?"

"Bullet in the back of the head. Softnosed .44-40 slug. Could have been a rifle or pistol bullet. So happens the sheriff said it was a rifle. They found a place in the brush where a man had waited for Jordan. There was knee and elbow marks in the soft ground and a dozen cigarette butts stuck in a row. He'd been waitin' there quite awhile. Jordan always rode that way. The killer knew that."

"You have any idea who did it?"

Tacos looked away. "I got a good job here. I like it. Comes a time when I'll have to leave."

"Wes wouldn't fire you, Tacos."

"It ain't Wes firing me that bothers me, Ken. If I shot off my mouth there might be someone else looking for me. I'd rather keep my mouth shut."

"Guthook man do it, Tacos?"

"*Quien sabe?*"

"As much as I hate Lon Naylor, I don't think he'd be the type to have a man dry gulched."

"You never know, Ken, you never know."

Ken nodded. He walked to the door. "I almost wish I had stayed away, Tacos."

"You got money comin', Ken. The old man didn't forget you. In some ways I always thought you was his favorite."

"Yeh. I can remember a few times when he wanted to

take a wagon tongue to my britches. We sure used to go around and around."

"Yeh, but you both liked it because you respected each other."

Ken opened the door and looked down the long slope to the tree-bordered river. "I still wish I had stayed away," he said thoughtfully.

"No," said Tacos. "You *had* to come back, Ken. They's some things a man just has to do. These things is worked out by a higher power than man, like the preacher says. You *had* to come back, Ken Macklin. It's writ in the book." Ken turned. "For better or for worse, eh, Tacos?" "Yep, for better or for worse." "I wonder which it will be?" *"Quien sabe?"*

Ken closed the door behind him and walked toward the house. It was then that he saw the two riders top the ridge and ride swiftly down the slope. He half closed his eyes. There was no mistaking her. She rode better than most men, and yet in a wholly feminine way. Her dark hair had been tied in a knot at the back of her neck and her hat hung from the chin strap. She wore a dark split riding skirt and a leather jacket. Miriam Harker. How old was she now? Eighteen, nineteen? With a start he suddenly remembered that she must be at least twenty-two years of age.

Ken waved a hand and walked toward the gate to open it. The boy rode closely beside his sister. Jobie Harker had grown tall and slim and he rode much like she did. They had both been born to the saddle. The boy was all in black, from boots to hat, and the morning sun shone on the well-oiled leather.

"Hello, Ken," she called out. "We heard that you had come home at last!"

"Hello, Miriam! Jobie!"

The boy waved a gloved hand. They rode through the gateway and he closed it behind them, then looked up at her. He was a little startled. She had changed, although the hair was still dark and lustrous as it had always been, and the lovely blue eyes, with the soft violet tinge to them, had a way of looking right through a man to weigh his hidden values.

If she had changed, her younger brother had changed still more. Jobie Harker slid from the saddle and gave his sister a hand. He was as tall as Ken but lacked the heavy muscles and the broad shoulders of Ken and Wes. He was slender as a rapier with the lithe quality of thin, well-tempered steel that distinguishes such a weapon. His face was thin, with almost a feminine quality to it, belied by the hairline of his Mexican dandy mustache. He stripped off a black glove and held out a slender hand to Ken. Somehow there was something about the boy that reminded Ken of someone. There was Harker in him and Castaneda too, but something else had moved in like a familiar spirit—an alien presence that might take over and drive the boy through life for bad rather than for good.

"Good to see you, Ken," said Jobie. His voice was flat and clipped, emotionless, and the eyes were hard and steady.

Then Ken knew. He was looking at a carbon copy of Steve Wascoe and the feeling was not good.

Miriam tilted her head to one side. "You've leaned out a good deal, Ken."

"I missed Tacos' good cooking, Miriam."

She glanced toward the house. "He doesn't cook for the people in the house," she said.

"I know."

Jobie slapped his glove against the side of his low slung Colt, mate to the other that also hung low and tied down from the belt. "You know about Estelle then?" he asked.

Ken nodded.

"She's a good wife to Wes," said the boy quietly.

Ken glanced quickly at him and met the cold challenge in the dark flat eyes. "Yes, I think so, Jobie."

"She's done a lot for the house."

"Yes."

"Don't you like it, Ken?"

Ken smiled. "It's not my style, Jobie."

The boy nodded.

How old was he now? Ken flipped through the files of his memory. Nineteen or twenty at the most. There had been a startling change in the kid who had hung around the house all day, reading books, and playing with his pets, brought in to him by the *vaqueros*. He had been sickly and sensitive, and yet no one had ever dared to show too much sympathy for his sickliness, for the bitter little challenge would rise in the dark eyes. Now that bitter little challenge had become the mark of the young man who stood before Ken, booted and spurred, and weighed down with twin engraved Colts, with mother of pearl handles.

"You must have covered a lot of miles in the past three years," said Miriam.

"Yes," said Ken. "Most of the Southwest. Been in Colorado and Wyoming too. I still like the Conchas country best though."

"You aiming to stay here?" asked Jobie as they walked toward the house.

"I don't think so."

"Get your money and get out, is that it?"

"Jobie!" said Miriam. She flushed.

Ken smiled. "He might have a point there. However, I also came home to see you two and Wes, Jobie."

The boy looked quickly at him and the veil almost dropped, but then it slid up again. "Not homesick I hope," he said sarcastically.

Ken opened the door for Miriam. "Yes, I think I was homesick, Jobie. However, since getting here, I'm not so sure about that."

"There's a rumor in town that you already had a run-in with some of the Guthook bunch," said the kid.

Miriam turned as she reached the far side of the kitchen. She eyed Ken's mouth.

"News travels fast," said Ken dryly. "Yes, I did have a run-in with some of them. I crossed Guthook land yesterday evening and was warned to stay off. I camped on the Double

H side of Skillet Crick. Evidently some of the Lazy J boys didn't think that was far enough."

"Was there any shooting?" asked Jobie.

"No. It was Jim Dana and two characters named Slim and Charley."

Jobie nodded. "They usually travel together."

"There was a fracas. Steve Wascoe came up and stopped it. He had Clem Brace with him and another man. Looked like a breed or dark Mexican."

Jobie glanced at Miriam. "Carancho, I'll bet."

"Yes," she said quietly.

"Carancho?" said Ken.

"Hawk," said Jobie.

"Also *buzzard*," said Ken with a faint smile. "That definition might fit him better if he travels with Steve Wascoe."

"Keep away from him," warned Miriam. "He does all Steve Wascoe's dirty work."

"That isn't true!" snapped Jobie heatedly. "Steve Wascoe isn't afraid of anyone around here. He's the fastest gun this country has ever seen." He glanced quickly at Ken. "And that includes Wes."

Ken shrugged. He looked at Miriam. She shook her head. Jobie was with his back to her and his eyes studied Ken. "Well, Ken?" he asked quietly. "That right?"

"I suppose so."

"And you too, Ken."

Ken's anger rose a little. "I didn't come home to get into stupid arguments about fast guns, kid."

"No," said Jobie softly. "You didn't, did you? But it didn't take long for you to brace up to the Guthook boys."

Miriam took Jobie by the arm and pulled him a little and the two of them walked into the hallway that led to the living room. Ken opened and closed his big hands. He had itched to take a swing at the cocky kid, but something had held him back and it wasn't those twin engraved Colts hanging at Jobie's thighs.

Ken followed the two of them into the living room. Wes

sat in his big wing chair again, elbows resting on his knees, staring into the fire, and there was a glass in his left hand and a cigar between his right fingers. A thread of smoke wavered up from it and hung about his slightly raddled face. Miriam stood by the front window looking down toward the Rio Frio, while Jobie sprawled in a big chair near the table.

"Estelle has a headache," said Wes to Ken without looking up. "I suppose you want to know what the old man left you."

"No hurry."

Jobie's eyes flitted from Wes to Ken and back again.

Wes flicked his cigar. "His will stated that you were to be left a cash sum, Ken. That or an interest in the ranch." He smiled faintly. "That is, if you thought you could run the Double H with me in partnership."

"I'm not sure about that, Wes."

The man's eyes studied Ken. "Meaning you don't *want* to run it with me?"

"You know better than that. It's this Guthook trouble hanging over the place that bothers me."

There was a faint sneer on Jobie's face.

"That all, Ken?" asked Wes.

"No. It doesn't appear to me that you're running much of a spread here anymore, Wes. I don't know why. Most of the horses are gone. Tacos said you have only a small *corrida*. Just a few cattle compared to the old days."

"So?" said Jobie.

Ken turned a little. There was always a challenge in the kid's voice. "I'd want to ranch, kid. The Double H is a good place to live and raise cattle and horses. Why let it go to seed? I'll take the money, Wes."

There was a long silence broken only by the dull crackling of the fire. "Well?" asked Ken at last. He hated this business.

"Tell him, Wes," said Miriam quietly.

Wes drained his glass. "Well, there was cash left in my care, but with getting married and doing all this sort of thing." He waved a hand to encompass the ornate living room. "Hiring a woman cook from Santa Fe, buying clothes for Estelle. A honeymoon in San Francisco. Other things, Ken. I used up almost all of the cash."

"I can wait," said Ken.

Wes laughed. "How long? I just can't raise that kind of money now, Ken."

"How much was it?"

"Ten thousand dollars, Ken."

Ken whistled softly. "I never knew the old man had that much cash around."

Wes refilled his glass. "He had more than that. I went through quite a bit of it before he was killed. Gambling debts mostly. Miriam and Jobie needed money. They wouldn't stay here."

"It wasn't my idea," said Jobie coldly and walked out of the room. They heard the rear door slam.

"That wasn't necessary," said Miriam.

Wes laughed sarcastically.

"Let's get on with this," said Ken.

"Truth is, Ken, I just haven't got the money for you."

"I can wait."

"No," said Miriam. "Tell him the rest, Wes."

Wes sipped at his drink. "I just don't know how to raise that money, Ken."

"You've got the ranch. One of the best in the Conchas country."

Wes nodded. "But I can't run it. I never was a rancher, Ken. The old man said that more than once after you left. Maybe I should have gone."

"You didn't," said Miriam.

Her brother looked at her, opened his mouth and then shut it.

Miriam looked at Ken. "Ken, why don't you make an agreement with Wes? Stay here and work the ranch. Get it on its feet. Then you can either stay on as partner or draw the cash and leave."

Ken rubbed his jaws. "I hadn't planned on staying."

"The Lazy J boys help you make that decision?" asked Miriam quietly.

Ken flushed. "Give me time," he said hotly. "I don't like the smell of things around here. Sure, I love this ranch and this country, but not to the extent that I'm going to sit atop a powder keg while someone fools around with a lighted match!"

Wes raised his head and his eyes held Ken's. There was a tragic message behind his eyes, but Ken turned away from the half drunken man and walked from the room out onto the front porch. He had hardly been home before things had started piling up. He heard Miriam talking to Wes in a low voice as he walked to the stables to get a horse.

CHAPTER FIVE

THE RIO FRIO purled along swiftly, making soft liquid music beneath the overhanging willows. The sun was up high and the New Mexican sky was dotted with fleecy white clouds hurrying on and on as they always did, trying to catch up with their own racing shadows that traveled down and up, across hills and streams, always ahead of the pursuing clouds.

Ken tethered the buckskin to a willow and walked along the soft bank of the river. Tacos had given him exact instructions as how to reach the place where Jordan Harker had been ambushed. Beyond the Rio Frio the Lazy J land rose in a wide swale, and at the top of the swale, half-hidden in a clump of brush and scrub trees, was the little crescent-shaped knoll where the killer had fired at Jordan Harker.

He looked up and down the valley of the Rio Frio. The area was at the farthest point from the ranch buildings of the Double H, in a sort of a pocket, formed by a bend of the river, that protruded well into Guthook land. The Double H side was lower ground, while the Lazy J side rose in successive swales and rises until it reached a range of low-mounded hills. Beyond those hills was the best grazing land in the Conchas country, owned by Lon Naylor, naturally.

A man could scout along the Lazy J side and never be

seen while he could see a man traveling on the Double H side of the Rio Frio. A killer could pick the time and place. They were never in any hurry. They were paid well and not interfered with, and when the job was done they left as they had come—in the darkness of the moon.

Something made him want to cross that shallow and swiftly-running stream. He had had hunches before. Sometimes they had kept him alive, so he had learned to pay attention to them. After looking up and down the valley he stepped into the river, waded across until he stood on the dangerous ground of the Lazy J. He emptied his boots and put them on again before slogging up the slope through the ground softened by the heavy rainfall in that country just the week before he had arrived.

He moved quietly through the brush until he was just below the crest of the little knoll, then dropped to his knees and worked his way quickly into the crescent-shaped hollow at the top of the knoll. From it he could see quite an expanse of Lazy J land, but when he turned to look west he was surprised. The view was far better than he had realized. He could see the valley of the Rio Frio for a mile in one direction and more than half a mile in the other, while across the high cut-bank beyond the Double H side of the stream, he could see clear to the ranch buildings.

Ken rolled a smoke and lighted it. He wondered how long the killer had waited there for the one shot that wiped out the life of the best man Ken Macklin had ever known.

Jordan Harker had been killed by a softnosed .44-40, hardly a rare caliber in the West of that time. And .44-40 cartridges were interchangeable between six-guns and saddle guns. A dozen butts had been thrust into the soft earth by the man who had waited to kill the rancher. It had been a good three-hundred-yard shot, downhill in uncertain moonlight.

Ken had a suspicion that Tacos knew more about the matter than he had let on. but men in that country were usually close-mouthed. They had to be, or a wagging mouth might be stopped forever by the simple application of a chunk of soft lead driven into the body by powder gas.

Something made him turn his head, and he saw three men riding swiftly toward the valley from the range of hills that concealed the rest of the Guthook spread.

As Ken rolled out of the hollow something caught in a button of his denim jacket. He gripped it with his left hand to rip it away and saw that it was a dirt-encrusted spur jangler —a little bell-clapped piece of metal usually worn on Texas-style spurs. Ken thrust it into his jacket pocket and crouched low as he ran for the river. He waded across and had just reached his buckskin when he saw the horsemen top the rise; but there were only two of them now. They spurred down the soft slope and rode toward the river while Ken Macklin prudently walked around his horse and stood, looking at them from across his saddle, with his hand resting on his sheathed Winchester.

"That you, Macklin?" called out a familiar voice.

"Yes, Brace."

"Thought we saw yuh over on this side."

"Maybe I was just being neighborly, Brace."

"What was yuh looking for, Macklin?"

"A hurdy-gurdy girl, *amigo.*"

Brace slapped his thigh. "Better'n ever! That's good, Macklin."

The other man quietly sat his horse, studying Ken from beneath the brim of his low-pulled hat. Ken glanced up along the ridge. Where was the third member of the trio? Maybe sighting along the barrel of a rifle with Ken as the target.

"Yuh busy, Macklin?" asked Brace.

"Not particularly. Why?"

"The old man wants to see yuh."

"What does he want?"

Brace shrugged and held out his hands, palms upwards. *"Quien sabe?* He never tells me nothing, Macklin."

Ken swung up on the buckskin. It had been three long

years since he had seen Lon Naylor, and there wasn't any desire in him to see the old bastard now, just a deep curiosity.

"Yuh coming then?" asked Brace.

Ken shoved back his hat and rested an elbow on his saddle horn. "I might, after I find out where that third horseman went to," he said.

Brace grinned again. He turned and rested a hand on his cantle, then waved his free hand back and forth. In a few minutes the third man appeared, waved at Brace, then rode along the crest of the ridge toward the north.

Ken waited until the man was out of sight before he crossed the Rio Frio. He glanced curiously at the man who was beside Brace.

"This is Dod Nellis," said Brace, jerking his head toward his companion.

Ken nodded. Nellis looked up. "Pleased, I'm sure," he said quietly, with an almost cultured tone in his voice. He was well dressed in dark clothing, plainly enough, but there was taste in it. This man was no twenty a month *vaquero*.

They all rode silently toward the Naylor domain.

Lon Naylor had built his feudal keep with an eye to beauty, and to safety. The buildings covered the only noticeable rise on the rolling terrain. Two storied, for the most part, built of adobe brick, well plastered, with thick, tile roofs. A deep earthen-banked reservoir reflected the sunlight. Ducks paddled peacefully about on the water. The fresh prairie wind moved the tall cottonwoods and willows. A Chicago Standard Windmill whirred steadily, pumping water into a stock tank.

The three horsemen loped their mounts to the gateway set into the high adobe wall that surrounded the central buildings. Ken shook his head a little as he looked about. Even in the old days it had been a magnificent place, but now Lon Naylor had outdone himself.

"*Bueno,* eh, Macklin?" asked Clem Brace.

Ken nodded. "Nothing like it anywhere else in this country," he said.

Brace spat. "I wonder why he's doing it?"

Ken shot a glance at the tough Texan. There was a cynical air about the man. Tough as he was, a mercenary, and in all likelihood a killer, there was something about the man that Ken admired. He said, "Some men like horses, some liquor and some the ladies. Lon Naylor just happens to like power and possessions."

"He's got 'em," said Brace.

"There's always time for a man to quit," said Ken.

Dod Nellis looked quickly at Ken. "Why?" he quietly asked.

"That's the way it goes," said Ken.

"I don't think so."

Ken felt for the makings. "Every man has his own goal," he said.

"What's yours, Macklin?" asked Nellis.

"I'm not sure."

"You will be, and then you won't be so critical of Lon Naylor."

"I won't likely kill a man to reach that goal."

Nellis smiled. "Seems to me you've done a little killing in your time."

"Meaning that fight in Conchas Corners?"

Nellis nodded. "That, and other events."

A cold feeling came over Ken. "I don't follow you," he said.

Nellis met Ken's direct glance with steady eyes. "What makes you think the past three years have been hidden, Macklin?" he questioned.

Ken slowly rolled a quirly. "I didn't know I was making history, Nellis."

Nellis smiled thinly. "You won't need me any longer, Brace," he said. "At least *today. Hasta la vista,* Macklin."

Ken nodded. He handed the makings to Brace, then

lighted his own cigarette. "Who's he?" he asked. "Pinkerton man?"

"Stock detective," said Brace.

"Hired killer you mean, don't you, Brace?"

"For Christ's sake, Macklin, take it easy!"

Ken grinned. He touched his horse with his spurs and rode toward the gateway. "Do I go in alone?" he asked over his shoulder.

"Suit yourself. Me, I'd rather have a troop of cavalry with me when I go in to see Naylor."

The man wasn't so far wrong at that, thought Ken, as he tethered the buckskin to the hitching rail in front of the big central building of the ranch. Ken walked up onto the wide, shaded veranda of the building and raised the big brass knocker molded into the shape of a steer's head. He knocked three times. In a few minutes the door swung open and he saw an aged Mexican eyeing him.

"Mister Naylor wanted to see me. The name is Ken Macklin."

The man nodded. "Follow me, *senor*."

They walked up the broad staircase to the second floor and the servant rapped sharply on a wide door set deeply into the wall. "Come in!" a dry voice called out.

The servant opened the door and stood aside. Ken walked into the huge room that was the aerie of Lon Naylor. It was big and drafty, warmed by a pinon log fire that blazed in the great fireplace. The plastered walls had been hung with Navajo rugs, Apache lances and war clubs, Spanish shoe stirrups fashioned of brass, muzzle-loading guns, buffalo rifles, bullet molds, quirts, beadwork, and so on. The place was veritably a museum of Southwestern antiques, relics and artifacts. How well it suited the white-haired old man seated behind the huge bare-topped desk near the great window that looked out across miles and miles of Lazy J land.

"You look tough, Ken," said Lon Naylor.

Ken smiled thinly. "No tougher than you, Mister Naylor."

The lined face cracked a little into what passed for a smile, but there was no mirth in the hard agate eyes of the man who was legend while he was still alive. Ken could not help but wonder once more how such a crusted old bastard had ever sired such a woman as Estelle.

Lon Naylor waved a hand toward a chair. "Set, Ken," he said. "What's your pleasure?"

"Rye?"

The agate eyes swiveled as Lon Naylor poured rye into two water glasses, for shot glasses might be considered an affectation in the household of the man who was the cattle king of the Conchas country.

"I know a helluva lot about you, Ken Macklin." The old man slyly smiled.

"You don't miss much, Mister Naylor."

"I didn't get to where I am without making a practice of knowing what goes on about me, Ken."

"I agree. Maybe you can fill me in on the death of my foster father."

There was a long silence broken by the ticking of the huge grandfather's clock that stood behind Lon Naylor.

Lon Naylor handed Ken a glass. "Is that why you came back?"

"In a way."

The old man sipped the rye. "It wasn't the inheritance then?"

"You know better than that."

"Yes . . . but maybe it was Estelle that brought you back, eh?"

"No. I would have come back long ago had she asked me."

"She's your brother's wife, Ken."

"I didn't know that."

The clock ticked on.

Lon Naylor swirled the rye in his glass. "I wish I could believe you, Ken," he said at last.

"It's the truth."

"Then you did come back to find out who killed Jordan Harker?"

"Yes."

"I thought so."

The old man always came to the point. You had to give him credit for that. Cruel but clean, like a surgeon's scalpel, that was Lon Naylor.

"It wasn't me, Ken," said Lon Naylor.

"This is the time that I wish I could believe *you*, Mister Naylor."

Lon Naylor swiveled his chair and hunched down in it. All Ken could see was the high back of the chair and the gnarled hand that held the rye glass. "You might not believe this, Ken," said Lon Naylor, "but I couldn't have killed Jordan Harker."

"Maybe not personally. You always kept your skirts clean, didn't you?"

The chair turned and the hard, bitter face looked at Ken. "I hated Jordan Harker's guts. Man to man, I would have looked forward to putting a bullet into his belly. But as for having him dry-gulched, that isn't my line, Ken."

"You talk big. The 'Guthook' treatment is known from one end of New Mexico to the other. Kill 'em, drop 'em on Guthook land, then claim they trespassed and were rustling. I damned near walked into one of those traps last night, Naylor."

Naylor drained his glass. "You did all right for yourself. Steve Wascoe said there would have been a helluva bloodletting if he hadn't showed up."

"He was right."

"Jim Dana never forgot you, Ken, with damned good reason."

Ken touched his battered mouth. "He faced Wes and me in Conchas Corners that day three years ago, shooting for belly shots. He got what was coming to him."

Naylor nodded. "Only the story has changed. Wes Harker has stolen the glory of that fight, Ken. You've been shoved back into the second row. It was Wes who killed those two men and maimed Jim Dana."

"So?"

Lon Naylor smiled as much as he could ever smile. "That's the way of it now. But you know, and I know, that Wes was so damned drunk he could hardly pull trigger."

"Go on."

"I can take care of Wes Harker, Ken. Jordan Harker knew that. I wasn't so sure about you. I'll admit I was damned glad to see you go instead of Wes."

Ken stood up and drained his glass. "I didn't come back for trouble," he said.

"Fact is, you did come back. I still want the Rio Frio. My daughter married a Harker. My *only* child. You wouldn't understand that, Macklin. You will, *if* you live long enough to have children. Now I have one more thing to say to you, take it or leave it. I don't know how much money Wes Harker owes you for your inheritance, but I do know he hasn't got it. I'm willing to pay you ten thousand dollars, no strings attached, to high-tail out of this country and never come back."

"Why?" asked Ken at last.

Lon Naylor refilled the glasses. "Because I see something of myself in you, Macklin, and I'm worried. I can take care of Wes Harker and the rest of them, but you, you're different. Get out of the Conchas country, son. Take your money and keep going, for as sure as I'm sitting here, either you or me will die in the next few months if you stay here."

Ken raised his glass and eyed the liquor. "I'll be around awhile," he said.

Lon Naylor stood up and raised his glass. "I knew you'd say that. Well, this is perhaps the way it should be. Watch your back, Macklin."

"*Gracias,* Naylor."

They touched glasses and drained them.

CHAPTER SIX

THE SUN was low in the west when Ken Macklin rode up the slope from the low-lands of the Rio Frio toward the ranch houses of the Double H. He drew rein sharply when he heard the staccato crashing of gunfire. He stood up in his stirrups to see the men standing near the big corral behind the stables.

Kneeing the buckskin on, he rode up past the big ranch house. He had been riding for hours, trying to evaluate his status in the deadly chess game that was obviously being played in the Conchas country. Lon Naylor was no fool and knew quite a bit more than Ken had realized, but Ken himself had never fully understood the complications that would arise upon his return to the Conchas country.

He slid from his saddle and tethered the buckskin to the corral fence just as another outburst of gunfire broke out. Ken walked toward the three men who stood near the rear of the corral wreathed in swirling gun smoke. There were Wes Harker and Tacos the *cocinero* and also a slim youth, dressed completely in black leather, who was reloading a beautifully engraved Colt. It was Jobie Harker with a self-satisfied look upon his thin face.

Wes turned as he saw Ken. He hiccupped. "Glad you

came back, Ken," he said a little thickly. "The kid here has been making us look pretty bad."

"Gawd dammit," said Tacos, "I ain't no gunslinger and never claimed I was!"

Jobie Harker slid the loaded Colt into its sheath, glanced at Ken, then turned quickly. A row of a dozen tin cans rested on the second rail of the corral fence, just about the height of a man's belly or chest. The kid crouched a little, snapped down his hands, and as they came up they held the twin Colts. Both guns rapped alternately, and almost as though by legerdemain, one tin can after the other was driven from the rail. When the kid's guns ran dry, he twirled them and slid them into their carved leather sheaths.

Ken shook his head. It had been an exhibition of fast precision drawing and shooting. Jobie Harker *was* good.

"Set 'em up again, Tacos," said Wes thickly.

The cook did as he was bid, then stepped behind Wes.

Wes spat. He wore but one gun, tied low. He eyed the line of cans. The kid grinned a little. "Go on, Wes," he challenged.

Wes went into a crouch and snapped his right hand down for a draw. The six-gun came up and cracked out. Three cans were driven from the rail but the shooting was erratic, and out of class with that of Jobie Harker.

Wes shook his head. "I used to do better than that," he said.

Jobie leaned back against a fence post. "Sure, sure," he agreed.

Wes peered at his brother. "You don't believe me?" he asked.

The kid grinned. "I've heard all about that famous gunfight, and of how *you* killed two men and maimed another. You and Ken here, the great *heroes* of the Conchas country!"

Wes looked away. He reached up and wiped the sweat from his puffy face. "Well, I used to be pretty good."

"You stink!" said the kid flatly.

"Now, Jobie!"

Tacos glanced quickly at Ken and then shrugged. Ken leaned against the fence. "I think you've had a little too much to drink, Wes," he said.

"That's my concern!"

"It's a little dangerous, isn't it, to be handling a six-gun in your condition?"

"I can do all right!"

"Sure. Sure."

Jobie took out a Colt and opened the loading gate. He reloaded the cylinder, but his amused eyes were on his brother. "Tell us how you and Ken blew hell out of the Guthook boys in Conchas Corners, Wes. How was it? *You* killed two men and blew off Jim Dana's right forearm, while Ken backed up your great play by wounding *one* man. Pretty good shooting for a man walking around with a bellyfull of rotgut."

Wes flushed darkly. He strode toward his younger brother and raised his fists, but the kid calmly closed the loading gate of his Colt, twirled the cylinder, stepped back and leveled the gun at Wes' belly. "You just stay where you are," he said coldly. "You're not going to lay a hand on me. You even so much as make a pass at me and I'll blow a hole in your guts."

Wes stopped. Sweat was running down his face. "You put up that gun," he said.

Tacos swallowed hard. He glanced at Ken. "Now, boys," he said.

"Shut up, you!" snapped Jobie.

Wes could break the kid in half with one hand, drunk or sober, but he couldn't handle a .44-40 slug in the belly.

Jobie stepped back and quickly slid the Colt into its sheath. He smiled thinly. "You drunken slob," he taunted. "It wasn't you who was the big hero of the Conchas Corners fight. It was Ken, and you know it. You've lied so damned much about it you believe it yourself."

Wes turned a little. "Tell him, Ken," he said.

Ken knew now that Wes actually believed he had done the most executing that smoky day in Conchas Corners.

"Tell him!" repeated Wes.

Ken looked at the kid. "Let's forget this thing, Jobie. You go on into the house. Wes is a little upset."

Jobie spat to one side. "The two big gunfighters," he said with a laugh.

Wes whirled and rammed a hand down for his Colt, but Jobie was too fast and his twin Colts seemed to leap from their holsters. Another man had been even faster. Ken Macklin had snatched up a short section of rail that had been leaning against the fence. He hurled it with all his strength a fraction of a second before Jobie pulled trigger. The heavy butt end caught the kid on the side of the head and whirled him about. One of his Colts cracked sharply and Tacos grunted in savage pain, then dropped to his knees, hung there poised for a second, then fell slowly forward on his face in the mud of the yard.

Ken leaped forward, drove Wes to one side by hitting him with a shoulder, then closed in on Jobie who was swaying back and forth trying to raise his guns again. Ken stepped to one side, twisted the left hand Colt from the kid's hand, then gripped his right wrist and drove it upward just as it exploded again. He ripped the gun away and hurled it clear across the corral fence.

"Damn you!" snarled the kid. There was pure icy hell in his eyes as he struggled with Ken. A left brought in a slamming jab that knocked Jobie flat on his back. As his eyes glazed he managed to spit at Ken like an angry cat.

"Jesus God," said Wes. "The kid is loco."

"You should have known better than to fool with him," said Ken. He dropped on his knees beside Tacos and turned him over. The washed-out eyes looked up at him, but they did not see, and they would never see again.

Ken stood up and took off his hat.

"He's not dead?" said Wes in a strange voice.

Ken nodded.

"This is a helluva mess."

Ken looked toward the house. Miriam was running toward them while Katie the cook stood on the porch twisting her hands in her apron.

"He's always like that lately," said Wes. "Looking for trouble, riding me about that Conchas Corners fight. It was *me* that did the killings, wasn't it, Ken?"

Ken turned slowly. "Shut up," he said. "You damned, drunken fool. There's a man lying here dead because of you and Jobie."

"You threw the rail at Jobie!"

"And if I hadn't he would have killed you, Wes."

"I had the drop on him."

"You had nothing," said Ken flatly. "Now a man is dead. A better man in his way than both of you put together. I'll have to get the sheriff, Wes."

Ken walked to the buckskin and swung up into the saddle. He looked down at Wes and Miriam. "Let him lie there," he said. "Cover him with a blanket or something. Tell Jobie to stick around for questioning." Ken kneed the horse away from the two of them and rode toward the gateway. He'd have to ride to Conchas Corners.

It was dusk when he reached that damnable place. Yellow lamplight threw squares of light on the boardwalks and the rutted streets. The bitter-sweet smell of woodsmoke mingled with the greasy odor of cooking hung over the town. Somewhere on the main stem a mechanical piano was grinding out a tinny tune.

Ken dismounted and tethered the buckskin to the rail near the sheriff's office. Conchas Corners had grown some in the past three years. It was the marketing place for the local ranchers, as well as the shipping point for their cattle.

He stepped up onto the boardwalk just as the first spit of rain came down with the freshening wind. He looked along the wide street to the main intersection—Broad Street and Cottonwood. It had been at that intersection that Ken and Wes Harker had fought the bloody little battle that was local legend by now. The fight was plainly etched in his memory and it would never fade. What had been puzzling Ken for a long time was how he had been able to muster up enough cold-blooded guts to step out into the street with his half-drunk foster brother to face the five men of the Guthook *corrida*. Ken knew he couldn't do it now.

He walked toward the sheriff's office and peered at the white card tacked to the door. "Out on posse," he read. "Be back Sunday morning. Signed, Milligan, Sheriff."

There was no use in him going back to the Double H, nor did he want to. So he walked into the nearest bar, not even noting the name, and stopped at the end of the long mahogany. The place was fairly well patronized. Several tables had the inevitable poker games in progress; a drunk dozed at a table near the rear of the place; three men stood at the bar, elbows resting on the edge, hands gripping shot glasses, eyes staring moodily at the back mirror, minds occupied with their own dark and dangerous thoughts.

"Your pleasure?" asked the barkeep as he polished the mahogany.

"Rye."

Bottle and glass slid to a halt in front of Ken. He poured a drink and raised it.

The barkeep eyed him. "You're Ken Macklin, aren't you?" he asked.

Ken nodded. In the silence that followed the big wall clock ticked steadily on. Men stopped playing cards and looked around and the three silent ones standing at the middle of the bar swiveled heads and eyes to look at Ken. A cold feeling came over him as he recognized Jim Dana, Slim and Charley.

The bartender polished the bar. "Heard you was coming back, Macklin," he prattled. "Gone quite a spell, wasn't you?"

"Yes."

"Been seeing the elephant, eh? Well, I always say a man

should get out and go afore he gets tied up in double harness with some filly. Now I—"

"Shut up, Benny," said Jim Dana.

The bartender paled. He glanced at Jim and he couldn't take his eyes from Jim's stub of an arm.

"You see something funny, Benny?" asked Jim.

"Who, me, Jim? Hell no, I don't see anything funny."

"Then what are you looking at my stub for?" The voice was icy and flat, almost as though a poised copperhead rattler had had the ability to speak.

The bartender's round fat face became beaded with cold sweat. "I—"

"You never seen a man with but one arm before?"

"Sure, sure, Jim. My Uncle Hank had only one—"

"Shut up!"

Ken hadn't moved all the time Jim had been baiting the bartender. The one-armed man was looking for trouble and it didn't take much to get him started on his vicious way. He had been bad enough before one of Ken's forty-fours had blasted his arm, now it evidently didn't take much to get the cripple ringey enough to peddle blood and death.

There was no sound in the barroom now beyond the ticking of the big wall clock and the occasional shuffling of a man's feet upon the sanded floor. Some of them wanted to leave, but to make a sudden movement in that room of impending violence might be fatal for the man who moved.

They instinctively knew that Jim Dana was more interested in getting at Ken Macklin than he was in baiting Benny. It was his way. Trouble was that the baited man paid a price for being in Jim Dana's murderous way.

Jim picked up his whiskey glass and threw the liquor into Ben's face.

"You got no call to do that, Jim," spluttered Ben.

"I ain't?" Jim's voice rose sharply. "I ain't? You tellin' me I ain't got no call to do that? You gutless bastard! You got a double-gun under that mahogany, ain'tcha? Get it out, Benny, if you aim to call me on what I done!"

Benny's face paled and his hands rested on the edge of the bar. The man was afraid but he wasn't a coward, and a frightened man can sometimes be more dangerous than a cool man. If Benny went for the double-gun and sprayed those loads out into that barroom, he might very well miss Jim and his *compadres*, but he might be dead even before his fingers tightened on the triggers.

"Take it easy, Jim," said Benny. "I want no fight with you." He glanced quickly at Ken. "You was all right until Macklin came in here."

"Macklin? What the hell has *he* got to do with it?"

Ken raised his head. "Let him alone, Jim," he said quietly.

"You taking on this fight, Macklin?" asked Dana.

"Let the man alone. If you want to pick trouble with me, I'm right here. This time you didn't get a chance to Indian up on me, did you?"

Jim spat to one side. "You was trespassin' then. Wasn't he, boys?"

Slim and Charley both nodded.

"That makes it right then, doesn't it?" Ken smiled.

"You sayin' it don't?"

Ken's hair-trigger temper slipped a little on the sear. "Look, Dana," he said softly. "You're getting to be a great talker. *You* were looking for the trouble, not *me*. Now, if you've got the guts you blow so damned much about, you just walk past me here through the door and walk south to the first intersection, then turn left and walk to the alleyway. I'll leave right after you and walk north, turning right at the first intersection to the alleyway. From then on we're both on our own."

"Listen to him," said Slim.

Charley spat. "Why'n't you go, Jim? You can handle him."

Jim Dana's face creased. It was one thing to brace up a man in a well-lighted barroom, when you were backed by two good gunfighters; it was another thing to walk out into the rainy darkness and up that muddy alleyway, looking for the man who had once outdrawn and outshot you in as fair a fight as any gunfighter could wish.

Ken had neatly turned the tables. Jim had to draw and shoot now, or else walk outside to meet Ken in the alleyway. There wasn't any other choice. Trouble is, he didn't *want* to make a choice, for he hadn't planned it that way. He knew it and he knew Ken Macklin knew it. There was one. other thing that tall, gray-eyed *hombre* standing there seemed to know, just as surely as though he looked into Jim's dark and innermost thoughts. Dana had changed since he had lost that arm. It had been one thing to Indian up on a sleeping man, himself backed by two gunmen, to take the sleeping man at a deadly disadvantage; it was another thing to have to face the man, now wide-awake, armed, and ready to fight.

"Well, Dana," said Ken softly, ever so softly.

Above the ticking of the clock and the soft, damp sighing of the wind against the frame building, came another sound: that of many hoofs churning the muddy street. Men's voices carried into the barroom, and then the door was pushed open and half a dozen men crowded in just behind Ken, led by big, bluff George Milligan, the sheriff. The big law officer took off his hat and shook it, splattering rain drops on the sandy floor.

Belly up to the bar, boys," he said to his soaked posse. "The drinks are on me." He grinned. "Come to think of it, they oughta be on the county."

"And they will be, eh, boys?" said a grinning deputy. "That's the Milligan way, ain't it?"

Dana slowly turned back to the bar and was sided by Slim and Charley. Ben wiped the bar and then hustled to where the posse had lined up with the damnedest look of relief on his round face.

"Hello, Sheriff," said Ken.

Milligan stared at Ken. "By God," he said. "It's Ken Macklin!" He thrust out a ham of a hand. "Glad to see you back, Ken. You interested in a deputy star?"

Ken shook his head. "Not right now, George."

"Sure could use you. We got news that Doroteo Navarez hopped a train south of here and got plumb away, so there wasn't no use in riding through all that wet to chase a train. I wired ahead and he'll get picked up. Hell of a name for a wife murderer, ain't it? *Doroteo!*"

The poker players had returned to their cards. They wouldn't open their mouths, not that night at any rate. The drunk snored on in rhythm with the clock. Suddenly Jim Dana and his two sidekicks downed their liquor and left the saloon. It was then that Ken took Milligan aside and told him why he had come to Conchas Corners.

Milligan shook his head. "Poor Tacos! Well, I been waiting for that damned kid to kill someone."

"It was an accident, George."

"Manslaughter maybe?"

Ken thought back. "No, I don't think so."

"The kid didn't draw his gun on his brother, did he?"

Ken felt for the makings. The swift deadly scene came back to him. It had been drunken Wes who had gone for his gun, to be outdrawn by his kid brother. Ken's act in hurling the piece of rail at Jobie had been the cause of Taco's death, but if he *hadn't* stopped Jobie the kid might have killed his own brother.

"Well?" asked Milligan quietly.

Ken looked at him. "Suppose we go over the whole thing when we get out there?"

Milligan nodded. His blue eyes studied Ken for a moment; he knew well enough that there was more to this simple tale of sudden and accidental death than Ken had let on.

CHAPTER SEVEN

T HE SKY was covered with low hanging clouds that threatened a renewal of the drizzle that had carried on through most of the chilly night. The Rio Frio had risen considerably during the night and it roared dully between its low banks.

There was a tense quietness about the ranch buildings of the Double H. Tacos had been placed in his little room beside the cookhouse. Doc Ives was examining the body, while Sheriff Milligan was questioning the involved parties in the fire-warmed living room of the big house.

Wes Harker sat in his big chair with his head between his hands, while his sister Miriam stood by the big front window, looking down toward the sullen rushing waters of the river. Ken Macklin leaned against the wall beside the fireplace, eyeing the straight, slim back of his foster sister. He had never been able to think of her as his sister, even though he had accepted Wes and Jobie as his brothers and Jordan Harker as his father.

Sheriff Milligan came out of the kitchen with a coffee cup almost buried in a huge hand. The cook's statement was tucked under his left arm. Katie hadn't had much to say. She claimed she had not seen the fatal shooting, only the results of it.

George Milligan placed his coffee cup on the table. "Now, how about you, Miss Harker? Tell me what you saw."

Miriam looked up with red eyes, for she had loved old Tacos. Her statement was short and simple. It was almost the same as that of Katie.

Milligan leaned back in his chair. "You didn't see who fired the fatal shot?"

"No."

Ken looked at her and knew she was lying.

Milligan nodded again. "Uh huh." He looked at Wes and Ken. "I'll take Job's statement now."

"I'll get him," said Ken. He walked to the kid's room and tapped on the door. There was no answer. He eased it open. The room was empty. The bed had not been slept in. A cold feeling came over Ken. He walked back into the living room. "He isn't in his room," he said.

"He didn't eat with us last night," said Wes.

"What about this morning?" asked the lawman.

Miriam and Wes both shook their heads.

Milligan stood up and rubbed his jaws. "You told him to stay here last night, Ken?"

"Yes."

"No one watched him though?"

Wes flushed. "We weren't talking," he said.

Miriam looked away. "He promised me he'd stay."

Milligan shrugged. "I'll have to send someone after him."

Ken felt for the makings and rolled a smoke. "Let me go," he said.

"Why? Some of my boys can round him up. The kid ain't slick enough to get away from my boys."

Ken raised his head. "He thinks he's killed a man. He won't hesitate to kill another if he has to.

Milligan half closed his eyes. "This is silly," he said.

"Job's only a kid." said Ken. "He won't understand."

Wes laughed dryly without mirth. "He doesn't think so. And he can shoot, Milligan. Better than you and me, maybe better than anyone around here, excepting Steve Wascoe."

A log snapped in the fireplace. The kitchen door opened and closed and Doc Ives came into the living room, tossing something from hand to hand.

"Well?" asked the sheriff.

"I heard that Job high-tailed it out of here sometime last night thinking he killed a man. One of the boys told me." Ives smiled a little.

"What's so damned funny?" growled Wes.

The doctor tossed a pellet of lead into the air and caught it. "I found this stuck against Tacos' wallet. He carried it in his left pants pocket. The bullet never made a hole in Tacos."

They all stared at him. "What killed him then?" asked Ken quietly.

"Heart attack. The shock of the bullet was too much, I guess. I'll report it as a heart attack, brought on accidently. Rough thing for a boy to carry on his conscience. He'll be glad to know he's innocent."

"Yeh," said Milligan. He rubbed his jaw again and looked at Ken from under shaggy brows. "You think he'd fight if cornered?"

"Yes."

Milligan paced back and forth "You say you'd go?"

"Yes."

"Go get him then." Milligan gathered up his papers, then glanced at Wes and Ken. "I'll need your statements."

Wes glanced toward the liquor cabinet and Ken shook his head out of sight of the sheriff.

"You were target shooting, is that it?" asked Milligan. "Job drew and fired. The shot struck Tacos and he fell. You didn't examine him, thinking he had been killed by the stray bullet, and didn't want to touch him until he had been examined by a coroner. Correct?"

Wes nodded and Ken followed suit.

"Beats me how the kid could have fired anywhere near Tacos," he said at last.

"Tacos had been setting up the tin cans we were using

for targets," said Wes slowly. "One of them teetered a little, and Tacos moved forward right into the line of fire."

Milligan nodded. "Well, this is about it then. I may have to have you in for the inquest. I'll need the kid for that too. The sooner the better."

Ken tossed his cigarette butt into the fireplace. "I'll pull out as soon as I can."

"Which way?" asked the lawman.

"Where would he go?"

The sheriff grinned. "Toward Mexico. Maybe he'll join up with Doroteo Navarez. Well, I can send another wire."

After Milligan had left, Ken went to the kitchen to get rations for his trip. He had no idea of where Job might have gone. The kid knew the country well enough and had been accustomed to taking long solo rides along the river bottoms and up the hills and mountains.

Katie silently filled a sack with the items Ken had requested and handed it to him. "The boy is innocent then?" she asked.

"Yes."

"Innocent of murder, or manslaughter, but not of the death of that man. Mister Macklin."

Ken looked quickly at her. "You seem to know a lot more than what you said in your statement, Katie."

She nodded and came a little closer to him. "I saw it all," she said in a low voice.

"It was still an accident."

"But not unavoidable."

"No."

"Where will you look for him?"

"In the hills and mountains, I suppose. He may be miles from here by now."

She nodded. "I knew he wouldn't stay here."

"How did you know that?"

She jerked a thumb over her shoulder in the general direction of the rest of the house. *"Her,"* she said.

"Miss Harker?"

"No. *Mrs*. Harker. She was in his room late last night talking to him."

"Tell me about Jobie!"

"Anyway, it wasn't long after she talked to him that he left. She's got a lot of control over that poor boy. It caused trouble between him and his brother. Maybe it caused Tacos' death too, in a long sort of a way. You mark my words, Mister Macklin, that boy is deadly, and she is going to use him. There's a smell about this place I don' like."

Neither of them had seen her enter the room. It was a way she had about her. She was like a cat in that respect. Ken saw her first and the cook's voice died away as she turned too.

"You have your notice, Katerine," said Estelle.

Katie bowed her head a little.

"Two weeks enough?" asked Estelle sweetly.

"No."

"I can't allow you more, not with your attitude and disloyalty toward your employers."

Katie smiled thinly. "I don't want any more, Mrs. Harker. I'd like to get out of here today."

"*Without* a recommendation?"

It was the way she fought; the Lon Naylor way. She had had plenty of time to learn his tactics.

Katie's face was set and white. Good jobs for a woman cook were not easy to find in that country.

Ken eyed Estelle. "Give her a recommendation, Estelle," he said quietly.

"I will not!"

He smiled thinly. "Yes you will. You talked Jobie into leaving here. Now, if I tell Wes that, you won't be in such a strong position around here, will you?"

Her eyes hardened.

"Write it, Stella," said Ken, using her nickname, the one she hated.

She turned on a heel and left the room.

"Thanks, Mister Macklin." said Katie.

"Forget it."

Katie turned. "She told the boy he was a murderer, but that if he pulled out in a hurry and stayed away for a time, the whole thing might blow over. She said he'd be safe enough, but that he'd have to watch his back." The words came in a rush from the woman.

"You didn't tell me this before."

"No. I didn't want to start any trouble."

He looked down at her. "You're sure you don't know where he went?"

She shook her head and she knew well enough that he knew she was lying, but why, he didn't know.

Estelle came in and threw the recommendation onto the floor. Katie began to reach down for it but Ken held her back. "Pick it up, Stella," he said softly.

She bit her full lower lip, and her eyes were like steel.

"Pick it up," he said again. "Show us what a *lady* you are, Stella. After all, old Lon paid plenty to give you the veneer of a lady at that fine school in Denver. You wouldn't let old Lon down now, would you, Stella?"

She hated to do it; God how she hated to do it, but she picked up the paper and handed it to the cook, then hurried from the room with a wild swishing of her skirts.

"Thanks, Mister Macklin," said Katie. She shrugged. "I'm glad to get away from here. The pay was good and the quarters were fine, but like I said before: There's a deathly smell about this place."

He left the room and got his gear, then carried it to the stable. He selected his own horse, the big, hammer-headed claybank that had brought him back to the Conchas country. He saddled it, sheathed his Winchester, then he stepped back and looked toward the door of the stable. There was Miriam coming toward him.

"I don't like this thing, Ken," she said. "He might fight, Ken."

"Oh, he'll listen to me. He used to listen to me years ago."

"He was only a boy then, and he admired you and looked up to you. Now he finds you, and men like you, only a challenge, a challenge to his new-found skills. He wants to walk big on this earth, Ken."

"We *all* do," said Ken softly.

"But with him it's almost like a sickness. He admires men like Steve Wascoe. He wants to be feared like Steve is feared."

"It has its points."

Her eyes searched his face. "Feared or respected?" she asked. "Which is best?"

"Respect," he admitted.

"You are respected, aren't you, Ken?"

He looked away.

"Ken?"

"Maybe."

"What happened out there?" she asked, swinging an arm as though to encompass the outer world, the world beyond the remote Conchas country.

He tightened the cinch strap of the claybank. "I have to get on," he said. "I want to be well up into the hills before dusk."

"You think that's where he went?"

"Good as any place."

She came close to him. "Pray God there will be no shooting," she said softly.

"I won't shoot at him, Miriam," he said sharply.

Her silence made him turn slowly. There was an odd look in her lovely eyes. "I wasn't thinking of that," she said. "It's him, Ken."

"He won't shoot at me."

"You've been gone a long time," she said simply. "Longer than you realize. He isn't the same, Ken."

"Someone has to go after him. Wes can't go."

He raised her chin with a big, hard hand and kissed her gently. *"Adios,"* he said. He, led the horse from the stable just as the rain began to patter steadily on the big roof.

Not until he was high on a ridge overlooking the ranch buildings did he look back. She was still standing there at the door of the stable looking toward him, heedless of the fine, driving rain that veiled the area between them. He raised a hand and waved. She waved. Then he hunched into the collar of his slicker and touched the claybank with his spurs as he rode toward the rain-gray hills.

Odds were that the kid had gone into the hills or mountains, north or west, either to ride that way, or to reach the railroad. From the railroad he could go northeast, or due south. If Milligan had sent on his wire the kid would be picked up on the train, whichever way he had decided to go.

The rain drove down hard as he entered the first winding notch and rode slowly north with a cigarette pasted in the corner of his thin mouth, protected from the rain by the down-pulled brim of his hat. The brim also cut down his vision, so that he did not see the lone horseman watching him from a hill to the east, nor did he see the wave of the man's hat to someone unseen, and the quick disappearance of the watcher from the sky line.

CHAPTER EIGHT

THE RAIN sluiced down in blinding sheets, and there was nothing to do but to give the claybank his head and trust that natural instinct would carry him through.

But it got worse instead of better and Ken finally slid from his soaked saddle and looked up in search of a place where he could lead the horse to safety; for in a little time the canyon would fill with raging waters carrying brush and trees, rocks, drowned cattle and coyotes: everything and anything, scouring the soaked ground like a great and merciless broom.

He worked his way up onto a ledge and talked quietly to the struggling horse. The claybank rolled his eyes and whinnied, and Ken raised his head. A noise was coming through the leaden lashing of the cold rain. The dull roaring sound that came down the canyon like a knell of doom was a pitiless warning that they did not have long to live.

There was nothing he could do for the fear-crazed horse. He drew out his sheath knife and cut loose his Winchester and its scabbard, casting them up the slope behind him. In minutes he had freed his food sack and blanket roll. The last thing he did was to cut loose the saddle, his favorite saddle of all time, a Frazier, and then he released the bridle reins and watched the struggling horse slide down the greasy slope to splash into the foot of yellow water that was already pouring down the canyon. The claybank galloped clumsily to the south, spurred by horrible fear.

Ken turned, heaved his gear further up the slope, then followed it, clinging desperately to branches, rocks and cracks in the rock faces until he was high above the canyon floor. Then he heard the terrifying roar of the flood as it smashed against the nearest curve of the canyon. He turned to see it mount the vertical wall, frothing and heaving like a maddened, insensate liquid beast, as it raged down the canyon after its helpless prey.

The water was five feet beneath his boot soles when at last it leveled off, flowed steadily, and then began to drop almost as swiftly as it had appeared. It was almost dusk.

He climbed higher and higher. The canyon was not familiar to him, and yet in a vague sort of a way he seemed to remember something about it. Which way had the doomed clay-bank taken him? He was high up the slope when he saw the faint line of masonry through the gloom and he knew that he was looking at relics of a forgotten past: the little dwellings built in the remote canyons of the Southwest by the Hohokam, or some such a loco name; the ancient ones who had been there long before the Apaches, Navajos, Pueblos and Hopis.

Well, it was better than nothing, and the chill of the wet wind was getting into his bones. He clambered over a terrace wall and peered into the nearest dwelling. The roof had long caved in. At the very end of the terrace he found a sort of a leaning-tower affair and the bottom room was in fair condition. He eased through the T-shaped doorway and stripped off slicker and denim jacket, shivering in the cold.

But Ken Macklin had hit the Stardust trail too many times to get concerned about his position. He was lost, at least until he could see sun or stars. He had shelter of a sort, food and water. He grinned wryly at the last. There was enough water in that canyon to float a frigate.

It was only a matter of an hour before he had his fire going, fed by dry as dust cottonwood and spruce beams and brush which had been driven into sheltered crevices by the strong canyon winds. His coffee and bacon were ready and his clothing was drying. He squatted by his fire, a lean lath of a man dressed in worn but serviceable long Johns, teetering on his boot heels as he chewed his bacon and sipped his coffee.

His blankets and clothing steamed, giving the low-ceilinged room a humid heat. He sat back against the wall and sipped his second cup of coffee. In times past he had hunted through many of the canyons of the Conchas country for deer and for strays and once for an escaped killer. He had seen the remote cliff dwellings a number of times and had done a little digging in them. But this group was new to him. The way he figured it, he was just north of the hills beyond Skillet Crick. It was going to be a long walk home the next day, *if* the rain let up.

He opened his eyes and looked up at the dim ceiling of the room. The fire had died away to ashes, with here and there a winking red eye of ember. He raised his head. A soft, cold sort of light seemed to show beyond the narrow T-shaped doorway. He threw back his damp blankets and walked to the entrance. The rain had stopped, and the clouds had drifted off letting the moon shine down upon the jumbled canyon country.

Now a new mood had taken over. There was a brooding quietness about the canyon; almost a mood of evil and impending danger.

Ken stepped back and picked up his Winchester, levering a .44-40 into the chamber. His extra cartridges had been in one of the saddlebags buried beneath the cold silt somewhere far down the canyon. But the magazine of the rifle was full, giving him twelve rounds, and his pistol cartridges were of course interchangeable.

Scanning the area slowly, he tensed as a bush moved, and it moved *against* the cold flowing of the pre-dawn wind.

Someone, or something, was up on that canyon brim, and he knew well enough that whoever it was knew that he was in those crumbling ruins.

He moved along the terrace, keeping to the shadows, then he moved behind one of the ruins, to climb up a slope of debris and reach an upper floor; He rolled over the eroded wall into the interior and bellied across to the outer wall, taking off his hat as he did so. He lay there for a long time watching the canyon brim. The wind and the moon played strange tricks with trees and brush, almost peopling them with figures of imagination, but he thought there was nothing human moving up there.

The moon was on the wane when he slid down the slope and reached the terrace. Suddenly there was a sharp blossom of orange-red flame. He hit the terrace as the gun flatted off, slamming its echo back and forth within the canyon. The softnosed slug struck squarely just behind where he had been standing, showering him with bits of the mud-facing of the building.

Ken bellied along the terrace. It had been tophole shooting: downhill, in vague light, at an indefinite target. He reached the end of the terrace and peered up at the brim just in time to see another one of those deadly orange-red blossoms sprout. This time the slug rapped the terrace wall and showered bits of rock and adobe into his face. Ken pressed low against the terrace floor. The bastard could shoot like one of Berdan's Sharpshooters.

Ken wormed his way back beside a building and lay with crossed arms, resting his chin on them as he studied that etched brim of rock across from him. It was at least three hundred yards across the great trough.

It was quiet now except for the soughing of the wind, and, as the moon dropped low, the terrace and the ruins became shrouded in the darkness of shadow. Ken crawled from his hide-out and over the terrace wall, sliding down the cold muddy slope until he was at the foot of the wall on his side of the canyon. He worked his way swiftly across the canyon and eyed the great, eroded wall above him. It would be damned outright foolishness to try and scale that in darkness with the rocks and earth loosened by the pouring rains.

There was nothing to do but sit it out until dawn.

The dawn light came slowly, and as it did so it lighted the western wall of the canyon, the one where Ken Macklin lay hidden with his Winchester cocked and ready in his hands. The light began to show details and then he heard the sound coming from above him, the sound of something sliding slowly down the wet slopes. He raised his head just in time to see two men move behind a great tilted slab of rock and not reappear on the far side. They would be watching the cliff dwellings on the far side of the canyon waiting for him to make a move. He could not recognize either of the two men, but one of them wore a slicker and the other a rain-darkened serape. Both of them had their hats pulled down low.

Ken eased himself from shelter and worked his way along the slope until he could almost look down upon the two men. All he could see was their hats. In a little while the two men moved, resting rifles on a rock ledge, while they watched the dwellings.

Neither of the men moved more than was necessary until, at last, one of them picked up his rifle and began to work his way with uncanny speed and stealth through the tangled brush and rocks down toward the canyon floor. It was the man who wore the serape.

The other man crouched low, and in a little while a thread of bluish tobacco smoke rose from his hiding place. Ken watched the serape-wearer reach the far side of the canyon floor and then vanish into a deep cleft that trended up the canyon wall.

Ken moved softly across the broken ground, and as he slid behind a rock ledge his boot heels loosened a rock that rolled down the slope with a rattling of loose pebbles. Bellying to the far side of the ledge, keeping low, peering through the brush, Ken moved swiftly. Just then he saw the smoker throw up his rifle to fire in the direction of the sound. The man never had a chance. Ken's slug hit him and drove him back beneath the rim of the ledge, and his rifle clattered to the rocks. Ken slid down the slope and looked across the canyon even as the last echoes of the gun shot died away. He could see nothing. The serape-wearer was lying low.

It was quiet now; a deathly sort of a quiet.

Ken wet his lips and peered down toward where he had dropped the first man. Nothing moved. But he wasn't about to poke his big nose down there to meet a softnosed slug.

Then he heard a sort of coughing grunt; a head arose and then dropped again. Lung shot, thought Ken. That man wasn't about to shoot now.

"Macklin," the voice came hoarsely from below the ledge where the wounded man was hidden.

Ken half closed his eyes. The voice sounded familiar.

"Macklin, for God's sake!"

Ken nodded. It was the blood hoarsened voice of Clem Brace.

"Macklin, yuh better come down here. Yuh got me fair and square. I won' shoot."

Ken eased his way down the slope, shoving his muddy rifle ahead of him, watching warily for any movement from across the canyon. He reached the ledge.

"That you, Macklin?" asked Brace.

"You know damned well it is."

"Yeh." Brace coughed thickly. "Nice shooting," he said.

"You weren't so bad yourself awhile ago."

"Wasn't me. It was him— Carancho."

Then Ken remembered the silent man who had been with Steve Wascoe that time along Skillet Crick. The breed, or whatever he was.

"What's the game, Brace?"

The man was silent for a time. "We followed yuh in here. We got orders not to let yuh come out and to be damned sure no one knew we was in at the kill. Yuh was to vanish completely." Brace laughed thickly. "Looks like it's me that's going to vanish instead."

Ken worked closer and then peered over the ledge into the pale unshaven face of the Texan, and what he saw on that face was enough to convince him that Clem had accurately forecasted his own end.

"If I can hogtie that buzzard up there I'll try to get you out of here, Brace."

"Yore a double-damned fool! Yuh won't get near him, Macklin, and yuh won't get me outa here either."

"I'll leave then and let him do it."

"Carancho?" Brace laughed again. "Jesus God yuh must be a nicer *hombre* than they give yuh credit for. That bastard would just as soon put the knife into me as bother to try and get me outa here. Well, I played their dirty rotten game. I guess I gotta make it up somehow."

Ken eyed the far side of the canyon. "Meaning?"

"I got nothing personal against yuh. It was orders. We was to kill yuh."

"Naylor's orders?"

"No."

"Steve Wascoe's?"

"I ain't goin' to tell yuh and yuh can't scare a dyin' man, *hombre*."

Ken looked at him. The Texan was true to his kind.

Brace raised himself a little. "Things was well organized afore yuh come back, Macklin. Now yuh got some of 'em scared and them that ain't scared is worried. I tried to scare yuh off and so did Jim Dana. Old Lon did too I guess. But yuh didn't scare. Something told me yuh wouldn't. Take my advice and get outa this country. Go on back and forget the Double H and that filly over there. She ain't nothing but loco weed for a man like you, Macklin. She's a Naylor, by God, and won't be nothin' else ever. Carancho and me left our horses up on the brim, half a mile due west, near a clump of trees. Yuh can't miss 'em. Take 'em both and get the hell outa this bloody Conchas country!"

"Who told you to kill me, Brace?"

Brace shook his head. "I'm not sayin'. Just get outa here! Pronto!"

"Who killed Jordan Harker?"

Brace closed his eyes and coughed thickly as the bright blood stained his mouth and unshaven chin.

The man wouldn't talk. Nothing on earth could make him talk.

Ken took Brace's cartridges and bent the barrel of his rifle between two rocks. Then he ghosted along the slope and slid down it to watch the far side where that damned wolf in human form, was lurking. He looked back to where Brace was hidden, waiting to die. There was no chance in him getting the man out of there. It would be a long lonely death for Clem Brace.

"Hey, Macklin!" Brace's voice echoed down the canyon. "I forgot to tell yuh yore on Guthook land again, and this time it ain't no-trick on yuh!"

A rifle spat high on the east wall of the canyon and the slug screamed eerily from the rocks inches from where Brace lay dying.

"Go to hell yuh breed bastard!" yelled Brace. "I hope Macklin gives yuh what he gave me!"

The gun flamed again, and this time it had an echo as Ken fired. The reports of both guns were followed by a thin yell from Carancho. Ken grinned.

He was two hundred yards down the canyon when he heard another gun report. This time the slug didn't hum through the air or ricochet screamingly from the rock. Clem had taken the short trail out.

Ken climbed the western slopes, concealed from Carancho by a bend in the canyon wall. His breath was thick in his chest when he reached the top, but there was no time to rest. He slogged through brush and catclaw until he found the horses, but instead of leaving with them, he found a secluded place within a hundred yards of the picketed horses. There he lay hidden.

The sun was at its zenith when Carancho came ghosting through the drying brush as silently as wind-driven smoke. Ken lay low and watched the man as he stopped and looked at the horses and scanned the surrounding terrain with slitted eyes.

Ken wet his lips and sighted his Winchester. It would be a close shot but he had creased wild horses in West Texas. He squeezed off his shot. The man whirled like a teetotum and fell heavily, while blood stained the side of his head.

Ken approached cautiously, for he knew this man was as deadly as a diamond back. For the time being, at least, Carancho was unconscious. Ken disarmed him of Colt, Winchester and knife. He carried the breed to one of the horses and slung him over the saddle, gagging him and then tying his wrists together with a reata found on the saddle, then securing him to the horse. He covered the naked form with the filthy serape, and mounted the other horse to lead Carancho to the south.

It was late in the afternoon when Ken Macklin looked down from a ridge toward the huge buildings of the Lazy J. He slapped the rump of the horse that was laden with Carancho, knowing the horse would head for the Lazy J corrals. He rolled a smoke and lighted it, watching the horse move steadily toward the buildings, and as it did so, he saw the contorted face of the breed staring at him with pure, icy hell in the dark basilisk eyes.

Ken kneed the horse away and rode toward the Rio Frio. He looked back toward the hills where Clem Brace lay stiff in death and waved a hand in farewell to a man who might have been a good *compadre* if he had been on the same side of the fence as Ken.

It would be war to the hilt from now on. But Ken still had not found Jobie Harker, nor did he know upon whose orders those two human wolves had followed him to dry gulch him.

Ken rolled another smoke as he reached the Double H side of the Rio Frio. He had failed to find Jobie Harker, or even get a sight of him. If Milligan's telegrams hadn't stopped the kid aboard the train, then he was still on the loose, and what was worse, still thinking he had killed a man.

But first he meant to corner Stella Harker and find out what she had said to the kid before he had lit out. It would probably be an interesting session. Ken smiled grimly as he sucked in on his cigarette and blew out the smoke. He was almost looking forward to it as a man looks forward to breaking a wild horse to saddle and bridle.

CHAPTER NINE

T HERE WAS a hushed quietness about the Double H as Ken Macklin walked up the soft, wet slope before the big house. There were no lights in the house and only the far bunkhouse had lights in it. There was a feeling of rain in the darkening air.

He walked around the side and stepped up on the, rear porch. It was almost as though he was at a deserted homestead rather than at what had once been one of the busiest ranches in the Conchas country.

The money from the place had been squandered by Wes, but the land was still there and always would be there. It was good land; as good as any in that country, barring the Lazy J. Old Jordan Harker's soul had been in that land as his body now was interred in it. Jordan Harker had left a strange legacy. The Double H had been a powerful factor in that country, but it was plain enough that it had been the leadership of Jordan that had made it so. His foster son had practically been driven from the country; his own eldest son was an alcoholic, and his youngest son fancied himself a gunslinger with a homicidal touch. That left Miriam. Ken had begun to realize that Jordan Harker's blood and spirit had passed on into the one female he had sired.

Jordan Harker's ghost remained to haunt the place until

his murderer would be exposed or killed. This was Ken's duty. He knew he could never leave until that was done.

Someone had given orders for Ken to get the notorious 'Guthook' treatment and had sent two experts in to do the job. One of them now lay blue-faced in death beneath the lowering skies, and the other had been shamed, as much as a man could be shamed, by being sent back naked and helpless as a silent message from Ken Macklin to Lon Naylor, or whoever had put the two killers up to their trade in the canyon country. Ken knew well enough that he had had more than his share of luck with him that day.

Lon Naylor had admitted bald-facedly that he still wanted the Rio Frio land. He had been willing enough to pay off Ken Macklin to get him out of that country. If he wouldn't leave, disaster was sure to follow.

Warning after warning, had been given to Ken Macklin. And he stood alone now, dependent upon his guts and his guns, faced by the toughest *corrida* in the Southwest, led by a man who was a living legend.

He opened the kitchen door. The place was cold and as quiet as a tomb. He walked into the big living room to start a fire. It was pleasant in a sense to have the big house to himself. He watched the fire creep over the logs in the massive fireplace, with a glass of rye in one hand and a cigarette in the other and his socked feet stretched toward the heat of the fire. He wondered where all of them had gone. It bid fair to be a wet night, and the roads were already soft and treacherous. Still it was pleasant to be alone with his teeming thoughts. He had had little enough time, since he had crossed the Conchas, to compose and arrange his thoughts.

There was an insistent impulse at the back of his mind to saddle up and get out of there, to ride east, west, north or south: anywhere to get away from the brooding shadow of blood that hung over the Conchas country. For he knew, as sure as he was sitting there, that the final events were swiftly shaping up, and unless he got out of there as swiftly as he had come, he'd be belly deep in gunsmoke and death.

Above the bittersweet odor of the burnt wood he had caught a soft and subtle fragrance, like the early summer flowers upon the plains. He raised his head a little, then sat upright. He wasn't alone in that darkened room. There was a full-bodied figure within five feet of him.

"Hello, Ken," said Stella Harker softly.

He stood up and eyed her. "When did you get home?"

She laughed quietly. "I was here all the time, you big booby!"

"Where are the others?"

She shrugged. "Wes went into town for a little gambling and a lot of drinking. That's where he usually goes when the going gets tough around here. Miriam left here shortly after you did. I don't know where she went. Maybe to look for Jobie."

"Up in the hills?" he said sharply.

She tilted her lovely head to one side. "What makes you think he went up into the hills?"

An odd feeling came over him. She was playing some kind of deep and dirty game; after all, she was the only child of Lon Naylor.

"Where is he Stella?"

"I don't know."

"You talked with him before he left. Perhaps you talked him into leaving."

"Maybe I did," she said defensively. "I didn't want him here. The sight of him annoys Wes."

"Why don't you give Wes a break?" he said earnestly.

"In what way?"

"Act like a wife. Try to get him off the bottle. Let Jobie alone."

She laughed and shook her head. "Coming from you, it's really funny, Ken. You loved me when you left here. I think you still do. What do you care if I make a fool out of that drunken wreck I married?"

He leaned against the side of the fireplace and fixed a smoke. She turned quickly and took two ready-made ones from a carved, wooden box on the table, placed them between her full lips and lighted them, taking one from her mouth and placing it in his mouth. He had never seen her smoke before, but as he watched her enjoy the tobacco he knew smoking was nothing new to her.

"Why *did* you marry Wes?" he asked quietly.

"You were gone, Ken."

"Cut that! You had plenty of chances to let me know how you felt about me."

She took the cigarette from her mouth. "My God," she breathed. "Listen to the man!"

"You played me like a trout. Just like you played all men who ran into your range."

She leaned forward. "Just what the hell do you mean by *that?*" she grated.

He flipped the cigarette into the embers. The taste of it had been spoiled by her lip rouge. It sickened him, as she had begun to sicken him.

She came close and studied him. "What's bothering you, Ken?"

"Many things. The murder of Jordan Harker. The mess being made of the Double H."

"And me?"

"In a sense."

She was almost touching him now and the warmth and fragrance of her full body seemed to flow over his senses. "What do you mean, Ken?"

He took her gently by the shoulders. She raised her face expecting to be kissed. He looked down at her. She was lovely, but there was something repulsive about her at the same time. The woman seemed to spread ruin and hatred wherever she walked. And blood would follow the hatred as surely as the night followed the day. His big hands tightened on her soft, rounded shoulders, and she opened her great, dark eyes. "Ken, you're hurting me!"

The hands gripped tighter and he felt her wince beneath the pressure.

"Ken!" she snapped.

"It's about time you and I had a little talk, Stella. You know where that kid went and I want you to tell me."

"Let me go, damn you!"

"You told the kid he was a murderer and all the time you knew well enough that the whole thing was an accident. You wanted that kid out of the way. Why, Stella?"

She kicked at him and yelled, "If I had a gun in my hand I'd blow out your guts!"

He walked toward her. "I almost believe you," he said. "You always were pretty good with a gun. Lon Naylor saw to that, didn't he? I can remember when you used to challenge some of the *vaqueros* to shoot against you, and you'd beat 'em every time. But maybe they were playing politics and didn't want to beat the daughter of the Big Boss."

She thrust the hair out of her lovely face. "I didn't have to take odds," she said. "I could beat most of them without even trying."

He looked down at her. "Now, Stella," he said quietly.

"Damn it! My name is *Estelle!*"

"Yes," he said dryly. "Estelle *Harker.*"

He bent over her and the mingled aura of warm flesh and perfume almost tempted him but he was held by the revulsion he now felt for this beautiful creature, who was ugliness incarnate in soul.

He gripped her by the arm. "Tell me, Stella!" he insisted. "Don't let that boy think he is a murderer. They won't take him without a fight, Stella, and he's good with those six-guns, as good as any man in this country. He'll shoot to kill before they take him. If I can find him I can talk him into coming back."

She laughed into his face, and his free hand caught her a stinging blow alongside the cheek. Her teeth sank into the outer flesh of his hand and he jerked it back. She pulled him toward her and he fell on top of her.

The front door swung open, and the draft from it caused the dying fire to flare up. Ken looked up into the taut and lovely face of Miriam Harker. He stood up. What he saw in her eyes was the destruction of an idol.

Stella struggled to her feet. She stared at Miriam defensively. "It was him," she said swiftly. "He came back and found me alone! He made advances! He was angry because I married Wes while he was gone! Look at him! The guilt is all over his face! It wasn't me, Miriam! I tell you it wasn't me!"

Miriam placed her hat on the table. "It seems to me the lady doth protest too much," she said wearily.

Stella walked toward her like a cat. "What do you mean by that?" she asked softly, but there was cold steel beneath the velvet of her tones.

The younger woman turned slowly. "I'd rather not talk about it, Estelle."

Miriam eyed Estelle. "If the truth be known," she said quietly, "he had more than a little help."

"I don't like your insinuations, Miriam."

"There's been nothing but trouble since you came here, Estelle, and before you're through there'll be a lot more of it."

Estelle swung from the hip, a full arc of a blow that caught Miriam flush on the left cheek, staggering her. Estelle laughed as she swung a left hand to strike the younger woman again. Blood trickled from the corner of Miriam's soft mouth as she went down and Stella kicked at her. Ken gripped Stella by an arm and swung her away. The fire showed her face as a mask of viciousness.

Miriam got up slowly. "Ken," she said quietly as she wiped the blood from her mouth, "let her go. She's got to learn a lesson sometime. Now is as good a time as any."

Ken stepped back and released the raging woman. She rushed at Miriam, and then Miriam stepped back a little, closed a small left fist and held her arm out straight, catching Stella flush on her wide mouth, staggering her, while an instant later a small but hard right fist struck the older woman on the jaw, driving her back against the front door.

Then Miriam closed in, alternating with hard, cutting blows to eyes, nose and mouth until Stella sank to the floor screaming pitifully, while the blood trickled from her nose and mouth.

Miriam smiled thinly." I wasn't raised with three brothers for nothing," she said over her shoulder. She turned and smiled a little at Ken.

Stella was up on her feet. She snatched up a heavy book end and hurled it at Miriam. It struck Miriam's shoulder and she winced in pain. Stella closed in now, like a bloody, raging fury, driving Miriam back across the room.

But the Harkers had fighting blood too. Miriam threw the older woman aside and gripped her by the hair.

It was then that Ken broke up the fight, sustaining half a dozen scratches and bites from both vixens before he shoved Stella toward the hallway door and pushed Miriam back into a corner.

Then suddenly it was quiet except for the heavy breathing of the two women and the crackling of the revived fire. Stella wiped the blood from her face. "I'm leaving," she said. "I've had enough of this hole and the fool people who live here. I'm going home."

"Good riddance," said Miriam. "I only hope we can rebuild the wreckage you've left behind."

"You'll rebuild nothing! You'll lose the Double H! You'll lose everything! Everything, you understand! I'll see that you're stripped naked before you leave the Rio Frio Valley!" She dashed out of the room.

Ken rubbed his jaws. "You'd better look to those cuts," he said. "I'll saddle a horse for her."

"Do you really think she'll go?"

He nodded. "I just can't help but wonder why she came here in the first place," he said thoughtfully.

When Estelle was ready, she mounted her dun mare

quickly and looked down at Ken. "I'll send someone for my things," she said coldly.

"Do you want me to ride with you to your father's house?"

"Why? Do you think anyone would bother Lon Naylor's daughter?"

"No," he said quietly.

She looked down at him. "Roll me a cigarette, Ken," she said.

He rolled a pair of quirlies, lighted both of them and handed her one. She sucked in on the smoke. "Why don't you pull out of here, Ken?"

"I can't right now."

"You'll never get that money out of Wes."

"So?"

She leaned forward a little, and he could see the livid bruises on her face. "Don't stay here and try to be a hero. This place is lost and so are the Harkers. My father will have the Rio Frio Valley before too long, Ken."

"You talk like him, Stella."

She smiled thinly. "He won't be here forever, Ken. Take my advice. Get out of here while you can, or throw in with my father. He doesn't like you, Ken, but he does respect you for a fighting man. The kind of man who could take over on the Lazy J when he is gone."

"Meaning?"

She smiled again. "Figure it out yourself. I haven't got anything against you, Ken." She touched her mare with her spurs and they jingled faintly. She rode down the slope without once looking back.

CHAPTER TEN

KEN MADE breakfast for himself and Miriam, while Wes, who had drunkenly stumbled into the house shortly before dawn, slept off the alcoholic effects. He caught himself looking quite often at this quiet young woman whom he had always considered as a sister, although their blood was not the same.

"I wonder what he'll say when he gets up and finds out she's gone, Ken?" said Miriam.

He shrugged. "He's better off this way. Do you think she ever really loved him, Miriam?"

"She doesn't love anyone but herself, not even her father, but she respects him. She respects anyone she can't browbeat or cozen into her way."

"Like you?"

She smiled faintly. "I must be the one exception. You seem to be able to handle her, Ken."

He waved a hand. "She handled me well enough before I left this country."

She studied him over the rim of her coffee cup. "It seems as though you've seen the elephant, as they say."

He nodded. "Enough to know that she isn't the girl I left behind me."

"Yes, she is . . . . Trouble is that you didn't know her for what she was then and you do now. She's dangerous, Ken, and you know it."

"She's a Naylor," he said simply. He glanced at Miriam. "Why did she marry Wes?"

"It was all you before you left. Then for a time she had half a dozen others hanging around. She got around quite a bit.

When she was away at school a few rumors came drifting back and her father brought her back. He should have left her there." She laughed without mirth.

"But why Wes?"

"As long as my father ran the Double H there was no chance of a Harker marrying a Naylor. You knew Dad."

"I should," he said dryly. "I can remember a few instances when I was chasing Stella."

She nodded. "Dad was the one thing that kept Stella, as you call her, away from Wes. But Wes was quite pleased that Estelle Naylor, the belle of the Conchas country, seemed to take an interest in him. It was about that time he started talking about how he had taken up the challenge of Jim Dana in Conchas Corners and led the way into that fight."

She looked up at him. "It was only after Dad was murdered from ambush that she moved in on Wes, *and* the Double H." She laughed bitterly. "Oh, the changes that woman made around here. Money and trouble. She alienated Jobie and Wes; she alienated Wes and myself. She sent Tacos out to cook for the men and brought in a cook from Santa Fe. One man after another left the ranch because of her. Wes took to the bottle, as you well know, and the ranch began to slide downhill. You might as well know the truth, Ken. It won't be long before we'll lose it altogether."

The land is still here," he said stubbornly.

"With a mortgage on it that we can't meet."

"What do you mean?" he asked sharply.

She nodded. "Wes borrowed a lot of money against the ranch. The note is due in a few weeks. We just haven't got that kind of money, Ken, and no way of getting it."

"Can't you renew the mortgage?"

She stood up and walked to the window. "Anywhere else we might have managed it."

"But there should be someone who can carry you along!"

She shook her head. "No," she said. "We'll be foreclosed."

"Let me see what I can do." He stood up and walked toward her. "Who has the due note, Miriam?"

She turned slowly. "You might as well know, Ken. It's Lon Naylor."

"Oh my God! He's wanted this land as far back as I can remember!"

"Yes. He could never get his grasping hands on it as long as Dad was here. Once Dad was out of the way the ruin began, instigated by Lon Naylor's own daughter. I really believe Stella Naylor married Wes just to ruin this place and put it into her father's hands, and it looks like she has succeeded, Ken. Maybe if I had left her alone last night we might have talked her into seeing her father on our behalf."

He shook his head. "No." The rottenness of the whole thing sickened him to the core.

"We'll have to find Jobie," said Miriam, breaking into Ken's thoughts.

"I'll go out again."

"I'll go with you."

"No."

"Why not, Ken?" she challenged.

He took her by the shoulders. "Because there's death out there, Miriam." He quickly told her of how he had been trailed and ambushed. "I may have to go on Guthook land again, and this time I might not get off so easily."

She shuddered a little. "That Carancho," she said. "You should have killed him, Ken. I shouldn't say that, but by letting him live, after what you did to him, you practically signed your death warrant."

He shrugged. "I've been beaten up and shot at since I

came back here. I've grown to expect it. Now go and rouse Wes. I want to talk to him."

As he listened to her talking to her brother and his sullen, thick-voiced answers, he sheathed his oiled Colt and placed his Winchester near the kitchen door. He heard her walking about in the living room. "Ken!" she called out.

"Yes?"

"You'd better come here at once!"

He hurried through the hallway, glancing into Wes' room to see the man sprawled on the bed. Miriam was standing at the big, front window looking toward the Rio Frio. "Look," she said quietly.

He looked over her shoulder toward the river. Three men were riding steadily toward the house. Rather two men and almost a grown man, for the third man was Jobie Harker, riding boot to boot beside Steve Wascoe, the man he had tried to ape in clothing, mannerisms, *and,* killing ability. The third man was the quiet man known to Ken as Dod Nellis: the man who had seemed to know something about the three years Ken had spent away from the Conchas country; the man who had been called a stock detective by Clem Brace.

Ken felt a cold finger trace the length of his spine. Those were three tough ones out there. There was no one to back Ken. The few hands on the ranch were out doing the chores, and even if they had been available, they weren't the type of hardcase *vaqueros* Jordan Harker had kept on the Double H in his time.

"What are you going to do?" asked Miriam.

He smiled faintly. "Do? Why, I'm going out to see what they want."

She nodded and stepped back. "I wish you had been here long ago, Ken," she said.

He smiled again. "Why, Miriam! That's the nicest thing you've said to me since I came back! But it means for the good of the ranch, doesn't it?"

She touched his face with a small cool hand. "Partly," she said.

He rolled a cigarette as he stood at the bottom of the steps watching the three horsemen. Jobie got down to open the Texas gate, let the two of them through, then closed the gate, mounted and rode up alongside Steve Wascoe again.

"Me and my shadow," said Ken to himself as he saw the boy beside Steve Wascoe.

They halted twenty feet from Ken. "Howdy," he said.

Wascoe and Nellis nodded but the boy did not move. His eyes coldly studied Ken.

"What can I do for you?" asked Ken. His eyes flitted past them, searching the willows and cottonwoods along the river, watching for a skulking figure with a long gun in his hands.

"There's no one back there," said Steve quietly.

"Did you think we *needed* anyone back there?" challenged Jobie.

"You riding with the Guthook boys now, Jobie?" asked Ken quietly.

"I ride where I please!"

Ken nodded.

"We were sent over here by Mister Naylor," said Steve.

"So? You want Mrs. Harker's things, is that it?"

Steve nodded. Then he leaned forward, resting an elbow on his pommel. "There's more to this visit than just that, Macklin." "Go on."

"Seems as though Mister Naylor doesn't like the idea of his daughter being beat up by a man, Macklin."

Ken stared at him. He took the cigarette from his mouth. "It wasn't a man, Wascoe. She tangled with her sister-in-law and found she caught a tiger by the tail. She couldn't hang on and she couldn't let go."

"Yeh," said Wascoe dryly. "Now you just get Wes Harker out here, Macklin."

"Why?"

The wind shifted a little and the windmill began to whirr and whine. A door slammed somewhere in the house.

"Because I was sent here to talk about what he done to his wife, is all."

"I said it was a fight between Estelle and Miriam."

Wascoe spat leisurely. "Bunk!" he said between his teeth. "Get Harker out here, Macklin. Pronto!"

"He's still drunk, Wascoe."

"Drunk or sober I want him out here!"

Ken spat now. "This is Double H land, Wascoe," he said thinly. "Now you take your two sidekicks and get out of here, at least until Wes is sober enough to tell you he didn't lay a hand on Estelle."

A thin, mirthless smile covered the lean face of the gunman. "Who's going to *make* us get off Double H land, Macklin?"

Ken wanted no part of the three of them, and if he went for his gun, two faster men than he were facing him, backed by an unknown who might be just as fast.

Jobie slid from his horse and started for the porch. "I'll get him, Steve," he said.

"Wait!" said Ken. "Look, kid, you've got no business with these *hombres*. Your brother didn't touch Estelle."

"That's not what she told me."

"She's lying, Jobie."

"What was that you said?" asked Wascoe.

Ken looked at him. "She's lying, Wascoe."

"She wouldn't lie to me," said the kid softly.

"She told you that you killed a man, didn't she?"

Jobie did not answer. He walked toward the house.

"Get back, kid," said Ken.

The dark eyes swept Ken's face. "I've killed my first man," he said in deadly seriousness, "and I won't hesitate to kill a second."

"Don't talk like a hero," said Ken. "Tacos died of a heart attack, not from one of your slugs. And if he'd died from one of your slugs it would have been considered an accidental death."

Jobie's face worked. He wanted to be a big man and he was in a helluva hurry to get there.

Wascoe swung down from his saddle. "Get your brother, kid," he said quietly.

Jobie walked three steps. The look in Ken's eyes held him back.

"Go on, Jobie," said Wascoe.

"Get out of the way, Ken," said Jobie, imitating Steve's flat, emotionless voice.

"No."

A deadly quietness came then. Wascoe had stepped away from his horse and stood there rubbing the back of his gloved left hand, feet spread a little apart, hat level with the thin eyebrows and eyes directly on Ken.

"Once more," said Jobie. "Get out of the way!"

"Look, kid," said Ken quietly. "They're using you. Estelle lied to you as sure as I'm standing here."

"Don't say that again!"

"She lied, *dammit!*"

The kid gave away his play with his eyes. Ken jumped to his right, getting Jobie between him and Wascoe, while he ripped his hat from his head, sailing it full into Jobie's face. Then he jumped forward, clamping a hard left hand down on Jobie's right wrist, holding the right-hand Colt in its sheath while his own six-gun cleared leather, was cocked and rammed hard into the kid's lean belly, driving some of the wind from him. It had only been a matter of seconds. Ken stared into the kid's wide eyes, inches from his own. "What are you going to do now, Jobie?" asked Ken coldly.

Wascoe turned angrily, and Ken stepped back with his gun wavering in a slow steady arc between the sickened kid and the gunslinger. "I said before that this was Double H land, Wascoe," said Ken. "Now get out of here!"

The hard eyes flicked down at the Colt and then up at

Ken's face. "Fair enough," said Wascoe. "But we'll be back, Macklin. We got a score to settle here, ain't we?"

"Git!"

The front door opened behind Ken and Wes Harker came swaying down the stairs. "Whoinell wants me?" he demanded thickly.

"Get back in the house," said Ken.

"Go ta hell! They want me? They got my wife! I'm going and get her!"

"Get back in the house!"

The kid's guts had come back. "We wanted you, Wes," he said thinly, "not Ken."

"You got me! You lookin' for trouble? I'll show yuh!" He slapped down for a draw. The kid jumped back, clawing for a Colt. Wes staggered toward him, trying to hold his gun steady. Ken sheathed his own Colt and reached to grab Wes just as he saw Wes' finger tighten on the trigger. Too late. A gun rapped and the slug struck Wes in the guts, spinning him about and dropping him. Ken turned to see Steve Wascoe in a crouch, the gloved hand holding the Colt from which a thread of smoke drifted. His eyes were like blue ice, and he was ready to fire again.

A sickening feeling came over Ken. The kid wouldn't shoot and neither would Nellis, and Wes was dying at Ken's feet. The gun blasted but Ken was untouched. Then he realized it hadn't been Wascoe who had fired at all. The report had come from the side of the house.

Ken turned. Miriam stood there with a smoking Winchester in her hands. "Ken told you to git," she said coldly.

Wascoe reached for his Colt.

"Leave it there," she said. "Jobie! Go into the house!"

He silently shook his head.

Wascoe swung up onto his horse. Nellis looked at him.

"You've just killed a man, Wascoe," he said.

"They know where to find me," the gunman said. He

turned his horse and rode swiftly toward the gate, followed by Jobie.

"Let him go," said Ken. He knelt beside Wes.

His foster brother opened his eyes. "I'm going, Ken," he said.

"You'll make it, Wes."

"No. It's just as well. I've made a damned mess of things. You had it settled until I butt in. Serves me right."

Ken looked up at Nellis. The man shook his head. Miriam began to sob.

Wes choked a little and blood trickled from his mouth. "I'm glad I'm going," he said. "Estelle left me and Jobie hates me. I've lost the Double H for the rest of you." He smiled faintly. "I even lied for years about being the big hero of the Conchas Corners fight." Wes weakly waved a hand. "The only thing I regret is that I didn't find the person who killed Dad. You find him, Ken, Promise me?"

"Yes."

Nellis glanced quickly at Ken and then at Wes.

"Whoever did the job knew Dad's habits real well and they planned his dry gulching that way. You find him, Ken."

"Yes."

Then a spasm shook the man's body and he was gone.

Ken stood up and looked toward the river. Steve Wascoe and Jobie Harker were just entering the willows.

"You going after them, Macklin?" asked Nellis.

"Yes."

"They'll kill you."

"Maybe."

"They will," said Nellis. He put on his hat. "Let me go up and talk with Lon Naylor. Maybe he'll have Steve taken into town."

"I doubt that."

Nellis shrugged. "Let me try anyway."

"What's your game, Nellis?"

The man smiled. "I have been working for Lon Naylor, but not as a hired killer. Lon Naylor hired me for two reasons. One of them was to find out who killed Jordan Harker."

Ken glanced quickly at him. "And the other?"

"I'm not at liberty to tell you. You stay here. If I can get the old man to have Wascoe taken to the sheriff I'll do it."

"And if he doesn't agree?"

The dark eyes studied Ken. "Then it's up to the sheriff, isn't it?"

"Milligan won't buck the Guthook *corrida,* Nellis." "Maybe." The big man mounted his horse. "I'm sorry about this, Macklin." He rode off leaving the two of them with their

dead brother.

CHAPTER ELEVEN

A LIGHT rain was falling on the Conchas country, dimpling the surface of the Rio Frio and pattering on the roof of the ranch house. Ken Macklin sat in the living room of the big house, looking into the dancing flames of the fireplace, trying to find the answers to the questions that teemed in his mind.

Joe Forrest, deputy-sheriff, came into the room. "I'm making out the warrant for the arrest of Steven Wascoe on a charge of murder, Ken," he said.

"Yes."

"They found Doroteo Navarez hiding out down south of here. Milligan was quite excited about locating him. Left right away."

"Right after he heard about Wascoe killing Wes," said Ken dryly.

"That ain't exactly fair, is it, Ken?"

"It figures. I know damned well that George Milligan would never go onto Guthook land looking for anyone, much less Steve Wascoe."

"Open and shut case of murder," said Joe.

Ken looked up at him. "Then you'll go right over there and pick up Wascoe?"

"Now I didn't say *that*. Milligan told me to stay close to Conchas Corners in case he needed me, so *I* can't go after Wascoe." Joe flushed. "Well, anyway, Milligan told mc I could swear you in as deputy, in case you wanted to go after Wascoe."

Ken stood up. He held up his right hand. "Swear me in, Joe, before I change my mind."

It was over in a matter of minutes. The star was pinned to Ken's jacket and the warrant was in his pocket. He was alone in the quiet living room of the house, listening to the thudding of hoofs on the road as Joe Forrest rode back to Conchas Corners, with the cold body of Wes Harker being carried in an undertaker's wagon behind him.

Miriam came into the room. "This is madness," she said. "They'll shoot you to doll rags, Ken."

He looked at her. "Maybe it has to be this way."

"You walk into that house over there and they'll kill you one way or the other, if you get as far as the house."

"I want Steve Wascoe, Miriam."

"It won't settle anything if he kills you."

"I'll take my chances on that."

"But the others! Carancho for one! Even Jobie!"

He smiled faintly. "Jobie isn't quite so sure of himself now." He looked into the fire. "Besides, something has been running through my mind. Something Dod Nellis told me."

"What is that?"

"You heard what he said. One reason Lon Naylor had hired him was to find out who killed Jordan Harker."

"Yes?"

"Why would he do that?"

"I don't know. Do you?"

He poured himself a drink. The memories of his talk with Lon Naylor came back to him. "He said he couldn't have had Dad killed. He said that, man to man, facing Dad, he would have looked forward to putting a bullet into his belly, but he would never have had him dry gulched."

She laughed without mirth. "Him? You believed *him* when he said that?"

Ken nodded. "Lon Naylor is a tight fisted,. battling old schemer, but he's no murderer. Sure, men have been killed on his range, but that was because his range is his kingdom, and maybe in most cases they should have been run off for rustling. Maybe Lon Naylor did the county a favor by getting rid of some of them."

She eyed. "You're changing, Ken."

"Maybe."

He downed his drink and then another. "I'd best be on my way."

"You won't get far beyond the Rio Frio, Ken!"

"Who said I was going to ride right up to the house and ask for Steve Wascoe like a little gentleman?"

"What are you going to do?"

He grinned. "Someone has to break the bugaboo of the Guthook. One man has to do it. I'll do it my own way, win or lose."

"You're mad!"

He looked down at her. "I have to do it. Don't you understand?"

"But what about me?"

She didn't mean her own protection or safety, she meant her deep love for the man who had been her foster brother and who was now the man she did not want to live without.

He drew her close and found the wonder of her lips and love.

It was dusk when he went to the stable to get a horse. The horse saddled when he heard the soft footfall outside of the building. Stepping back into a stall, he drew his Colt.

A figure darkened the doorway. "Macklin?"

Ken did not answer although he recognized the voice, for some men could shoot accurately at the sound of a voice.

Dod Nellis raised his arms to show he did not hold a gun. "Macklin?" he queried.

"Yes. Come in."

The detective walked into the stable. "You play it cozy," he said with a slow smile.

"I've kept alive more than once by doing so."

Nellis nodded. "Cigar?" he asked. He extended a case. Ken helped himself to a short six and they both lighted up. Nellis looked at the star on Ken's jacket. "So it's true then?"

"Yes."

"The news came out to the Lazy J."

"I figured it would."

Nellis eyed the end of his cigar. "I know you're not fool enough to ride onto Guthook land big as life and twice as ugly. You aim to do it one way or another though." Nellis leaned against a post. "You're up against big odds. Steve Wascoe is tough enough, but he's backed by Carancho, Jim Dana, Slim, Charley and even your own brother."

"Foster brother," corrected Ken.

"No matter. You like that kid. You could have gunned him down easy enough. Jesus God, Macklin, you move like a cat when you have to."

"I said I'd stayed alive by watching what I did."

"Yes," said Nellis thoughtfully. "Over on the Horsehead Crossing of the Pecos was one time."

Ken stared at the man in the dimness, but there was no expression on the detective's face. Still, he might have heard of that hassle by hearsay.

"Then there was that barroom brawl in Tascosa," said Nellis. "How many men died that night, Macklin?"

"You seem to know, Nellis."

"Five, I think. Two of them by your gun."

"I'm not sorry about that."

"You shouldn't be. There are other things I know about you."

"Who put you on to this, Nellis? Naylor?"

"In a way. He really didn't know much about it though."

"He just wanted to keep an eye on me, is that it?"

"Don't flatter yourself. Lon Naylor practically forgot you until you came back. Only when you came back you ran into him and his kingdom across the Rio Frio. That made him watch you again."

"Figures."

Nellis sucked in on his cigar and blew a smoke ring. "The old man pays well, Macklin. I told you one reason he hired me was to find out who killed Jordan Harker. The other reason is one I didn't want to mention in front of anyone else. But I'm going to tell you."

"Why me?"

"I'm not quite sure. Would you like to know what it is?"

"You seem to want to tell me."

Nellis nodded. "How much do you know about Mrs. Naylor?"

"She was a Castaneda; Luz, half sister to Dolores Castaneda who married my foster father. I never knew her. I was a baby when she left this country. She was Estelle's mother. Fact is I can hardly remember Mrs. Harker. She died giving birth to Jobie. They say she was a wonderful woman. Jordan Harker never forgot her."

Nellis relighted his cigar and eyed Ken over the flame of the lucifer. "And Luz Naylor never came back again did she?"

"Not to my knowledge. They say she died down south somewhere of alcoholism." Ken laughed shortly. "Anyone who lived with old Lon probably *had* to drink if they couldn't fight him."

"They say the feud between Lon Naylor and Jordan Harker started because of the land brought to Harker by his wife."

Ken nodded. "That's about the size of it. The Castaneda Grant was rather cloudy, although it had been recognized by the Territorial Government. The sisters had been agreeable enough about it. Luz was the eldest and she agreed to take the eastern part of the Rio Frio, while Dolores took the western side. Luz got the best of the deal, although the western side is top land. You'd think Lon would have been satisfied."

Nellis shook his head. "They never are. It gets to be a disease with them. Yet, for all his money, he lives almost like one of his hands. There are times when he takes his old soogans and goes to sleep out on the bare ground because he can't sleep in that mausoleum of a house he built. He still likes his hogmeat and beans."

"I wonder what drives him on? He's getting along now, Nellis."

The detective looked up. "Old Lon wasn't too nice to his wife, Macklin. He even admitted that to me. The old man's conscience has been bothering him for some time now. He hired me to track down Mrs. Naylor. You were right. She died of alcoholism in El Paso not too long after she left Naylor. Naylor had me verify that story."

"I'm sorry to hear about that."

"I talked to the nurse who was with her when she died. She told me an odd story about the last words of Mrs. Naylor. Seems as though old Lon wanted a son back in those days. A son to carry on the tradition of the Guthook. A Naylor!"

"Sounds like him," admitted Ken.

"He was out on the range when he heard about the arrival of his first-born. A girl."

Ken shrugged. "That's the way it goes. He got a dandy too."

"It was a helluva blow to Lon Naylor. He accepted the little girl, but he never accepted Luz Naylor after that. She left and drank herself to death. But I found the nurse, as I told you, and she said Luz Naylor, as sick as she was, and in delirium most of the time, began to laugh near the end. She laughed like a madwoman and said that she had paid Lon Naylor off in his own coin, and that she had left a living curse on him. It got me interested. I almost forgot I was working for Naylor."

"Pride of profession no doubt," said Ken dryly.

"I've got a few angles left to work out. I'm on my way to

the county seat now to check into some records. I want you to do one thing for me."

"Yes?"

"Stay away from the Lazy J until I get back."

Ken shook his head.

"It's a little thing to ask."

"Wascoe killed my brother almost in cold blood. I want him, and I want my other brother to come home where he belongs."

"Very commendable," said Nellis, "but it can wait."

"Look, Nellis," said Ken quietly, "you said you had two reasons for working for Naylor. One to find the killer of Jordan Harker and the other to find Mrs. Naylor. You did the second, and inasmuch as you don't seem too much interested in the first, it's up to me to take over."

"Maybe the two of them tie in together. Did you ever figure it that way?"

"No."

"I have a feeling they might. Now wait until I get back, will you?"

"No."

Nellis shrugged. "I'll ride as hard as I can and hope to God I find out what I have been suspecting for some time, and I hope I get back in time to stop bloodshed."

"You'd better ride like the wind then, Nellis, because I'm pulling out of here this night."

Nellis nodded. He knew he couldn't stop this big, determined man.

Ken held out his hand. "Thanks for coming over," he said.

"Forget it. I only wish I could help you now. It might be too late by the time I get back."

"That is as it may be, amigo."

"*Vaya con Dios,* Macklin," said Nellis.

"*Vaya con Dios.*"

Ken led his horse out of the stable and rode toward the south to vanish into the darkness.

Nellis relighted his cigar. There was something about that big man that was vaguely familiar, yet he had never met Ken Macklin before Macklin had returned to the Conchas country, nor had he ever seen a picture of him. "Strange," he said. He mounted his horse and rode off to the north.

Ken cut north after midnight through the hills, forded Bravo Crick, and rode out on Lazy J land. He bypassed a line camp in a wide loop of the creek, then trended northeast, through low, naked hills devoid of any cover, until just before dawn when he entered a *mal pais* country.

It was a veritable hell of catclaw, acacia and wait-a-bit bush, interlaced with sharp-edged rock and stubby trees. It was almost impassable and no one ever ventured out that way if they could avoid it. But it did have one great advantage. The sprawling headquarters of the Lazy J were spread out in full view not more than two miles from the rim of this treacherous country.

Ken had picketed his horse in a deep draw where there was grazing and water. He himself lay flat beneath an overhanging ledge of rock with Jordan Harker's old German field-glasses in his hands, studying the movements at the group of buildings.

It would be a tough nut to crack. The odds were immense. He'd have to face Wascoe, Jim Dana, Slim, Charley, Carancho and possibly even Jobie Harker. Ken closed his eyes and the idea to divide and conquer crept into his mind.

Ken rubbed his unshaven jaws. The idea was splendid, the execution extremely doubtful. Lon Naylor kept what was his. No man had even been taken from Guthook land unless Lon had willed it so. More than one man on that range rode with a price on his head. Lon Naylor paid well and asked but two things from his riders: Fighting ability and loyalty. His gold purchased those two things from some of the toughest hardcases in the Southwest.

Hours drifted past as the sun arose and began to warm the wet earth, and still Ken Macklin lay in his hide-out watching those distant buildings. If he did get into action he would sure as hell lose out. He'd wait until darkness and then make his play. Win or lose he'd have to make his play, for the Guthook men would be sure some time that day that Ken Macklin had left the Double H with a star pinned on his jacket. They'd be waiting for him.

CHAPTER TWELVE

T HE DARKNESS came slowly across the range, and as it did so a dark figure left the *mal pais* and trotted steadily across the softer ground to a winding arroyo that cut across the land like a great gash. The arroyo eventually ran into the north branch of Bravo Creek, which in turn flowed just behind the main buildings of the ranch. Lon Naylor had planned well, for his buildings were up high, affording a clean sweep of the surrounding country. Ken had often wondered what the old man had intended when he had built that place, for it was built for a siege, and it could withstand a siege. Manned by Guthook men with plenty of food and water, as well as ammunition, it would take a strong force, and probably nothing less than artillery to breach those massive adobe and rock structures. Now one man was going to try to do the job.

He reached the creek and waded along the western bank of it until he could see the nearest bunkhouse, patterned after the main building. Yellow lamplight showed from the narrow windows. Ken walked softly up the bank and to the rear of the bunkhouse, flattened himself against the rear wall and peered into the nearest window. Three men sat in the bunkhouse near the stove. Slim, Charley and another man whom Ken did not know, but he looked as though he had been cut from the same cloth and pattern as all the other Guthook *vaqueros*.

The window was partly open. Ken bent his head to listen. The strange man was speaking. "Steve wants me to take a look at that *mal pais* country along with Carancho when the moon comes up."

Charley spat against the stove. "He thinks Macklin might be in there, Red?"

The man shrugged. "I suppose so. I don't like that country even in the daytime and. besides, I'd rather ride with a damned rattlesnake than that Carancho. He gives a man the creeps."

Slim nodded. "Macklin made a damned enemy for life outa that breed. He shoulda killed him like he done Clem Brace. Bad enough he lets Carancho live, he has to send him back here nekkid atop his hoss. Yuh can't make an Indian lose face that way. Besides, Carancho is a breed, and that seems to make 'em worse."

Red picked up his rifle and walked to the door. "Who's up at the house?"

Charley looked up. "The old man, Steve Wascoe, Jim Dana and the Kid."

Ken faded into the darkness as Red came outside and closed the door behind him. The redhead halted to look toward the *mal pais* hills. The view was the last thing he remembered for quite some time, for a steelshod rifle butt hit him silently just behind the left ear.

Ken carried the man into an outbuilding, trussed and gagged him, took his Colt from its holster and thrust it through his own belt. Then he stepped back, and as he did so he thought he saw something move near the doorway.

He didn't have long to wait, for the dim figure raced toward him on silent feet. Instinctively Ken bent his upper body and met the onrushing man with a shoulder into the belly. It was Carancho, armed with a wicked looking cuchillo, aiming to let out Ken's life blood with it.

Carancho struck a post as he was hurled back but he

managed to swipe at Ken with the knife and the tip of the blade slashed through the front of Ken's jacket. Ken sidestepped as Carancho came in again weaving a pattern of cuts and slashes. Ken backed away. His breath was harsh in his throat but there was no sound from the breed as he forced Ken backward, ever backward.

Ken's overwhelming desire was to draw and shoot, but he held tight to his discipline, for trading a dead breed wouldn't bring in Steve Wascoe.

Ken's back struck the wall and the breed lanced in. Ken closed in thrusting his left leg into Carancho's right side, and at the same time gripped the knife wrist and pulled it back and down with all his strength. Carancho grunted, the first sound he had made since he had attacked Ken. He went down on his back and Ken slammed right hook after right hook into the breed's sweating face until the man yelled hoarsely. Ken who had the knife now, drove it hard into the man's back, felt him stiffen, then stood up over him with the sweat dripping from his own face. It had been a damned close thing.

He dragged Carancho behind a row of sacks, wiped the blood from the packed earthen floor, then threw the knife over another pile of sacks.

Red and Carancho had been gotten rid of, and it wasn't likely that they would be missed. They would assume the two men had gone to the hills on their manhunt.

Slim and Charley were still in the bunkhouse when Ken peered in. The stove was still going. Ken swung up onto the roof and crawled to the chimney. He stuffed the pipe with his bandana, then crawled behind a pile of lumber that had been stacked upon the roof to dry. Suddenly he heard muffled cursing from inside the bunkhouse as the smoke poured back into it. In a few minutes a ladder thumped against the side of the bunkhouse and Slim appeared, walked toward the chimney, and the Colt butt met his head just as he reached out to see what was plugging the chimney. Ken tied and gagged him, then walked to the far side of the roof, held on by his hands and dropped lightly to the ground. He circled the building and waited just outside the door. Smoke drifted through the open doorway.

"Gawd dammit, Slim!" said Charley. "Ain't you clearin' that?"

There was no answer. Charley walked outside. Ken struck hard, but not true, for the surprised man went down on one knee. "What the hell?" he said. A boot heel connected firmly with his jaw and stopped his questioning.

Ken took care of Charley as he had the others, depositing the man in a shed beyond the bunkhouse. Then he climbed to the roof, removed the bandanna, climbed down the ladder to the ground, removed the ladder and shut the bunkhouse door.

Now he had to get into the house before the moonlight flooded the surrounding grounds, but he still didn't know if Steve Wascoe was in there or not. He made his way, crouching low, until he reached the gateway that opened into the walled garden along the southern side of the house. It would still be dark within those grounds, but when the moon arose he would easily be seen by anyone on the wide balcony that ran around three sides of the house.

He had just reached for the gate latch when something made him turn. There was a slight figure within five feet of him. It was instinct that made him go for his gun this time, for the figure was Jobie Harker.

"Ken!"

He stared in bewilderment, for Jobie had spoken in a woman's voice, the voice of his own sister, Miriam.

"It's me, Ken!"

He reached out and drew her close within the shelter of the gateway. "You came close to stopping lead," he whispered harshly. "For one awful moment I thought it was Jobie I had drawn on."

"I wore his clothing," she said quickly.

"What are you doing here?"

She looked up at him. "You were here alone," she said simply. *"Someone* had to help you."

"For the love of God," he husked.

She gripped him by the front of his jacket. "I won't leave you. Ken."

He turned without a word and eased open the gate. He padded in, followed by Miriam, until he was within the shelter of shade trees and shrubbery at the far side of the garden. "Stay here," he said quietly. He walked to the house, pulled himself up and over the wall, and dropped his feet to rest on the narrow paved ledge that banked the creek that flowed just behind the house. He could see the lighted window of the room in which Lon Naylor spent most of his time when he was at home.

It was simple enough to scale the house wall by standing on the garden wall and reaching up for the edge of the balcony flooring. He stopped to listen when he stepped over the low railing. There was a lighted window to his left, probably Estelle's room. He looked down and saw an indefinite shape in the shrubbery. He couldn't help but grin at the trick he had played on her. She'd stay there until he was sure he had Steve Wascoe under control.

He padded along the balcony until he was close beside Estelle's window and then he peered into the room. She was pacing back and forth on the thick carpeting, clad in a low-necked dress, with her lovely hair piled high atop her shapely head. Bruised as her face was, she was still a beautiful sight for any man, unless he knew her as Ken Macklin knew her. She stopped near the window and lighted a cigarette, then resumed her steady pacing, leaving rifted bluish smoke hanging in the big room about her. If it had been anyone else, Ken might have thought it was her conscience bothering her, but not Stella Harker nee Naylor. She was plotting something or the other, if Ken knew her at all.

He stepped back behind a thick abutment. Time was fleeting and he hadn't located his man as yet. The moon was silvering the eastern range tips. Then the door a few feet away from him swung open and Estelle Harker walked out upon the balcony and gripped the railing with her hands, looking down into the garden, deep in thought. Suddenly she stared directly at Miriam Harker's position. She opened her mouth to cry out.

Ken took his long chance. "Stella," he said quietly.

She whirled. Her eyes narrowed. "Ken! What are you doing here?"

He smiled. "You asked me once why I didn't pull out of the Double H. You said I might be able to throw in with your father."

She studied him. "Are you lying to me, Ken? If you are, so help me God, I'll scream bloody murder and in a minute Steve Wascoe, Jim Dana and Jobie will be up those stairs."

Gracias, he thought. *You've located them for me.* But he wasn't through with *her* yet. In a sense she was the most dangerous of the lot—the female of the species.

"Look, Stella," he said quickly. "I know the Double H is lost. I won't get a damned dime out of it. Wes is dead now. Jobie likes it here from all evidences. Your father will take over the Double H and this ranch and the Double H will be the biggest spread in New Mexico. A man could live like a king here, Stella."

She flipped her cigarette butt into the garden while she eyed Ken. "Come on inside," she said.

He glanced down into the garden as he did so. There was no sign of Miriam.

Estelle closed the door and pulled down the shades. She lighted two cigarettes and place one in his mouth as she sat on the arm of his chair. "Tell me more," she said softly. She tapped the star on his jacket. "What's this foolishness?"

"You know that Wascoe killed Wes."

She nodded. There was no sign of sorrow on her oval face. "Wes was a damned fool. Jobie told me the whole thing." She smiled thinly. "You're lucky you got out of that one."

"Yes. You said your father would have the entire Rio Frio Valley before too long. I didn't believe you at the time. Since then I found out who holds the note on the Double H. It's hard to beat old Lon at that game."

She glanced quickly at him. "Who told you about that note?"

"Miriam."

She puffed out a ring of smoke. "It just so happens that my father doesn't know about that note . . . yet."

He stared at her. "What do you mean?"

She blew another ring of smoke. "*I* made that deal." She smiled. "Loaned my drunken husband the money with the ranch as security. Now he's dead, his heirs haven't got the payment money, so the Double H is mine now, Ken."

"It is probably yours in part anyway, Stella, now that Wes is dead."

Her eyes were flint-sharp. "I didn't figure on that at the time! Now the whole ranch will be mine."

"A little dirty wasn't it? The way you worked it?"

She sniffed. "I thought I had something due me to pay for Wes' drunken pawings." She grimaced.

"When do you intend to tell your father?"

She smiled again. "When I'm ready. I outsmarted him this time. For years he's been trying to get his hands on that land but it was little Stella who finally got it."

It was all Ken could do to keep the intense revulsion from showing on his face.

She tilted her head to one side. "You really want Steve Wascoe, don't you?"

"Yes."

"Supposing I let you get your hands on him? You'll never take him at gunpoint and you know it, Ken."

"I figured on taking my chances."

She laughed as she lighted another cigarette. "The three of them are sitting downstairs in the living room right now. Go on. Go down and get him, Ken ... if you're fool enough to try."

"You might have something there, Stella."

She picked a piece of tobacco from her full lower lip and looked at it. "I can get him up here if you like, Ken."

There was no need to ask her how she'd do it. It would be simple enough.

"He's always had an eye on me, Ken, but wouldn't make a pass at me because of my father."

"Loyalty or fear, Stella?"

She smiled. "You figure it out."

"What's the price I have to pay?"

She sat down on the arm of the chair again. "I told you I had nothing against you. I'll need a real man here beside me when I take over the Lazy J. You'll do nicely."

"Gracias," he said dryly.

"Agreed then?"

He nodded. She stood up, adjusted her gown and walked to the door. "Wait outside on the balcony," she said archly. "In five minutes I'll have him in a position where he can't draw. You can bet on that." She opened and then closed the door behind her.

"I'll bet I can," said Ken. He walked toward the balcony door and stumbled over something. A pair of little boots, beautifully figured and carved, with silver Texas spurs on them. Stella's boots. She had worn them the night she had left the Double H. He stepped over them and then stopped short. Something was missing from one of them. He stared at the left boot. It had a silvered jangler on it; the right boot did not. He felt in his pocket and brought out the dirt-encrusted jangler he had found on the little crescent-shaped knoll where Jordan Harker's killer had patiently waited, smoking at least a dozen cigarettes.

Ken wet his dry lips as he knelt on the thick carpet and placed the jangler he had found beside that of the jangler on the left boot. It was a perfect match. A cold feeling came over him. The marksman had been damned good, far better than average, for it had been at least a three-hundred-yard shot, downhill, in the moonlight, and the softnosed slug had struck Jordan Harker in the back of the skull. He stood up and something else came back to him in a swift rush of memory; the night he had been alone with Stella Harker in the living room of the big house on the Double H. He remembered then of how he had mentioned Stella's skill with the long gun and of how she used to beat the Lazy J *vaqueros* in matches with rifles.

"*For the love of God,*" he whispered to himself. It was impossible, but the evidence was there, and since he had returned to the Conchas country he had learned to know what Stella Harker could do if she had to.

He heard voices in the wide hallway outside and he slipped through the doorway onto the balcony, softly closing the door behind him. He peered through a narrow space and saw Stella laughing as she looked back at Steve Wascoe who stood there with his hat in his hands, looking about that sumptuous room. She had kept her word then.

Ken stepped back a little and felt for his Colt. He'd have to go in there with gun in hand for he couldn't take chances with Steve Wascoe no matter what the man was doing. He'd take the both of them in. Wascoe for murder and Stella Harker on suspicion of murder. It was a dirty way to do it, but when you dealt with dirt you had to get your own hands into it.

He had his Colt halfway out of its sheath when he heard the quiet, hard voice just behind him. "Just drop it on the porch, Macklin. You won't be needing it."

Something hard and round was thrust hard against the small of his back. He dropped the Colt. For Jim Dana would shoot to kill without any compunction whatsoever.

Jim kicked on the door. Steve Wascoe opened it with gun in hand. "*Buenos noches,* Macklin," he said coldly. "We been wondering when you'd show up."

Ken looked over the gunman's shoulder into the set face of Stella Harker. "You double-crossing bitch," he said thinly.

Jim brought his Colt barrel down hard alongside Ken's head, staggering him. He felt the hot blood trickle from the laceration and he stared dazedly at Stella. There was a faint, icy smile on her lovely, oval face.

"We take him to the old man?" asked Jim.

Steve turned to look at Stella. She shook her head. "Not yet. I want to go in and talk with him. He respects Ken even if he doesn't like him, and he might get ideas. You understand, Steve? Take him downstairs into the living room. He can sit and make small talk with his foster brother, Jobie."

CHAPTER THIRTEEN

THE KID was seated at the massive living room table, with a shot glass in his left hand, staring moodily at the partly empty bottle that stood on the table. He looked up as Ken was shoved into the room. "Why didn't you have enough sense to stay away from here?" he asked.

"I could ask you the same thing, Jobie."

The kid scowled. He refilled his glass. "Wes would have killed me and you know it."

"What chance did he have? Drunk or sober he didn't have a chance against you, Jobie. You're fast and accurate. Better than Wes ever was."

The kid's dark eyes studied Ken. "It was an accident, wasn't it, Ken?"

Ken glanced at Steve Wascoe. The gunman was watching the kid. Between Steve Wascoe and Stella Harker, the kid was powerless. No chance of him helping Ken now. He was as rotten as they were, and perhaps worse for he had turned against his own blood.

"*Wasn't it*, Ken?" insisted the kid.

"Tell him, Macklin," said Wascoe coldly.

Ken looked at the kid. "Steve Wascoe could have placed

a bullet anywhere he wanted in Wes. He could have shot the gun out of his hand if he had had a mind to, but he *had* to kill him."

The icy, blue eyes of the gunman flicked at Ken and then down at the star Ken wore. "You'll never live long enough to get off the Guthook," he said softly.

They heard her heels tapping on the stairs and then she was in the room. Her face was like a carved, ivory mask. "We'll have to get rid of him," she said quickly.

"Who, the old man?" asked Jim.

"Damn you! I mean Ken here!"

Jim grinned. "Well, the other can always come later."

"Shut up!" snapped Wascoe.

The kid emptied his glass. "What do you mean, Estelle?"

She walked to him and placed a hand on his shoulder. "Don't you understand, dear? As long as he's around he'll cause trouble. Now we don't want that do we?"

"No, Estelle."

"What *do* you want, Jobie?" asked Ken harshly.

The kid stared at him, opened and closed his mouth, then got up on his feet. "I can't go ahead with anything like this," he said.

"You're in on it, kid," said Wascoe. "You'll do as you're told!"

Jim shoved Ken toward the front door of the huge house.

"Where are you going with that man!" a cold voice broke in.

Jim turned. Lon Naylor was coming slowly down the stairs, bareheaded and unarmed, and behind him was Miriam Harker. While they were all busy Miriam had climbed up to Lon's room in the hope that the old man could prevent any disaster.

They all looked up at the old man. Stella, Wascoe, Jobie, Jim and Ken Macklin.

"He came for me, Mister Naylor," said Steve.

"Because you shot and killed Wes Harker on his own land?"

"Yes."

"Then you had better go with him, Wascoe."

A minute dragged past.

"No," said Wascoe softly.

"I give the orders here. I'll get you the best lawyer in the territory."

"No, Mister Naylor."

Lon Naylor came down a few more steps. "You go with Macklin," said Lon Naylor.

"Dammit! No!"

Lon Naylor's face worked. "I'll call in the rest of the boys," he said quietly.

Estelle laughed. "What boys? *These* are your boys, Father."

The hard eyes studied her. *"My* boys? No, they seem to be *yours* now, Stella."

"Steve isn't going with Ken Macklin."

Lon Naylor gripped the balustrade. "I give the orders here," he said.

She laughed. "Why don't you give up? I'm going to run the Lazy J *and* the Double H from now on."

He nodded. "I heard about that double-dealing of yours. I knew nothing of it, Ken."

Ken nodded. "I knew that."

The old man eyed him. "Let Macklin go, Wascoe. My daughter can take over the place, but let Macklin go. I can't see this man killed. There's been enough bloodshed around here."

"Listen to him!" jeered Jim Dana.

The front door swung open and they all turned to see Dod Nellis standing there. He looked down at Jim's drawn gun and then at Ken. "I knew it," he said. "But thank God I got back in time."

Dod Nellis came forward and as he did so, Steve Wascoe

neatly plucked his Colt from its holster, but the big man showed no expression on his face.

Nellis paused at the foot of the stairs. "I just came back from the county seat, Mister Naylor. I've discovered something that seems incredible, yet it is so. I became so interested in the story of Mrs. Naylor that I almost forgot to work on the mystery of Harker's death."

"Go on, Nellis," said the old man.

Dod Nellis turned. "Luz Naylor died of alcoholism in El Paso, but before she died she confessed something that has been a secret for almost a quarter of a century. She hated her husband and knew he had wanted a son, but she gave instead a daughter."

Lon Naylor looked at Stella and she looked away from his steady gaze.

Nellis shoved back his hat. "She left Lon Naylor a daughter all right, but it was not his daughter!"

"What do you mean?" demanded Stella harshly.

The detective looked up at Lon Naylor. "Luz Naylor bought a girl baby from a drunken woman who was passing through this country and substituted that girl baby for her own son. Mister Naylor, you've been raising a daughter that is not your own!"

"And what of my son?" asked the old man faintly.

"He lives," said Nellis. "He was wrapped in a serape that had the name Macklin on it and left where Jordan Harker could find him, for Luz Naylor knew Jordan Harker better than she did her own husband, and she knew he would raise the boy to hate you as Jordan Harker hated you! Your own son might some day kill you, Naylor. It was what she wanted. To pay you off in your own coin, a living curse on the man she had married and whom she hated."

In a matter of seconds it seemed that Lon Naylor aged ten years. He stared at Nellis and then at Ken. "God," he husked, "she must have hated me."

"Why not?" said Stella. "Look at you!" She raised her

head. "This is all very pretty but I've gone too far now to leave here a pauper without a name."

"So?" said Lon Naylor.

She turned to Steve Wascoe. "We'll lose everything if this gets out, Steve."

The gunman nodded. He looked at Ken, then at Nellis and Miriam and then finally at Lon Naylor. "Dead men don't talk," he said softly.

Where did Miriam come from?

Ken caught Miriam's eye. "Now, Ken!" she cried. She flipped a Colt through the air toward him and it smacked hard into his open palm.

"Watch out!" yelled Jim Dana.

Ken whirled and struck hard at Steve Wascoe with the barrel of the Colt driving him back against the wall, half-stunned. Jim thrust his pistol forward, but Ken dropped to the floor and fired upward. The slug caught Jim in the breastbone, smashing him back toward the living room.

Nellis ran forward, but Steve Wascoe fired, and the big detective went down with a smashed left shoulder. The gun smoke rifted through the hallway.

"Get him, Jobie!" shrieked Stella.

The boy was in between Ken and Steve Wascoe now, facing Ken.

"Get him!" screamed Stella again.

"Get out of the way, kid!" snapped Steve Wascoe.

The kid whirled. "Shoot, damn you!" he said.

Wascoe knew the chips were down. He thrust his pistol forward to fire but the kid was too fast. His twin Colts cleared leather and spouted flame and smoke from hip level, and half a dozen softnosed forty-fours literally cut Steve Wascoe in half.

Ken stared at the kid. He had faced Steve Wascoe when the gunman had had his Colt in his hand and had drawn and fired before Wascoe had fired once.

The smoke lifted and wavered in the draft. Two dead men lay in their blood. Dod Nellis groaned in pain. Miriam ran down the stairs to help him. Jobie Harker looked at Ken. "I'm sorry, Ken," he said.

"Why, kid? You saved my life."

Jobie looked down at Steve Wascoe. "He killed my brother," he said simply. He slowly unbuckled his gunbelt and dropped it to the floor. "I'll never carry a gun again," he said.

Lon Naylor looked at Stella. "Well?" he said.

She stared at him. "You'll have to give me something," she said. "You can't let me go out into the world with nothing."

"Agreed."

"I have a note on the Double H. It'll be mine because they can't pay off in time."

Lon glanced at Ken. "My *son* can pay off that note if he likes."

Ken nodded. He walked toward Stella. "As deputy-sheriff of this county I arrest you for suspicion of murder."

She stepped back a little. "What do you mean?"

He studied her expressionless face. "You waited for Jordan Harker along the Rio Frio the night he was murdered.. You shot at him with a forty-four rifle from the swale overlooking the creek. It was the only way you could get rid of him. You had to do it yourself, Stella, because you couldn't trust anyone else to do it for fear of blackmail."

She stepped back to the main door. "You can't prove that," she said.

"I can, Stella. The game is up."

She reached for the door handle and turned it, pulling open the huge door. A spit of rain came in to wet her hair; then she was gone, running madly through the silvery veil of rain, with her high heeled shoes slipping and sliding in the gravel of the walk.

"Get her!" said Nellis.

Ken shook his head. "How far do you think she'll get?" he said quietly. He turned to look at his father.

Lon Naylor drew Ken close. He did not seem able to talk. "I want to be alone for awhile, Ken," he said.

They watched him walk up the stairs, a tired old man.

The rain beat down upon the Conchas country. It would take a lot of it to wash the blood away, but it would raise the streams and bring the grass to make the cattle fat and the horses sleek, and that was the way it should be.

MASSACRE CREEK

FOREWORD

There are persistent frontier legends about Confederates who refused to surrender after Appomattox. Some of General Joe Shelby's men moved through Texas after the war, living off the state, several thousand un-reconstructed Rebels, going to Mexico to offer their sabers to Maximilian. Some got through.

Somewhere in Sonora, on the lonely Mesa of the Bell-maker, there are two families descended from Confederates who had left the United States after the Civil War rather than take the oath of allegiance. Their intermarried descendants speak no English.

There is a tale from the Powder River country of Wyoming. It tells of a column of thin gray-clad ghosts who followed the bloody Bozeman Trail up into Montana in the summer of 1865 and settled there. Whether they were ghosts or living men we do not know. The answer has been lost through the passage of time. But they were Confederates.

Perhaps there were men like Sabin Shay and his 'Galvanized Yankees'. Quién sabe? *Who knows?*

CHAPTER ONE

The dry west wind scurried across the barren earth of Kansas and rattled grit like buckshot against the warped walls of the prison hospital. The sun had died long ago in a welter of rose and gold to the west and the new moon had not risen to soften the harsh landscape. The noise of the wind sounded like the scrabbling of bony fingers to Sabin Shay as he wiped the sweat from his face and looked across the body of the dead boy at Surgeon Hamish Hume, late surgeon, Provisional Army of the Confederacy.

Hamish Hume scratched his lean jaw with stained fingers. "Putrid blood," he said quietly, his soft burr hardly apparent. "A common after-effect of erysipelas. The disease got into the bloodstream, Sabin."

Sabin Shay passed a big hand through his thick dark hair. He looked down at the wasted body of his kid brother. "This damned Yankee prison," he said hoarsely. "Miles might have had a chance if that bastard Khuyper hadn't kept him so long in that guardhouse cell."

The surgeon shrugged. He eyed the broad-shouldered man across from him, noting the dark circles beneath the hard gray eyes. "Aye, but it was only a matter of time. We did all we could."

Sabin drew the sweat-soaked sheet across the drawn face of the dead boy. "Yeh! Miniated tincture of iron, alternated with quinia and emulsion of flaxseed. God!"

Hume washed his capable hands in carbolic solution. "You need rest, Sabin... You've been on duty here for twenty-four hours. There was nothing else you could do."

Sabin smashed a big right fist into his left palm and looked about the little improvised prison hospital. It was tenanted by the agonized bodies of his men. A full quarter of the old cavalry company fought various stages of erysipelas, typhus, typhoid and enteric fever. Two typhus cases had died of pneumonia that very day while Miles Shay fought the last long battle for life. The guttering candle lanterns cast alternate sweeps of shadow and light over the sick men. The mingled stench of carbolic, raw wood, sweat and fecal matter hung in the room like a miasma.

"Filthy," Sabin Shay said. "Rotten food. A few piddling medical supplies. That Yankee bastard is trying to kill us off. Why don't he line us up and execute us? Get it over with! Three months now, Hamish. Three whole stinking months of this! All because we fought his damned volunteers to a standstill and put a slug through his shoulder. I know what to do!"

The lean surgeon wiped his hands and leaned against the wall. "You could have been sent to the officers' prison at Alton, Illinois. You might have been exchanged or paroled by now."

Sabin's hard eyes held the blue ones of the Scot. "You know why I ripped the bars from my collar and the braid from my sleeves. I couldn't let the kid come here alone. Before God, if I'd known this was going to happen, I would have fought to the last with my bare hands. But Miles was wounded. I *had* to stay with him! Khuyper killed him here the same as if he'd gutshot him!"

Hume put on his faded gray coat. "No. The war killed the boy. He was worn out from poor food and exposure before he was captured. The wound was dangerous. It welcomed disease into his body. The boy was doomed."

Sabin walked to the door, seeking a change in air. His hands opened and closed spasmodically. He looked across the little prison compound, past the barracks, almost as though he could see through the high pine wall into the quarters where Captain Frank Khuyper sat at his ease.

A deep-toned infantry G bugle sounded out on the parade ground of little Fort MacNaughton. The wind was cold but it did whisper of the vast plains to the west. Of Kansas, Nebraska, Wyoming and Utah. The country Sabin Shay knew and loved so well. It also whispered ghoulishly of what Sabin Shay would do to Captain Khuyper.

Floor boards creaked as Surgeon Hume came up behind Sabin, carrying with him the fused odors of carbolic and strong tobacco. "The boy might have been killed by Kiowas or Comanches in some unnamed skirmish. Disease is prevalent in the Confederate forces. One way or another he might have died. It was in the throw of the dice, Sabin."

"I'm still alive."

Hume nodded. "You've got a constitution like a grizzly. Your years on the plains made a strong man of you. The boy was a scholar, a musician, too delicate for the rough life."

Sabin shook his head. "He wanted to serve with me. He was a mere kid when I went to New Mexico with Sibley. I was just a sergeant then, but when I came home to convalesce from the wound I got at Valverde, I had lieutenant's bars on my collar. He was all for enlisting right away. I prevented him. Then I received orders to form an independent company for service against the Kiowas and Comanches. He showed up at our camp on the Pease River, hot as hell's fire to enlist. I ordered him home, but he swore he'd enlist elsewhere. He was old enough. I had to take him."

"He had a lot of you in him, Sabin. You were younger than he was when you went west to fight Indians. Tell me? What did you expect from a Shay?"

Lantern light glistened from the polished rifle barrel of a sentry as he paced the catwalk above the big compound gate. Power seemed to flow down to Sabin's hands from his broad shoulders. He felt as though he could easily scale that wall, smash the sentry into a bloody jelly, and then go to find Khuyper.

"I'll not be here much longer," the surgeon said quietly. He raised his face to let the cold wind dry the sweat which dewed it.

"You're taking advantage of General Order Sixty?"

"No. Surgeons can be released without exchange or parole through an agreement between the two governments."

"You'll go back to Texas?"

Hume hesitated. "No."

Sabin eyed him. "So? What are you driving at?"

Hume felt for a cigar and lit it. The quick sulphurous burst of the lucifer accentuated the planes of his face.

"I've been asked to take the oath of allegiance to the United States."

Sabin leaned forward. "You won't do that!"

Hume shrugged. "I'm not a fire-eating Rebel, Sabin. I'm still a British subject. I could just as easily have joined the Union forces in the beginning. It so happened I was in Texas at the time and was carried away by good whiskey and noisy local patriotism. I've regretted my decision."

"I can't believe it of you."

Hume eyed his cigar appreciatively. "A doctor is dedicated to the service of humanity, whether they wear blue or gray clothing."

"A damned Galvanized Yankee!"

"Call it what you will. I plan a long life dedicated to help the suffering, Sabin. The war has been on almost four years. The Confederacy is fighting a losing battle. They're doomed."

"We're not licked!"

"No?" The surgeon smiled wryly. "There speaks the stout

heart. But the facts are as plain as the long Scottish nose on my face. New Orleans fell in '62. Gettysburg and Vicksburg broke the back of the Confederacy back in '63. The Federal blockade has strangled Confederate commerce. It's a lost cause, my bitter friend."

"God," Sabin said. "Coming from you—"

"I'm a canny Scot. I can see the handwriting on the wall. One hundred and twenty years ago my people learned a bitter lesson at Culloden. They fought well. They always do. But they were outnumbered, facing finely equipped troops and lots of artillery. Courage and blood could not sway the balance, and God knows, they had more than their share of that. There is a striking similarity between them and the South."

"You'll be executed if the Confederates capture you in a bluebelly uniform."

"The odds are against it. I'm not staying here, nor am I going back to the States. The Federals need surgeons along the Oregon Trail. That's where I'm heading."

Sabin looked away. Hamish Hume was one of the few men he had ever met in his wandering life who seemed to fit into Sabin's idea of real friendship. Now the quiet Scot had destroyed the one worthwhile thing Sabin had found at Fort MacNaughton. With Miles dead, and Hamish gone, there would be nothing left at the fort but the bitter days and the lonely nights. Marianne Bascomb had not written from New Orleans since his imprisonment months ago. There was nothing left now but his hate for Frank Khuyper.

"One more thing," Hamish Hume said as he flicked the ashes from his long nine. "I've been promised that I will never be used against the Confederate forces; only against the Indians on the frontier, with the Federal forces holding them in check along the Oregon Trail. It should be interesting."

"A Yankee trick."

"No. I might add that the Federals are anxious to have Rebel prisoners take the oath of allegiance for service against the Indians. You could do it, Sabin. You know the Plains Tribes better than most men. How about it?"

"Go to hell, you turncoat bastard!"

Hume threw away his cigar. "You're overwrought, Mr. Shay! I'll overlook that remark. Get some sleep. You're wasting precious health." The surgeon turned on a heel and strode away.

Sabin walked into the reeking hospital. He stopped by the cot of Driver Ellis, a rawboned trooper from the banks of the Neches. The foul odor of excrement clung about Sabin as he eased the big man over and patiently cleaned the filth from him as if he were a child.

"Galvanized Yankee," he muttered.

Driver opened his lusterless eyes. "Yuh say Yankee, Cap'n Shay, suh?"

Sabin nodded. "Take it easy, Driver."

The lantern light showed the fiery acrid humor of erysipelas on the head and face of the big man. St. Anthony's Fire was what Hume called the characteristic rose rash. That was like Hume, to have a name which fitted everything like a glove, in his precise, logical mind. Hume had a solution for everything. His decision to take the Federal oath of allegiance had been the result of his cold logic. A logic that filled Sabin with more disgust than the excrement on his hands.

CHAPTER TWO

The men of Shay's Independent Frontier Company stood with bared heads, leaning against the strong cold wind. The early morning sun was a cold globe in the cloudless sky. The post cemetery was on a slope overlooking the waters of the Smoky Hill. A curious Kansas Indian sat his gaunt pony across from the cemetery, and *then* whipped it into motion as he saw the raw pine box being lowered into the grave.

Trooper Blalock Lott, a backslidden sinner who had once been an elder of the Campbellites, raised his thin hands and looked upward, speaking in a gravelly voice. The words of the Twenty-Third Psalm cut across the murmur of the wind. Sabin picked up a clod as Lott finished, and crumbled it into the grave. One after the other, the remaining members of Shay's Company crumbled earth atop the coffin of Trooper Miles Shay.

Sabin turned away. "Sergeant Kester," he said, "mark it in the book. Private Shay, Miles, from Duty to Died of Disease in prison."

Sabin strode away, never looking back, but the clear ring of the shovels and the hollow thumping of the clods on the pine box followed him to where the guards leaned on their long Springfields, watching the ragged Confederates bury another of their dead.

There were now eleven graves in the little prison cemetery. Sabin remembered them all. Donaldson, Doxmude, Fettis, Fischer, Kleinschmidt, Moss, O'Hara, Olney, Pratt, Wolfe and Shay. How many more of them would lie there before the rest gained their freedom? Many of the company had been killed or seriously wounded in the bloody little fracas at Badwater Creek. Sabin's orders had been to pursue and attack a raiding party of Kiowas which had come down on the Pease in the light of a late fall moon. They had struck the Kiowas near Badwater Creek, and had scattered them, killing half of them, but Shay's Company had suffered too.

Sabin's men had been short of ammunition when they ran into a strong reconnaisance force of Kansas Volunteers. John Easterly, Sabin's second-in-command, had been downed. A giant Yankee had bayoneted the wounded officer and pitchforked him over his head. Sabin's last pistol shot had smashed the killer's face into a red jelly. Miles went down with a terrible wound. There had been nothing to do but to surrender to the strong Yankee force.

There were times when Sabin wished he had fought to the death, ripping with teeth and claws, to end up buried in an unmarked grave beside John Easterly. But Sabin had ripped the bars from his collar and the braid from his sleeves and surrendered as an enlisted man so as not to be separated from Miles.

Sabin waited for his men and marched with them into the compound. He looked back over his shoulder just before the gate closed behind them. A tall officer was standing on the porch in front of headquarters, watching them. The wind ruffled the silken blond hair which he wore in a long cut.

"That cold-eyed Yankee sonofabitch," said little Warner Giddings, Sabin's company trumpeter.

"I'd like to get my hands on him," said gaunt Norton Fraser. "No Comanche would beat me in torturing *him*."

The gate slammed shut behind them and the sentry yelled down from the catwalk, "Scatter, you Rebel bastards!"

"Hell with you!" Giddings yelled back.

The guard cocked his Springfield. "I'll put a ball through your belly!"

Giddings grinned. "Never saw a Yank yet that could hit a man from that range."

"Shut up," Sergeant Kester said. "Yuh might get fooled."

Sabin went into the barracks while the prisoners policed the compound. Miles' empty bunk still stood beside the window, next to Sabin's bunk. Sabin took the battered tin box from beneath his brother's cot. The lid was awry. Sabin had locked it the night he took Miles to the hospital. The lock had been pried open. He flipped back the bent lid. The little roll of shin plasters was gone, as well as the lone gold piece. The silver-chased claspknife was gone too. It had been a gift from laughing Sally Ross, the girl who had kept Miles' heart back in San Antone; the girl who had stitched the company's swallow-tailed guidon with the Star of Texas on it. Miles had been guidon bearer, almighty proud of the crossed flags sewn just above the elbows of his shell jacket. And that guidon had singled Miles out for the Yankee bullets on the Badwater.

Big Matt Duggan came into the barracks. It was like him to loaf while the others did their share of the policing. Duggan dropped on his bunk and laced thick fingers behind his dirty reddish hair. Sabin placed the battered tin box on his bunk and stared at the big trooper.

"Sure sorry about Miles," Duggan said loudly.

Sabin nodded.

"That little Ross filly back in San Antone will shore take it hard."

If I find that knife on you, Sabin thought, I'll break your thick neck like a matchstick.

One by one the prisoners drifted into the cold barracks. No firewood had been issued for several days, although the post woodyard was well stocked with it. The men all came in except little Phin Harris. Kester tapped the roster book with a dirty fingernail. "I entered it, sir," he said.

"*Sir,*" Duggan mimicked.

Kester whirled. "We agreed that Cap'n Shay would keep command here," he said.

"Bull chips," Duggan said as he excavated a bit of breakfast sowbelly from between his stained teeth.

Kester glanced angrily at Sabin. Sabin shook his head. Kester was an old Regular who had served in Texas and New Mexico before the war.

"We're a-dyin' here like flies," Duggan said morosely. "Driver Ellis ain't got long to go. When do we get exchanged, Kester?"

Kester shrugged. "Damned if I know. What about it, sir?"

"There's some slip-up," Sabin said. "They claim we're not regular troops of the Confederacy. I tried to write to Texas for confirmation. The letter was kept here in the files."

"That bastard Khuyper again," Kester said.

"I could'a been in the Fifth Texas in Virginia," Duggan said. "Them's the fightin' fools of the Lone Star State." He looked at Sabin. "I gotta get drunk and end up in *this* outfit. Shay's Independent Frontier Company! Jeesus!"

"Yuh would'a had, yore butt shot off at Antietam or somewheres," Warner Giddings said.

"What the hell does a windjammer like you know about war?" Duggan yelled.

Giddings spat. "I'd like to wrap that ole horn around yore dirty neck, Duggan."

A half mad light flickered in the pale green eyes of Matt Duggan as he sat up. "I got bobcat bristles on my belly," he said ominously. "I'm an eye-gouger an' a fighter from who laid the chunk. Anyone here wanna try me?"

"Shut up," Norton Fraser said. He squatted beside Sabin. "We got to get outa here, Cap'n Shay," he said. "If'n we don't, we'll all be a-killin' each other afore the Yankees do."

"I know," Sabin said quietly.

Fraser scratched in his ragged beard. "Now I figger it thisaway: Jump the guards some dark night. Take their guns. Break for the corrals to get hosses."

"Then what?" Kester asked.

"Head for the Arkansas."

"The country's alive with Kiowas and Comanches. The Yanks got posts all over."

"We kin travel at night."

"With troopers from half a dozen places on our tail? You're loco."

"Damn it, Kes!" Fraser said hotly. "Yuh want to join them boys in the cemetery?"

"Hell no!"

"Then let's talk business."

It was the old routine. Talk about impossible escapes to keep their minds from rotting like their bodies. Between the well fed, splendidly equipped Yankees and the bloodthirsty Kiowas and Comanches, they didn't have a tinker's chance in hell.

"Yuh ain't said much, Cap'n Shay," Fraser said.

Sabin closed the tin box. "You know the odds."

"What about headin' west?" Corporal Lockerby asked.

"More Injuns," Fraser said.

Duggan yawned. "Dirty, thievin' scum," he said. "We could go through 'em like a dose of Glauber's Salts. They ain't no match for Texicans."

Sabin eyed the big man. "The Pawnees have enlisted as Yankee Scouts along the Oregon Trail," he said. "Beyond them are the Teton Sioux and the Cheyennes, and the Arapahoes are no cinch either."

Duggan's thick lips curved in a slow sneer. "I forgot yuh was an expert on Injuns," he said. "How are them Cheyenne squaws anyways?"

Sabin went white. Duggan knew more than Sabin had expected.

Kester cursed. "I'll take him on," he said.

Duggan sat up again and flexed huge muscles. "Come on, Kes. I'll change that ugly face of yourn."

Sabin got to his feet. "Forget it, Kester," he said. "We'll settle nothing by fighting amongst ourselves."

"Yes, sir."

"*Yes, sir,*" Duggan mimicked. "My God!"

Sabin felt cold sweat run down his sides. It was only a matter of time before Duggan irked someone into a bloody rough-and-tumble, and Sabin wasn't so sure he could take the big man. Sergeant Tim Downey had tangled horns with Duggan their first week in prison. Duggan had beaten him to a pulp. His wounds had brought on the erysipelas which had eventually sent him to his grave.

"You're due for hospital orderly," Sabin said to Duggan.

Duggan grinned. "I ain't goin' in *that* pesthole. Turn or no turn. Get some other damn fool to go."

Sabin looked about the room. The drawn faces avoided his. It was always so. "I'll go," he said. He walked outside into the cold wind, hating the thought of going to the hospital, but disliking the tension in the barracks still more.

CHAPTER THREE

S urgeon Hume looked up from his desk in the little office. "Where's Duggan? We need wood and water."

"I'll get it," Sabin said. "Duggan refused to come. That man's a real troublemaker."

"I know." Hume plucked at his long lower lip. "What's wrong, Sabin? Are they talking escape again?"

Sabin nodded.

"The bloody fools. None of them is in condition."

"Well, it keeps their minds off their troubles."

Hume leaned back in his chair. "Phin Harris is working as mess orderly in the officers' mess," he said a bit too casually.

"So?"

"I ate there this morning, Sabin. At the invitation of Major Donaldson. He's from the Military Division of the Missouri. From the Inspector General's Department."

Sabin waited, frowning, puzzled. Hume cleared his throat.

"You may as well know, Sabin. Phin Harris took the oath this morning. He's volunteered to fight Indians."

First there was a shock, because one of the men had given in to the Yankees. And then Sabin realized that it was only Phin Harris. He broke into a grin.

"He'll be a great help," he jeered. "Hell, it's an omen that the Indians have the sign on the Feds. Signing up Phin Harris. My God, how hard up can they get?"

Hume relit his cigar. "I'll have to agree on Harris. But–"

"You, though. You're still going through with it, Hamish?"

"I am," Hume purred, and then Driver Ellis raised his huge, shaggy head from his pillow. "Gawd damn yuh, Surgeon Hume!"

Sabin walked to the sick man. He prepared wet applications for the rose flush. In the next cot, Jim Foster was breathing harshly. Sabin looked over his shoulder at Hume.

"Foster's in relapse," he called.

Hume got up. "We'll blister," he said.

Together they treated the typhus case by blistering the length of the spine with ammonia and mustard. Hume wiped his hands and sighed. "You might have made a good doctor, Sabin."

"I might have made a lot of things."

"I know. But it's a pity. As a doctor you would understand that men are men, regardless of whether they wear blue or gray. Political issues aside—oh, the devil with it." He smiled and produced two fresh cigars. "Have one, Sabin. One of Major Donaldson's supers."

"Yankee weeds," Sabin growled, and then his head snapped up as he heard loud voices in the barracks. Wood splintered. A man screamed thinly. Warner Giddings appeared at the door.

"Cap'n Shay, suh!" he yelled. "Matt Duggan is a-killin' Phin Harris!"

Sabin burst through the doorway into the barracks. Matt Duggan stood in a corner holding the shattered leg of a table in one huge, freckled paw. Now and then he stabbed the splintered end at the ring of faces which tried to close in on him. Behind him, Phin Harris was crouching in the corner, with his thin arms protecting his head. Blood dripped from his face.

"Get back, you bastards!" Duggan yelled. "I'll fix this Galvanized Yankee." He swung the table leg and stabbed viciously at the cowering little man behind him. He twisted his free hand into the loose folds of Harris' huck shirt and dragged him to his feet, stabbing at him with the club. The little man's left nostril was ripped raggedly up to the bridge of his nose. His lips were a bruised mass. His left eye was closing, swollen and bloody.

Sabin shoved a trooper aside. "Get out of that corner," he told Duggan.

Duggan whirled like a great cat, driving Harris back against the wall with his rump. Harris went down and Duggan trampled him with his big shoes. "This stinkin' little bastard took the oath!" Duggan roared.

Sabin reached for the club. Duggan grinned and swung. The club lashed down on Sabin's left forearm. The club rose again and skinned the left side of Sabin's head.

"Bastard—bastard—bastard!" Duggan chanted.

Sabin reeled back, bumping into Lockerby. Lockerby jumped in front of Sabin, took a smashing blow on the head and went down. The rest of the men scattered away from the yelling giant.

Sabin pushed in. He danced back and forth, avoiding the swift blows, his breath thick in his throat. He dashed the blood from his left eye. He was out of condition. They all were with the exception of Matt Duggan who seemed to have the terrible vitality of a grizzly in his huge stinking body. Harris tried to crawl for cover but Duggan battered at his rib cage with his feet. Sabin timed a blow. He managed to paste Duggan's lips and teeth together in a bloody mass, but his knuckles were cruelly ripped by the stained teeth.

Duggan spat blood and moved in on Sabin with the terrible set smile of the mentally unbalanced. Sabin hooked a left to the belly and brought his head up beneath the blocky chin. Duggan's mouth snapped shut. A wild blow of the club sent Sabin to his knees. He rammed his head into Duggan's groin, wrapped his long arms about the thick legs and up-ended the big man. Duggan's head smashed against the wall, rattling the whole flimsy building. He went down. Sabin got to his feet and smashed home a boot to the jaw to make sure the giant stayed down.

"Jesus," Warner Giddings said. "What a bloody fracas."

Sabin swayed to the nearest window, thrust his head out and spewed a sour mess on the bare earth.

"The guards!" Kester said.

Sergeant Schmidt came into the barracks, followed by a file of Kansas militia with bayonets fixed on their Springfields. "Godt damndt Rebels!" Schmidt yelled. "Killing each odder! Maybe it iss goodt!"

Fraser threw a chair at the big German. One of the militiamen, his thin face drawn with fright, lunged at Fraser. Kester parried the thrust with his arm, throwing the soldier off balance. The needle bayonet rammed into the wall. Fraser snatched up another chair and swung it. Sabin closed in on him and smashed him to the floor with an uppercut.

Then, suddenly, it was all over. Four men lay in their blood on the dusty floor. The militiaman yanked his bayonet from the wall. Schmidt drew his big issue Colt from his holster and cocked it. The clicking of the hammer sounded loud in the sudden quiet.

Schmidt looked from one face to the other. "What iss?" he asked.

Kester wiped the sweat from his face. "Harris came for his things. Duggan somehow knew he'd taken the oath. He went after Harris. The rest of us tried to break it up. Harris mighta been killed."

"One less Johnny Reb," said a militiaman.

"Shudtup, you!" Schmidt barked. "You ain'dt as goodt a soldier as some of these men. Gedt that Harris and that Duggan to the hospital yedt."

Sabin wiped the blood from his face and walked outside.

Schmidt came up behind him. "You'd better have Harris taken to the regular post hospital," Sabin said.

"For why?"

"He's one of you now," Sabin said quietly.

The pale eyes of the German held Sabin's. "Yess. You are hurdt too."

"I'll be all right."

"Take that Harris to the dispensary!" the sergeant called. He tapped Sabin on the chest. "You tell dese men to take it easy yedt. Next time maybe somebody shoodt. Dese militiamen is nervous. They don'dt like Rebels. They think you are wildt animals."

"Dirty Dutchman," said someone in the background.

The burly German ignored the remark. He strode toward the gate followed by the shambling militiamen.

Sabin dabbed at the blood on his face. "Schmidt is all right. He's a Regular. I think it gripes him to be in charge of the stockade and those strawfoot militia."

Sabin walked to the hospital. Hume was working over the unconscious Duggan. "I hear he might have killed you," he said over his shoulder.

"Damned Yankee fools—letting Harris come back into the stockade."

Hume jerked a thumb toward a chair. "Sit down and take it easy. You'll need a few stitches."

Sabin sat down wearily. He wondered how long he would be able to stand the gaff. Maybe he could make a break himself. Yet he didn't want to leave his men. Besides, there was Frank Khuyper to deal with. He had kept Miles in a cold stone cell in the guardhouse when the kid was still weak from his wound because Miles, in his sickness, had broken some minor prison infraction.

Hume finished with Duggan and set to work on Sabin. Afterwards he washed his hands in the blood-tinted water of a basin. "Lie down for a while," he said.

Sabin dropped on a spare cot and looked up at the sagging ceiling. His head throbbed and his lacerated knuckles stung like fire. There was little hope for his men being paroled or exchanged. Khuyper claimed they were little more than guerillas. The bloody memories of Quantrill and his raiders were still fresh on the war pages of the history of Kansas. The shifting border line between the Confederacy and the United States in that area was infested with Jayhawkers, wild Indians, deserters and conscription dodgers, and both Federal and Confederate governments had given short shrift to any men who were not part of recognized military units.

It looked as though Shay's Company would rot at Fort MacNaughton, eating half-raw food and dying of disease. As though to mock Sabin, the westerly wind crept into the sour-smelling room and teased him with its freshness.

He dropped off into a restless sleep.

CHAPTER FOUR

It was full dark when he left the hospital. He walked to the water trough and bathed his face. Someone approached through the darkness. He turned and saw Sergeant Schmidt.

"Shay," the non-com said, "you are wanted at headtquarters yedt."

"Why?"

"You will find oudt. It iss nodt Captain Khuyper who wishes to see you. It iss Major Donaldson."

Sabin wiped his face on his shirttail. "More trouble?"

Schmidt just grunted.

Sabin walked with the big German to the gate. They passed through it and crossed the gully bridge to the parade ground of the fort. Somewhere a trooper was singing. The odor of fresh bread hung about the post, awakening hunger anew in Sabin.

Schmidt stopped in front of headquarters. The window light reflected from his polished buttons and the crossed sabers on his forage cap. "There hass been hard fighting at Petersburg," he said.

"So?"

"General Lee cannot escape."

"Why are you telling me this, Schmidt?"

The German shrugged. "The war will soon be over. General Sherman hass marched from Atlanta to Savannah midt sixty thousand men. Savannah iss now a base for the Union."

There was a cold feeling in Sabin, not brought on by the searching wind which penetrated his thin clothing. He had heard that Lincoln had called out 300,000 more men. It was said that the Union had almost a million and a half men in uniform.

Schmidt jerked his thumb at the stockade. "It is nodt goodt to see men penned up like animals. Soon I go west on die Oregon Trail. I wass hoping that you and your men would be free by then."

"Thanks, Schmidt."

Schmidt waved a beefy hand. "Come. The major iss waiting."

Schmidt ushered Sabin into headquarters and into an office. Sabin's hands closed into fists. Frank Khuyper stood by the window, immaculate in a fine broadcloth uniform. His long blond hair had been carefully brushed to bring out the deep wave in it. There was a cold handsomeness about the sonofabitch. Even Sabin had to admit it. The man's uniform fitted perfectly, emphasizing the breadth of his shoulders and the leanness of his waist. The thin line of his white collar accentuated the faint ruddiness of his skin against the blue of his dress blouse. The thought came to Sabin that here was a man who fancied himself a real stud.

Major Donaldson coughed. Sabin jerked his gaze away from Frank Khuyper and found himself looking into a pair of cool, steady gray eyes. Donaldson was chunkily built, with a fringe of curling burnsides framing a square, stern face that fairly shouted "Regular." Sabin took him to be a real man and a first class soldier.

"Wait outside, Schmidt," said Donaldson.

Khuyper shifted his gaze from a roller map and eyed Sabin. Donaldson indicated a chair with a jerk of his thumb.

"Sit down, Captain Shay."

"The man is a guerilla, sir," Khuyper said in his smooth voice. "I haven't seen fit to use his assumed rank."

Donaldson shrugged. "We have no sure knowledge that he *isn't* a Confederate officer. Until we know for sure, Khuyper, we can afford him the courtesy of his rank."

A faint flush tinted the fine skin of Captain Frank Khuyper.

Donaldson leaned back in his chair. "I hear there was quite a fracas in your barracks, Shay."

"It was a damned fool thing to let Harris come back there after taking the oath," Sabin said shortly.

Donaldson glanced at Khuyper. Khuyper turned his head slightly. Donaldson smiled.

"Why did you surrender as an enlisted man, Captain Shay?"

"I wanted to share the fate of my company. My brother was seriously wounded. I couldn't very well leave him to the tender mercies of a Yankee prison."

"Humm. Well, there is no news on your exchange or parole, captain."

"We're entitled to it, major."

"Our government has changed its policy," Donaldson said.

"Why?"

"Simple enough. The South is outnumbered. We can afford to leave our men in Rebel prisons. The South can't spare the men in Federal prisons. The Confederacy is being bled white of manpower."

"They'll last."

"No. The desertion list in the Confederacy is unbelievably high."

Donaldson hooked an arm over the back of his chair.

"We have no proof that your company was a part of the regularly constituted forces of the Confederacy."

"We are part of the Northern Military Sub-District of Texas, Brigadier-General Henry E. McCulloch commanding."

"You have been listed as guerillas."

"A lie thought up by Captain Khuyper."

Donaldson's eyes were icy. "Take care in what you say!"

"I accuse him of destroying company records which would have proved our status," Sabin said.

Khuyper laughed. "You have no right to accuse anyone of anything. The only difference between you and Quantrill is that he at least had the honesty to ride under the Black Flag."

Donaldson slapped a hand down on the desk. "Dammit! I've had enough of this quibbling!"

"Then get to the point," Sabin said, "or let me go back to my men."

"Don't try me, Shay! I've had enough from you arrogant Rebels." Donaldson controlled his temper. "Captain Hume will take the oath of allegiance tomorrow for service along the Oregon Trail."

"Interesting," Sabin said with cold politeness.

"Hume thinks a great deal of you, Shay. He has told me of your knowledge of the Plains Country. You were out there from '54 through '59?"

"Yes."

Donaldson lit a cigar, eyeing Sabin keenly over the flare of the lucifer. "Were you in the Army?"

"No. I scouted for Sumner in '57 against the Cheyennes between the Platte and the Arkansas. Later I served in the Utah campaign of '58."

"You know the Sioux then?"

"The Otchenti Chakowin; the Seven Council Fires."

Donaldson's eyebrows went up. "You speak their tongue?"

Sabin shrugged. "Enough to get by, with plenty of sign language to help out. I also speak a little Cheyenne and some Pawnee."

"I see. Things are rough along the Oregon Trail. Seven hundred miles from Westport Landing to Fort Laramie, with one and a half graves figured for every one of those miles."

"It never was a pleasure jaunt."

"The Sioux and Cheyenne are as thick as buffalo gnats along the Trail. The Arapahoes are doing bloody work west of Fort Laramie."

Sabin grinned. "You're said to have a million and a half men in your army. You should be able to hold the Indians in check."

Donaldson turned to the map behind him. "Before the war we had regulars out there. Tough in the prat. Disciplined. The hostiles respected them."

"So?"

"Now all we have out there are volunteers. Their discipline is not of the best. Most of them are guarding the roads and the telegraph line from South Pass to Julesburg. But we need experienced Indian fighters."

"I hope you get them."

Donaldson flushed. He was used to respect, and he wasn't getting much of it from Sabin Shay. "We expect bloody trouble on the Trail. The Indians know we're in a life and death struggle with the Confederacy. There has been hell to pay in Colorado. Last fall. Major Chivington of the Colorado Volunteers struck the Cheyennes under Black Kettle at Sand Creek. It was a hideous slaughter of innocents."

"Get to the point, Donaldson."

Donaldson frowned. "I want you and your men to take the oath of allegiance to the United States for service along the Oregon Trail."

"*Wa nee chee*," Sabin said. "No!"

"You have the word of the government that you will not be forced to fight against the Confederacy. Hume and Harris have already taken the oath."

"Hume is a British subject. Harris is nothing more than a damned clay-eater."

"Your brother is dead. Most of the men of your old

company are dead or will die of disease before the end of the war."

"We can thank Captain Khuyper for that!"

There was a silence.

"Yes," Khuyper said thinly. "I wish to God you were *all* dead."

Donaldson waved a hand. "Please leave the room, Captain Khuyper."

The handsome officer closed the door behind him. Sabin looked steadily at Donaldson. "That sonofabitch deliberately caused the death of many of my men, including my own brother."

"So? I understand your men were in poor physical condition when they came here."

Sabin leaned forward. "Did Khuyper tell you he marched us here on foot from the Badwater on half rations?"

Donaldson's teeth closed hard on his cigar. "I don't suppose you've heard of Andersonville prison in Georgia?"

"A little," Sabin said.

Donaldson raised his voice. "A filthy pesthole where over ten thousand Federal soldiers died in indescribable filth!"

Sabin hesitated. In a minute they would be shouting attach other. This was getting neither of them anywhere.

"You're an officer," Donaldson said more temperately. "We need you to influence your men to serve on the frontier. Sound them out. Ask them to take the oath. Within a week we'll have them on the way west, mounted on good horses, with the clean wind to blow the prison stench from their nostrils."

Sabin shook his head. "Call my guard," he said.

Donaldson placed a sheet of paper in front of him. "Read that—and *think* about it."

Sabin read the paper and turned white.

"Yes," Donaldson said. "By order of the commanding general, Department of the Missouri, you and your men will either take the oath or stand court-martial as guerillas. You have no records to prove your existence as a Confederate unit. Quantrill has set a bloody precedent for you." Donaldson's blocky face lost just a bit of its granite sternness. He tugged at his sideburns and coughed as if embarrassed. "Captain Shay," he said, "I'm afraid that unless you take the oath, Frank Khuyper will have his pleasure. Because if you are found guilty of being guerillas, the only fate you can expect is the firing squad—every last man of you."

Cold sweat ran down Sabin's sides in rivulets. He sat absolutely still and watched Donaldson take a letter from the top drawer of his desk.

"I met a Colonel Bascomb, his son, and his daughter Marianne in Westport Landing," the major said. "Miss Bascomb heard I was traveling here. She asked me to give you this letter."

Sabin took the letter. The faint odor of jasmine rose from it. He watched Donaldson stand up.

"The Bascombs are traveling west along the Oregon Trail to make a new home in Oregon," Donaldson said.

Sabin stared at the letter. The last one he had received from her had come from New Orleans just before he left San Antonio for the Pease River. She had mentioned nothing then of traveling west, but only that she was sick of the domineering Yankees who had occupied the city since May of 1862.

Hamish Hume was asleep on a hospital cot. Sabin sat down at the surgeon's desk and split open the letter.

Westport Landing, Missouri February 25,1865 Dearest Sabin:

I have received no mail from you since you left San Antonio for frontier service. The news of your capture came to us from a paroled prisoner. We send our best wishes to you and Miles before we leave on our great adventure— for we are embarking on the Trail to Oregon! Father is arranging for our wagons and supplies for the long journey. We will soon leave for Fort Laramie. I am thrilled at the prospect of seeing wild Indians and the vast open spaces of the Plains.

My brother Stacy, poor boy, is with us. Stacy received his parole at New Orleans in the late summer of 1862, in case you did not know. The poor boy became quite ill of fever while held in a Federal prison. Of course it was difficult for Father to get permission to leave New Orleans and come north to Westport Landing, but as you know, he had *great* political influence in Washington before the war, and his old friends did not forget Colonel Clay Bascomb! He managed to find a way, the old dear, just as he *always* does.

We are looking forward to a fresh start in Oregon and Father has plans for a great manor there where I can be the lady of the house. He says the future of this country is in the West. I must close now, as a seamstress has come to fit me out with some traveling costumes. Is there no way you can be paroled or exchanged? You always loved the Great West, and I know that Oregon would be the place for you to settle down and make the mark in the world of which you are capable. Need I say more, Sabin?

Take care of yourself and remember your old friends from the Crescent City. Perhaps we will see you again. . .

With Love,

Marianne

Sabin felt cold now, and not just because the sweat had dried on his body. Old Colonel Bascomb knew which side his johnnycake was buttered on. Getting out of the South while the getting was good, eh? It was like the old bastard to grease his way out of a mess and turn up smelling like a magnolia. Sabin was willing to bet he had most of his wealth with him, too. He had given Sabin a hard time before the war, demanding to know what plans he had for a future if he figured on marrying Marianne. Stacy had swaggered around in his gaudy militia uniform, lording it over Sabin, although Stacy had joined a home guard outfit which was not required to serve outside the state. That was "poor" Stacy all over. He had sure learned from his dad.

But Marianne. . .

Sabin leaned back in his chair, thinking; of her. The great

blue eyes and the honey-colored hair. The smooth lips and skin. The full breasts and long legs. Marianne had held nothing back from him; there was a hot flame beneath that glacial beauty. Many times he had seen her oval face smiling in the embers of bivouac fires. Too many times. It wasn't good for a man in the field, and Lord knows it wasn't good for him now, in prison.

He sighed and glanced at Hamish Hume. Still asleep. He got up and went to a cabinet and took out a large bottle. It was labeled Poison. He had seen Hamish Hume label it. He sniffed it, then poured some of the "poison" into a tin cup. He sipped and smacked his lips.

Bourbon, he thought. Compliments of Major Donaldson, probably, like his goddam cigars.

Outside, the wind seemed to whisper from the dark reaches of the West. From west Kansas, Nebraska, Wyoming, Utah and far Oregon. It spoke softly of the muddy Platte, the Sweetwater, the Big Sandy, the Snake and the Umatilla. It hinted at roast buffalo hump broiled on the embers, and of the Shining Mountains and the Big Country. But most of all it brought to Sabin Shay the faint, clinging odor of jasmine.

CHAPTER FIVE

I n the slow days which followed, Sherman won through to Savannah, and Lee was penned in Petersburg.

And here in this grim Yankee prison Big Driver Ellis wasted and died. His huge body and tremendous strength had been no match for the rosy filth of erysipelas and the fatal blow of blood poisoning. Jim Foster put up a good fight against typhus, living through the chills and fever, the racking pains and prostrations, the purple rash, only to succumb at last to pneumonia. Jim left a wife and five kids on the banks of the Nueces.

Hamish Hume had left the stockade to wear Federal blue. Ellis and Foster joined the line of mounded graves. Matt Duggan returned to the barracks, silent and morose, keeping to himself, half insane with hatred. But it was gaunt Norton Fraser who argued against any plan of release other than that of a clean break from the stockade. The tough Texican could see only one way out, and half a dozen hotheads backed his wild idea.

Fraser's chance came when an epidemic of intestinal trouble hit the regular garrison and prisoners from the stockade were needed to carry on some of the fatigue details of the post. Fraser and his six conspirators volunteered en masse one afternoon to unload supply wagons which had just rolled in from Fort Leavenworth, and Sabin Shay volunteered with them. The eight ragged Rebels marched to the quartermaster wagon yard under the guard of four militiamen.

Fraser worked next to Sabin, carrying boxes from the wagon into the warehouse. "Now don't get any ideas of stoppin' us," he said in a low voice.

Sabin jerked his head. "You damned fool. If you make a mistake like this it will be your last."

They placed the box on a pile. Fraser wiped the sweat from his face. "I'm sorry yuh volunteered with us," he said. "Me and the boys has it all figgered out. My advice to you is to get sick and go back to the stockade. Yuh try to stop us, Cap'n Shay, and you'll get hurt."

Dusk came slowly, forming shadows. Here and there in the fort yellow lamplight held back the darkness. A corporal rounded a building. "All right, Rebs! Back to the hawg pen! Quick march there!"

The prisoners obediently fell in and slogged toward the stockade. Sabin marched behind Fraser and ahead of Morton. The stockade gate creaked open. The corporal of the guard was just ahead of Fraser, in a hurry to get rid of his charges and take off for the mess hall. Fraser shot a glance at Sabin. Sabin shook his head. Fraser spat. Then he jumped directly behind the corporal like a great lean cat. Sabin ran forward but one of the prisoners thrust a foot between his driving legs. He hit the ground hard, bruising his face.

Norton whirled the corporal around and smashed a blow home to the jaw. He jerked the Springfield from the nerveless hands as the non-com went down. The prisoners moved silently and swiftly. Two to a man. One of the guards on the catwalk stared at the struggling men and then discharged his piece into the air, awakening echoes among the low bluffs across the Smoky Hill. He rammed home another cartridge, cocked and capped his piece and discharged both slug and ramrod down at the men below. The heavy slug struck Palley in the chest. The ramrod pierced his throat and stuck, equal lengths quivering before and behind. He went down with a grunt.

Sabin rolled from under the mass of stamping, thrusting feet. Three of the guards were down. Sam Farber staggered from the fight and collapsed against the stockade wall, gripping a smashed shoulder. Fraser broke loose, followed by MacGinnis, DeVries, Danby and Lewis.

Men yelled through the darkness. Feet thudded on the hard earth. The guard came up on the double. Fraser fired directly over Sabin's head, blinding him with the flash and heavy smoke. He crawled to one side, rubbing at his eyes. From somewhere he heard the impact of the bullet like a stick being whipped into thick mud and the coughing grunt of a man hard hit. The roaring voice of Sergeant Schmidt broke through the din, flailing his men into effective action.

Rifles spat steadily and Sabin's eyes cleared until he could see. Smoke drifted between the buildings. Sabin stood up beside a low building. A tall man raced across the parade ground with a stubby carbine in his hands. It was Captain Khuyper. Danby snapped a shot at him. Khuyper raised his carbine as though on the range. He fired. Danby went down as though pole-axed. The four remaining escapees ran for the corrals. But they hadn't figured on Frank Khuyper. He fired again. DeVries skidded face downward along the ground.

"Oh God!" Lewis yelled. "He's got one of them Yankee repeaters yuh load in the mornin' and shoot all day!"

Those were the last words Lewis spoke on earth. A slug drilled him through the head. Schmidt led his men behind a building and opened a flanking fire. MacGinnis threw down his rifle. Fraser sprinted for the corrals. A volley spoke from the militia rifles and the tough Texan jerked as the .58 caliber slugs riddled him.

Khuyper saw Sabin's movement. He snapped a shot at him. Sabin winced as a splinter ripped the skin of his left arm. Khuyper stalked toward MacGinnis. MacGinnis looked desperately over his shoulder. He held up his dirty hands.

Khuyper fired deliberately from the hip. The soft slug plowed into MacGinnis' belly. He doubled forward. The Spencer rapped twice more. MacGinnis' head smashed like a dropped egg.

Sabin Shay ran forward. Khuyper stood there in the wreathing smoke like a man in a dream and began to feed cartridges into the butt gate of the Spencer. Schmidt's detail doubled up through the smoke and slammed the big gate shut. Khuyper looked up and saw Sabin. He raised the carbine. Sabin gripped the hot barrel with his left hand and drove a fist against the officer's jaw, jerking the carbine free as Khuyper went down.

Something hard jammed into the middle of Sabin's back. "Drop that Spencer," a voice rasped behind him. He dropped the repeater.

Khuyper shook his head and wiped the blood from his mouth. "You'll swing for this, you Rebel bastard."

Major Donaldson came across the parade ground. Behind him the companies were forming under the whiplash of non-com's voices. Lantern light gleamed on bayonets.

Donaldson stopped in front of Sabin. "Did you know about this break, Shay?"

"I heard rumors."

"Why didn't you try to stop it?"

Sabin smiled coldly. "I have no authority here. Besides — have you ever tried to reason with an angry Texan?"

"There will be hell to pay for this."

Sabin looked past the officer at Khuyper. "Yes," he said, "there *will* be hell to pay."

Donaldson rammed a fist into his other palm. "Damn it, have you made up your mind about taking the oath?"

Sabin looked at the bloody bundles which had once been his men. Khuyper, in his cold hatred, would make the rest of his company pay in blood.

"Give me until reveille tomorrow," he said. "You'll have my answer then."

CHAPTER SIX

I t was a silent group that clustered around Sabin's bunk after a tasteless mess. Seven men lay outside on the cold ground, covered with their ragged blankets. Five of them had been killed outright. Farber and Danby had died of their wounds. Sabin looked the survivors over grimly. Hard-pratted Texans for the most part, with a leavening of men from Arkansas, Tennessee and Missouri who had gone to Texas before the war. Men from the banks of the Brazos, Trinity and Colorado.

"You saw what happened this evening," Sabin said.

"It was a good try," Todd Shatter said.

"Mebee yuh should'a gone with 'em," Al Carroll said. "Fraser was loco to try."

Sabin held up a hand. "We've lost most of the company since the days on the Pease. Our chances for exchange couldn't be worse. We'll sit here and rot with Khuyper goading us until this company won't even be a whore's memory in San Antone."

"So what do we do?" Duggan sneered. "Write to that rail-splittin' gorilla Lincoln?"

Sabin ignored him. "You might as well know how the Confederacy stands. Lee is bottled up in Petersburg.

Sherman has sixty thousand men in Savannah ready to go after Little Joe Johnston. The South is bled white."

Sabin looked through the window. The wind seemed to be calling again. "West of here, clear to the Pacific, there is land for the taking."

"Ain't much takin' we can do," Blalock Lott growled. "Penned in the lion's den as Daniel was."

"Them lions didn't chaw on him did they?" Warner Giddings asked.

"Maybe they didn't have a Khuyper amongst them," Ames Lockerby said.

Kester took the bull by the horns. "If you'll shut up and listen, you'll learn somethin'. The only way we can get outa here is by takin' the oath." He stood up before anyone else had a chance to speak. "Now I know what you're thinkin'. You're goin' round and round, talkin' about damn fool escape tries like Fraser did. Now listen to the captain here."

There was a pregnant silence in the drafty room.

"Major Donaldson has authority to recruit us into U. S. service," Sabin said quietly. "We can be out of here in a matter of days, headed west, with good horses and guns, and with supplies for the taking. There's a helluva lot of country out there. I know. I've been out there and so have some of you."

"I ain't listenin' to no treason," Chase Corby said. "Even from *you*, Cap'n Shay!"

"Hear him out," Kester said. "We're all in this calabozo together. None of you thick-skulls has figured out a way. Now listen to a man as has."

This was the crucial point. One wrong word and the scales would tip down against Sabin. Most of these men were like quicksilver on a platter-running every which way. Quick loyalties and quicker hatreds. Yet they said nothing as they sat in their rags eyeing Sabin.

Sabin stood up and paced back and forth. "Let's face the truth. We're dying like flies here from disease. You saw what happened to Fraser and his hotheads. One more loco break like that and Khuyper will have a blood fiesta. There's nothing here for us but disease and death. Out on the Oregon Trail, with good horses and equipment, we'll at least have a chance to live. In a blue uniform, yes, but we'll be *men* again, not prison sheep!"

Warner Giddings heaved a sigh. "I alius wanted to see the Oregon Trail," he said, "but I sure never wanted to see it dressed in Yankee blue."

Cobb Howell, the tallest man in the company, stood up. "I'm fer it. Damned if I want to die like Driver Ellis or get gutshot by Khuyper. And when the time comes out there, Gawd help any bluebellies as gits in my way!"

Matt Duggan touched his scarred face and looked coldly at Sabin. "I'm starvin' here. Nothin' to be gained by sittin' here like sheep ready for the slaughter. I'm fer it too."

Sabin walked out into the starlit night and waited. After a while Kester came out and joined him.

"It's done," Kester said. "They'll all go."

"*All* of them?"

"Who'd stay after what happened to Fraser and his boys?"

"I hope to God we're right."

Kester laughed. "No one leads those *ladinos* around by the nose." He looked at the barracks. "They all have two reasons. An inward one and an outward one."

"What's yours, Charlie?"

"I've been doing a lot of thinking. I joined the Regulars in '46 and wore the blue until '61. Fifteen years is a long time to wear one uniform. I'm a professional. I guess it doesn't make much difference to me in the long run. The South can't win now. I'd have re-enlisted again after the war if the Federals would let me in."

I wish my reason was as simple as that, Sabin thought.

"How about you, sir?"

Sabin shrugged. "I think I'll turn in," he said.

"Well—" Kester hesitated. "Well, good night, sir."

The oath-taking was over. Shay's Company had taken it

like so many children swallowing a dose of sulphur and molasses, vile-tasting stuff but a necessary evil which cleans the bad humors of winter from the blood. And now, in the cold barracks, the converted Rebels eyed the pile of equipment which had been issued to them.

"Before Gawd," Warner Giddings said as he surveyed the gear on his bunk, "No wonder some of them Yankees fight so mean. After gittin' into all these fixin's a man's like to be mean enough to beat his own Granny with a stob of kindlin'."

"You never had it so good," a grinning Yankee said from the doorway.

Sharps New Model 1863, .52 caliber, cap-and-ball carbines with Maynard tape primers were placed in racks. Pull throughs and other cleaning gear fell to the Texans. Colt Model 1851 caliber .36 cap-and-ball six-shooters had been issued along with sabers made by Ames of Chicopee, Massachusetts.

"What do yuh do with these?" Jonas Gilpin asked as he hefted the saber.

"Ride the redskins down with 'em," Cob Howell said with a grin. "At best they may be right handy to toast bread over a campfire."

Warner Giddings, kid that he still was, got into his new regalia first. He looked down at the nine rows of yellow braid set horizontally across his chest. "I have to be a trumpeter," he said dolefully. "Lookit the buttons. Forty-four of 'em!"

Kinston Forbes grinned. "What with the sun shinin' on that and your horn," he said, "there ain't ary Sioux between here and the Big Horns that won't set his sights on yuh, Warner. Yore positively outstandin', sonny."

Sabin drew up the high-waisted trousers and put on the thick shell jacket. He held the forage cap, with its shiny brass saber ornament, in his hand for a few minutes, and then he put it on and looked in the mirror. He saw a lean face, with set gray eyes, staring at him from beneath the vizor. A curious uneasy feeling came over him.

Blalock Lott drew his pull through out of the barrel of his Sharps. "I had my mind set on one of them load-in-the-morning-and-shoot-all-day-Spencers like that bastard Khuyper has," he said. "But the Lord has provided and I accept with a glad heart."

"That'll stop a Cheyenne," Lockerby said as he worked his high collar together and hooked it.

"Cheyenne?" Lott said. "How about a Yankee?"

Sabin turned. "Enough of that talk," he said.

Duggan pulled on his new boots. "We don't take no orders from you, Shay," he said. "Private Shay, that is."

The men looked at each other and then at Sabin. "He's still company commander in my book," said tall Cobb Howell.

"Go to hell," Duggan said.

Howell eased back the hammer of his new Colt. "One of these days, Duggan," he said softly. *"One of these days."*

Giddings buckled on his belt. "How come they call us Galvanized Yankees?"

"When iron is galvanized," Sabin said, "it turns from blue to gray. Or the other way around. I forget."

The men stood about inspecting each other in their thick blue shell jackets. To an outsider the hard-faced Texans were Union cavalrymen. But they carried a guidon of a different pattern in their hearts.

Ames Lockerby came into the barracks. "I just heard somethin' interestin'," he said. "Seems as though Captain Khuyper can't bear to part with us boys. He's been relieved of duty as post commander here and he'll be second-in-command under Donaldson."

Nothing was said, but everyone in the room knew how everyone else felt. Howell's face cracked into a wide smile. "Gawd," he said, "I feel my luck changin' already."

Sabin sat down on his bunk and pressed his right hand down on the ticking. Inside the mattress was the guidon he had ripped from the bullet-splintered staff at the Badwater and carried beneath his shell jacket all the way to Fort MacNaughton. Two broad horizontal stripes, the upper white, the lower red, and a vertical blue stripe set against the staff, carrying on it the single white star of Texas. It was still stained with Miles' blood. Someday, somewhere, somehow, it would fly again in the breeze. He felt as sure of that as he was sure that Frank Khuyper did not have long to live.

CHAPTER SEVEN

The Oregon Trail stretched on either hand as far as the eye could see. Double sets of ruts forming a great roadway a hundred and more yards in width littered with filthy rags, broken bits of wood, smashed glass and decaying garbage. Dotting the barren earth were piles of manure: horse, ox, mule and human. The ceaseless wind blew the rags about, pinning them capriciously to clumps of brush or harrying them across the dusty flats. Floating high overhead, like a scrap of charred paper, a lone buzzard eyed the long line of blue clad soldiers who had halted at right angles to the trail.

Sabin Shay held the bridle of his big bay. The bay kept jerking his hammer head. "Take it easy," Sabin said. The wind fluttered the arm-length cape of the greatcoat he wore, exposing the bright yellow lining. In the long days of travel from Fort MacNaughton the restlessness in him had some-what abated. The column had crossed northwestern Kansas and the southwest tip of Nebraska. The South Platte was miles behind the column, and the North Platte was beyond the Trail, revealed by a low line of dusty trees.

Charlie Kester shook his canteen. "Platte water," he growled. "You chew it instead of drink it."

Warner Giddings grinned. "Best way to drink that

water," he said, "is to empty it outn' yore canteen and fill the canteen with forty-rod."

"Some humorist," Kester said sourly. "How come every company has to have one, Cap'n Shay?"

Sabin shrugged. "They're like saddle sores and diarrhea, Charlie. They're issue."

One hundred and fifty troopers waited, standing to horse, while in the distance a dozen troopers topped a rise and vanished from sight, scouting ahead. Major Donaldson was with them, leaving the troopers in charge of Captain Frank Khuyper. Khuyper was studying a thin thread of dust or smoke which wavered up far beyond the rise.

"Injuns?" Aaron Fitch asked Sabin.

"*Quien sabe?* Emigrants maybe."

"Helluva country."

"Ain't no worse than some parts of Texas," Giddings said.

"Yuh alius run off at the mouth like that?" Fitch demanded.

"Seven days a week," Giddings said brightly.

"Six days shalt thou labor," intoned Blalock Lott.

Sabin leaned against the big bay. The column was mixed. A few regulars, quite a few Kansas Volunteers, the rest Galvanized Yankees scattered throughout the squads. Miles behind them a battalion of Kansas Volunteer Infantry slogged through the dust, followed by the supply wagons. Sabin thoughtfully eyed the thin streamer which stained the bluish membrane of the sky. It was smoke. An emigrant campfire maybe. Or skulking Arapahoes or Pawnees.

A lone trooper rose above the ridge and hammered down toward them, raising a thread of dust from the hard earth. The horse's hoofs drummed steadily. Then the trooper dipped out of sight as though the earth had swallowed him. Minutes later he surged up out of the hollow, galloped to Khuyper and circled his horse on the forehand, speaking swiftly and pointing toward the smoke. Sergeant Schmidt stood up in his stirrups. "Shay!" he bellowed. "On the double, you!"

Sabin mounted the bay and spurred it toward the officer, drawing rein beside Schmidt.

"Major Donaldson vants that you shouldt come to him yedt," Schmidt said.

Khuyper's cold eyes studied Sabin. During the days on the trail, Sabin had felt those eyes on him constantly. Sabin nodded and spurred toward the trooper.

"Private Shay!" Khuyper said.

Sabin turned in the saddle.

"Haven't you learned how to soldier yet?"

Sabin saluted. Khuyper let him hold the salute and then slowly returned it. Sabin followed the Yankee trooper. The trooper grinned, revealing even white teeth. "Bit of a rasper, isn't he?"

Sabin nodded.

The trooper looked back. "I've served under plenty officers, good and bad, but there's something about that sonofabitch that gives me the crawls."

"I know."

"The name's Jim Lester."

"Sabin Shay."

"Pleased to meetcha," Lester said. "How do you like wearing blue?"

"It fits and it's warm."

"Nice bunch of fellas, you Texicans."

"We get by. What's doing up ahead?"

Lester shrugged. "Donaldson found something. Sent for you. That's all I know."

"Indians?"

"Yes."

They rode down a long slope. Donaldson was on the far side of the hollow, lying on his belly in the dry grass, studying something with his field-glasses. The scouts stood to horse in the hollow. The sun reflected from their scaled brass shoulder epaulets.

Sabin dismounted and handed the reins to Lester. He

slogged up the slope in his stiff new boots. "Sir," he said to the major.

Donaldson moved. "Lie down. Take these glasses. Look at that smoke."

Sabin took the glasses and studied the smoke. It rose from the far side of a low knoll. "Two wagons," he said, "One of them burning."

"See any signs of life?"

"No, sir."

Sabin began to sweep the slopes, back and forth, until a slight movement caught his eye. "I've found something, sir." He passed the glasses to the major. "To the right of the wagons. Near that rise."

"I'll be damned! A wolf!"

Sabin shook his head as Donaldson lowered the glasses. "Wolf headdress worn by an Indian."

"You've got abnormal vision."

"Maybe I developed it out here to keep alive."

"Arapahoe? Sioux? Cheyenne?"

"No. Pawnee."

Donaldson looked relieved. "Good! They're our friends. Good scouts. Hate the Sioux and Cheyenne like poison."

Sabin took the glasses. "Pawnees," he said. "Brainy, wide ranging, expert horse thieves as well as liars and extortioners. Loudmouths."

"You know them that well?"

"Enough. I knew the Skidis better than the others. Stayed in a Kitkaha village once during a blizzard. They treated me fine and then followed me and stole two of my pack horses."

"Some of them were enlisted as scouts last year under Captain McFadden."

Sabin shrugged. "I wouldn't consider them as allies."

"They hate the Sioux and Cheyenne, as I said."

Sabin smiled faintly at the officer. "You're a little naive, begging your pardon, sir. They fight with you because they hate you less than the Sioux and Cheyenne."

"What do you suggest?"

Sabin eased his collar. "Ride over there and take a look-see. Best send a courier back to have the column brought up here. Don't let them graze their horses too far from the column, sir."

"Thanks." Donaldson slid down the hill and relayed the order.

Sabin and Donaldson rode west, followed by the scout detail. The smoke had thickened, and the wind raveled it out, bringing with it the odor of burning wood and leather, mingled with hot metal. There was a clinging, underlying odor, sickeningly sweet. Human flesh being cooked. Sabin knew it well.

Donaldson and Sabin put themselves ahead of the jangling troopers. Sabin glanced back at the bright brass shoulder epaulets on their shell jackets. They had rolled their greatcoats and fastened them to their cantle packs "Some sight," he observed. "The sun shining on those epaulets."

"They're regulation," Donaldson said.

"Where, sir? Against Jeb Stuart? Mosby? Wheeler?"

Donaldson frowned. "I see what you mean."

"Remember, the Sioux don't use sabers, sir."

Donaldson nodded. He studied Sabin. "How do you feel?"

"Warm and well fed."

"Is that all?"

"That's all, sir. Except that I'm damned curious about that smoke."

Donaldson dismounted below a rise and walked up the slope. Sabin ran after him as he reached the skyline. He jerked at the major's belt and dragged him down. Just as he did so the boom of a heavy rifle sounded. A slug whispered inches above their heads.

Donaldson paled. "Whew," he said. "That was a near thing. Thanks, Shay."

Sabin crawled up behind a clump of grass and took off

his forage cap with its bright brass insignia. He parted the grass and looked west. A rickety wagon was smoldering two hundred yards away. The axles had collapsed, dropping the bed to the ground. The osnaburg tilt was still smoldering. The traces had been cut and lay on the sloping ground like coiled snakes. Another wagon was fifty yards beyond the first. A wisp of powder smoke drifted away from it.

"Someone's still alive," Donaldson said.

"Damned good shot too." Sabin studied the ground. Some cloth fluttered against a bush. A heap of cloth lay behind a clump of sage. He lay still, resting his chin on his hands.

"We'll go forward," Donaldson said.

"No!"

"There are no Indians in sight."

"That's the time to look for them, sir."

Sabin took the glasses. The good German lens picked out every detail. The heap of clothing behind the bush was a dead man, more likely a boy. A charred mass clung to one of the rear wagon wheels. Sabin swallowed dryly. A man had been lashed to the wheel while the wagon roasted him in hot flame.

Sabin shifted the glasses. The wolf was gone. He handed the glasses back to the major. "I think the Pawnees are gone, sir."

Donaldson cased the glasses and jumped up. He waved his arms and hit the ground just as the rifle spat flame from the intact wagon. The slug keened overhead. Sabin grinned. He stood up and waved his cap and then ran fifty feet to one side, waved the cap again and then dropped as the rifle spoke for the third time. Then Sabin slowly rose erect and stood there. This time there was no shot.

"Let's go, sir," he said.

They rode slowly toward the wagons. Sabin half-cocked his Sharps. The major held his issue Colt. One hundred feet from the wagons Sabin drew rein. "United States Cavalry!" he called out. He glanced at the body behind the bush. He had been right. It was just a kid, no more than sixteen, with a bloody pipe ax buried in the back of his skull.

The osnaburg tilt moved a little. A slender man came out, cradling a long-barreled Sharps in his arms. A wide-brimmed hat flopped over his face.

"Are you all right?" Donaldson asked.

The slim man came forward and grounded the rifle, lifting the hat brim from in front of the face.

"My God!" the major said.

"Amen," Sabin said quietly.

It was a young woman, dusty of face and with powder-stained hands. "Are you two alone?" she asked. "There are about fifteen of them around here. Indians I mean."

They dismounted. "Look around, Shay," the major said.

Sabin slid from the hammerhead bay and loosened his issue Colt in its holster. He glanced curiously at her as he walked past, Plain looking, with auburn hair tied up beneath her dusty hat. The eyes caught and held his attention. Almost too big for the oval face. Hazel . . . reddened by trail dust. Her firm breasts pushed out against the thin huck shirt.

The rest of the scout detail rode up as Sabin ascended a rise. To the west was Hat plain, stippled with Russian thistle and sagebrush. Dust raveled up from a ridge. Someone was driving horses at a fast clip. He saw no sign of life except the lonesome buzzard which had beat its way west against the steady wind, and now hung high overhead as though inhaling the odor of the feast it expected. Sabin went back down to the wagons.

The troopers had covered the boy with a blanket. Two of them were cutting the half-charred corpse from the wagon wheel. The young woman had removed the hat from the coiled helmet of her hair. Now and then the troopers glanced at her. One of them picked up a shovel lying beside the burning wagon.

"They were Pawnees," she said in a monotone. "Dad wasn't afraid of them. Some of them had been with the

wagon train as scouts. They were friendly enough then. My
father became ill. Too ill to move. The wagons went on
without us. This morning we knew the Pawnees were
watching us. My brother wanted to go on but Father had
gotten worse. I rode ahead to get help. Then I heard the
shooting. I rode back too late. The Pawnees were driving off
the stock. Freddie was lying behind that bush. You saw my
father. He was too sick to know what they intended, I guess.
A few of them came back to get me. Then they saw your
dust. They rode away."

The shovel grated against the earth. A horse shied and
blew, dancing away as the troopers carried the dead boy
past him.

"Your name?" Major Donaldson asked.

"Katherine Williams. My father was Seb Williams. We're
from Pike County, Missouri. We were going to Oregon." She
bit her lip to hold back the bitter tears. "Why did they leave
us? Why?"

Sabin looked away. It was a helluva big country for two
wagons, a woman, a boy and a sick man. Some bastard had
gone on and left them.

Donaldson stripped off his gauntlets and slapped them
against his left hand. "I'll make a report on this."

"It won't bring back the dead," Katherine Williams
said.

Donaldson flushed. "Connelly!" he called out.

"Yes, sir!"

"Ride back to the column. Tell Captain Khuyper to
bring them up. We'll bivouac here. Smartly now!"

Connelly galloped off, looking apprehensively at the
brooding ridges.

Sabin unhooked his canteen and proffered it to the girl.
"You can wash a little with it if you like," he said.

Her eyes held his. "Thank you, sir."

"The name is Shay. Sabin Shay."

"Thank you, Sabin Shay."

The sun died in a welter of rose and gold. Dust rose from

the beating of hooves as the column threaded its way down
the far slope. The graves were almost done.

The girl appeared at the back of her wagon, now wearing
a threadbare but neat gingham dress. Trooper Lester whistled softly as he saw her. Sabin turned quickly. In a short
time she had done wonders. Her hair had been uncoiled,
brushed and recoiled. A bonnet hung from its strings at the
back of her neck. Sabin caught a flash of white stockings as
she placed small feet on the ground. The dress seemed to
have lifted up her young breasts.

She came to Sabin and handed him his canteen. "I'm
afraid I used it all," she said.

"It's all right, ma'am."

She did not look at the covered bodies, but watched the
troopers ride toward the bivouac area.

"Who was the wagon master of the emigrant train?"
Sabin asked.

"There really wasn't any."

"So? It isn't wise to travel without some kind of organization."

She closed her hands tightly. "It was organized. We were
delayed at Westport Landing when Father became ill. Our
own train went on without us. We joined a private train
which was going through to Fort Laramie. They had paid
guards."

"A private train?"

"Yes. Owned by one family. Nine wagons and a Dearborn. They had ten men as guards and a few Pawnees as
scouts."

A curious feeling came over Sabin. "Whose train was it?"

"Colonel Clay Bascomb's. He said they couldn't afford to
wait for us. I think he thought Father had cholera. That
wasn't so."

Sabin's face darkened. He could almost see the imperious
face of Colonel Bascomb with its immaculate goatee and
curling mustachios. The smooth plump face and the ice-chip

eyes of Marianne's father. It was like him, the self-centered sonofabitch.

A wolf howled far from the north. A moment later another answered it from the west, closer to the camp. Then a third one howled from the south. The Pawnees were out there, ringing the camp area. Waiting, waiting, waiting.

CHAPTER EIGHT

The bivouac fires had smoldered low, leaving a thick scarf of smoke hanging in the windless air. The prairie night was velvety soft, prophesying the slow oncoming march of spring. It was chilly away from the fires, and those men who had taken to their blankets lay muffled like mummies, heads resting on horse-stinking saddles, forage caps low on their noses. Now and then a fire flared up, revealing the eyes of the horses on the picket lines like moist jewels.

Sabin Shay sat huddled in his issue blanket, at the mess fire of his squad. The Yankees of the squad had gone to their blankets, leaving Sabin with Charlie Kester, big Cobb Howell and little Warner Giddings. Giddings slowly polished his spang new trumpet. There wasn't a windjammer in the column, footslogger or yellowdog, who could match Warner Giddings when he put spit into a horn.

The infantry fires were beyond the cavalry fires, close up under the knoll. The beetle crushers hadn't had much to say since they pulled in long after dark, furred with dust. A good many of them were Johnny Raws, marching on feet that had swollen, then blistered, then developed into a raw mass, all one with socks and shoes.

A lean figure picked its way between the sleeping men

and stopped beside Sabin. He looked up into the face of Hamish Hume, now wearing first lieutenant's bars on his blouse. The green sash of the Medical Department circled the waist of his single-breasted frock coat. "How does it go, Sabin Shay?" he asked.

"Set a spell," Cobb Howell said. "There's good Yank coffee in the pot, suh."

Hume sat down on a saddle. "I've been treating diarrhea, constipation, scalded feet, blisters and indigestion," he said. "Yankees are no different from Johnny Rebs, it seems. In that respect anyway."

The shrieking laugh of a coyote came out of the black velvet far beyond the fires.

Cobb Howell spat. "Damn Pawnees," he said. "What they figger on doin' out there?"

"Snap up a stray horse," Sabin said.

"You're sure they were Pawnees?" Hume asked as he filled a cup with bitter coffee.

Sabin nodded.

"Arapahoes raid around here, don't they?"

"Yes. Farther west as a rule."

"Treacherous bastards," Kester said.

Now they could hear the wolves far out, beyond the fire reflections, talking among themselves.

"Makes a man feel queerlike," Kester mused, "hearing them, knowin' they're humans like us."

"Ain't nothin' crazier than a white man," Giddings said as he adjusted the yellow worsted cord on his trumpet. "Look at us. Fight like hell against the bluebellies— then we *jine* 'em. Yuh figger thet ain't loco?"

Howell spat into the fire. "We got us a reason."

"Shut up, Cobb!" Kester snapped.

Hamish Hume studied the quiet men with his sharp eyes. "What's going on here?" he asked.

Sabin yawned. He wasn't sure where Hume stood in the matter of his new loyalty. "I ever tell you hombres about the Pawnee Crazy Dog Society?"

"Uh-uh," Kester said swiftly. "Tell us."

Sabin grinned. "They go out ahead of their battle line, stripped to the buff, with feathers hanging from their privates. They tie their privates to a rope and fasten the other end to a stake in the ground. By God, they'll stay there too, to fight, unless one of their friends cuts the rope."

"Helluva a note if a friend got too excited and cut too close," Kester said. "Hawww!"

But Hume kept on watching Sabin. There was little Sabin could conceal from the canny Scot.

A trooper came to the fire. "The major wants to see you, Shay. On the double!"

Sabin yawned. "Double time yourself," he said. He dropped his blanket and stood up behind Hume. He shook his head warningly at his three comrades and then placed his right hand over his mouth before he walked away.

Donaldson was seated on a carpet camp stool under the patched wagon tilt which served him as a tent. He returned Sabin's salute. "I've been listening to those damned wolves out there," he said.

"Pawnees, sir," Sabin corrected.

"Same thing." Donaldson peered intently at Sabin. "I'm an old soldier, Shay. I can smell trouble in an organization long before it breaks."

Sabin raised his head a little. "Sir?"

"I don't like the way your Texans look at Captain Khuyper."

Sabin grinned. "I've seen a good many of your Yankees do the same thing, sir."

Donaldson grunted angrily. "Watch your tongue! There isn't much discipline in you or your men. I often wonder how you ever had any control over them at all."

"They *love* me," Sabin said dryly.

For a moment anger struggled for control of Donaldson's face and then he smiled. "Touché!" he said. "I had no business saying that, Shay."

"Forget it, sir. You didn't ask me here to talk about Frank Khuyper."

Donaldson drummed his fingers on his camp table. "Things are easy now. But today we got a taste of what's in store for us. I've got to get this column through to Fort Laramie in good shape. But I haven't a really decent scout in the whole organization." Donaldson paused. "I'd like you to take over as my chief scout until we reach the fort."

"Why, sir?"

"You know the Plains Indians. Surgeon Hume has told me quite a bit about your experiences with the Sioux."

"Cheyennes, sir."

"Same thing. Although I hear the Cheyenne women are considered the beauties of the plains."

Sabin studied Donaldson. *How much had Hume talked?*

"What do you say, Shay?"

"I'm just a yellowleg trooper, major."

"Then I must order you to take the detail. I had hoped you'd volunteer."

Sabin smiled. "Yon can order me to take it, sir. I'm too old a soldier to volunteer for anything."

Donaldson glowered a little but made his peace. "Fine. Report to me at dawn. You can pick your own men. Good night. Shay."

"Good night, sir."

"Shay!"

Sabin turned.

Donaldson shoved a box of cigars toward him on the table. "Light up," he said gruffly.

Sabin took a super. He nodded. "Thanks, sir."

Outside the tent, Sabin paused to light his smoke. He stood there in the darkness, remembering. He had lived with the Cheyenne for a time, in the winter of 1857-1858. He had been damned sick with fever and a Cheyenne girl had nursed him. He had been a long way from Texas, and young, and a hell of a lot more romantic than he was now. So he had drifted into living with her. Pretty Hands was her name, and she had been no more than sixteen when he married her. The Cheyennes in the sub-band of Little Eagle had accepted them as man and wife. That is, all of them had except Standing Bear, son of a Sioux father and Cheyenne mother, who lived with his mother's clan amongst the Cheyennes. Standing Bear had wanted Pretty Hands. Sabin had taken her. Standing Bear had left to live with the Sioux where he was known as Mato Najin in their tongue.

Sabin had left Little Eagle's camp in the spring, planning fully and sincerely to return. That summer he met Marianne Bascomb, and Pretty Hands faded from his mind. . .

Sabin looked about the sleeping camp and then at the tent of the major. *How much did Donaldson know?*

The bivouac had quieted down. The only movements were the occasional stamping of a horse and the pacing of sentries. The supply wagons were neatly aligned, with Katherine Williams' wagon a few yards beyond the last one. Sabin threaded his way between sleeping men. A guard stepped out from behind the end supply wagon.

Sabin halted. "How is she?" he asked softly.

The guard was a Yank infantryman. His hair was whitish gray beneath his forage cap. "She's all right, Johnny."

Sabin nodded. "She's had a helluva time."

The older man leaned on his Springfield. "Yeh. The major picks me out to stand guard. Me and Jonas Scribner. Guess he figgers we're too damned old to be much interested."

Sabin grinned.

"You goin' to smoke all of that seegar?"

"It's yours."

"Thanks. I'll cut off the tip and chew the rest. Man can't smoke on guard but he sure as hell can chew."

There was a faint movement in the brush beyond the wagon. Sabin handed the guard his cigar. "Mind if I look around in the brush?"

"You got more guts than I have, Johnny. Not with them

Pawnees prowlin' around, I don't. Go ahead—but one thing, Bub! Don't try to git into that waggin!"

Sabin drew his Colt and padded into the brush. He stopped fifty feet from the wagon to listen. The wolf howling had died away. Maybe they were in closer now, hoping to pick off a stray. Sabin waited. The guard drifted off behind the line of supply wagons, his jaws moving steadily. Minutes drifted past and then Sabin heard a faint scraping noise. He caught a furtive movement not fifteen feet away. Sabin reversed his Colt and held it by the long barrel. He bent his knees to lower himself.

Then he saw the dark outline of a man inching along on his belly. This was no Pawnee, slick with rancid grease, and with roached hair. The odor of sweat-soaked wool came to Sabin. The soldier raised himself to hands and knees and stared at the wagon, turning his head slowly from side to side like a questing bear. He did not see the tall grim man watching him. He stood up and padded toward the wagon with one hand outstretched to part the osnaburg.

Sabin moved fast. He thrust his Colt beneath his belt, gripped the soldier by his blouse, whirled him about and crashed a big fist against his jaw. There was no outcry. The man never knew what hit him.

Sabin crouched over the fallen prowler and looked about. There was no movement in the wagon. He dragged the man into the brush and squatted beside him, raising the head by the shaggy hair. He swore silently as he looked into the brutish face of Matt Duggan.

Sabin snapped out the blade of his caseknife. Methodically he cut through the thick leather belt and slashed the shell jacket here and there. He cut the laces of the heavy issue shoes and slashed the leather into ribbons. He inserted the point at the bottom of the trouser legs and ripped the heavy material all the way up to the knees. Then he carefully cut out the crown of the forage cap. He grinned as he contemplated the wreckage. Matt Duggan would have hell's own time with his non-coms and officers in the morning.

CHAPTER NINE

The long dusty column was climbing from the plains country into the plateau country, the transition marked by the curious spindle-shaped Chimney Rock which rose from a cone of talus rock.

"Seems to me I've seen one like that somewhere before," Jim Lester mused as he rode beside Sabin and Cobb Howell.

Cobb Howell shifted his chew of spit-or-drown. "Hellsfire, Yank," he said, "yuh never seen a woman with one like thet."

Lester grinned. "You ever been in Chicago, Reb?"

Sabin turned in his saddle. The point detachment of the column was a good two miles behind them, marked by a streamer of dust. They had traveled the Coasts of Nebraska at a steady pace, eating up the long miles. Somewhere back there was Katherine Williams.

As though reading Sabin's mind, the Yank trooper spoke up. "Funny thing about that girl back there insisting on going on to Fort Laramie, all alone with that one rickety wagon."

"Guess she had nowhere's else to go," Howell said.

Sabin thought of the girl's answer to Major Donaldson when he had mentioned the fact that Katherine could go back with the first military unit they met traveling east.

"No, major," she had said quietly. "Dad wanted to go to Oregon. It was all he had in his mind after he was discharged from the Army in '62. I'll go on. I can take care of myself."

Sabin wondered if she had known about Duggan prowling about her wagon. Duggan was now tramping behind a wagon, his wrists lashed together, tied to the axle by a length of rope, eating dust. He had been afraid to tell what had happened to him. He would have gotten far worse punishment if his superiors had found out he had planned to molest the lone girl in the column.

There was little for Sabin and his detail to do except watch the distant smoke or dust threading up against the clear skies. Sabin had picked out some Yankees for his scouts, along with Cobb Howell, Ames Lockerby, Gus Feichter, Jesse Tinsley and Chase Corby. Donaldson had seen to it that the ex-Rebels were accompanied by Yanks three to one, with the exception of Sabin's personal detail.

Sabin had a feeling that they were riding in a huge bowl, with the dim rim peopled by hostiles. But the Indians wouldn't jump as strong a column of yellowlegs and walk-a-heaps such as the one now traveling west beneath their slitted eyes.

The days had been fairly mild for March. There was no haze as yet. Everything stood out clearly, deceptive as to distance.

"Hey!" Lester said. "Look there!"

Sabin looked up. A lone horseman had appeared on a ridge ahead of them, outlined against the sky, as though etched there by a master hand. The pony was painted for war and his tail was tied up. The warrior wore a bonnet. The wind fluttered the many feathers. He sat there, less than half a mile away, watching the three scouts. Sabin drew rein and felt for his fieldglasses. He drew them out and focused them. The face of the warrior swam into view. It was eagle-like, the whole silhouette thrust out, saddle-leather in color. The nose was imperious and immense.

"Pawnee?" Lester asked in a curiously strained voice.

Sabin shook his head. "The warbonnet should tell you that, Jim."

"Cheyenne then?"

"No. He has the four-pointed sacred star on his shield cover. Arapahoe."

Cobb Howell spat. The juice made a sound like that of a pack of playing cards dropped in the thick dust. "They ain't such a much," he said.

"Bad enough," Sabin said. "They don't give a damn for prestige. They like booty. Shifty bastards."

"He friendly?" Lester asked.

"Not with a warbonnet on."

"Maybe he's hunting."

"On a white horse? No. Bad medicine for an Arapahoe."

Lester eyed Sabin. "Where'd you learn all this?"

"I lived with the Cheyennes for a time. The Arapahoes are allies of theirs. Curious though, they don't speak the same language, and don't intermarry. Good fighters, the Arapahoes, but not on a level with the Cheyenne and Sioux."

The warrior raised a heavy musket. The weapon bellowed, driving a thick cloud of smoke ahead of it. The slug whipped past Jim Lester. "The sonofabitch!" Lester said.

He set the steel to his dun. The big horse shot forward.

"Come back!" Sabin yelled.

Lester unsnapped his carbine from its sling and capped it at a dead run. The dun's hoofs drummed on the hard earth. The warrior slung his rifle and took his lance in hand. Lester came on, riding hard.

"What do we do?" Howell asked.

"Set tight. That red bastard ain't alone."

"That figgers."

Lester fired at a hundred yards. The warrior forestalled the trooper by turning his pony away and hanging over the far side. The slug went wild. Lester slung his carbine and ripped out his saber with a slither of steel, drawing his Colt with his left hand. The Arapahoe turned tail and vanished over the ridge. Then Lester was atop it, eager saber extended. He too disappeared, leaving a wraith of dust to mark his passage.

Sabin dismounted. "Get in that hollow, Cobb," he said. "Maybe you think we ought to back his play?"

"God no! He's a loco Yank, ain't he?"

They led the horses into the hollow and capped their Sharps. There was no sign of Lester. Then a rifle popped.

It was followed by the snapping discharge of a Colt. Then silence.

Sabin dropped to the ground and slid his Sharps forward. Minutes drifted past. He looked back. The point was not in sight.

"There he is," Howell said.

Sabin turned. The warbonneted warrior was back on the skyline, watching them. He shook his lance and then held up a dark scrap of something. Sabin fixed his glasses on the dark object. It was a dripping scalp. Some of the blood stained the white side of the horse. His guts boiled a little. He had liked Jim Lester. "He's done, Cobb," he said.

Cobb snapped up his rear sight and slid the movable sight slide upward to clear the V notch which was set at two hundred yards. "I figger he's a lot closer than when we first saw him," he said.

"Two hundred and fifty yards."

"About thet." Cobb settled himself. "Wisht I had my old Hawken rifle my pappy give me when I growed up."

The Arapahoe sat there, evidently waiting for another sortie. Cobb had been the best shot by far in a company of better than average marksmen. He let out half of his breath and tightened his big hand on the small of the stock. The carbine barrel wavered, then settled. The big hammer snapped down. The carbine roared dully, driving smoke ahead of it. The Arapahoe moved. He was too late. The 475-grain slug smashed into his naked chest, driving him from the back of his pony. The pony buck-jumped and vanished over the ridge, dragging the corpse behind him. There was nothing left on the ridge but the war-bonnet, its feathers fluttering in the wind.

Cobb shifted his chew and spat. "These Beecher's Bibles ain't bad little guns," he said. "I didn't think I'd get him."

"Look," Sabin said.

The ridge had sprouted a score of warriors. The sun shone on greased hides and the brass trim of weapons.

"There they are," Howell said as he reloaded. "Salt, pepper, and gravel in the grease."

Sabin squeezed off, parting the feathers of a warbonnet. Howell fired as Sabin reloaded. His bullet struck a paint pony. Sabin fired as Howell reloaded. Most of the warriors flowed down the far side of the ridge, leaving eight warriors who spread out in a crescent, circling down the ridge at far range.

Howell glanced back over his shoulder. "Here comes the point," he said. "Burnin' leather."

The dozen troopers pounded up heavily with a jangling of saber sheaths. Sabin looked up into the flushed face of Frank Khuyper. The Arapahoes cautiously withdrew, but stayed on the near side of the ridge.

"Where's Lester?" Khuyper asked as he wiped his face.

"Dead, sir." Sabin stood up and reloaded.

"Dammit! Where?"

"Beyond the ridge, captain."

"You let a few skulking Indians cut him off?"

Sabin capped the Sharps. "There are a helluva lot of them beyond that ridge," he said quietly.

"I see just eight!"

"I said there were more—*sir*."

Khuyper turned in his saddle. "Corporal Ames!"

The non-com kneed his horse close to the officer.

"Get back to the column. Tell the major we're going to teach some Cheyennes a lesson."

"Arapahoes," Howell said.

"Shut up!" Khuyper rasped.

Sabin frowned worriedly. He hated Khuyper's guts but he had nothing personal against the sweating troopers. "Stay put, sir. They won't attack."

Khuyper checked the caps on his Colt. "I can ride through a hundred of them with these men. The stinking scum!"

Faces were taut beneath forage cap vizors. The men looked nervously at each other and then at the ridge. The eight warriors sat there, speculating on what the Long Knives planned to do. Maybe the Long Knives would bite on the oldest dodge in Plains fighting. Set a trap and draw the soldiers into it. Then surround, circle in close and cut them down. It usually worked fine. It had failed with the scouts. Maybe there was still a chance.

Khuyper waved his pistol at Sabin. "Mount!"

"The major ordered me to avoid contact, sir."

"Dammit! I said 'Mount!' "

Sabin grew tense as Khuyper aimed the Colt. "I'm sorry, sir. I have my orders, sir."

Howell moved a little. The hammer of his Sharps double-clicked back. The muzzle moved to cover Khuyper. Khuyper looked from one to the other of the two ex-Rebels. "Sit there then, you yellow-bellied Rebel scum!"

Khuyper struck his spurs in deep. The big gray lurched forward. The troopers clattered on behind the impetuous officer. Sabin watched them as they plowed up the ridge, sabers extended, Colts held at the ready. The Arapahoes fired a few scattered shots and then spread out to both sides, lashing their ponies out of the way, and then over the ridge. Khuyper breasted the ridge, slowed down, and then waved his Solingen saber. The detachment vanished from sight.

A few seconds passed. Then shots crackled. Smoke drifted up.

Cobb Howell spat. "Right smart doin's over there, Cap'n Shay."

The dust was rising from the east where the main column hotfooted forward toward the sounds of shooting.

"Here they come," Cobb said.

The troopers had reappeared, but not all of them. Khuyper was leading the way, stabbing home the steel. Seven men were behind him, riding as if the devil was on their heels and the fires of hell had been freshly stoked for them.

The troopers clattered to a dusty halt and slid from their saddles, jerking their carbines from their slings without orders. Khuyper sheathed his blade with a ring of steel. His breath was thick in his throat as he looked up the ridge.

"Damn fool," a trooper said in a low voice to Sabin. "There was forty of them Arapahoes over that ridge. In the draws. They come up outa them like screeching devils and cut us to ribbons. Kelly, Hansen, Finster, Ross and Ollinger won't draw this month's pay. The crazy, glory hungry bastard!"

A single frenzied scream, cut off short, drifted to them on the wind, and then there was nothing but the rustling of the dry bunchgrass and the stamping of the lathered horses to break the silence.

The column came up in a veil of dust. Donaldson drew in his gray. "Well, Captain Khuyper?"

Khuyper said, "Arapahoes, sir. I tried to cut them down. They outnumbered us. I lost five men."

Donaldson turned to Sabin. "Didn't you warn him?"

"I did, sir."

Khuyper shot a look of feral hate at Sabin.

"The oldest dodge on the plains," Donaldson said. "I saw it through my glasses. Captain Khuyper, return to your company!"

Sabin watched Khuyper go, and loved it.

"Skulking Pawnees behind us," Donaldson growled. "Arapahoes ahead of us. What next?"

Sabin swung up on his horse. "Just the Sioux and the

Cheyennes, sir. Let me tell the major that they'll raise more pure, unadulterated hell than any Pawnees or Arapahoes."

Donaldson eyed the deserted ridge. "Will you scout ahead?"

"That's my job, sir."

"Watch yourself."

Sabin rode forward, followed by Howell. They ascended the ridge, dismounted, and wormed forward on their bellies. The Arapahoes had vanished. Dust rose from the north. But the warriors had left something for the troopers to meditate on. Sabin focused his glasses and then lowered them quickly.

He and Howell mounted, waved the column on, then rode down into the vale of death and mutilation. The Arapahoes had done their work thoroughly, with savage relish. Eyes had been gouged out and placed on rocks. Noses, ears and chins had been hacked off. Teeth were scattered about like bloody kernels of corn. The men had been gutted and their entrails dragged out. Hands and feet had been hacked from the bodies. Their privates had been severed and placed on the hacked faces. Ribs had been separated by slashing axes. Arrows stuck up like grisly growths from the softer parts of the bodies. There were puncture holes in every sensitive part of the corpses.

Donaldson spurred down beside the scouts. "I'll divert the column," he said thickly.

Sabin shook his head. "March them past, sir. Let them see what the Plains Tribes do for vengeance."

"Vengeance?"

"Have you forgotten Sand Creek, sir? I heard there were many lodges of Arapahoes there."

Donaldson nodded. "Yes. You're right. The men will be marched past."

The column, horse, foot and wagons, was led past the sprawling mess of bodies. Some of the younger soldiers spewed their bellies empty on the bloody grasses. Sabin waited until he saw the rickety wagon of Katherine

Williams. He rode toward her and stopped beside it as she drew rein on the ridge.

"Turn here," Sabin said quietly.

Her face was tired beneath the dust. "Why?"

"There's been fighting."

The horses shied at the thick odor of fresh blood in the air. Sabin tethered his horse to the tailgate and walked to the front of the wagon. "Move over," he said. "I'll drive."

She did not speak, but slid across the warped seat. Sabin touched up the team and drove it south, behind a low ridge. The wind hummed through the wires of the telegraph line and stirred the dust in the ruts of the Oregon Trail. Half a mile west Sabin could see where the telegraph line had been cut and dragged by horses. Two poles and been hacked down.

She wiped the dust from her face. "I didn't thank you," she said.

"For what, Miss Katherine?"

"For stopping that soldier from coming into my wagon."

"You saw—"

"Yes." She touched her hair. "I was all right. I had a loaded pepperbox pistol."

He grinned. "Sure you can take care of yourself, is that it?"

"I always have."

"Why don't you go back? Haven't you relatives in Missouri?"

"No."

"Friends?"

"Most of them are already in Oregon."

He drew rein half a mile past the place of death and wound the reins about the brake handle. "We'll wait here," he said. They would be burying the bodies now.

What was it Donaldson had said? *For the seven hundred miles of the trail there are one and a half graves per mile.*

The wind moaned through the telegraph wires. Behind them some of the troopers had appeared, riding slowly toward the trail. The white tilts of the wagons showed up over the ridge.

"You plan to go to Oregon alone?" Sabin asked.

"Yes."

"It's a long way."

"It's a long way back. Not in miles but in thoughts."

"I see," he said. "What will you do out there?"

"Teach school if I can. I'll find work."

"What about Colonel Bascomb?"

Her hands closed tightly. "If I were a man I'd seek him out," she said.

"Let him alone. He's not to be trifled with."

"You know him then?"

"Yes. I know him."

She leaned back against a wagon bow. "His daughter paid me to help her," she said. "She's beautiful."

He nodded. "I know."

She turned her head to scrutinize him more directly. "You are a strange man, Sabin Shay."

He smiled. "Why do you say that?"

"You're not a Yankee."

"No."

"Jonas Scribner said you were a Galvanized Yankee."

"Do you dislike me for that?"

"All I know is that you've been kind to a woman who is alone in the world."

"Gracias," he said dryly. "I was brought up right, I suppose."

"Yes. Beneath that hard face there seems to be a gentleness, Sabin Shay."

He shrugged and got down from the seat. He looked up at her. "Take my advice. Find a man and get married if you insist on going through to Oregon."

"I need no man!"

"So? You'll see. You'll be all right to Fort Laramie. You must make your own way from then on."

"You'll stay there?"

"Who knows? The Yanks may want us to—"

Cobb Howell cantered up and drew rein. He doffed his cap. "Afternoon, Miss Katherine."

"Good afternoon, Cobb Howell."

Cobb eyed her in appreciation. "The major wants we should scout ahead, Sabin."

He untied his horse and mounted, kneeing it close to the girl. "It's dangerous out here, Miss Katherine. Keep your guns handy. I know you know how to use them."

"It's more dangerous where you're going."

He smiled. "Most of my life has been that way, Miss Katherine. But I'd like you to have a future." He tipped his cap and followed the big Texan along the telegraph line. After a while he looked back. She waved to him.

CHAPTER TEN

I t had been over seven years since Sabin had seen old
Fort Laramie. He had equipped himself there in '58 for
the gold rush to Cherry Creek, two hundred miles
south of the post. He had still been weak from the fever
which had struck him down in the early fall of '57 while
hunting in the Cheyenne country.

Donaldson's dusty column lined up on the parade ground
while Donaldson went to arrange quarters for them. Sabin
stepped out of ranks and took inventory. Old Bedlam, the
two-story stone officer's quarters had received a fresh coat
of whitewash. The fort squatted on a huge paw-shaped bluff
with the pewter colored waters of the Laramie washing its
base. New barracks had been added, and at the foot of the
bluff, to the northeast, he noticed many additional buildings:
quartermaster storehouses, a post office, commissary warehouse, a mill yard, laundry, Sadler's workshop, quartermaster
quarters, a blacksmith shop, teamster's quarters and a corral
with blockhouses at opposite corners. Lines of Sibley tents
bellied in the fresh breeze.

The original walled fort, Old Fort John, was now used as
the commanding officer's quarters. Behind the quartermaster storehouse, Sabin saw lines of emigrant wagons.

He walked past the barracks and looked down on them.

Sway-backed Conestogas, smaller models of the same effi-
cient type, Studebakers, and a miscellaneous group of
bastard types. At one end of a line of nine splendid modified
Conestogas he spied an anachronism—a covered Dearborn,
shining in the sun. His heart caught. Colonel Bascomb had
nine wagons and a Dearborn in his private train. *She was
here!*

"Shay!" bellowed Sergeant Schmidt. "You think maybe
you don'dt haff to stay in ranks yedt?"

Sabin grinned as he strolled back to the ranks. Schmidt
had big fists planted on his hips. "You men listen here! You
haff been on the trail many days! Diss place is to gedt rest
and fix op equipmendt yedt! There iss vimmens here! Vhite
vimmens and redt vimmens!. Dere ain'dt no way I can vatch
you twenty-four hours a day! You vill fool mit dese vimmens
and gedt into trouble yedt! This I cannot shtop! But vhen
Virst Call comes, you vill be in the ranks, ready to do a day'ss
vork, or I vill show you who iss the boss here! There are
plenty of vagon wheels to lash you to! There iss plenty of
sandt to fill your haversacks so you shouldt carry it roundt
and roundt the parade groundt! Drunk, sober, or just plain
lazy, you vill act like soldiers yedt, or Manfred Schmidt ain'dt
topkick of diss J Company oudfidt! Remember diss!"

"Damn Dutchman," Cobb Howell said out of the side of
his mouth.

"He knows his business," Sabin said. "I'll give him credit
for that much."

Donaldson came back to his command. Orders rippled
out. The infantrymen slogged off to an empty barracks. The
wagons rolled down to the area near the Q.M. warehouse.
The cavalry led their horses to the corrals and then carried
their mass of gear to a line of faded, sagging Sibleys.

Sabin dumped his gear on a rickety cot and inspected his
new quarters. The canvas was riddled with scorched holes
from careless firemaking. Cobb Howell stooped to get into
the tent. "Damn!" he said. "I thought these Yanks had good
equipment. This tent would make a good fish net."

"Thank the Lord for small favors," intoned cadaverous Blalock Lott. "I'll match you for the cot nearest the door, Brother Howell."

"Stable frocks!" yelled a non-com out in the company street. "Let's get at them horses, Johnnies! You ain't in no Rebel critter company. You're in the U. S. Cavalry, by Gawd!"

"*Cavalry*," Howell sneered. "The dumb booger can't even pronounce it right. Should be *calvary!*"

Warner Giddings stumbled into the tent laden with his gear. "Damn Yankees take soldiering serious," he said. "Yuh see them Pawnees down behint the officer's stables? Must be a hunnert of 'em. Pawnee Scouts."

Cobb Howell twirled the cylinder of his Colt. "One of these days," he said, "I'll help that little Williams gal to even up the score."

Sabin glanced toward the Dearborn as he trudged to the stables carrying his horse-cleaning gear. A woman was riding sidesaddle toward the line of wagons. She wore a modish riding costume of Army blue. A forage cap was tilted to one side of her honey-colored hair. The sun glinted on the crossed saber insignia on the cap. Sabin stopped and stared hungrily at Marianne Bascomb. There had been a time when Marianne had promised a kiss to every Confederate who would bring her news of killing a bluebelly. Times had certainly changed in the family of Colonel Bascomb.

The horses had been cleaned and fed. The Sibleys had been swept out. The bunks had been made and the equipment had been cleaned and put away. Sabin had bathed in the cold river and had hacked away his beard. He hooked the collar of his jacket and placed his forage cap on his head.

Blalock Lott sat on his bunk in his baggy gray drawers, industriously cleaning his carbine barrel. He eyed Sabin and then winked at Cobb Howell. "The bird of paradise goes forth," he said.

Howell lay on his bunk with his hands behind his head. "Keep away from them squaws," he said with a grin, "or they'll leave yuh with a memento of Fort Laramie yuh ain't about to like."

Warner Giddings blew gently into his trumpet. "Hell," he said. "He ain't foolin' with no breed doxie. I seen him eyeing that filly riding about here with the forage cap on her *cabeza*. Capn' Shay likes class."

"Shut up," Sabin said sourly. "You bastards talk too much."

He left the tent and struck off toward the parade ground. A quartermaster corporal had told him the Bascombs had taken up quarters in an unused officer's quarters. Trust old Colonel Bascomb to deal himself in on the best.

The sun was long gone. Lights had sprung up all over the sprawling post. The wind was cold as it swept across the bluff. Sabin looked down at his uniform. He wondered what Marianne Bascomb would think of Private Sabin Shay, United States Cavalry. She always did have a penchant for epaulets, sashes and swords.

A slim man leaned against a post in front of Bascomb's quarters, puffing at a cigar. He wore a wide-awake hat on the back of his fine blond hair. A neat broadcloth suit with the trousers tucked into polished Hersome gaiters. A splash of white linen showed at his throat.

Sabin stopped. "Good evening, Stacy," he said quietly.

Stacy Bascomb straightened up. "This is Officer's Row, soldier," he said coldly. "Are you here on duty?"

Then the Louisianian bent his head forward and stared at Sabin. "You called me by name. By God! It's Sabin Shay!"

Sabin nodded. "I just came in with Donaldson."

Bewilderment showed on the handsome spoiled face of Stacy Bascomb. "You? In a Yankee uniform? What is this?"

"They call us Galvanized Yankees, Stacy."

Bascomb threw away his cigar. "Damned traitors!" he snapped.

Sabin went cold. "What are *you* doing here on a U. S.

post? Where's your militia uniform, Stacy? The nice clean one that never got stained by sweat, mud and blood?"

Bascomb jerked his fine head. "I was paroled," he said, "according to the rules of war."

"You know a helluva lot about war, militiaman."

Thin lines were etched on Stacy's face. He slid his right hand inside his coat.

Sabin grinned. "You haven't got the guts to draw on me, sonny. I'll take that hideout gun away from you and break your head with it. Where's Marianne?"

"Inside. You'd better keep away from her, Sabin. Father won't like it."

"I'm worried."

Stacy Bascomb withdrew his hand. Then he smiled thinly. He bowed. "Mister Shay," he said politely, "do present yourself. Marianne may have something to say to you."

Sabin walked past the immaculate Louisianian. He tapped on the door while Stacy lit a fresh cigar. The flare of the lucifer illuminated the sly grin on his face.

A gaunt woman opened the door. "Yes?"

"I'd like to see Miss Bascomb."

"Who's a-callin'?"

"Tell her it's a good friend."

The woman shrugged and plodded on flat feet into a rear hallway. Sabin looked about. A fire crackled on the hearth. Soft rugs covered most of the rough wooden floor. The place was of field officer grade.

A door opened and Marianne Bascomb came into the room. Breath caught in Sabin's throat. She had gained beauty in the years since he had last seen her. Her figure had filled out. She wore a low-cut silk dress which exposed the deep cleavage between her full breasts.

"Sabin Shay!" she said. "What are you doing heah in *that* uniform?"

He held out a hand, wanting to touch her. She made no effort to approach him. She looked from side to side in confusion. "This is a shock," she said.

"I've come from Fort MacNaughton, Marianne. I'd hoped you'd be here."

She placed a hand at her throat. "I don't understand."

"It's simple. I took the oath of allegiance and enlisted for frontier service."

"But you had your own company, Sabin! You were a Confederate officer!"

He grinned ruefully. "Now you don't think the United States would give me bars after my fighting them for nearly four years!"

Lord, but she was beautiful. The hard days on the trail had done nothing to harm her freshness. Sabin stood there, almost like a schoolboy, turning his forage cap round and round in his big hands, devouring her with his eyes.

She flushed. She knew what was in his mind. She had held nothing back from him in the old courting days. Now he was here like a lean, wind-burned ghost, wearing an alien uniform, expecting her to feel as she had in New Orleans.

She looked past him. "Father is due back here any moment," she said. "We're to dine with Colonel Collins."

"I saw you this afternoon," he said desperately.

She walked to a window. "You can't bring back the past, Sabin."

"Why? We were in love. We were to be married when the war was over."

She turned her head a little. Her fine white teeth pressed into her lower lip. "So many things have changed," she said uncertainly.

A wave of utter loneliness swept over him. He walked close to her, fearing to touch her, not knowing how far he would go.

She raised her head. "Father plans a new life in Oregon," she said quickly.

"I may be planning that very thing myself, Marianne."

He placed his hands on her smooth white shoulders. For a moment it seemed as though she might come to him and then she moved away from him.

"What's wrong, Marianne?"

She spoke over her shoulder. "Father and Stacy don't want me to associate with old friends."

"I see," he said quietly.

She whirled around. "It isn't what you think! The Confederacy is doomed! There was nothing to be gained by staying in New Orleans. Father might have been ruined. He was clever enough to get his family out of there and get permission to come west. He can't afford to take chances now, Sabin."

It hit him like a dose of canister. Then he came back fighting. He stepped close to her, slid his left arm about her waist and pulled her close. Her head went back and her full lips met his in a long bruising kiss that had the old-time fire in it. Then she pushed at him frantically. "Things have changed, Sabin. They've changed, I tell you!"

He turned her face toward his and kissed her again. Then he pressed his cheek to hers, feeling the wetness of tears. "We can start again," he said softly. "Out in Oregon."

She broke away from him. "Father mustn't see you here."

He smiled. "Dear Stacy has already seen me."

She waved a hand toward the door. "Please go. I'll tell Father that you came by to see me and I sent you away."

"But you *haven't*, Marianne."

Her lips parted. "No. I'll get word to you when I can see you."

He closed the door behind him. A man walked toward the quarters. Sabin walked across the porch. Stacy Bascomb grinned in the shadows. "Heah comes Father, Shay," he said with relish. "It's a damned good thing for you, suh, that he didn't come in on you and my sister."

Colonel Bascomb stopped short when he saw Sabin. "Sabin Shay! Befo' God, suh! What are you doing heah?"

Sabin bowed. "I might ask you the same thing, sir."

Bascomb slowly took the cigar from his plump lips. "A damned Galvanized Yankee!" he said.

"A Reconstructed Rebel," Sabin said in return.

"Suh?"

Stacy moved out of the shadows. "He means you, Father."

Colonel Bascomb looked quickly about to see if anyone was within earshot. "You will watch that kind of talk, suh!" he said furiously. "Furthermore, my daughter is not for your sort."

Sabin slanted his forage cap on his head. "*My* sort? What must she think of a man who would deliberately desert a sick man out on the trail—a man who died because of your callousness?"

Bascomb dropped his cigar. His mustaches and goatee seemed to bristle. "You mean Williams, suh? The man was hopelessly ill with Asiatic cholera. There was no hope for him. None at all, suh. I did not want to endanger my family."

Sabin shook his head. "He had pneumonia. The Pawnees came down on them near Chimney Rock. They killed the boy and tied the father to a wagon wheel. Then they set the wagon afire. He burned alive, Bascomb!

Katherine Williams was saved from a hellish fate because we came up just in time. *You* talk about *my* sort? Look into your own soul, Bascomb. God help you when you realize what you've done!"

Stacy came forward and faced Sabin. "I'd ask you out, suh," he said stiffly, "if you were a gentleman!"

Sabin's right hand cracked across the handsome face in front of him. "You haven't got the guts of a cottontail," he said. "Get out of my way."

Bascomb raised his left hand to his stinging face. Shock filmed his blue eyes. His father shifted a little.

Sabin shouldered Stacy aside. "Colonel," he said quietly, "keep your hands out of your pockets."

Clay Bascomb slowly took out a silver cigar case. "Get out of heah," he said softly. "An enlisted man has no business heah unless he's on duty. I'll have you thrown into the guardhouse, suh!"

"No need. I'm going." Sabin turned on a heel. He walked across the parade ground, then down the slope toward the tent lines. He skirted the end of the wagon line where slab-sided men and gaunt women moved about. He looked toward Katherine's wagon. She wasn't in sight.

A big infantryman from the Kansas Volunteers leaned against a wagon. "There's one of 'em now," he said to some emigrant men lounging near him. "One of them Texicans who joined up."

Sabin walked past. The Kansan grinned. "He was an officer from what I hear tell," he said loudly. "Another damn Rebel crawlin' back into blue before the war ends. State's Rights! Hawww!"

Sabin stopped.

The Kansan was big and cocky. He thrust out his chest "Well?" he challenged.

One of the civilians grinned. "He looks right purty in blue," he said.

"Shore does," said another with a wink.

Sabin eyed them. "I don't see you two clay-eaters in uniform," he said. "Are you bounty jumpers or just plain yellow?"

The soldier waved a restraining hand at the two red-faced civilians. He swaggered close to Sabin. "I'm your oyster," he said. "Leave the boys alone, Galvanized Yankee. I hate the guts of any man as turns against his country, even if it is that stinkin' Confederacy."

All the accumulated hatred for the Bascombs welled up in Sabin like a deep maroon flood. He smashed a left into the Kansan's gut and followed through with a right uppercut which snapped back his opponent's head. The soldier crashed back against the wagon and went down. He shook his head. One of the civilians snatched up a broken wagon tongue and swung it at Sabin. The jagged tip slashed Sabin's face. He went under the tongue and smashed two blows home to the gut. The man grunted and dropped the wagon tongue. He went down on one knee and Sabin finished his interest in the fight by planting a heel against his slack jaw.

Sabin whirled to meet a wavering attack from the first civilian. It was easy. Hate powered the swift blows. The man went down with a smashed nose. "I had enough," he yelled.

Sabin stepped back and looked at the crowd. "Anyone else?" he asked thickly.

A gaunt bearded man came forward. "I'm Sam Nelson. Wagonmaster. Go back to your quarters, soldier. We got nothin' against yuh. Clem Barton and Bill Ryland are troublemakers."

"Thanks." Sabin looked down at the bloody human wreckage he had created. Somehow he felt better.

Katherine Williams stood beside her wagon as he walked away. "Let me bathe that face, Sabin Shay," she said.

"I'm all right."

"Please," she said.

"Forget it. You're amongst your own people now. They don't like Galvanized Yankees."

"I speak for myself, Sabin."

He walked away into the shadows.

CHAPTER ELEVEN

Trouble came to roost on the roof tops of lonely Fort Laramie, flapping its ragged wings in sensuous pleasure, scanning the curious mixture of humans which inhabited the post. There were hard-shelled Abolitionists and Kansas Free-Soilers; Union Volunteers from Kansas, Ohio, Iowa, Michigan and Missouri; tobacco-spitting emigrants from a dozen different states; veteran regulars and green militia. Now a new ingredient had been added to the mixture. Lean-jawed, hard-pratted men of a different breed, somehow alien in dusty blue. Men who looked as though they had been living in a smoky suburb of hell for too long a time.

Trouble had seen the likes of these men before. Fighting at the Alamo, Goliad and San Jacinto. Tangling with whooping Comanches and Lipans. Leading the wild assaults of Lee's infantry as members of the famed First, Fourth and Fifth Texas of Hood's Division, coupled with the Third Arkansas, rated as some of the best shock troops in the Confederate Army.

These new inhabitants of Fort Laramie were no Johnny Raws, who had yet to pop their first caps in battle. There weren't many of them, but it had been said that they would charge hell with a bucket of water. Trouble looked at the lowering sky. Rain always played hell at these Western outposts. Good! The rain would set the mood just fine.

The rain started gently, pattering on the shake roofs and stippling the shallow waters of the Laramie. It marbled the windows of the post buildings and changed the color of the faded canvas tents. It slicked the talmas of the men on guard. By noon it had begun to soak the post thoroughly. Then it shifted into a heavier downpour as the Thunder People loosed their eerie shafts of lightning across the streaming hills. The gutters ran and pools formed in the low spots on the wide parade ground. Now it was a real, rousing rain.

Pay call had blown at Fort Laramie that afternoon. The eagle had flown over and deposited two month's pay. Trouble patiently added this to the brew. It couldn't be more perfect. Rain and payday. There was one more vital ingredient. Whiskey. There was plenty of it at the sutler's. The soldiers had money and no duties to perform. The brew was ready for the tasting.

Cobb Howell splashed through the mud of the company street and entered the sagging Sibley. He shot a hard glance at the perforated canvas. Blalock Lott perched on his bunk, huddled under his talma, gloomily smoking his pipe. Warner Giddings was counting his pay. Sabin Shay was covering his bunk with one of the Yankee shelter halves. Cobb spat out into the streaming street.

"I'm buyin'," he said, "I'm sick of lookin' at your constipated faces."

Lott looked up. "The demon Rum has no appeal to me, as a rule, Brother Howell, but it seems to me that a little spirits might help me. Take a little wine for thy stomach's sake, and thine infirmities."

Giddings slid his pay into his pocket. "I'm game," he said.

"I'll pass," Sabin said.

The three Texans splashed up the company street. Here and there another Texan came out of a tent and followed them. Sabin hooked his talma and slanted his forage cap over his right eye. There was no damned use staying in the tent. The wind bellied the soaked canvas and flapped the fly.

Sabin waded through the mud toward the emigrant wagons. He hadn't seen Katherine Williams since the evening of his fight with the Kansan and his civilian allies. He had been damned short with her. He scratched on the canvas of her wagon.

A slab-sided emigrant woman poked her head out of her dripping wagon. "She ain't there, soljer," she said. "Went up to the fort. That Bascomb woman sent for her."

Sabin walked up the greasy path and came out at the eastern end of Officer's Row. The rain slanted down finely. The low sutler's building was ablaze with lights. For a moment Sabin was almost tempted to get a drink or two, but he didn't want Katherine to listen to his apologies and smell the liquor on his breath at the same time. He slogged toward Bascomb's quarters. He'd wait until she was free. Liquor had been flowing like the rain all day and both soldiers and civilians were carrying plenty of the potent stuff. There weren't enough women to go around at Laramie; particularly a good-looking woman like Katherine Williams.

Old Bedlam, the bachelors officers' quarters, was well lit up, and the music of a gay polka came from the dance orchestra. Sabin stopped beside one of the streaming windows. He looked in at the small dance floor, packed to the nines with dancing couples. He saw Marianne Bas-comb, with flushed and laughing face whirl by in the arms of a captain, and then a shock hit him as he recognized the face of Frank Khuyper bending over that of Marianne.

He turned away into the rain and darkness. It all figured. A woman like Marianne would be fair quarry for every bachelor officer on the post. Frank Khuyper was handsome enough to catch any woman's eye.

Suddenly Sabin wondered about Katherine Williams. The emigrant woman had said Marianne had sent for Katherine. Yet the dance had been on for quite some time.

She should have been back with her own people by now.
Sabin walked swiftly toward the Bascombs' quarters, feeling
uneasy.

The living room of the Bascombs was dimly lit. Sabin
stepped up on the porch, raised his hand to knock, then
lowered it. He didn't want a scene with the old man or Stacy.
Khuyper still had the power to give him a bitch of a time,
and one word or two from Clay Bascomb would start the
persecution.

Sabin peered through a rain dappled window. There was
a low settee in front of the blazing fire. A shapely head
showed above the back. A man stood at the end of the fireplace with his arm resting on the mantel, talking to the
woman. For the second time within a matter of minutes
Sabin felt a ball of ice in his gut. The woman was Katherine
and the man was Stacy.

It hit him hard. He wanted to smash in the door and grip
Stacy by his smooth throat and squeeze his rotten life out of
him. He wanted to take Katherine Williams. His big hands
opened and closed at his sides. Then reason regained the
saddle, slipped the bit in his mouth, and led him away.

He walked down Officers' Row to the magazine at the
far end, and stepped into the shelter of the overhanging roof
to wait for Katherine. Minutes ticked past. Now and then
he stepped out into the drizzle for a better view but there
was nothing but the rain, the beating of the orchestra in the
dance hall, and the din from the sutler's store.

Half an hour passed. Then he saw her walking toward
him. He stepped out into the rain just as a man burst out of
the sutler's and splashed past. "Oh, man!" he said as he raced
past, "There's hell to pay in the sutler's. Some of them
Galvanized Yankees tangled with some of the Kansas and
Missouri boys. Old Silk the bartender is out cold!"

The guard broke from the provost-marshal's building
and double-timed through the rain toward the sutlery.
Sabin lost sight of Katherine. He walked toward the
sutlery. The guard was wasting no time. They were used to

pay nights at Fort Laramie. Carbine butts thudded home, laying a bloody carpet of drunken battlers on the dirty floor.

The sergeant of the guard surveyed the havoc. "Dammit, Silk," he said to the weaving bartender. "We ain't got room for *all* of 'em in the guardhouse."

Silk spat bloodily. "Just clear 'em outa here, Donovan. That's all I ask. I'm closin'!"

The guards were grinning as they hauled the subdued battlers to their feet and shoved them through the doorway into the soaked street. Sabin saw Blalock Lott. His face was battered and bloody. Big Cobb Howell rubbed abraded knuckles against his hips and winked at Sabin. He stooped and slung little Warner Giddings over his shoulder. The kid was out cold.

The shambling drunks weaved past Old Bedlam. The porch was crowded with the finely dressed ladies and immaculate officers of the post, eyeing the doleful procession. Sabin walked behind the guard. He saw Marianne Bascomb.

Frank Khuyper came to the edge of the porch. "What happened, sergeant?" he asked harshly.

Donovan saluted. "Payday is all, sir."

"Lock them up. Every mother's son of them." Khuyper's hard eyes spotted Sabin. "That tall one! Why isn't he under guard?"

Donovan turned quickly. "*Him,* sir? He wasn't mixed up in the fracas."

Khuyper bit his lip. "Place the rest of them in the cells. Bread and water. Buck and gag them!"

Donovan looked curiously at Khuyper. "I'm sorry, sir. But the colonel has standing orders for these payday Donnybrooks. Unless someone is badly hurt we usually send the boys back to their organizations."

Khuyper fumed. "Discipline seems to be damned loose around here."

Donovan couldn't help but speak up. "The men involved

in the fight came in with Major Donaldson's command," he said.

Khuyper went white. Marianne Bascomb slid a smooth arm under his. "Frank," she said, "we have the next polka."

Sabin grinned. Khuyper saw the grin. For a moment it seemed as though he would tear himself away from her to vent his cruelty on some of the poor sots standing in the pouring rain. Then he followed her inside.

Donovan spat. "Now you misbegotten sons of hardcase bitches! You thick-headed sons of Belial! You cotton-mouthed slobs! Get back to your quarters and thank God for an understanding commanding officer!"

"Scratch my hairy rump," said Warner Giddings from Howell's shoulder.

Donovan nodded at a big private of the guard. "Take that one," he said, and eyed the rest of the Galvanized Yankees. "Anyone else?"

There was no answer. The guard carried Giddings toward the guardhouse.

Donovan inflated his barrel chest. "I'm a Regular," he said. "I don't like volunteers and militia. But I'm a Yankee. I hear of anymore trouble outa you Galvanized Yankees and I'll run the whole damn lot of you in."

"Go to hell, Donovan!" Giddings called back.

The battered Texans stood in the rain watching Giddings being taken to the pokey. "Never could keep his mouth shut, that boy," Howell said.

Sabin walked with them down the greasy path. He stopped at the foot of it. "I'll see you later," he said, and went toward the dripping wagons.

He hunched deeper in his talma as the rain sluiced down. His head snapped up as he heard a woman scream from an outbuilding near the wagon line. Two men were fighting savagely in the darkness. One of them thudded a club down on the head of the other then raised the club for a killing blow as his opponent went down into thick mud. Sabin closed in behind him, reached over his shoulder and snatched away the club. The man whirled. Sabin saw the dim contorted face of Matt Duggan. A sour stench of whiskey flooded over him. He chopped hard with the club. Duggan fell down over his victim.

Sabin stepped back. Katherine Williams stood in the doorway of the outbuilding, holding her ripped dress together with shaking hands. "He followed me from the Bascombs," she said.

Sabin knelt by the side of the man Duggan had felled. It was Sergeant Manfred Schmidt. His swollen face was blood-streaked. He opened his eyes. "It wass you who savedt me, Shay?"

Sabin nodded.

"Thanks. Gedt the guardt. This man shouldt be in the guardt house."

Sabin trotted up the path to the guardhouse. Donovan was at the door having a smoke. "Sergeant Schmidt was attacked by Trooper Matthew Duggan," Sabin said. "I dropped Duggan. Get down there and get him in the wagon yard before he comes to, or it will take most of your guard to subdue him."

Schmidt was leaning against the outbuilding when Sabin returned. "I prefer charges," he said thickly. "That man iss not righdt in the headt. You agree?"

"Yes."

Schmidt picked up his mud-plastered cap. "He might haff killdt me. I don'dt forget, Shay."

Sabin watched Schmidt walk off into the darkness. He turned angrily to Katherine. "I once told you to find a man and get married if you intended to go on to Oregon," he said harshly.

She fumbled with the front of her dress and then pulled her cape over the wreckage. "I need no man," she said.

"I said you'd be all right until we reached Fort Laramie. This sort of thing can happen any time. There are many men here without women. There are women who will play along with them. Most of these men don't know the difference between a good woman and a bad one."

"Do you?"

He stared at her. "Yes. I think I do."

She walked toward her wagon. "Are you still in love with Marianne Bascomb, Sabin Shay?"

He felt as if he had been slapped hard across the face. "You know about us then?"

"Yes."

"Who told you?"

She stopped at her wagon. "Stacy."

"He would."

She looked curiously at him. "I suspected as much. I've been helping her with her hair and wardrobe. Once I mentioned your name and she said she'd known you very well in New Orleans."

Sabin leaned against the wagon. "You seem to be on friendly enough terms with the Bascombs after what they allowed to happen to your father."

"Stacy explained to me that his father had an inordinate horror of Asiatic cholera. Stacy's mother died of it when he was a boy, and Colonel Bascomb worshipped her. He lost his head and left us. I've tried to forgive him, Sabin."

"My God," Sabin said involuntarily. He controlled himself. "I'm sorry, Katherine."

She touched his face with a cool wet hand. "You always seem to be around when I need you."

She put her hands on his shoulders, drew him down and planted a soft kiss on his mouth. Then his loneliness swept over him again. He drew her close and kissed her hard. She tried to push him back but he kissed her again and again, stopping only when her hand cracked wetly against his face. "Let me alone," she said. "You're like all the rest."

Sabin walked away with the fires still flaring in his mind. He looked back at her. She was so damned alone, and fair game for a smooth talker like Stacy Bascomb. Sabin wondered if he should tell Katherine the real story of

Therese Bascomb. He knew the facts, all right. Colonel Bascomb had been just as much responsible for *her* death as he had been for Katherine's father and brother.

Lott was asleep in the leaking tent. Howell was hunched in his talma with a bottle between his wet knees. Sabin took it and drank deeply. "To hell with everything," he said.

Lott opened one discolored eye. "Amen," he said.

The rain beat down steadily. Trouble had had a good day. He shook the water from his ragged wings and flitted silently north through the sluicing rain. Up there in the north, Sioux, Cheyennes and Arapahoes were hunching in their wet lodges, bitterly re-telling the tales of the white man's perfidy. The odds were with him.

CHAPTER TWELVE

At any ordinary Army post, in any ordinary military district, Matt Duggan would have been tried properly by general court-martial. But this was Fort Laramie on the Oregon Trail. Somehow the formal court-martial became a drumhead affair—and somehow Captain Frank Khuyper became a member of the court, while the presiding officer turned out to be the sort of over-age-in-grade, whiskey-sodden political time-server who could be "spared" from more rigorous tactical duties.

The court could do nothing less than sustain the charges of attempted rape and assault upon a non-commissioned officer with a deadly weapon. The facts and the witnesses were on hand, and the verdict had to be Guilty As Charged. But after the witnesses departed, after the officers of the court were free to talk at leisure over a comradely drink, prior to passing sentence, something went wrong.

Next day, Matt Duggan's head was shaved. Then he was drummed out of the service to the tune of the Rogue's March. He had been given a dishonorable discharge with ritual trimmings, and that was all. Duggan took up his residence among other scum who lived with "Ration Indians"— lazy fullbloods and diseased half-breeds—beside the Laramie, downslope from the officers' stables. The Galvanized Yankees came to a high Texas boil inside their blue-belly uniforms. They talked of killing Matt Duggan.

Sabin Shay took it hardest of all, but he had to stay calm.

"Listen," he said. "I know it's a mockery of justice and I know Khuyper's behind it. But hear this. Khuyper did it in the hope that we'd bust loose in garrison. He'd like nothing better than to see us kill Duggan. Then he could have us hanged for it."

Warner Giddings knitted his brows in strenuous thought.

"Well," he said, "leastways it shows how a fellow can get out of this dirtyshirt blue. Now suppose I was just to up an' gunwhip some bluebelly non-com—"

"No!" Sabin said. "In Duggan's case, Khuyper had it easy. He could remind those fools that Federal prisons in the East are already bulging with Rebels. He could predict that they'll all be turned loose automatically, once the war's over, the criminal as well as the noncriminal. He could point out that transport back over the trail is in such a fix that taking the cost and trouble to ship a guarded prisoner back East would be virtually a crime in itself. He could argue that a Rebel who'd taken the Federal oath would be a pariah in Texas right now, and that with a dishonorable discharge from the Federal Army thrown in, he wouldn't even dare to go home. You see?"

"I guess so," Giddings said. "He tricked them into thinkin' the easy way out was just to turn Duggan loose here, stranded-like. But why wouldn't it work—"

"For the rest of us? Because a second crime would expose their mistake and they'd have to get tough. Slug a non-com, Warner, and they'll put you behind bars for a long, long time. Kill Matt Duggan and you'll hang. Khuyper knows it. Now don't play into his hands—any of you. We've got to wait. Understand?"

They understood. They left Duggan alone. And they waited.

The roads were still too muddy for travel. The emigrants

still camped at the post, having babies, squabbling amongst themselves, raising hell in general. A few cavalry patrols splashed off on the muddy roads. The telegraph line went out regularly as the Indians cut it. Katherine Williams worked for Marianne Bascomb, and Marianne Bascomb worked on Captain Frank Khuyper, and Matt Duggan got himself a job as teamster with Colonel Bascomb.

Robert E. Lee attacked Fort Stedman on the Union right at Petersburg, according to a telegraph dispatch from the East, and failed. General "Jube" Early ran afoul of Phil Sheridan at Waynesboro and lost most of his command. Sheridan cut the Virginia Central and the James River Canal. "Cump" Sherman was chasing Joe Johnston as the strong Federal force under his command moved toward Fayetteville for the eventual junction with U. S. Grant.

Sabin Shay went about his duties with a sickness in his soul. The South had no hope left now. He knew it and the men knew it. All they could do was go on waiting, biding their time for the chance to leave this fort behind and strike out West for themselves.

At night, Sabin always walked across the parade ground to the edge of the Laramie bluffs and spent a while alone, staring blindly west into the windy darkness. A man cannot follow a flag for four years and then suddenly admit that the flag no longer exists. Soon the smoke-blackened, shot-torn Stars and Bars would be a trophy in the Yankees' hands. But he had to get used to the idea, to cure his soul sickness, to search out a new aim in life that meant more than just a purposeless flight into the Western nowhere.

He was trying, but it would take time.

CHAPTER THIRTEEN

abin picked up the heavy ration box and hoisted it to his bruised shoulder. He settled it and trudged out of the stifling warehouse into the quartermaster wagon yard. Cobb Howell poked his head out from the rear of the wagon. "How many more of them damned boxes?" he asked.

Sabin plumped the box down on the tailgate.

"Watch that box!" roared a corporal. "You'll be eating some of those rations out on the trail starting tomorrow!"

Cobb wiped the sweat from his face and spat at a lantern hanging on the warehouse wall. "Yuh know what *yuh* kin do, yuh Yankee snotnose," he said in a low voice.

"That's the last," Sabin said. He wiped his dirty forehead with the back of his left forearm. "What time is it?"

Cobb dropped from the tailgate into the churned mud of the yard. "I heard Call To Quarters awhile back. Ain't time for yuh to make the dance, Sabin."

Sabin looked down at his filthy stable frock. He itched. He needed a shave. "I told Katherine Williams I'd pick her up at eight for the enlisted man's dance."

Cobb shifted his chew of spit-or-drown. "Yeh. There's a skunk in the woodpile, Sabin. That slick Bascomb kid prob'ly whispered a few choice words into Khuyper's dirty ear. Worked fine too. Here yuh are standing in manure and mud, smelling near as bad as the manure, when you're supposed to be squirin' Miss Williams to the dance."

The two-striper sloshed through the mud. "That all?" he snapped.

"We ain't standin' here whilst there's work to be done!" Cobb said in mock horror. "Now you know thet, *sir!*"

The corporal bent his brows. Cobb had been riding him all evening, and he wasn't quite sure what to do about it. "All right," he said. "Haul your butts outa here. See you get cleaned up, too. We head west at dawn."

Cobb thrust out a thick arm. "Forward to glory!" he crowed.

Sabin couldn't help but grin as he trudged through the mud with the big Texan. It was hard to beat Cobb Howell down. If he liked you it was easy to handle him; if he didn't like you, he could give you hell's own time.

"There ain't been nothin' but trouble for you since Stacy Bascomb's been butterin' up Miss Williams," Cobb said.

"There was plenty of it before we ever got to Fort Laramie, Cobb."

Cobb shot a sideways glance at him. "Yeh. But you been gettin' it from all angles. It's a queer world, Cap'n Shay."

They entered the company street. Cobb placed a hand on Sabin's shoulder. "One of these days yore luck will change."

"What the hell are you driving at?"

Cobb stopped and faced Sabin. "Bad enough Khuyper had it in fer yuh at MacNaughton. Now he's squirin' Miss Bascomb around. That filly is enough to unhinge a man's mind, ef'n she has a mind too, and it shore looks like she has."

Sabin flushed. "Take care," he warned in a low voice.

Cobb shook his head. "We're amigos, Cap'n Shay. I want thet yuh should know that all the time. But yuh got a bot fly borin' into yuh with this Bascomb woman. It ain't right. What with her switchin' that rump of hers all over the post and hangin' on to Khuyper's arm like he was God hisself."

Sabin swung from the hip, but Howell had been expecting it. He blocked the hard blow with a thick forearm and wrapped a bear hug about Sabin. Then he spoke with his face a few inches away from Sabin's. "Damn yuh! The boys been wrathy about yuh. They know what's been eatin' yuh. Can't yuh see what's goin' on? Now *listen* for a change, instead of talkin'!" Cobb stepped back and placed his hand on his hips.

Sabin controlled himself.

Howell looked up and down the quiet street. Most of the men had gone to the dance thrown for those leaving the post for duty on the trail. "Yuh ain't nothin' but a draggle-assed high private in the rear rank of a John company, Sabin. Not *Captain* Shay, of Shay's Independent Frontier Company! That Bascomb gal is wise. Her old man got her outa New Orleans whilst the gettin' was good. Headin' for Oregon and a new life. Now is she goin' to take up with a Galvanized Yankee out there? Hell no! Not whilst she can hitch herself to *Captain* Frank Khuyper. By God, Sabin, she may still like yuh. *Love* yuh, for all I know. But there ain't no place in her nest fer yuh. Get *thet* through yore hard *cabeza!*"

"Go to hell," Sabin said sourly, and walked toward his tent.

He cleaned himself swiftly and scraped off his beard. He dressed and left the tent. He found Howell sitting on a box at the end of the street, sucking at his battered pipe. Howell grinned at Sabin. "A fine night," he ventured.

Sabin stopped. "Somewhere along the line," he said, "You seem to have forgotten that I asked Katherine Williams to the dance tonight."

"Appears like I did. Howsomever, Cap'n Shay, I been with yuh quite a spell now. I saw yuh read that jasmine smellin' letter damned near every night whilst we was on the trail to here from Fort MacNaughton. I've seen yuh look at Marianne Bascomb. Mebbe yore foolin' yoreself. Anyways, I figgered it out, sittin' here, that a man's got a right to do what he thinks is best. Good luck to yuh."

Sabin walked up the path to the parade ground. He looked toward Officers' Row. The Bascomb quarters were well lit up. *He* was probably there. Sabin stopped and lit a cigar. He had learned plenty about Frank Grayson Khuyper since the column had left Fort MacNaughton.

Khuyper had been a law student in 1861, and in 1862 he had enlisted in the Kansas Militia, rising swiftly to the rank of first sergeant. In 1863, Jim Lane of Kansas had used his influence to have a second lieutenant's commission presented to Khuyper. By the fall of 1864, Khuyper sported the twin bars of a captain without having seen any more action than a skirmish against some guerillas at Harneyville. The only spot of glory on his record was the defeat and capture of Shay's Independent Frontier Company on the Badwater, with Shay's Company almost out of ammunition and badly cut up after defeating a large band of raiding Kiowas.

The war was almost over. Too much rank and not enough glory had rubbed off on Frank G. Khuyper. The rumor around the post was that Khuyper planned to make his home in Oregon after the war. With a brevet commission and an honorable war record he would be in solid with the Union men of the new territory. A beautiful, gracious wife, with money of course, would shine beside Frank Khuyper as he began the long climb to political heights. The study of law was almost essential for political prominence. That . . . and money. Colonel Clay Bascomb had plenty of that last item.

Sabin strolled toward the big barracks where the dance was being held. He stepped up on the porch and leaned against a post. Every window held its little group of lonely enlisted men watching the fortunates inside. Their eyes studied each woman, thin or fat, plain or pretty as though each one was a goddess temporarily visiting earth to ease the harsh burden of frontier duty for a pitifully short spell.

Sabin looked over the clumps of heads at the nearest window. Katherine Williams was dancing with Stacy

Bascomb. She wore a dress he had never seen before. She was far prettier than he had ever realized, and her eyes were all for Stacy Bascomb. Then Sabin stiffened, taking the cigar from his mouth. Naturally he recognized the tall, broad-shouldered officer standing on the sidelines, near the sweating orchestra. Frank Khuyper. But it was the woman beside him, standing with white-gloved hand resting posses-sively on Khuyper's arm, who riveted Sabin's attention. It was *her*. She looked like an exquisite Dresden figure.

Sabin devoured her with his eyes. She was like a bird of paradise compared to the other women in the hall. Sabin walked to the door, kept open because of the heat in the place. He walked in and took off his forage cap. He stared steadily across the crowded floor. Suddenly she saw him.

Sabin placed his cap on a hook and skirted the crowd. He came up behind the couple. Khuyper did not see him. "May I have the honor of the next dance, Miss Bascomb?" Sabin asked with a bow.

Khuyper whirled. Hot blood rushed up beneath his fine skin. "Shay," he said, "you're on detail."

"I was, sir. Finished a few minutes ago."

Khuyper seemed almost ready to strike. "Miss Bascomb is here with an officer, Shay."

Sabin smiled. "I know, sir. Nice of you to honor the enlisted men's dance. Very nice indeed, Captain Khuyper, sir."

Sabin had him then, and Khuyper knew it. Sabin took Marianne as the next dance started. Halfway across the floor she glanced back at the raging captain.

"Sabin," she said. "He hates you. Why did you do this tonight?"

He grinned. "It's the privilege of any enlisted man, isn't it? One of the few times in his miserable life when he can dance with the chosen few. Besides, we're leaving tomorrow. I had to see you."

"Why? We may never see each other again."

"We're both moving west."

She looked away. "They say the Indians are gathering in great strength along the trail. Colonel Collins refuses to give Father permission to leave until things are safer. Sabin, it's *so* dangerous out there."

A side door was right beside them. Before she knew what he intended, he swung her out on the wide side porch. The porch was deserted. He drew her close and kissed her. She pushed him back. "Sabin! You're mad! He's insanely jealous!"

He raised his head. "He's *insane*. I'll agree to that. How can you associate with a madman like that?"

She bit her lip. "There's so much pressure on me. From Frank. From my Father. Even from Stacy. I seem to be some kind of chattel. Father seems to think I should marry Frank. Frank plans to settle in Oregon after the war. Father says it will protect our future there."

Sabin felt cold all over. "That man is responsible for the death of my brother. Many of my men died in filth and neglect because of him. Some of them were shot down in cold blood. Why? Because he was wounded at the Badwater. Because we fought them to the last cartridge. Any honorable man would have forgiven us that last hard fight. But not *him!* It was a personal affront to his ego. He'll never be satisfied until he sees to it that every last one of us Galvanized Yankees is killed off. One way or another."

"Take me back," she pleaded. "I don't know what to do, Sabin. *Before God, I don't know what to do!*"

He gave it up. They walked back inside. "Thank you for the dance, Miss Bascomb," he said, and bowed. As he walked away he could feel the cold shaft of Khuyper's eyes boring into the back of his neck. The odd thought came to him that Marianne Bascomb would someday wake up to the fact that she had married a monster. Too late, of course. Then she could do one of three things. Leave him. Kill him. Or do what her mother had done in years gone by when *she* realized what kind of man she had married. Somehow Sabin knew it would be the last. God help Marianne Bascomb.

Katherine Williams stood near the front door of the hall, smiling at a red-faced corporal. Sabin stopped in back of the non-com, "This dance is mine, corporal," he said.

The corporal seemed almost relieved as he walked away. Sabin bowed formally. "I'm sorry," he said. "I was placed on extra fatigue. Did Giddings tell you?"

She nodded.

He looked down at her pretty gown. "I've never seen that before," he said.

She blushed a little. "I was helping Miss Bascomb. Stacy asked me to attend the dance with him. She insisted I wear this."

"Where is the gallant Stacy?"

She nodded across the teeming floor. "At the punch bowl."

"Stacy likes his liquor." "Oh, be quiet!" she snapped.

Sabin grinned. "Look, Kathy. I'm sorry about the whole thing."

She frowned fiercely at him. "So? Is that why you went to *her* first like a bee after pollen? Simpering and smiling? Sometimes you make me sick, Sabin Shay."

"Sometimes I make *myself* sick, Miss Williams." She looked away and then laughed. "Somehow I can't really get mad at you. There are times when you look so stern and angry, then suddenly you seem able to play the fool without much effort."

"A neat picture of my whole life," he said with a sigh.

Stacy Bascomb skirted the edge of the crowd with two brimming punch glasses in his fine slim hands. His face reddened when he saw Sabin. "What are *you* doing here?" he blurted.

Sabin ignored him. "This is our dance, Katherine," he said.

"Please," she whispered. "I need the work from Miss Bascomb. *Please*, Sabin. Don't make trouble."

Sabin stepped aside. Stacy smirked. The kid was half

drunk already. Sabin walked outside and felt for a cigar. It had been a damn fool stunt to rile Khuyper.

Sabin saw Warner Giddings leaning against a post. The light from the hall glittered on the rows of braid festooning his narrow chest. He grinned at Sabin. "Through for the night?" he said. "Yes."

Giddings nodded. "I got a bottle of forty-rod," he said, "and I ain't about to hog it myself. I'd admire to have yuh help me kill it, Cap'n Shay."

Sabin smiled. "Never let a comrade down yet," he said. He took Giddings by the arm. "Where does the execution take place?"

"In the tent. Ole Howell sent me up to see how yuh was."

"Well, thank you."

"I looked in and seen yuh with Miss Bascomb and then with Miss Williams, Cap'n Shay. Two purtiest gals at the stompin'. How do yuh do it?"

Sabin grinned. "Easy," he said. "I just grab an earring and stick it in my pocket. Then they have to follow me around."

They ambled down the graveled pathway. Giddings glanced back at the brightly lit hall. "Quite a difference between them two fillies," he said, and neighed like a small, pleased horse. "Yore a lucky man in some ways, Cap'n Shay."

"How so?"

"I never seen Miss Bascomb look at that skunk Khuyper like she does at you, nor I never seen Miss Williams look at that Bascomb brat the way she does at you."

Sabin placed an arm around Warner Giddings' thin shoulders.

"Boy," he said solemnly, "after the war is over, Shay's Independent Frontier Company will live again. By God, we'll form us a reunion-type marching and drinking club for holiday parades and such. And when that glorious day comes, remind me to promote you to corporal."

Giddings tilted his head. "Shore will. You really think that day will come, Cap'n Shay?"

Sabin increased his pace. "Certainly. Let's get that bottle. I feel like I've got a heap of drinking to do before dawn."

They had a heap of drinking to do before spring, it turned out. Not that it changed anything, or anybody. Every human being on the post seemed to be frozen into his own set role throughout a winter that would never end.

But winter did end. Spring came early to Wyoming that year. Summer arrived in a rush. And the troops took to the field. . .

CHAPTER FOURTEEN

ort Laramie lay over one hundred and fifty dusty miles behind Donaldson's command. Far to the north, tall nimbi towered over the dim hills. Eerie sheet lightning played across the clouds scarring them brightly.

Sabin Shay drew rein on a rise ahead of the slow-moving column. The supply wagons bounced and joggled in the ruts of the road. The dust threading up from the mules and horses hung over the sweating infantrymen who slogged ahead of the wagons. One cavalry company led the column, while another closed up the rear, eating the dust. Now and then the vagrant wind tattered the dust and brought the sound of rumbling wheels and thudding hoofs to Sabin.

For two days there had been no Indian sign. No lone warrior sitting his paint horse on an elevation watching the passage of the column on the Great Medicine Road. There had hardly been a day on the long journey where at least a dozen warriors had been seen eyeing the Mila Hanska, the Long Knives, as they slogged along. But there had been no slashing raids by the Crazy Dogs, Dog Soldiers and Stronghearts.

Sabin rode on. A mile ahead of him he could see Cobb Howell and Uh-sah-wuck, Spotted Horse of the Pawnees, watering their horses at a buffalo wallow. Far on the northern flank of the column other cavalry scouts were paired up with Pawnees. Ames Lockerby and Si Webster were out there somewhere.

He joined Howell at the wallow. "Just look at this buffalo tea," Howell growled.

The water was brown, and an odor of ammonia rose from it. Sabin shook his canteen. "I'll do without it," he said. "Never could figure out how a buffalo can stand in water, peeing and crapping into it while he's drinking it."

Spotted Horse was a thick-bodied man, wearing a cast-off issue undershirt hanging over his breechclout. His moccasins were worn thin. His hair was roached and from it depended a single feather. He looked like a typical Fort Laramie "ration Injun," but he was a warrior of some standing in his home village of Arikararikuchu. He was a member of the Two Lances, entitled to wear the black moccasins during ceremonial occasions, for he had consecrated the buffalo four times.

Cobb jerked his head at the Pawnee. "Gabby, ain't he?"

Sabin chuckled. He nodded at the Pawnee. "How does it go, brother?"

Spotted Horse glanced at the lightning-riven clouds. "No good. Voice of Great Spirit. No good."

"You have seen the enemy?"

"No Cha-ra-rat."

"What the hell is he saying?" Howell asked.

"No enemy."

"Time to look for 'em is when you don't see 'em." Cobb took out three cigars. "Last of my stock from the sutler. Light up, Cap'n Shay."

Sabin and Cobb lit up, but the Pawnee stuffed the dry tobacco into his mouth and munched on it.

"Look at that," the big trooper said.

Sabin drew the smoke into his lungs. "Few Pawnees can smoke. They have to qualify in some ceremony."

"Queer ducks."

"Matter of opinion. We whites have some queer notions ourselves."

Howell stood up and pointed east. "Column's gainin'. You want to wait and report?"

"Hell no!"

Howell shoved back his forage cap and wiped the sweat from his face. "Khuyper been rawhidin' you again?"

"Naturally."

Cobb Howell rubbed his hand against his holster. "First gunfight we get into with them Sioux, I'm hopin' Khuyper gets in my way."

"You may have to get in line, Cobb."

They mounted and rode west, followed by Spotted Horse. The Pawnee's eyes moved constantly, studying the terrain. Three miles from the buffalo wallow he kneed his mouse-colored mare close to Sabin. He thrust out an arm, pointing down a long slope toward the sluggish coil of the river.

"What's up?" asked Howell.

Sabin looked west. Beyond a loop of the river he saw a group of buildings set back from the road. "That must be Sage Springs Station."

"Sho! that's where we're headin' ain't it?"

Sabin nodded. "It's called Fort Bowen now."

Cobb scowled out across the great shallow bowl of country, ringed by low hills, with ridges of naked rock like dislocated bones, thrusting themselves through the shallow soil. "Hell of a place. Nothing but sky and hills. Every Dog Soldier in Wyoming can sit on them hills an' look down into your mess tin to see what you're eatin'."

Sabin relit the stub of his cigar. "I don't like the looks of this place. See those hills near the ford? A natural place to ambush anyone traveling the road."

They rode down the slope, eyeing the hills. A coyote loped through the brush and vanished into a draw. A thread of smoke drifted up from the old stage station to stain the clear sky. The wind had shifted, bringing a breath of cool air from the north where the nimbi brooded over the mountains.

Spotted Horse half-cocked and capped his rifle. He shifted his lance sling from his right to his left shoulder.

"Take a look into those hills," Sabin said.

The Pawnee kicked his heels against the sides of his horse and rode north of the road to circle in on the hills. Antelope jacks rose up out of the brush and raced away from the Pawnee.

"How many men the Yankees got in that station?" Cobb Howell asked.

"About a platoon."

"Infantry?"

"Cavalry."

"That so? Where's the hosses?"

Then Sabin knew what had been bothering him. The big corral, set off to one side of the station and back from the main buildings, was as empty as last night's bottle of rotgut.

They left the road and flanked it a half mile to the south. The dust rose from the grass. Spotted Horse was out of sight.

An icy finger of loneliness seemed to trace a wavering line down Sabin's sweaty back. An air of brooding hung over the shallow valley, as though it was hiding some dark secret.

They drew rein a quarter of a mile from the river. The Pawnee came out of the hills, riding swiftly. He held up something as he neared the two white men. It was an ankle-height moccasin. He gave it to Sabin. Sabin examined it. "Sioux," he said quietly.

"Cha-ra-rat," Spotted Horse agreed.

"How the hell do you know it's Sioux?" Howell asked.

"Lazy stitch. Isosceles and right-angled triangles. See how they've been combined into hour-glasses, diamonds and two-pronged forks? The Cheyenne designs are similar."

Cobb nodded. "There's dried blood on that skin fringe at the heel."

Sabin looked at the little fort across the river. There was

still no sign of life. The bastards must be asleep. The three scouts rode toward the ford.

The wind shifted, blowing from the fort.

"My God," Cobb Howell said.

The wind had brought a sweetish rotten smell to them. The wind-borne horror was sending them a silent message. Howell's horse shied and blew at the edge of the water. There was something in the shallows. Something covered in greenish blue cloth. A dead soldier, the bloated body taut against the soaked cloth.

Spotted Horse kneed his horse away from the two white men as the corpse seemed to move. The pent-up body gas was forcing itself out. The foul stench drifted to the two white scouts.

Howell stood up in his stirrups. "Look," he said. "In the eddy. Three more of 'em."

Sabin turned to the Pawnee. "Stay here," he said. He knew damned well it was a useless thing to say, because the Pawnee wouldn't go near that silent fort.

The two white men rode across the ford and drew rein a hundred yards from Fort Bowen. The doors were closed and the windows shuttered. The tendril of smoke still drifted from the huge rock chimney. The odor of death thickened about the two scouts.

Sabin unsnapped his carbine swivel and capped the Sharps. Howell followed his example. They touched spurs to their horses. They encircled the fort. There was no sign of life. The wind banged a loose shutter and Sabin's nerves jumped.

Sabin slid from his horse. "Stay here, Cobb," he said.

"With pleasure. I'll cover yuh."

The last fifty feet to the front door seemed an eternity to Sabin. He shoved at the thick door with his carbine butt. It swung open on creaking hinges. Then the full blast of the charnel house hit him. He gagged and turned away. He slipped his scarf up over his nose and mouth, took a deep

breath of fresh air, and walked into the big common room of
the station.

Men were scattered about the floor like bundles of
bloody rags. A pipe-ax protruded from the back of a
sergeant's head. A corporal lay near the door with his feet and
right hand hacked off. Arrows bristled from everybody. Sabin
felt a sour flood well up in his throat. He crossed the stinking
room. A man lay near the fireplace, but his body wasn't
swollen tight against his clothing. He lay on his back near the
smoldering fire. Bits of a broken ammunition box were half-
burned in the fire. Sabin knelt and touched the dead man's
face. It was still warm. The poor bastard had been severely
wounded, and his hands were twisted in the blood-soaked
undershirt. He had evidently lived there for several days in
that rotten tomb, unable to move, feeding the fire as a silent
message to whoever might come near the station.

Sabin counted ten dead men in the big room and four
others in a smaller room. The Sioux had gone through the
station like beer through an open bung. He came out of the
back door. Cobb Howell beckoned to him. He pointed out a
mass of horse tracks behind the corral in a soft area near the
walled springs. "Musta been about a hundred of 'em," he
said. "How was it in there?"

Sabin pulled his scarf from his face. "Like the Alamo
after Santa Ana got through with it."

"Wonder how it happened?"

"*Quién sabe?* They might have got careless. The Sioux may
have broken in at dawn and got every damned one of them,
even those that broke for the river bottoms."

Blue-clad horsemen topped the ridge across the river.
They drew rein. The setting sun flashed on fieldglasses as an
officer studied the fort. Spotted Horse had ridden along the
river and was swimming his horse across. He came out of
the river and rode his dripping horse in tight little circles,
pointing to the hills behind the fort.

Sabin whirled. There were war-bonneted warriors against

the sky line. Over a hundred of them. Laughing at the stupid
Mila Hanska below them. They had taught the Long Knives
a lesson. Then to the west and the north, other horsemen
appeared. Cheyennes, Sioux and Arapa-hoes.

Cobb Howell looked at the advance guard of the
column. He began to sing.

"Come home, John, Don't stay long. Come home soon
To your own Chick-a-biddy."

The advance came swiftly down the hill. A trumpeter's
mount shifted into an easy singlefoot to ease the trumpet-
ing. The clear notes of the C horn filed across the valley.
Then the first company showed up on the ridge.

The hostiles watched the Long Knives until they
reached the river. Then they vanished as quickly as they had
appeared.

Howell wiped the nervous sweat from his face. "It's as
hot as a Dutch oven with the biscuits burnin'," he said.

The advance threw up sheets of water tinted bloody by
the dying sun. The bloated corpses bobbed in the miniature
waves.

Sabin waited for Lieutenant Teale. He saluted. "Mr.
Teale," he said, "the garrison has been wiped out. Four
bodies in the river. Fourteen in the station."

Teale paled. "No survivors?"

"We haven't found any, sir."

The troopers shifted in their saddles as the fetid stench
drifted to them through the open door. They looked
nervously at each other and then at the hills where a wraith
of dust marked the passing of the hostiles. They felt like
Christian martyrs in a great natural Coliseum, with the
blood-hungry eyes of two hundred hostiles glaring down at
them.

Teale dismounted and eased his crotch. "Was the spring
fouled?"

Cobb Howell nodded. "Two dead mules in it."

Teale turned. "Sergeant Carmody! Haul the mules out of
the spring. Finch! Ride back to Major Donaldson and tell

him what's happened. He'd better jump up some dust getting down to the river. We don't know where the hostiles are."

Finch spurred toward the river. Teale walked to the door and poked his head in. Suddenly he turned and spewed a sour flood out on the ground. "Oh, Lord," he spluttered. "That's Jim Hartnett in there with his men. Jimmy and I enlisted back in Kansas three years ago."

The sun was almost behind the hazy hills as the column wound down to the river and crossed it. Troopers of the advance had looped picket lines about the feet of the dead men and had hauled them out into a hollow beyond the station. Most of them lost the beans and bacon from their last meal before they finished the job.

When the sun went down the wind carried the shrieking laugh of a coyote down to the nervous men at Fort Bowen. Then the cry was repeated from hill to hill, so that they knew they were ringed by a great circle of the finest natural horsemen in the world, patiently waiting another chance to cut the Mila Hanskas to bloody ribbons and send them across the Shadow Waters.

CHAPTER FIFTEEN

They had buried the eighteen bloated dead in the neglected post cemetery. The buildings had been scrubbed and disinfected. But the aroma of death still clung stubbornly as though to remind the living that death was always close.

Major Donaldson sent out patrols with orders to go no farther than the first line of hills. Too many men had ridden over the hills in that country to vanish from sight forever, or to be found in undignified death, slashed and mutilated. The telegraph line was still out, although Corporal Kerr tested his key every hour. The hostiles had been clever enough not to touch the line within sight of the post, hoping that some of the Long Knives would ride over the eastern hills to trace the break. The post itself was safe enough. The hostiles knew better than to ride into the fire of Walk-A-Heaps sheltered behind log walls. They wanted the slow-riding horse soldiers to come out after them.

There was no news from the east, and the garrison had no knowledge of what was going on farther along the line. Perhaps there was nothing but a string of charred station ruins with blackened corpses silently garrisoning them.

The post flag snapped in the strong wind every day, reminding the soldiers that this was indeed an outpost of the United States, but to all appearances, they might have been the first men on a silent, menacing planet, thousands of miles from Mother Earth.

A quiet new enemy showed its scabby head at Fort Bowen. One by one, men fell prey to fever, aches and nose-bleeds. Rashes and rose spots appeared on their abdomens. Hamish Hume diagnosed it as typhoid.

Sabin waited outside the small hospital one day for news of Charlie Kester.

Hume wiped the sweat from his face with one hand as he felt for a cigar with the other. "Typhoid," he said. "Charlie's tough. It's the major I'm worried about. He's had a relapse. Hemorrhages."

"That leads to—"

"Yes."

"We can't afford to lose him. If Khuyper gets in the saddle there will be pure hell to pay around here."

"I've heard that he wants to send out a patrol to find that break in the telegraph."

Sabin spat. "You know why. The bastard is dying to get a message from Marianne Bascomb."

Hume raised his eyebrows. "It's gone that far?"

"You know damned well it has! He'd sacrifice good men to get that line through just to hear from her."

"I've asked for you as temporary medical orderly."

"Thanks," Sabin said dryly.

Hume grinned. "You're welcome. Fennessey got into the medical alcohol last night. Man, but he was fighting drunk!"

"He's regretting it. Khuyper has him lashed to a wagon wheel out in the sun."

"I'll stop that. The man won't live."

"Here's your chance. Here comes Khuyper now." Sabin snapped to attention as Khuyper stopped in front of Hume.

Khuyper stared at Sabin. "Have you no duties?"

"I was on guard last night, sir. The second night in a row —sir."

"Captain Khuyper," Hume said quietly, "The typhoid

may spread. It may have been caused by water that was used five to fourteen days ago. Typhoid usually requires a minimum of five days after infection for the fever to start."

"What are you doing about it? We can't afford to have men lying about in hospital, Hume."

Hume flushed. "Treatment requires careful nursing. All excreta must be destroyed. I'll need screening of some sort for my patients. I believe the flies spread the disease."

Khuyper laughed. "*More* of your fine theories."

Hume raised his head. "I don't tell you how to screen an infantry column with cavalry, nor how to establish Cossack posts. Please don't question my theories as a medical man!"

Khuyper shrugged. "You'll have to do the best you can with what you have."

"I'd like to have Trooper Shay detailed as a medical orderly to replace Fennessey."

Khuyper glanced suspiciously at Sabin. "Why?"

There was a dryness in the Scot's tone as he answered. "He had good opportunity to learn his business at Fort MacNaughton, you may remember."

Khuyper's mouth drew into a tight line. "I'm in command here. The man has been assigned as a scout. I may have need of him very soon."

"For what purpose?"

"An eastern patrol, Hume. I want that telegraph line repaired. For all we know the war may be over." The cold eyes flicked over Sabin's set face. "I'd like to hear of Lee's surrender." Khuyper wanted Sabin to rise to the bait. He had plenty of wagon wheels exposed to the blazing sun.

Hume looked east toward the hazy hills. "A dangerous business, Frank."

"Soldiering is always dangerous business," Khuyper said, as though *he* had seen plenty of danger while in uniform.

Hume rubbed his lean jaw. "The major will not allow any such patrol."

Khuyper smoothed down the front of his blouse. "Will he recover, do you think?"

Hume looked again at the plum-colored hills. "You might as well know now as later. I do not think so."

Khuyper straightened. "Too bad. Keep me posted, Hume. I've got to get this garrison better organized while I have the time." He strode away, vastly pleased with himself.

Hume rubbed his hands on his trousers as though to rid them of something unclean. "Bloody swine," he said.

Sabin nodded. "He's like a buzzard floating low over something that's dying, waiting for his chance."

"I hope to God Donaldson recovers. If he doesn't, Sabin, Khuyper will sign your death warrant by sending you over those hills." Hume relit his cigar and closed his eyes as if weighing a decision. "There is a way," he said softly.

"What do you mean?"

"The nights are dark. Khuyper pokes about the post at all hours. The hostiles are close in at night."

Sabin shook his head. "The time will come for me to kill him, Hamish. But I want him to *know* who killed him."

Sam Donaldson died shortly after the notes of Retreat died amongst the shadowed hills. Twenty-five hard years of wearing the blue. Top man of the Class of 1840. He had lived through the tornado at Punta Rasa in 1841 as junior officer of the old Eighth Infantry, when Camp Caloosahatche had been obliterated. He had participated in the battles of Palo Alto, Matamoras, Monterey and Buena Vista under Taylor in the Mexican War. Later he had transferred to the dragoons and served at half a dozen different frontiers posts. In '61 he had been wounded at Wilson's Creek, as a captain of cavalry. In '63 he had been promoted to major and brevetted lieutenant-colonel. His army account was now closed: *"Donaldson, S.M., Major—from Duty to Died of Disease."*

The Army is an old institution. The old Regulars are wise in the ways of officers. In time some of that sage wisdom rubs off on the Volunteers. Some of the men had liked Donaldson; others had disliked him. But every one of them had respected him. There is a difference. Now Sam Donaldson had gone and Frank Khuyper had taken his place. A subtle demoralization seemed to hover about the fort. For none of the men liked Khuyper.

Furthermore, all of the men knew his record. There was no question of his personal courage. Let him kill himself in a wild dash for glory against the waiting hostiles. But Frank Khuyper had proved once before that he could and would take other men to die needlessly with him. And Khuyper wanted a brevet. He had no chance of getting it against the Rebels now, but there were Indians aplenty. A man could shoot for record and glory out in Wyoming almost any day of the week. The rumor in the sanitary sinks of isolated Fort Bowen was that Frank Khuyper wouldn't waste much time in his search for the strumpet Glory.

One hour after evening mess on the day Sam Donaldson died, Sabin Shay stood booted and spurred with Troopers Phin Harris, Aaron Fitch, Ames Lockerby, Ben Carver, Harry Banning and Jonas West. Spotted Horse stood by his mouse-colored mare. Harris, Fitch and Lockerby were former members of Sabin's company. Carver, Banning and West were a poor selection of the Kansas Volunteer Cavalry. With the exceptions of Lockerby and Spotted Horse, they were not men with whom Sabin wanted to face a circling ring of Sioux and Cheyenne horsemen.

Khuyper came from his quarters and stamped his feet on the hard earth as though enjoying life to the fullest. He drew in deep lungfuls of the fresh air, and then he looked at Sabin. "You're in charge, Shay," he said. "West is a former telegraph operator for the railroad. You have your tools and key, West?"

"Yes, sir," West said sourly.

"Good. I want that line in. Understand?"

"How far shall we go?" Sabin asked.

Khuyper folded his arms and cupped his chin in his left hand as he looked at the eastern hills, almost as though some spirit was communing with him. "Two days at the most. No dawdling! Don't think you can hide in the hills and kill time, and then come crawling back here saying you can't find the break."

Sabin said nothing. He saluted and left before the temptation to say too much overcame him.

The patrol crossed the dark river, followed by the eyes of the men in the picket post. "I'll bet we won't see them boys again," said a lean private. "How come Khuyper puts a Galvanized Yankee in charge?"

A corporal spat a stream of tobacco juice into the river. "That's easy. He hates his guts. I heard a sanitary sink rumor at Fort Laramie that Shay used to spark that Bascomb filly. Even before that, though, Khuyper hated his guts. Shay and his men were prisoners at MacNaughton. They say Khuyper was responsible for Shay's brother dying there. I don't like Rebels, Harry, but I'm damned if I ain't on Shay's side."

Harry nodded. "Khuyper's a brassbound sonofabitch. I sure ain't looking forward to serving under him. Things weren't so bad with Donaldson in command."

"Uh-uh." The corporal yawned. "But you forgot one thing, Harry."

"What's that?"

"The Sioux, Cheyennes and Arapahoes up in them hills. They ain't going to make it easy for *anyone* out here."

The patrol rode up into the dark hills. There was no talking. Just the creak of girths, squeak of saddle leather and the soft thud of hoofs in deep dust.

On the ridge, Sabin looked back at the yellow lights of the fort. Khuyper had worked things out pretty well. He had to admit it. If the patrol survived, they'd mend the break in the line so Khuyper could hear from his light-o'-love. If they didn't survive, Khuyper would be rid of Sabin Shay.

I'll come back, Sabin told himself. I'll come back and see *him* dead.

He wished he believed it.

CHAPTER SIXTEEN

A girth-high mist shrouded the shallow creek. Sabin shivered in his one blanket. It was almost dawn, and they had bivouacked beside the creek an hour ago, chewed cold cooked rations and fed their horses with good oats from the nosebags. The wind moaned faintly through the creek bottoms and whined about the telegraph line. They had found no break. Sabin planned to stay hidden during the day and ride on after dark.

Sabin stood up and walked about the area. Carver, one of the two guards, was asleep with his back against a tree. Phin Harris, the other guard, was shivering under his blanket. He said, "I don't feel well, Cap'n Shay."

"You're in good company," Sabin told him.

Sabin circled through the little camp. He glanced at Fitch's blankets. Then he strode over to them. They had been filled with heaps of long grass. Sabin went to the horses. One of them was missing. Fitch had pulled foot. Sabin walked to the edge of the creek and listened. No sound of hoofbeats penetrated the windy darkness beyond the camp.

Spotted Horse materialized like a ghost.

"Fitch is gone," Sabin said.

"No hear anything."

"Scout along the creek."

Spotted Horse disappeared into the darkness. He was back in twenty minutes. "Horse tracks in mud. Man ride southeast. Fast."

Sabin nodded. He hoped Fitch had enough sense to hole up during daylight.

The dawn filled the eastern sky with cold light. Sabin walked up out of the bottoms and looked east out over the rolling plains. Ames Lockerby came up behind him. "Yuh see him, sir?"

Sabin shook his head.

"He's loco. Them hostiles will pick him up."

"I know. To hell with him. It's the rest of us I'm thinking about."

"Spotted Horse is along the bottoms. Phin Harris says he's sick."

"He usually is."

They stood there for a long time, talking aimlessly to ease the strain. The sun came up. Suddenly Sabin caught the odor of wood smoke. A thread of bluish smoke drifted up above the low trees. Sabin cursed and plunged down the slope, and through the shallow creek. Banning, Carver and West were squatting about a fire. Sabin shoved West aside and kicked out the fire.

"What the hell is the matter with you?" West yelled.

"You fools! Every damned hostile in the hills may have seen that smoke!"

"We was only going to make coffee," Carver said.

Banning hiccupped. "Damn Rebel thinks he's a corpril or somethin'. I say we're Union men. We ain't about to take orders from no damned Galvanized Yank."

Lockerby cocked his Sharps. "Get up, you bastards."

Sabin looked up at the sky. The smoke was drifting with the morning wind. "Boots and Saddles," he said, "We'll head south along the bottoms and then come out in those low hills."

West stood up. "I say we go back to Fort Bowen."

"Shut up," Lockerby said.

West flexed his muscles and shoved Sabin. "I ain't saddling no horse. I'm heading back."

Sabin hit him with a short right and knocked him over the embers of the fire. "Get up," he said softly. "Get up or I'll break your jaw with my foot."

West got up and held his jaw. "I ain't forgetting this," he said.

They led the horses up the creek, splashing through the shallow waters. Two miles from the bivouac they met Spotted Horse. He pointed south. "Cha-ra-rat. Chase Fitch. No good."

Sabin slogged up the rise. He saw specks far out on the plain. Six of them. One ahead and five behind. Dust threaded up behind them. He couldn't distinguish Fitch, but he knew the Pawnee was right. As he watched, Fitch's horse went down and then the five specks closed in on the speck on the ground. Aaron Fitch would never see San Antone again.

"Now what?" Lockerby called.

"I say we go back!" West yelled.

"Through them hills?" Phin Harris said. He wiped cold sweat from his narrow face.

Sabin mentally cursed Frank Khuyper, Aaron Fitch and the three stupid Yankees who had started the fire. He led his horse up the creek and halted where the trees thinned. Indians knew better than to camp in creek bottoms, but they also knew it was a habit of the white men. The hills he had planned to hide in were two miles across an undulating plain. There was scant cover, but they'd have to risk it.

Lockerby covered the three Kansans with his Sharps. They led their horses out into the open. The wind rippled the short grass. Banning took a drag at his canteen. The men looked up at the low hills. They felt naked. It was a hell of a big country and a long way from the walls of Fort Bowen.

Sabin and Spotted Horse dropped back. They were two

hundred yards behind the others when it happened. It didn't seem quite real. The thin line of horsemen shot out of a hidden draw like a shaft driven by a one-hundred-pound bow. Indians. Sioux. Stripped to gee strings, covers stripped from their war shields, feathers rippling with the speed of their motion. The rising sun shone on the brass trim of carbines and rifles.

Banning turned greenish white. West swung up on his mount and spurred it toward the creek. Carver fumbled with his carbine sling. Lockerby hooked his reins over his left arm and cocked his carbine.

There was death in the swift advance. Painted and feathered death, sweeping down in a long arc to cut between the two small parties of Long Knives.

Phin Harris screamed. He dropped his carbine and ran away from his horse. He ran straight toward the mouth of a draw to the west. He ran full on into a group of warriors. A muzzle-loader spat a chewed slug into his chest. With hardly a change in gait, a burly warrior sank a pipe-ax into Harris' skull as the little man pitched forward. The warrior swung down, whipped out his knife, neatly circumscribed the narrow skull and ripped off the reeking scalp. Then he straightened up on his pinto and raced after his mates.

The two sickles cut in on the three troopers. Carver went down with a shaft driven into his breastbone. Banning turned his face away from sure death and retched out a sour flood of liquor and food. A lance drove in behind his left shoulder blade, smashed him down, and jerked free, dripping blood.

Lockerby got off one shot. He whipped out his Colt and dropped a claybank. The rider hit the ground running and caught a ride behind one of his mates with hardly a change in pace. Then the dust swirled about Ames Lockerby as he fought alone. His Colt spat four more times. The hostiles drew off, circling like a great wheel, with only a leg and arm showing over the tops of their lathered mounts. Lockerby shook his free fist at them and then jammed his pistol muzzle into his mouth. The report was muffled as he blew the top from his head.

Sabin drew his Colt and shot his bay. Spotted Horse killed his mouse-colored mare. They dropped behind the quivering bodies. Sabin thrust his Sharps forward, raised the sight and fired. The big slug drove a buck from his horse.

Spotted Horse fired and slowly reloaded. He looked at Sabin. "No good. Uh-sah-wuck knew all time. Gods angry—"

The Pawnee stripped to his gee string. He slapped his chest as he eyed the enemy. The hostiles had drawn off. Wet scalps dribbled blood down the sides of their lathered ponies. West had made the creek and was nowhere in sight.

Sabin wet his lips. Twenty of them sitting their ponies out there. There wasn't a chance now. Fear spread a green mucous over his mind. His guts tightened and then relaxed.

The dead men lay like bloody rag bundles under the sun. Their faces had loosened like watery pie dough. The hostiles swung away from the dead and circled widely. Sabin fired his Sharps and missed. He cursed as he lowered the breech and slid in another cartridge. He'd have to settle down. This was for the record.

Spotted Horse fired. A pony buckjumped and shot out of the circling line. His rider jumped clear as the pony went down.

A war-bonneted Sioux shook his shield four times toward heaven. "*Co-oco-o!* Get ready!"

Then the first charge came like a bolt straight from hell, almost up to the two men lying behind the dead horses, only to split and race away, with the hostiles hanging onto the far side of their ponies. Sabin had wounded a buck while Spotted Horse had dropped another pony. It was good strategy, for Indians of the Plains hated to fight afoot.

Three warriors drew off to one side. One of them was barrel-chested, with strong bowed legs which clung to the barrel of his horse like thick clinging vines. There was something vaguely familiar about him. He was a warrior of proven standing. There could be no doubt about that. And he was talking war—big war. He had enough of foolishness. The trio rode back to their mates.

Sabin wet his lips. Sweat soaked into the thick wool of his uniform. "No reserve and no support," he said to himself.

Spotted Horse did not look at him. The Pawnee seemed to know he was going to die. Like all primitive minds, his was still open to the whispering of the fates.

Three times the glory charge came, led by the stocky warrior Sabin had singled out. Three times the charges split. Two warriors were down, one of them dead, the other thrashing about with a shattered leg. The hostiles drew off. This was getting serious. Too many men had been lost. The two behind the bullet-pocked horses must die.

For the fourth time the screeching warriors came in. Sabin heard a sound like that of a stick being whipped into thick mud. Spotted Horse grunted. He fingered the bluish hole below his left ribs, eyeing the flow of blood. He squinted at the dust-shrouded horsemen and then cut a ten-foot length from his issue picket line. Slowly and deliberately he tied it about his lean waist and then to the haft of his lance. He coughed. Blood trickled from his mouth. He slapped his chest as he stood up.

"I go," he said thickly.

Spotted Horse carefully stepped over his mare and walked fifty feet toward the watching warriors. He thrust his lance into the ground, leaning heavily on it as he did so. Then he slapped his chest and stood there defiantly with his knife in his left hand and his Colt in his right.

Sabin reloaded. The Pawnee was doomed and so was he.

The charge came like a freshet. Spotted Horse emptied his Colt as calmly as if he were on the range. Then he sank down on one knee, still facing the enemy. Blood flowed from a scalp wound, half-blinding him. He began his death song.

The enemy call came clearly on the wind. *"Co-oco-o! Get ready!"*

Sabin fired as they came on. There was a spume of dust and a splattering of foam as the warriors drew up in front of the lone Pawnee. Forehooves thrashed as the ponies flung off. A warrior drew back the string of a horn bow. The loosed shaft struck Spotted Horse full in the center of the forehead, quivering with vibration. The barrel-chested warrior hooked his bow over one arm and flung his lariat. The loop settled about the neck of Spotted Horse, jerking him off his feet. The Pawnee was dragged, bouncing and jerking, behind the horse of the man who had killed him. Another warrior had snatched the coveted lance from the earth.

The sun beat down mercilessly as the hostiles gathered out of range. Sabin Shay looked at them from under the vizor of his slanted forage cap. The long road was ending. He felt curiously calm now. He had seemed to know all along that the patrol would be wiped out. Spotted Horse had accepted it by his way of death. *A man of men, Spotted Horse.* A man could always die like a man.

He sweated there for an hour while the warriors squatted in the shade of their ponies. There was no hurry. They would get him. One Mila Hanska, lying behind two swelling horses, eyeing the others who had died. It was good to let him wait and think about the manner of his death.

There was one amongst the warriors who sat alone, watching the white man behind the horses. He did not move very much, that big soldier. The warrior hoped he was not dying. In the last wild charge, the warrior had looked full into the sweating face of the white man and had known who he was. Wakan Tanka had at last brought back the white man who had wronged him. It was good. He stood up. *"Co-o-co"* he said in his deep voice.

Sabin raised his head. A dull ache had begun to thud across his temples. His vision swam a little as he watched the warriors. They mounted and began riding slowly toward him. He braced himself. Time for one carbine shot and five from the revolving pistol. The last slug was for himself and to hell with posterity.

Then they burst into swift action, racing down on him. One warrior didn't make it. A fifty slug smashed his chest. A Colt slug smashed a brown arm. The rest closed in shrieking their courage word. *"H'gun! H'gun! H'gun! H'gun!"*

Sabin stood up to die.

Four more shots blasted out of the Colt before a lance ripped across his arm and a lathered pony knocked him to one side. The Colt was gone. He snatched up his Sharps and reversed it. Three warriors slid from their sweating mounts to count coup by touching him. One of them went down with a smashed shoulder. He knocked the second cold. The third was a barrel-chested buck with a face as hard as flint. He ducked under a swing of the Sharps, touched Sabin with his left hand, screaming for a count of coup. Then, as he swung up the warclub, he shrieked his name twice for Sabin to know.

"Mato Najin! Mato Najin! Standing Bear! Standing Bear!"

The last thing Sabin remembered was the glancing blow of the warclub and the rush of greasy bodies bearing him down on the bloody grass. A rifle butt thudded behind his ear and he collapsed into a bottomless vortex that whirled him around and around, giddily, until he went into the little death of unconsciousness.

The sweating warriors waited for Mato Najin to strike the death blow. Standing Bear stepped back.

"No," he said huskily. "This Long Knife is for the little torture fires. I have spoken."

A pock-marked warrior frowned. "He went down like a man," he said.

Standing Bear slid his hand down to his knife. "I say he lives long enough to scream under the little torture fires. Do you question me, Lame Deer?"

Lame Deer hesitated. Some said that Mato Najin was sick in the head. He was a great warrior and a great horse thief, but something in his eyes did not seem right. Lame Deer shrugged and stepped back.

Standing Bear felt the blood wash through his brain. It was always so after a hard fight. This one had been harder than he had expected. But there were many others of the white soldiers in the little fort to the west. More coups and more scalps. Glory for Mato Najin. Now Wakan Tanka had rewarded a favored son by placing in his hands the white man who had stolen Pretty Hands from him so many colds ago. It was good. *Everything* was good. It was the time of war.

CHAPTER SEVENTEEN

S abin opened his eyes to look up at a lowering sky. An oxhide drum seemed to be beating at the base of his splitting skull. He turned his head a little, cautiously fingering the bloody hump behind his left ear, and saw a young buck squatting nearby with a Sharps across his naked thighs. The guard tried not to show his curiosity in the big white man, but it was hard to conceal.

The rest of the warriors were acting like kids, ripping through the pile of bloody clothing and equipment they had gathered from the broken bodies of the dead. Sabin wet his gummy lips with his tongue.

"What will they do with me, brother?" he ventured in rusty Cheyenne.

Blank surprise showed on the broad face of the young buck. "You speak the language of the Dzi-tsii-tsa, Long Knife?"

"It is so. You are of The People. Yet most of the others are of the Seven Council Fires."

"It is so. They are of the Border People. Those Who Camp By Themselves."

Sabin remembered now. They had fought like the Hunkpapas, the grimmest of the mighty Sioux Nation. He said, "That is Standing Bear who leads?"

The Cheyenne nodded proudly. He shifted the Sharps so that the muzzle centered on Sabin. The big Long Knife had fought like two bears.

"How is it that you speak the tongue of The People?" he asked.

"Many colds ago," Sabin said, "I lived with the band of Little Eagle."

The warrior tilted his head to one side. "But you are a Long Knife! An enemy!"

"*Hou!*"

"Maheo was good to us today," the buck said.

Sabin glanced at the bloody wreckage of his patrol. Maheo had indeed favored the Sioux. "How are you called?" he asked.

"Swift Runner."

The first fat drops of rain struck the dusty earth. Sabin struggled upright as the warriors swung up on their ponies and lashed them toward him. Standing Bear was heavier than Sabin remembered him. A warrior now of many coups. In the old days there had been a sullenness about him coupled with an air of uncertainty. Now it was gone. Standing Bear had a hard face, the face of a fighting sub-chief. Pride, endurance, cruelty and experience had etched themselves deep—and also, contempt for Sabin showed very plainly.

"Dog," Standing Bear said. "White dog. I have waited long."

Sabin spat deliberately to one side. "Give me a knife, Loud Talker," he said. "Face me and fight."

The chief spat full into Sabin's face. Two warriors slid from their mounts and hustled him over to Ames Lockerby's horse. They practically threw him up on it, swiftly lashing his ankles together under the barrel of the horse. Sabin felt the saliva run down his cheek. He closed his fists as they lashed his wrists together, and an odd thought struck him. Frank Khuyper and Standing Bear resembled each other in no physical respect whatever, yet they were alike under the skin. Khuyper had done well. He had delivered Sabin Shay into the hands of his Indian blood brother.

Hours later the warriors topped a ridge and hammered down a long slope, throwing gobs of mud from the hoofs of their ponies. The rain had increased steadily all day. Sabin's crotch felt as if it might split any moment. There had been no food or water for him, although the warriors had gnawed at *wasna* while they rode.

In the bottoms, along a sluggish creek, there were at least fifty lodges. The smoke drifted from the smoke holes and hung like a thick scarf amongst the cottonwoods and willows. Many ponies were herded in a meadow across the rain-stippled creek. Paints, palominos, spotted grays, mouse blues, buckskins, bay coyotes, dun coyotes and pure whites.

The raiders flourished their fine new weapons and scalps coated with drying blood. They slid from their wet ponies as the people gathered about them. A pock-marked warrior cut Sabin's ankles loose.

"Mani! Mani! Walk! Walk!" the pock-faced warrior barked.

Sabin felt lonely as a hawk as he walked through the pressing crowd. A stone glanced from his shoulder. A squaw spat in his face. Pock-face shoved him into a sagging teepee. He sat down beside the cold ashes of the fire-hole. He had nothing to look forward to except the "little torture fires" which would be kindled at his staked-out hands and feet and allowed to move up as his extremities burned away. The Women's Society would pour hot fat on his flesh and force him to drink bowls of urine. They were worse than the men.

Sabin peeked through the flap. The camp was mixed. Sioux, Cheyenne and Arapahoe. A warrior stood guard at the front of the tent. The rain pattered steadily and leaked through the smoke vent.

A cold wind swept through the bottoms, billowing the sagging teepees. The warriors were all under cover, being cared for by their womenfolk. Sabin was safe for the night at least. He lay down on a tattered buffalo robe and went to sleep.

A hard hand shook him awake. He blinked in the dim light. A fire was flickering into life in the firehole. He stared at the hatchet face which hovered over him. "Little Eagle," he said quietly.

"It has been many colds since you have been in the country of The People, Lone Hunter."

"I have traveled. I have been to war, my brother."

Little Eagle squatted beside Sabin. "Maheo has frowned on The People. It is *emeoestove*—the time of war here also. The Seven Council Fires mean to close the Big Medicine Road. Here there are many Dzi-tsii-tsa, O'ho-omo-io and Hi-na-nae-inan, ready for war."

Cheyenne, Sioux and Arapahoe, thought Sabin. "You do not like the thought of war, my brother?"

"It is so. I am an old man. I have few ponies left. Once I was a Crazy Dog, with many coups. Now I am an old man whose voice is weak in council. But the Hunkpapas pray to their Big Holy and the Thunder Music of the Hi-na-nae-inan is heard always in the hills. The Long Knives travel the Big Medicine Road. It is not good."

Sabin rubbed his numb wrists against his chest. "You have not forgotten how we hunted the buffalo, my brother? How we shared the good hump meat? Have you forgotten?"

Little Eagle's eyes were pools of melancholy in the light of the quickening fire. He bowed his head. "That was many colds ago. Standing Bear never forgot you. He is leader here now."

Sabin held out his hands.

Little Eagle looked away. "There are many strong voices here. They feel their power. They have stopped travel on the Big Medicine Road. They have captured many fine weapons from the Long Knives. The young men cry for war and the newly risen chiefs will lead them to drive the Long Knives from this land."

"You have not said you will help me, my brother."

Little Eagle stood up. He dropped a piece of wasna onto

the robe. "It is in the hands of Maheo. Good-bye, Lone Hunter."

A great loneliness settled upon Sabin. There was no expression on the lined face of the old chief. "I am an old man," Little Eagle said as he paused by the door flap. "My two strong sons have gone to the Land of Shadows. There is nothing left for me in life. You were like a son to me, Lone Hunter."

"It is so, Little Eagle."

"I do not want to see you die like a dog for the cooking pots."

A faint spark of hope grew in Sabin. Then Little Eagle was gone. Sabin gnawed at the pemmican the old man had left. The rain sluiced down steadily. The warriors would stay close to their fires, leaning against their backrests, playing the moccasin game. If the rain died out during the night, the next day would be the last on earth for Sabin Shay.

CHAPTER EIGHTEEN

The Thunder People were in fine fettle. A vicious rain slashed at the lodges while lances of lightning shot through the night and forked into the buttes. The creek began to roar as the waters rose steadily.

Sabin's guard came into the teepee and crouched near the door, praying in a low voice. The Blue Cloud People were brave in battle but deathly afraid of nature's manifestations.

"Maheo is angry," Sabin ventured. "He will wash away *hesec,* the blessed mother soil."

Rivulets of water were trickling across the lodge floor. One of them hissed into the firepit, raising steam.

"Maheo is angry," Sabin persisted, "because The People have dared to raid the Big Medicine Road and cut the talking wires."

Thunder rumbled in the hills. Lightning shot across the streaming sky. The rivulets coiled like snakes across the lodge floor. The Cheyenne eyed them. The Long Knife had said Maheo might wash away the blessed mother soil.

Lightning flashed and snapped angrily close to the lodge. The odor of the discharge filled the air. The Cheyenne fled from the lodge and vanished into the night.

Sabin rolled up on his knees and then to his feet. The

thongs about his wrists were too strong to break or loosen. He peered from the teepee. The village street was thick with mud. There was no one in sight. Sabin lay on his back and propelled himself through the greasy mud by thrusting with his heels. The creek roared by close to the lodges. Sabin hunched his shoulders against a tree and worked himself up to his feet. The horses were beyond the creek, huddled against a low bluff.

Sabin worked his way into the rushing waters, swaying as the current tore at him. He did not see the blanketed figure which followed him from the village. Ten feet from the far shore he went under, rolling over and over with the force of the current. Panic shot through him as he fought on the greasy bottom to get on his feet. His lungs were ready to burst and his senses reeled. Then his head reached the surface long enough for him to draw in a deep breath. He crashed his shoulder against a fallen tree and started to go under again. Then something twined in his thick hair. It pulled hard and hurt like hell. He yelled, filling his mouth with water.

Then he was up on his feet again, plowing through the thick bottom mud, following the punishing pull on his hair, until he floundered out of the water. He fell over a rock and sprawled face downward in the cold mud, drawing air deep into his chest. Then his wrist bonds suddenly gave way. They fell loose as if cut. He looked up at the blanket-shrouded figure which stood over him. "Who are you, my brother?"

There was no answer.

"Little Eagle?" asked Sabin. The figure was too slight for that of the old chief.

The eerie lightning shot across the sky. Then the mysterious hooded figure suddenly threw back the flap of blanket which concealed its face.

"For the love of God!" Sabin said.

There was no mistaking her. Pretty Hands. Older, but even more attractive with her added years. The lightning faded away, leaving them together in the streaming darkness.

Sabin lurched to his feet, rubbing his swollen wrists, not knowing what to say or do.

"Come," she said quietly. She led the way through the trees. Half a mile from the camp she led him into a brush-shielded cave which cut deep into a sheer bluff facing the rushing creek. She gripped his hand with her small wet hand and led him on in the ebony darkness with a sureness which showed that she had been there many times before. She made a hard right turn. She released his hand. He stood there in the blackness. Then she struck a light and lit a torch which jutted from a cleft in the wall. She gazed at him with liquid eyes.

Sabin drew her close. She did not resist. He felt her full unhampered breasts against his wet chest. He raised her face and kissed her. But there was no response. The old fire was gone. She pressed him back with the slim, lovely hands which had given her name.

"I saw you, Lone Hunter," she said, "as they brought you into the village."

Shadowed sadness softened her face. Sabin reached for her, but she drew back.

"Why did you never come back?" she asked.

There was no use in lying. The simple directness of Pretty Hands had always disarmed him before. *"Emeostove,"* he said. "The time of war came for my people."

"The white man's war began four colds ago," she said gently.

She had him there. He had left her in the spring of '58. Sabin glanced back toward the cave entrance and then at the flickering torch. "I've got to get out of here," he said.

"I know. Standing Bear has it in his heart to hear you scream like a white woman."

"I'll need a horse and a gun."

She nodded. She did not move.

Sabin slapped a hand against the damp cave wall. "Well" he snapped. "I *meant* to come back! There were many day's journeys between us! The war started!"

Her liquid eyes held his. "You could have taken me with you," she said.

Sabin leaned back against the wall. His nerves were fraying. The massacre of his patrol. The shock of being captured by the Indian who hated his guts. The certainty of a death by torture. His life being saved by Pretty Hands. It had unsettled him so that he wasn't sure he could go on. There was just one thing he did know—he *had* to get out of here fast.

She came close to him. "You will take me with you now?"

"Yes! Yes!" he said. "Only hurry!"

She came closer to him and slid her arms about his neck, drawing his head down. Her lips sought his in the way he had taught her to kiss him in the days long ago when she had been a naive girl. Sabin kissed her. She snuggled close and the cold realization came to him that she expected to be loved, then and there, as proof that he really wanted her to go with him.

Thunder thudded in the skies. Sabin placed his hands on her shoulders and gently pushed her back. "The People will be looking for me," he said swiftly. "There is no time, Pretty Hands."

She clenched her little fists. He hadn't fooled her a damned bit. But she turned and walked from the cave. Sabin put on a dry, greasy shirt he found in the back of the cave along with a miscellaneous pile of junk. The only weapon the junk pile yielded was a short bar of rusted iron. He doused the torch. He felt his way to the mouth of the cave and waited there, listening to the thrashing of the brush.

He leaned against the wall of the cave, debating whether or not he should take off through the woods on foot and to hell with help from his former squaw. Yet he was too beat to get far without a mount. He'd have to wait for her.

There was a darting movement. He barely caught in the corner of his eye. He whirled, raising the iron bar, but it was too late. A squat, barrel-chested buck held a huge revolver inches from Sabin's gut. The lightning revealed the pitiless face of Standing Bear.

Sabin dropped the bar into the mud. The lightning flickered away, leaving the two of them standing there in the streaming darkness. Sabin's stomach drew up into an icy ball. Damn the girl! Her delaying had allowed the sub-chief to find him.

Standing Bear shifted. "Turn," he said.

Sabin turned, feeling the pistol muzzle press at the base of his spine. There was a chance the revolver might be too wet to fire, but it was too long a chance. The odds were that Standing Bear would march him back to the village. The sonofabitch wanted him to die slowly. Maybe he should make a break. It would be better to die with a bullet through the back than from the little torture fires.

The muzzle pressed harder and then Standing Bear fell heavily against Sabin. Sabin whirled in time to see Pretty Hands standing over the fallen chief.

"He is not dead," she said. She held up a heavy Savage revolver and touched the barrel with a slim forefinger.

Sabin drew her close. There were no horses in sight. She gripped him by the slack of his shirt and led him through the darkness to where a blocky gray stood with hanging head.

Sabin took the Savage from her hands and slid it inside his shirt. He stood there, not knowing what to say.

Pretty Hands motioned toward the camp. "The People are to gather here," she said. "There will be at least five hundred warriors. The Big Medicine Road is to be closed forever by the warriors of Standing Bear."

Sabin considered going back to the cave. His hands gripped tighter. It would be easy to get rid of Standing Bear right now.

The thunder almost drowned out her voice as she spoke again. "Do not fear that I will go with you, Lone Hunter. My heart tells me you are not the same man who shared my lodge many colds ago."

He could not think of a thing to say that would make sense.

"Good-bye, Lone Hunter," she said.

He bent to kiss her, but she fled into the wet woods like a startled deer. He swung up on the gray. "Pretty Hands!" he called. The wind tore the words from his mouth and scattered them into meaningless fragments of sound. The Thunder People chuckled as they drove their great arrows of lightning across the tumultuous skies.

Sabin headed west, upstream, riding by instinct. Far behind him, Pretty Hands padded softly back toward camp. She walked with her head down, listening to the tiny squishes of water in her moccasins, thinking the little thoughts that held away the big sadness. Standing Bear had not seen her. He had known she would take her white man to the cave, but he had not seen her and he could not prove a thing. She smiled bitterly into the black night. Standing Bear would not speak even if he could prove that she had helped Lone Hunter to escape. Not with that lump on his head. Not when The People would know that she preferred Lone Hunter as her lover.

She was safe. She was alone again. She walked on, softly, toes turned slightly in, Indian fashion. And as Indian women had done since The People came to exist, she cried silently, dry-eyed, letting the tears run down her throat, so that not even the trees could see.

CHAPTER NINETEEN

abin Shay came out of the hills at dawn, a gaunt lath of a man, riding an exhausted horse. Smoke drifted up from Fort Bowen. Sabin's breath caught in his throat. Among the many wagons there, he could distinguish the fancy Dearborn in which Marianne Bascomb lived on the trail.

He led the bay to the ford and rode it across. A corporal raised his rifle as he stepped out of the little picket station. He said, "Hand over that pistol, Shay."

Sabin cocked a curious eyebrow at him. "What's up?"

"Get that pistol, Josh," the non-com said over his shoulder to a private.

Sabin handed over the clumsy Savage. "What is this?"

"West got back alive. Said you led the patrol into a trap and then deserted."

"He's a damned liar!"

"Maybe. But we got orders to arrest you on sight. You're in a mess, man."

"I've been in a mess ever since I took the oath."

"That figures. You could have avoided that too."

"How so?"

The burly non-com smiled leisurely. "Taken the oath of allegiance to the Old Flag back in '61," he said.

He marched Sabin into the headquarters room. Khuyper sat at his desk. Sergeant Schmidt looked up from the eternal paper work of a topkick long enough to warn Sabin with his eyes.

Khuyper leaned back in his chair. "Now I suppose I'll get some cheap heroic story of escape from bloodthirsty hostiles."

"Not from me, sir."

"Where were you?"

"The hostiles jumped us ten miles or so east of here. Lockerby, Fitch, Banning, Carver and Spotted Horse were killed. I was captured."

"West claims you led the men deliberately into a trap and then deserted."

"He's lying."

Khuyper swiveled his chair and glanced through the window. He spoke over his shoulder. "Donaldson was too soft with you and the rest of the Rebel scum. I'm going to make an example of you, Shay."

"I'm entitled to a hearing."

Khuyper whirled and smashed a hand flat down on his desk. "You're entitled to absolutely nothing! This is war! The penalty for desertion is the firing squad. You deny that?"

Sabin shifted. The guard half-cocked his rifle.

Khuyper thrust out an accusing finger. "You'll be bucked and gagged until such time as I decide your penalty."

"There are regulations, sir. I'm innocent until proven guilty-"

Khuyper stood up. "Get this through your thick Rebel skull. *I'm* the regulations here. We'll see how easily you talk after a few days of gagging!"

Sabin was marched to the improvised guardhouse. They walked past one of the outbuildings. Marianne Bascomb sat in a chair while Katherine Williams brushed the beautiful blonde hair. Katherine glanced at Sabin, gasped, started to speak, and then didn't. Stacy Bascomb lolled on a cot beyond her, grinning.

They tied Sabin's wrists and ankles together. They forced his lashed wrists down in front of his knees and thrust a stick over his left forearm, under his knees and over his right forearm. A trooper said, "Open your mouth, Shay," and then he looked at his mate. "God, but I hate to do this to a man, Martin."

"Go ahead," Sabin said.

Martin swore. "It's been hell around this outpost of Hades ever since that Bascomb doxie got here and got Khuyper in heat."

They closed the door behind them. Sabin eased his back against the wall. He tried not to think. The thing he needed now was sleep.

The cell was dark when Sabin heard the rattling of the bolt. A lean figure crossed to Sabin and placed a plate and cup on the floor. The man lit a candle stub. Sabin looked into the gaunt face of Kinston Forbes. "That sonofabitch," the Texan said.

Forbes untied Sabin. Sabin pulled the soaked gag from his mouth.

"The boys are ready to break," Forbes said in a low voice.

"No!"

Forbes squatted beside Sabin and spooned food into his mouth while Sabin worked his stiffened muscles. "There's a score of us, countin' you, Cap'n Shay. Ain't no hostiles kin cut *us* down if we fight like Texicans."

"The hills are crawling with them."

"They don't fight at night. We figger we kin break out of here after midnight, get hosses and make for the hills. Comes daylight we kin hole-up and ride on after dusk."

"To where?"

"West, o' course. Mebbe we kin—"

"No, Forbes! It's not time."

"Look, Cap'n Shay! Khuyper's been ridin' hell outn' us Galvanized Yankees. Burial details. Loadin' details. Latrine diggin'. Extry guard duty. Hellfire! He even had some of us clean out the cabin thet Bascomb filly lives in. To top it off, so help me, we had to dig a privy for her special use. We got us a bellyfull."

Sabin drank deeply. "I say it isn't time."

Forbes grunted. "Yore first rate in our book, Cap'n Shay, but we sorta knowed yuh wouldn't go fer the plan. So we formed a committee. Me, Charlie Kester, Cobb Howell and George Fletcher. We aim to go, and we aim to take yuh with us."

"Let me talk to your committee first."

"All right. I'll get the boys to come here."

"Dammit, no! Khuyper will gag and buck the lot of you!"

Forbes chuckled. *"Him?* Hell! He's dinin' with thet Bascomb filly tonight. He don't see nothin' but her figger and them come-to-bed-with-me eyes of hern'. These Yank guards is all right. The Yanks hate Khuyper about as much as we do. Three of 'em went over the hill the night yuh went out on patrol."

After Forbes left the cell, Sabin paced back and forth. The guard looked in now and then but made no effort to see that Sabin was bucked and gagged again. It seemed Forbes was right about the feeling of the Yankees against Khuyper.

The conspirators showed up shortly before Tattoo. A bottle passed from Cobb Howell to the guard. He cached it under a loose board along the eaves and then unlocked the cell door.

"How are yuh?" Howell asked.

"About beat," Sabin said.

"We can't figger how yuh made it back here."

"I'll tell you the whole story some other time. Right now I want to talk against this break."

Kester pulled at his lower lip. "Things have gone from bad to worse. Bascomb and the emigrants had a rough time. Lost six waggins near Sandy Crossing. One of them was Katherine Williams'. Seven emigrants and four soldiers were killed. The waggins was supposed to stay at the Platte Crossing, but Bascomb had his way—as usual."

"Tomorrow afternoon," Howell put in, "some of us has

orders to cut firewood along the crick. We aim to steal food and cache it out there. We kin take care of the guards tomorrow night and light out on the hosses."

"Supposing the alert goes out?" Sabin asked.

"We'll git us a passel of Yankees as well as the hosses," Fletcher said.

"Fools," Sabin said angrily. "Can't you wait until the hostiles pull foot? They're sitting up there waiting for any movement from the fort. Be patient, can't you? No Indian was ever born who'd sit out a siege like a white man. If there's no easy loot for the taking, they'll wander off. Let's wait."

"We ain't!" Kester snapped. "We stay here much longer and someone will kill Khuyper."

Howell leaned against the wall. "Maybe the cap'n is right. We're a helluva long ways from safety out there."

"It ain't goin' to git any safer," Fletcher protested.

Sabin played his last card. "Maybe Khuyper will let the wagon train proceed. Maybe we'll be ordered to go with it. Our chances would be better."

"Fine chance of him doin' thet," Fletcher said.

"He knows we're the best Indian fighters he has. He isn't about to let Marianne Bascomb go on without giving her the best protection he can."

Kester nodded slowly. "That makes sense. I got to admit it."

George Fletcher sighed. "I'll agree to wait a few days. But that's all."

Howell walked to the door. "Three days is the time limit. No more."

Kester waited behind the others. He gripped Sabin by the shoulder. "When that young woman got here all she did was ask about you and then looked up into them damned hills."

"Marianne?"

"Her?" Kester spat. "Lordy, no! I mean the Williams gal." He walked out into the darkness.

CHAPTER TWENTY

K huyper's threats against Sabin never materialized. Without explanation, on the second day, Sabin was released and told to report to Sergeant Schmidt.

Schmidt eyed Sabin's swollen wrists. "Godt verdamnt! Sometimes I think this Khuyper shouldt haff been in the Prussian army yedt. There, such treadtment iss expected!"

"You don't like it, Sergeant Schmidt?"

Schmidt slapped a big hand down on his packing crate desk with such force that a nail popped out. "No! I servedt mine time in the old country as a boy. Lashes ve godt. Breadt und vater ve got. Like dogs ve vere treadted. It iss nodt goodt to treadt soldiers like dogs. Soldiers are men!"

"Thanks," Sabin said dryly.

Schmidt grunted. "Wass it nodt for the lady, Shay, you vouldt still be in the guardhouse yedt."

"Miss Williams?"

"Der liddle vun? No. The vun midt yellow hair."

"You mean Miss Bascomb?"

"Ja. She leads Khuyper aroundt like a liddle dog on a chain. Such a fool he iss for that voman."

"What happens to me now, sergeant?"

Schmidt leaned back in his chair. "Der hills iss still full

midt Sioux. Many uv der men are sick midt typhoid. I godt to make out duty rosters midt nodt enough men to do it midt. A sergeant-major's job I godt midt first-sergeant's pay."

"It's the old army game, Schmidt."

"Ja! I tell Khuyper ve needt scoudts to see what dem Sioux iss going to do. Maybe that iss vhy he ledts you oudt."

"I see. Maybe I was better off in the cell."

"Gedt cleaned up. Repordt for duty."

Sabin got stiffly to his feet. The sergeant jabbed a thick finger at him. "Shay! Don'dt you gedt any ideas on going over der hill. You gedt caught and you vish you'dt never been born!"

Sabin walked outside. It was a clear day. The rains had washed the skies and the heat had not yet formed a haze on the sharply outlined hills. Sam Nelson, the emigrant wagon-master, was checking the wheels of a Conestoga.

"Glad to see yuh out," Nelson said.

"Gracias."

"Damn fools," Nelson grumbled. "I told these bastardly emigrants to put three-inch tires on their wagons back at Westport Landing. We got enough wedges in some of these tires to raise Chimney Rock. Sand gets in 'em and works 'em loose."

"How long do you figure on staying here?"

"The ground is still soft. But it will be all right in a day or two. But movin' is out."

"How so?"

Nelson spat a streamer of amber. "Reason is that moon-eyed Khuyper is sparkin' that Bascomb female."

"The hills are full of hostiles, Sam."

Nelson shrugged. "We got plenty good riflemen. If Khuyper gives us some cavalry we kin make it. O' course we'll have losses, but these Pukes and Suckers is anxious to git to Oregon and they're willin' to pay the fiddler's fee to git thar. Trouble is, that Bascomb has better waggins and better animiles. I kin only move as fast as my slowest waggin.

Bascomb kin make miles to my yards with his rollin' gear. He's been workin' on Khuyper to let him go on with a strong cavalry escort."

"And to hell with the emigrants."

"Yeh."

"So you'll sit here a while."

Nelson scratched in his beard. "Supplies is low. I figgered we might get by on buffler out thar. Ain't seen any. Guess the hostiles druv 'em off."

"I didn't see any. Just buffalo skull circles."

Nelson nodded. "The hostiles figger the Big Holy will bring back the buffler if they make them circles."

Sabin rubbed his wrists. "Time is running short. Khuyper will either have to let you go or turn you back to Laramie."

"The hell he'll turn us back! I aim to talk to him and that stuck-up Bascomb bastard. There'll be hell to pay onct I get 'em together."

Sabin went on to his tent. Warner Giddings was dozing on his blankets. Sabin cleaned up and then drew a set of arms and equipment from the quartermaster. He folded the Lone Star guidon in the bottom of his haversack. Almost five months had passed since it had snapped in the breeze. He had made himself a rash promise about it, just before he left Fort MacNaughton. Now he wondered if it would ever fly again, even as a nostalgic symbol.

Uneasiness hung like a pall over little Fort Bowen. The telegraph line was still out. Now that Marianne was with him, Khuyper made no effort to get it repaired. Fort Bowen was a good setup for Frank Khuyper. He had two companies of cavalry and a company of infantry, along with a small detail of quartermaster and medical service men. He was in complete charge of his little world, and except for the menacing tribesmen in the hills, it was a good world. He drank of Colonel Bascomb's liberal supply of bourbon and smoked his inexhaustible dear Havanas. And to top it all off, Marianne Bascomb seemed to have accepted his suit.

Khuyper was alone in his happiness and confidence. The other officers knew a showdown would soon be due. Of the hundred and twenty-five troops at the crowded post, a fifth were in the hospital. Sam Nelson worried himself sick. Some of his wagons were in bad shape. His draft animals were not allowed quartermaster forage but must be pastured along the river under a skeleton guard of troopers and emigrants.

Typhoid had struck amongst the emigrants. Two children had died, and a score of the adults were prostrated with it. Khuyper had the emigrant wagons moved behind the station in a motte of cottonwoods to quarantine the civilians from post limits. But, paradoxically, he allowed the Bascomb wagons to remain on the post proper, and issued forage to Bascomb for his draft animals.

Sabin came off herd guard at midnight the day of his release. Lamplight showed in Khuyper's room. Sabin glanced through the window. Khuyper was playing poker with Colonel Bascomb, Stacy, and Lieutenant Teale. A bottle stood on the table and blue tobacco smoke rifted in the drafty air.

A low light was burning in Marianne Bascomb's quarters. As Sabin passed, he heard a low voice call his name. He stopped and saw her standing in the shadows wrapped in a dark cloak.

"What is it, Marianne?"

"Are you all right, Sabin?"

"As well as can be expected, I reckon."

"No one expected to see you come back, Sabin."

"It was close," he admitted.

Jasmine drifted to him. "I'm afraid," she said. "I want to leave this terrible place. The odor of death seems to be everywhere. Yet I'm afraid to leave."

"It's one or the other, Marianne. A bitter choice."

"The typhoid is gaining, Surgeon Hume says."

"You're safe enough."

"Father is afraid of Asiatic cholera. He says it would spread like wildfire through the post."

"There are no symptoms of it."

"Many people have died of it on the trail."

Sabin waved a hand. "The Oregon Trail is no pleasure jaunt."

She seemed to want to talk with him. She leaned back against the wall, letting her cloak swing open, revealing a filmy nightgown. A sort of sickness grew deep inside of Sabin. He suddenly realized how long ago it had been since he had had a woman. Marianne was a real piece of feminine goods.

She placed a hand on his forearm. "They say you know this country better than any other man here."

"Yes."

She came close. "Couldn't you take me away from here? We could ride at night. They say the Indians won't fight at night. You could get me through, Sabin."

"What of your father and Stacy? What of Frank?"

"They don't seem to be too concerned about my well-being!"

"And I should be?"

She rested her head against his shoulder. The pungent odor of spirits mingled with the jasmine and suddenly he knew why she wanted him. "Have you forgotten *everything?*" she asked.

"No."

"Then come in. I want to talk with you."

"I'm on the ragged edge around here. I can't take chances."

She looked up at him and smiled.

"You either come, Sabin, or I'll scream. You know what Frank would do to you. I talked him into releasing you. One scream and he'll have you shot."

She was so damned skillful in getting her way. Sabin followed her into the dimly lit room. There were two cots in it. One of them covered with silk, the other with coarse trail blankets. Katherine wasn't there, but Sabin knew she had been staying with Marianne.

Marianne shut the door and placed her back against it. "She's with those filthy emigrants," she said. "Nursing. If Father knew he'd discharge her. He pays her well to help me."

"Nice of him," Sabin said dryly.

"You didn't expect me to live without help?"

"No, Marianne. I'm surprised you get along with *one* maid. How many did you have in New Orleans? Five or six?"

"Oh, shut up! I don't seem to know you anymore."

The air was thick with the mingled odors of perfume, women, and oddly, liquor. He picked up a slim bottle. "Vermouth," he said.

She filled two glasses. "It helps my nerves."

Sabin sipped the liquor. He had heard often enough that her mother had been a heavy drinker. Absinthe. She had taken to the wormwood distillation after she learned that the colonel had a quadroon mistress. In time Therese Bascomb's mind had become deranged. Delirium and idiocy had followed.

Marianne downed two drinks quickly. "Will you take me?" she asked again.

"I'm in the Yankee army now."

"I'll forgive that. I don't know how you had the stomach to take the oath, but it doesn't really matter. The war is almost over. I forgive you, Sabin."

He walked to the door. "The last damned thing I want from you, Marianne, is forgiveness."

She gripped his left arm with surprising strength. "Damn you! You always were so high and mighty! Yet you took advantage of me when I was a mere girl!"

"I took—" Sabin couldn't help but laugh. "How many were ahead of me?"

She slapped his face with her free hand. Sabin gripped her wrists. "Listen," he said quietly. "You got into this mess with that sanctimonious father and puling brother of yours. Now get yourself out of it."

Tears filled her eyes. She pressed against him. "God, Sabin! Help me! I don't know what to do!"

"You've got Frank Khuyper."

"Damn him! Damn my father! Damn Oregon!"

She dragged on his arm, pulling him with her, pulling him down atop of her as she fell loosely on Katherine's bed. He felt her full warm body through the thin gown. She wrapped her arms about his neck and pulled him close, thrusting her body up against his in a paroxysm of released passion. The liquor-wet lips mashed against his. The old desire swept over him, and then suddenly cold reason gripped the bridle reins and hauled back on the bit. He started to get up. She ripped the gown from her full breasts.

The door opened. Sabin broke away from the thrashing woman beneath him. He turned to look into the taut face of Katherine Williams. Marianne sat up and laughed at her. "You see?" she asked. "He's just like all the rest of them!"

Katherine closed the door. "Get out of here, Sabin Shay," she said. "You're in enough trouble as it is."

"Get out of here yourself," Marianne said thickly.

Katherine reached for the door handle but she kept on looking steadily at Sabin.

"Please," she said.

Marianne laughed. "I've seen Stacy pawing *you*." She stood up, swaying back and forth. She reached out and plucked at the shabby dress. "Look at you," she said. "God alone knows what Stacy sees in you."

Katherine pushed Marianne's shaking hand away. "Maybe he sees a lady," she said quietly.

The Southern woman swayed and passed a hand across her eyes. "I—" She staggered slightly. "I feel sick."

"Please go," Katherine said to Sabin Shay. "Unless you want to see her in worse condition than she is."

Sabin shrugged. "Why don't you get out of here?" he asked. "Go back to the wagons."

She shook her head. "No. They've given me work here. I

have no way to get to Oregon alone." Her eyes held his. "You never really loved her, did you, Sabin?"

Marianne had dropped onto the bed. She beat steadily with small fists against the blankets. "Oh God," she whimpered. "I want to go home. I want to go home."

Sabin opened the door. Katherine came out with him. "I'm sorry for her," she said.

Sabin tipped her piquant face. He kissed her lightly. "You can forgive anything from anybody," he said.

She turned away. "Don't be too sure about that." She closed the door behind her.

Sabin did not see Matt Duggan watching them. Nor did he see the big man walk swiftly toward Khuyper's quarters.

CHAPTER TWENTY-ONE

The white worms writhed in Stacy Bascomb's gut that morning after his drinking bout with Frank Khuyper. He felt deathly sick, but he knew he must kill Sabin Shay. What had started out as a boredom-dispelling dalliance with Katherine Williams somehow had developed into a powerful desire for the independent Missouri girl. Like all his kind, Stacy needed a strong and vital woman as a leaning post through life. She was poor but she was as different from the gaunt, slatternly Puke and Sucker women as a blood filly differs from a draft colt.

Stacy had been protected throughout his useless life by his father's position and wealth. His mother had left him in the care of a faithful, pampering mulatto nurse. Marianne had always showed spirit and determination, but Stacy, as he grew older, developed a taste for bourbon, cards, quadroons and octoroons, with a pure black now and then to vary the course. He had inherited his mother's taste for liquor and his father's craving for women, and to give Stacy *some* credit, he damned near outdid the old man. The one thing he had not inherited from either side of his family, nor shared with his sister, was a leavening of fighting spirit. In short, he had a yellow streak down his back as wide as his narrow shoulders.

Stacy Bascomb had inherited *one* thing from his father: an ability to scheme his way through life letting others do the dirty work. Matt Duggan was a tool fashioned to fit Stacy's hands. Duggan, rough and ignorant, with a half-mad light in his muddy green eyes. Built with a muscular and bone structure that could give him the edge in a bloody rough-and-tumble, groin-kneeing, eye-gouging battle. It would be easier to pay for a simple knife thrust in Sabin Shay's back, but Stacy wanted to see the bloody wreckage of the man who had slapped his face at Fort Laramie, the man who now had the inner track with Katherine Williams.

The trick would be to arrange for Matt to get at Sabin in some isolated, secluded place. There would be a way. Trust Stacy Bascomb to find that way.

A sickly moon lit the eastern sky. It was quiet about Fort Bowen. Entirely too quiet. Sabin came off guard to find a note pinned on his bunk. It was from one of the emigrant women, and it stated that Katherine Williams had suddenly taken ill and wanted to see him. She was at the wagons, in the quarantine area.

Sabin left the tent, thrusting his Colt beneath his belt. He passed through the motte of cottonwoods. A sentry clumped along the western edge of the motte. Otherwise the place seemed. . .

Something moved behind Sabin. Something hard pressed into the small of his back.

"Walk over toward the crick," said a familiar voice. "Don't get no funny ideas of makin' no break, Shay."

The pistol jabbed hard into Sabin's kidney.

"Walk," Matt Duggan said.

After they were screened by brush and trees, near the river, Duggan stopped. Two dismantled emigrant wagons stood to one side. "Throw that Colt into the bresh," Duggan said.

Sabin disarmed himself and turned.

"Easy," Duggan said.

"What's on your mind, Matt?"

"I ain't forgot yuh, yuh dirty sonofabitch. Long as the other boys was around, I couldn't take no chances. I had to bait my trap with some nice cheese like that note."

"When did you learn how to write?"

Duggan chuckled. "The Williams filly taught me."

Duggan placed his pistol on the lazy-board of one of the wagons. He spat on his hands. "I'm agoin' to take the starch outa yuh, Shay."

Sabin shifted. The man never had been normal. "You're loco, Duggan. Those hills are crawling with Sioux."

"They don't fight at night."

"They hear a racket and they'll be around."

"Racket? Hawww! I'll smash yuh, Shay."

Sabin sighed. "Come on then."

He came on with short, plunging strides, pumping both thick arms like pistons. They smashed Sabin's guard aside. He went back, trying to block with forearms and elbows. He hit the ground from a right that struck like a pipe-axe. He got the boot twice before he made it to his feet.

Duggan wheezed laughter as they circled. Then he came on again. Sabin locked the thick arms under his elbows and brought up his knee into Duggan's groin. He broke free as Duggan grunted in pain, then lanced a left to Duggan's meaty jaw as the man doubled over. He chopped both hands at the base of the shaggy neck. Duggan crouched and ran awkwardly away.

Sabin took his own turn laughing. "Come on back, king-pin!" he jeered.

Duggan snatched up something from the grass. It was a rusted pitchfork with the center tine broken off short. His lips drew back from his yellow teeth. He held the shaft in his right hand, halfway down, as he advanced in a crouch.

Sabin glanced at the pistol lying on the lazy-board. He darted for it but Duggan drove in hard with the fork. The tines hit the wagon. Sabin snatched back his arm an instant before they struck.

Sabin backed off, wetting his lips. If he ran he'd get it in the back like a harpoon. Duggan lunged. A tine scraped through Sabin's shirt, raking his left side. He gripped the shaft but Duggan backhanded him, driving him down on one knee. Sabin rolled over just as the fork plunged into the soft earth where he had been downed. Something rolled under him. He snatched up a four-foot length of heavy chain as he got to his feet.

Duggan charged. Sabin whirled the chain. The end smashed against Duggan's face. He gasped as he staggered sideways. Sabin swung again, catching Duggan across the chest. Duggan retreated, glancing at his pistol. He tried for it but Sabin moved like a cat. He got between the big man and the wagon. Duggan was hurt. His breath came harshly in his throat. He gripped his fork and held it like a musket at port arms, waiting for Sabin's attack.

Sabin darted to one side. Duggan thrust. Sabin reversed, backlashing with the chain. It whipped about Duggan's skull, the tip flicking into his left eye. Blood splattered from his face. He yelled hoarsely as he clapped his left hand against the smashed eye.

Sabin moved in, chopping with the doubled chain, raining blows on head and shoulders until Duggan went squirming back against the wagon. Duggan dropped the fork and ran in panic. Then he tripped over a broken wheel and went down.

Sabin threw the bloody chain away. Duggan groaned as he pawed at his eye. Then he began to fumble in his shirt. He was up on his feet with the knife in his hand before Sabin could grab the chain. Duggan's bloody face was like a mask straight from the steaming slums of hell. Then Sabin saw the knife clearly in the moonlight. He could not mistake it. It was the silver-chased knife which had been stolen from Miles' effects as he lay in the hospital.

There was no pity and no fear in Sabin now. He retreated before the half-blinded giant. Then he stooped and snatched up the pitchfork. Duggan seemed to be in a daze, but he did see the poised fork. For a second he stood there, and then he whirled, throwing the knife into the brush. He ran.

Sabin cast the heavy fork. One of the tines struck deeply beneath the left shoulder blade. Duggan hurtled on, carried by the force of the blow and his own momentum. He went down, dead before he hit the ground. The fork shaft swayed a little as the big body twitched.

Sabin wiped the greasy cold sweat from his face. He hawked and spat to get rid of the sour taste in the back of his throat. He found his Colt and the knife. Then he dragged the heavy body to the waterside and rolled it in.

Sabin padded through the brush. He stopped. That tree over there had a shadow that was far too fat for it. Sabin cocked the Colt. Then he heard the faint sound of breathing.

"Come on out," he said.

The man stepped out into the moonlight. It was Stacy Bascomb. The whole plot was etched on his face. He had stationed himself there to watch Duggan commit mayhem and murder on a man he couldn't fight himself.

"What's wrong with you?" Stacy asked shakily.

Sabin slid the Colt beneath his belt. "Your champion failed," he said softly. "The show was spoiled, wasn't it?"

Stacy looked beyond the set-faced man in front of him. "I'll call out to the guards," he said. "I saw you kill him."

Sabin's left hand caught the trembling Stacy full across the mouth. His right drove Stacy to his knees. Then Sabin had him by the shirt front with his left hand bunched into the fine material. His right cut the handsome face into bloody ruin. Stacy sagged down on his knees, gripping Sabin about the thighs. "For God's sake! Stop! Stop!"

Sabin dragged him to his feet. He whirled him about and planted a boot against his rump. Stacy Bascomb groveled on his hands and knees. Again and again Sabin booted him until the bloody-faced wretch scuttled through the woods to the shelter of the fort.

Sabin went to his tent. His mates were asleep. He

stripped to the waist and examined the gash across his left ribs. It had been too damned close. One day he'd grip Stacy's scrawny neck until he gasped like a dying chicken. Sabin walked outside and let the fresh night wind dry the sweat on his body. But the wind could not blow away the foulness of Fort Bowen.

CHAPTER TWENTY-TWO

T he hand gripped Sabin's shoulder. He opened his eyes and came up on his blankets, fighting hard.

"Hold it, Shay!" the voice roared.

The mists cleared. Sabin saw the angry face of Corporal Kinzie. "Sorry," he said.

Kinzie shook his head. "Get dressed," he said. "There's hell to pay. Khuyper wants to see you."

"Uh-oh. Why?"

"Matt Duggan was found on a sand bank in the river with a pitchfork sticking in his back. Someone said you were seen near there last night."

Cobb Howell, Warner Giddings and Blalock Lott stirred uneasily. "That's what you was afraid of, cap'n," Cobb said. "So help me none of us done it, though."

"I know," Sabin said, and winked. "Just keep your mouths shut and wait."

Khuyper was in his quarters with Colonel Bascomb. Stacy stood against the back wall. His face was swollen almost beyond recognition.

Khuyper did not return Sabin's salute.

"Teamster Duggan was found dead this morning," he said. "You were seen near the emigrant wagons shortly after midnight, and then seen again coming from the woods beyond the wagons. What have you to say?"

Sabin looked past him at the battered Stacy. "Nothing, sir."

"You deny being there?"

"No, sir."

Colonel Bascomb puffed at his cigar. "I would like to prefer charges against him, suh."

"Military or otherwise?" Sabin asked.

"Damn you!" Khuyper snarled. "Keep a civil tongue!"

Stacy pointed at Sabin. "I saw him, I tell you," he said thickly. "It was him all right."

"Go to hell," Sabin said.

Khuyper stood up. "I formally charge you with the murder of Teamster Matt Duggan. I hereby warn you that anything you say hereafter may be used against you."

"You'll need witnesses," Sabin said.

"You admit you did it then?" Stacy said eagerly.

"Stacy, you scaly bastard, I wouldn't even admit I was *here* to you."

Colonel Bascomb said, "If you were a gentleman, suh, my son would ask you out."

Sabin laughed. "Him? He hasn't got the guts of a louse. At least a louse will bite."

Stacy's hands clawed empty air. He said, "You—" in a strangled voice, and couldn't finish.

Khuyper looked at Corporal Kinzie. "Place this man Shay in the guardhouse. Bucked and gagged as before. That will keep his tongue—"

The door opened, interrupting him. Katherine Williams walked in. Khuyper eyed her suspiciously. Stacy seemed to be looking right through her worn dress.

"I understand Trooper Sabin Shay is being charged with murder," she said. "It isn't true."

Khuyper actually went pale. "Get out of here," he said.

She lowered her head. "You have to hear me out," she

said, almost whispering. "I know he could not have killed Matt Duggan."

"Can you prove it?" Colonel Bascomb sneered.

"Yes. I know where he was from the time he came off guard until after one o'clock this morning."

"Huh?" Khuyper recovered quickly. "Where was he?"

She moistened her lips. A deep flush spread from her throat up to her hairline.

"Well?" Khuyper snapped.

"He—was with me. In one of the emigrant wagons."

Stacy swallowed hard. Colonel Bascomb worked his cigar from one side of his mouth to the other. Khuyper just stared.

"She's lying," Sabin said.

She shook her head. *"He's* lying to protect my reputation. He was with me."

The three men glanced at each other. Khuyper sucked in his breath.

"Get out of here!" he said hoarsely. "Get out of my sight —both of you!"

Outside, Sabin caught Katherine by the arms and shook her gently. "You know what you've done to your reputation?" he said.

"Yes."

"Thanks. I was in a bad spot in there."

"You seem always to be in bad spots. I know they hate you."

"You've made a choice bit of juicy gossip."

She looked toward the distant hills. "This is such a clean country," she said softly. "Too bad the people living out here cannot see how close they are to God."

They walked toward the wagons. Women nodded to Katherine. They respected her now for her work among the sick. In a short time they would treat her like dirt.

"It was a courageous thing to do," Sabin said.

She glanced sideways at him. "You did kill him, didn't you?"

"Yes."

"Why?"

"He meant to kill or maim me. This is a clean country, as you say, but it's a tough country too. Kill or be killed. The strong survive. The weak turn back or die."

"My father once said that the cowards turn back and the weaklings die."

"It's so."

"I was a fool to come on, Sabin Shay."

"Maybe it was meant to be. I'm a fatalist, Katherine."

He left her at the wagons. He found Cobb Howell sitting on his blankets eating from his meat can.

"Yuh heard the news?" Howell queried.

"*I'm* the news, Cobb."

"Yeh. I know the girl saved yer skin. But what I meant was, the telegraph line is through."

"So?"

"A patrol from the east repaired the line. Sent a message the hostiles are swarmin' like buffalo gnats east of here, headin' for the fort. Half a thousand of 'em. Real whoppin' war party. Pony tails tied up and warpaint on their rumps. Led by a sure-'nough fighter too. Standin' Bear."

It had to come, Sabin thought.

"Salt, pepper and gravel in the grease," he said.

"Amen."

"We can hold them off here."

"Mebbe." Howell spat. "A rumor down to the sanitary sinks is thet Khuyper has been talked into escortin' Bascomb west outa the danger area."

"Bascomb? How about the emigrants?"

Howell scraped his fork in the bottom of his meat can. "Damn lousy fixin's they feed yuh here," he growled. "Yuh know how Khuyper feels. I hear from the cooks he's figgerin' on takin' enough calvary to protect Bascomb. Bascomb's animiles kin haul them fine waggins of his twict as fast as the emmygrants kin go."

Sabin nodded. It was like Khuyper and Bascomb. Khuyper was a small edition of God at Fort Bowen.

CHAPTER TWENTY-THREE

Once Frank Khuyper made up his mind, with pressure from Clay Bascomb, he got into action at once. He chose the best horses and the best shots amongst the men for his escort company. Fifty men were to go along with Lieutenants Teale, Carlson and Burgeen, the best officers in his command.

Command of Fort Bowen fell to bumbling Captain Seb Horton. He was an expert in Army paperwork but in nothing else.

Angry talk bubbled and boiled in the emigrant camp. Khuyper refused to take them along. Sam Nelson tried to have a message sent to Fort Laramie concerning the matter, but the line had gone dead again. Fort Bowen had but half a hundred men fit for duty and most of them were infantry. Khuyper lined up his command at dusk. Sabin saw Marianne Bascomb helped into her sumptuous Dearborn. The story was that she was ill, but Sabin knew she was hallseas over with vermouth and fear. Sabin started as he saw a slim woman come from the emigrant camp carrying a carpetbag. It was Katherine Williams.

Sabin stopped her. "You're not going with them?"

"Yes. I'm going, Sabin."

"But why?" he asked desperately.

"There is no work for me here. Colonel Bascomb offered to double my wages if I went along to help Marianne. She's ill."

"Drunk," he said.

"Judge not, lest ye be judged, Sabin Shay."

"For God's sake, woman! Your chances of surviving out there are no better than they are here. Possibly worse."

"My reputation *has* suffered here. I want to go on to Oregon."

"I thought you hated their souls."

"I did once. It doesn't matter now."

"Is there no way I can make you see the light?"

Her clear eyes held his. "There may be."

"What is it?"

She looked away. "You must know that yourself."

Sabin shoved back his forage cap. "You've got me licked," he said.

"Shay!" roared a sergeant. "Shay! Dammit! Where are you?"

Sabin turned. "Good-bye Katherine," he said quietly.

She nodded and walked toward the Dearborn. A teamster handed her up into the coach. She slammed the door shut and let down the canvas blind.

Sabin stood there watching the train pull out. The shadowy wagons and troopers disappeared into the purple darkness. In time there was nothing left to mark their passing but a smell of bitter dust in the night air.

Sam Nelson had called a council of his men. They demanded an escort from bumbling Seb Horton. Horton was flustered. This went beyond precise paperwork. It called for the judgment of a uniformed Solomon and Horton was far from being that. He flatly refused the use of any troops, claiming, quite rightly, that he could not afford to lose any men at all.

Horton did send out scouts at dawn. They returned at noon with a report that the immediate hills were empty of hostiles, but that they had seen much dust to the west, in a great valley beyond the hills. Khuyper had served one good purpose in some minds; he had drawn the hostiles after him.

Nelson saw his chance. He marshaled his wagons in the late afternoon. Half a dozen of the worst ones had been stripped to furnish parts and ironwork for better vehicles.

Their poorest horses and mules were slaughtered for extra meat. Horton grudgingly allowed Nelson the use of an extra supply of trade rifles which had been stored in the little post and overlooked by the raiders.

Sabin spoke with Nelson before he left. "You're sticking your neck out, Sam."

Nelson shifted his chew. "I'm leadin' these people to Oregon. Sojers or no sojers. Might be that Khuyper has led the hostiles off."

"There's enough of them to go around," Sabin said.

"Hellfire. I fit Injuns afore yuh was outa diapers!"

"You'll lose your hair, Sam."

Nelson snorted. "I ain't kissin' Horton's fat rump for no favors. We got extry rifles now. Most of the wimmen kin load and shoot. I'll get through!" He stamped off.

The emigrants pulled out at dusk, as Khuyper had. A line of emigrant outriders surrounded the wagons, but it was pitifully thin. Many of them were boys. They rode as if they had learned to ride on plowhorses. If the hostiles, the finest light cavalry in the world, swept down on them, they wouldn't have a chance.

Sabin found Cobb Howell, Charlie Kester and George Fletcher in his tent when he returned.

"Meeting," Kester said. "Kinston Forbes is on guard duty."

Sabin dropped on his blankets and accepted a cigar from Fletcher.

"This is our chance," Kester said. "We can pull out of here before Horton knows a thing. The hostiles will be after those wagons like trout after grasshoppers. What do you say, Cap'n Shay?"

"I'm thinking of those women and kids out there," Sabin said.

"Yankee squaws and Yankee kids," Fletcher said.

"Americans," Sabin said

"Listen to him!" Fletcher jeered.

"Shut up!" Kester said.

Sabin chewed at the dry cigar. "Supposing I talk Horton into letting us go after the emigrants? He has no damned use for Galvanized Yankees."

"Fat chance," Cobb Howell said.

"If we make a break we lose men. We haven't enough as it is to break through the Sioux. I can grease the way if I can talk him into ordering us out."

Fletcher rubbed his jaw. "He's stupid, but he ain't *that* stupid."

"You're an expert on stupidity," Kester said dryly. "Go ahead, Cap'n Shay. You've been using your *cabeza* while we've been milling around."

Sabin went into headquarters. Horton was presiding behind Khuyper's old desk. He drummed on it with fat fingers. "What's your angle, Shay?" he asked suspiciously.

"Khuyper may be cut off. That's *his* responsibility. But those emigrants were *your* responsibility. If Nelson gets wiped out, the department commander will place the blame squarely on your shoulders, sir."

Horton was badly shaken. Sweat dewed his fat face. "I'm up for promotion," he said as though to himself.

Sabin timed his next words. He knew Horton secretly feared the lean Texans, and there were too many of them left at the little post to give him much peace of mind. "The Galvanized Yankees are trained Indian fighters, sir. You could send us to help Nelson."

Horton reacted as if Sabin had read his mind. "Do you take me for a fool?" he shouted. "Get out of here!"

Sabin saluted and walked outside. Seb Horton paced back and forth. He had never trusted those hard-eyed Texas bastards. Shay had been right when he had said Nelson was the post commander's responsibility, and that placed the blame for any misfortune squarely on the shoulders of Sebastian Horton.

Sabin paused fifty yards away from headquarters in sight of the front door. He didn't have long to wait. Horton's plump figure showed in the doorway.

"Shay!" he yelled. "Round up Mister Degnan and Mister Kretch along with Sergeant Schmidt! Get them here on the double!"

Sebastian Horton had clutched at a straw. Once Sabin's idea had made itself secure in his mind, he had adopted it as his own. First Lieutenant James Degnan, an infantryman whose chief claim to military fame was the fact he had been the best poker player at Fort Laramie, was to be in charge of the 'Flying relief column' as Horton fatuously termed the little force. Second Lieutenant August Kretch was in charge of the cavalry. He had never heard a shot fired in anger within half a mile of himself.

Horton assigned two escort wagons to carry the dozen infantrymen he had allowed Degnan. There wasn't any doubt in the Texans' minds as to why he was sending them along. It was Sergeant Manfred Schmidt who worried Sabin the most. His pale blue eyes kept Sabin and his grinning Texans under constant inspection. Sabin knew damned well that Schmidt would fight them alone if he had to, to keep them under the colors of his adopted country.

Hamish Hume leaned against the corral wall to watch Sabin place his cantle and pommel packs on his bay. "So you're on your way West?" he asked quietly.

Sabin nodded.

"There is something going on here I do not like," Hamish Hume said. "There is a lot of land out there."

"I've been there, Hamish."

"I'd like to go along."

"Saddle a horse."

"It isn't as easy as all that. There's plenty of responsibility for me here. Thank God I sent ten men back on duty in the last two days."

"The post is safe enough. The hostiles won't buck up against walk-a-heaps firing rifles from a rest, and behind stout walls. They respect that type of defense."

"But how about you? Those officers are a poor lot."

Sabin leaned back against his saddle. "My men can take care of themselves out there."

"This is good-bye then."

"I'm not dead yet."

"No," Hamish Hume said. "But dead or alive, I am not sure I will see you again."

Sabin grinned. "We'll see each other again, Hamish. It's in the cards."

"Perhaps." Hume gripped Sabin's shoulder. "You must act before you think. I wish it were otherwise. You're a young man, Sabin. A man with great capabilities and a fine future, if you can find yourself. Good-bye, my friend." The surgeon walked off into the shadows.

A lonely feeling crept over Sabin as he led his bay to where the detail was lining up.

Horton bustled out of his office. "Now, Degnan and Kretch, you must be wary. Use discretion. Remember those emigrants are depending on you."

Kretch looked as though King Arthur had just invited him to sit at the Round Table. Degnan swung up on his horse.

"Mount! Fours Right! Walk Ho!"

They filed down the fort road and turned left on the river road. In a few moments they were out of sight. Horton turned to his officers. "Corral all stock. Double the guards. Shutter the windows. Place combustibles in all outbuildings ready to fire them in case of attack."

Lieutenant Cope saluted. Lieutenant Rogers grinned. "How about a little game tonight, boys?" he asked.

Horton drew himself up to his full five feet seven inches. "Sir!" he barked. "I am in full charge of a military post of the

United States Government! There will be no laxity in discipline here! No frivolity! To your posts!" He bustled into his office.

"My God," Rogers said.

Cope smiled at him. "Funny thing, Norton. The fat little bastard *means* it too. God help us all."

CHAPTER TWENTY-FOUR

The sun was just tipping the hills when Sabin and Cobb Howell returned to the little column. "Sir," Sabin said to Lieutenant Degnan, "there are hostiles between the Bascomb train and the emigrant train. They seem more interested in the Bascomb train."

Degnan bit his lip. "They're after Khuyper then."

"I think so, sir."

"How many of them?"

"It's hard to say, Mister Degnan. We saw about fifty, but there must be many more of them in hiding."

Degnan was more worried about getting caught than he was of helping the emigrants. "Damn Khuyper!" he snapped. "With our combined commands, and both trains together, we might have had a better chance."

"It's too late now," Sabin said.

Degnan nodded. "We'll rest here. No fires. We'll go on in three hours."

But it was closer to noon when they moved on through cut-up land, crossed by shallow streams and broken by low hill masses. The men were nervous, constantly shifting in their saddles to scan the brooding hills. At dusk they reached a low, Hat-topped hill. They bivouacked off the skyline and again ate cold rations. Sabin, Howell and

Kinston Forbes went out on a scout. They could see no lights in the great valley, but the emigrants couldn't be far ahead. Nelson must have been pushing them to overtake Bascomb's outfit.

Forbes shifted his chew and spat. "This is our chance," he said quietly.

Sabin turned. "The wagons aren't safe yet."

"To hell with 'em."

"Damn you, Forbes. You haven't got the sense God gave a louse!"

"Watch what yuh say, Shay."

Howell kneed his bay in between them. "Cut it," he said.

Forbes thrust out his chin. "He's been agin us ever since he got tied up with that Williams filly. We're out far enough now to make our break."

"We wait!" Sabin snapped.

Forbes spurred his horse close to Sabin. His heavy carbine rose and fell. Sabin slid from the saddle and lay still.

"Kinston!" Howell roared. "What for did yuh do thet?"

"Listen," Forbes said coldly. "We're pullin' out. You go back and get the boys. Yuh can work it out."

"What about Cap'n Shay?"

Forbes grinned. "He's goin' with us. Conscious or unconscious. Now git the boys. We can be miles on the way by dawn. Jump up some dust, amigo. *Vamonos!*"

There was a faint suggestion of the false dawn in the sky when Cobb Howell and the Galvanized Yankees jingled up through the darkness. They brought a prisoner with them, lashed and gagged atop a rangy bay. Sabin squinted, trying to identify the captive. His head ached as though he had been on a tequila bust.

"For God's sake!" Forbes yelled. "What for did yuh bring Schmidt along?"

Howell slid from his saddle and eased his crotch. "It was either bring him or kill him."

Charlie Kester walked over to Sabin. "It was easy. There was only three beetle-crushers on guard. Cobb Indians up on them, buffaloes them, and then gets the boys together. Degnan and Kretch was asleep. Only Schmidt gets wise. We had to take him along."

Sabin fingered the knot on his head. "Well, you've got everything the way you all wanted it."

"Yuh sound riled," Jesse Tinsley said.

"I am. Those emigrants might need us."

"They didn't even know we was out here," Fletcher said.

"They know the hostiles are," Sabin said quietly.

"Let's move out," Kester said.

"Where to?" Jerry LaValle asked.

Without bothering to answer, Kester took Sabin's weapons from Forbes and handed them to Sabin. "Lead out, sir."

Sabin holstered his Colt and gripped his carbine. "I'll go along. I haven't any choice. But you bastards can do your own commanding. I'm no longer your officer."

Kester said, "This is what you wanted, back at Fort MacNaughton, Cap'n Shay. We're free now. We've got plenty grub and good horses. We pinched three mules and loaded them with supplies."

"I *said* he was riled," Tinsley said.

Sabin swung up on his horse and kneed it close to Schmidt. He took the gag from the non-com's mouth. "Gott verdamnt!" Schmidt roared.

Sabin cut loose the sergeant's wrist bonds. *"Vamonos,"* he said.

Schmidt rubbed his wrists. "No. I go along. I gedt my chance. I arrest you all yedt."

"Go to hell, you Dutch bastard," Fletcher said.

"Cherman I am! I go along!"

Forbes raised his carbine. "Git!"

Sabin drew his Colt and twirled the cylinder. "The first man who harms him gets it in the belly," he said coldly.

Howell shrugged. "Let's pull foot. Let him go."

They rode west, passing the non-com. But Schmidt was a man with a one-track mind. He rode on a hundred yards behind the pack mules, unarmed and alone, but determined that he'd bring those men back to the fold. In his book they were United States Cavalrymen, and by God, Manfred Schmidt was going to bring them back if he had to dog them clear to Oregon.

CHAPTER TWENTY-FIVE

The heat covered the deep draw with a hot blanket. The horses stood with bowed heads near the water hole. The men dozed on the ground with forage caps tilted over their eyes.

Sabin lay at the lip of the draw, studying a movement across the valley through the fieldglasses Howell had stolen from Degnan. "It's them all right, Cobb," he said over his shoulder. "Dog Soldiers. Crazy Dogs. Strong-hearts. Massing behind that hill. I swear I saw Standing Bear talking big out in front of them."

Kester took the glasses. "The emigrants are still at the crick. You think the hostiles are after them?"

"Uh-uh. Not now. Nelson is in his defensive circle."

"Where in hell is Khuyper?"

"On the far side of that rocky hill, I'd say."

"The hostiles are after him then?"

"Keno."

"What do we do?" Howell asked.

"Sit tight," Sabin said.

Manfred Schmidt sat on a rock beyond the waterhole. Howell grinned. "Bullhead, ain't he?"

"You have to admire him," Sabin said.

Kester wiped his sweaty face. "You want to take a closer look at the war party?"

"Might as well. I sure as hell can't sleep with all this going on."

They rode west, keeping behind the line of hills. A half a mile from the hill they saw the Bascomb train. The wagons had been formed into an irregular square. The sun glinted on metal. A line of cavalrymen had formed in front of the wagons. A thin line of warriors faced them from the west. Sabin could see a mass of warriors formed in a draw to the north, unseen by the troopers because of a slanting ridge.

"That Khuyper," Kester said. "What's he planning to do?"

Sabin wet cracked lips. "He's going to charge them. The fool!"

The troopers moved out at a walk, stepped up to a trot, and then suddenly broke into a fast run. The wind tore the brazen notes of the Charge into ragged shreds. The thin line of hostiles parted. They fired from the far side of their ponies. The troopers drew up, reformed, then charged back toward the wagons. The hostiles scattered again, winding the big cavalry horses.

The thin line drew off to one side and waited. Khuyper led his sweating men on again. They went up the rise, hell-for-leather, pistols at the ready and sabers flashing in the sun. Up, up and over the rise after the retreating bucks. Then the main body of hostiles moved, slowly at first, and then with a massed charge that struck the troopers like a load of buckshot at close range. Dust veiled the clash. Pistols popped like grease in a gigantic skillet. Then Sioux, Cheyenne and Arapahoe rifles roared.

The troopers shredded down the bloody slope, riding wildly, looking back over their shoulders with white faces. A third of them were gone. Warriors cut in to snap up stragglers. Then a thin sickle of racing brown horsemen shot in between the retreating troopers and the wagons. The scattered troopers pelted over a rise to the east of the wagons and looked back to see a great wheel of warriors between them and the wagons, beginning the slow circling attack which would tighten and tighten until the Cossacks of the Plains would be firing at pointblank range into the wagons.

Sabin groaned. Khuyper had done the one thing he should never have done. He had allowed his force to be bloodied and then cut off from the wagons. Sabin stood up.

"What the hell's the matter with you?" Kester said. "Get down!"

Sabin gripped the reins of his bay. "Go on back," he said.

"Where yuh think you're goin'?" Howell asked.

Sabin jerked a thumb toward the surrounded wagons. Rifle flames dotted the thick dust. Sabin swung up and spurred the bay down into the draw which led toward the fight.

"A strange man," Cobb said as he shifted his chew. "I don't hardly know him no more."

Kester snorted. "You dumb bastard. Don't you know what's the matter with him?"

"Can't say as I do right now."

"It's that girl."

"Sure. Sure. I know thet. But he ain't about to give her much help going down there alone."

Kester rubbed his jaw and looked back toward the district draw where the Galvanized Yankees waited for darkness. "Yeh," he said quietly. "Let's get back to the boys. I got some talking to do."

Sabin picketed the bay in a draw. He bellied up and hid out in a clump of brush. Some of the hostiles weren't more than two hundred yards from him. They had drawn off from the wagons for a breather. Reeking scalps hung from bloody lances. They had scattered the Mila Hanska with little loss to themselves. The people in the wagons were soft for the killing.

Sabin studied the terrain with his glasses. Here and there he spotted the lone body of a scalped trooper. Sabin estimated Khuyper's losses at about fifty percent. The rest of his demorialized men were scattered through the broken country to the south. Sabin lowered his glasses and rested his head on his forearms. He had never felt so alone in his whole life. There was no chance to break into the circle of warriors and get her out of the wagons. He had thought of starting a fire in the grass, but it wasn't dry enough to sustain a real covering fire. That left one alternative. Get close to the wagons, look for Katherine, and kill her before those hot greasy hands touched her body.

The warriors began a slow rifle fire against the wagon defenders. They wriggled through the grass and rocks, firing and then moving on to a new position. Sabin raised his glasses again. The fine German lens picked out the broad face of Standing Bear. The chief was squatting with a group of veteran warriors. Sabin fingered his Sharps. The range wasn't impossible, but killing Standing Bear would not stop the attack, and it sure as hell would stop Sabin Shay.

Minutes ticked past. A steady leaden rain of fire thudded against the Bascomb wagons. There were about twenty-five men in the smoky square—and two women.

Sabin sensed, rather than saw, the movement behind him. He turned slowly, raising himself up on one elbow. They were all there, sitting their sweating horses. Every living Texan from Sabin's old company, looking up at him with expressionless faces. Charlie Kester kneed his horse toward the bottom of the slope. "You said you weren't our officer, no more, Cap'n Shay, but you can't get rid of us as easy as all that."

Sabin slid down the slope. "Get these men out of here! The draws and ridges are crawling with Sioux and Cheyennes!"

Cobb Howell grunted. "My maw alius said I'd come to no good end. Helpin' Yankees! Jeeesus!"

Tim Casey shoved back his forage cap. "We was figgerin' on goin' west."

"We are," Kester said. "Right through a passel of Sioux."

Warner Giddings grinned at Sabin. He tapped his shining trumpet. "I ain't had much chance to use this horn."

"Makes a man sick," Forbes snapped. "Here we got a chance to cut stick and we got to fool around the business end of a war party."

"Sit here on yore butt then," Giddings said.

Jesse Tinsley shifted his chew and spat juicily. "I got an eye on one of them Puke fillies back there in Nelson's waggins. 'Pears to me, if'n these hostiles take Bascomb's waggins, there ain't goin' to be anything to stop them from takin' Nelson's waggins but we 'uns."

Sabin glowered balefully at them. "Get out of here," he said. "We haven't got a chance against these red bastards."

"Listen to him," Cobb Howell said.

"Lost his guts," Gus Feichter said.

Jesse Tinsley rode forward and handed Sabin a lance. "Picked this up on the trail," he said. "Might make a good guidon staff if'n a man *had* a guidon."

Sabin stared at the expressionless dusty faces. "You damned romantic fools," he said. He reached inside his shirt and took out the stained and torn guidon of Shay's Independent Frontier Company. He fastened it to the Indian lance. The wind snapped it out.

"Never thought I'd see thet again," Todd Shatter said.

"I'd admire to carry it, suh," Chase Corby said.

Sabin handed him the guidon.

"I aim to get those women out of that wagon ring," he said. "Anyone who wants to leave can do so."

No one moved. *"Bueno!"* Sabin said.

"This is all very well," Kinston Forbes drawled, "but I ain't about to go chargin' out there whistlin' The Yellow Rose Of Texas whilst them hostiles pepper hell outa me. They's too many of 'em, Cap'n Shay, and yuh damn well know it—*suh!"*

The steady sound of the rifle fire came to them fitfully as the vagrant wind shifted. Sabin wiped the sweat from his face. "If we wait much longer, Kinston," he said, "there won't be any reason for us to go out there at all." They looked at each other and then away, each man trying to hide the sudden fear in his eyes.

Sabin jerked his head. "Cobb Howell! Take a *pasear* to the west, keeping well to the north. See how far back the hostiles are."

Cobb saluted and spurred his horse up the draw. Sabin nodded at Kester. "Keep the company here. If the hostiles come this way, drop back under cover, but don't put up a fight unless there's no chance of breaking away."

"Yes, sir."

"I'm scouting south. Somewhere around here there's a place where we can break through."

Sabin led his horse south along the draw. Now and then he bellied up to the top of the draw. They were still soft-ening the defense of the wagon ring. Now and then a wisp of smoke would snake through the grass and hover until the distant sound of the shot caught up with it. A white man lay in front of the wagons clutching a rifle. Sabin knew he was dead.

A mile from the waiting company he came upon a dun horse grazing in the draw. The dun's saddle had slid to one side and blood showed on its flank. Beyond the horse a trooper lay on his back, both bloody hands gripping an arrow shaft which protruded from his right side.

His mouth and eyes were open. Flies buzzed lazily about them and his reddened hands.

Sabin ground-reined the bay and padded up the draw. He began to belly up the slope. Then he felt, rather than heard, the movement behind him. He turned, sweeping back the hammer of his Sharps. It was too late. Frank Khuyper stood there with a cocked Colt in his hand, the muzzle centered on Sabin's belly. Sabin lowered the Sharps very slowly. Khuyper looked wild. Six troopers, dusty and sweaty and fear-ridden, were huddling in the bottom of the draw. Sabin stood up and raised his hands.

"Where's your commanding officer?" Khuyper snapped.

Sabin wet his lips. The hand holding that pistol was shaking from suppressed rage. "I have none, sir," he lied.

"Deserted again, eh?"

Sabin glanced at the men. Khuyper had led them into a trap from which only fantastic luck had saved them. Some of them were looking up the draw, telegraphing their wish to get the hell out of there in a hurry and to hell with the hindmost.

"I was separated from Mr. Degnan's command," Sabin said.

"You're alone then?" Khuyper asked craftily.

"Yes."

"You lie, you Rebel bastard!" Khuyper said. He thrust out his free hand. "There's a unit up this draw. Who's in command?"

"I don't know, sir."

Khuyper raised his head. "Then we'll damned well find out, won't we?"

Sabin shrugged. He walked to his horse and gripped the reins. Khuyper walked up behind him. "Take us to them," he said. "Under cover. You understand." He shoved the pistol muzzle against Sabin's back.

They slogged up the draw. Yellow dust wreathed up about them. Sabin glanced back. He could have sworn there was one less trooper behind the officer.

Half a mile from the waiting Galvanized Yankees, Khuyper came to a halt. "Corporal Kostby!" he called.

The non-com came forward.

"Keep the men here. Shay! Up that rise!"

Sabin walked up the rise, hearing Khuyper puffing behind him. At the top of the rise they dropped. They could see one of Sabin's men on guard. The rest of them were in the draw. Wind had wrapped the guidon about the lance pole.

Khuyper nodded. "There's enough," he said to himself.

"Sir?"

"Enough, combining my men and those men there, to take the Sioux in the flank."

Sabin glanced down into the draw. Not one of the troopers was left. Nothing was left but a wraith of yellow dust to mark their passage.

Khuyper talked on. "I hurt them with that charge. I bled them. One more and I'll have them."

Sabin eyed him. There was something radically wrong with the man. Sabin eased down the slope a little. Khuyper moved swiftly. There was nothing wrong with his reflexes. The Colt leveled on Sabin's head. "Don't move, damn you! You're going along. We're all going down there again."

"You'll never come back," Sabin said.

"*I'll* get back."

Sabin tried to shift so as to reach his Colt but Khuyper's eyes drilled into his. Then the officer stood up. "What guidon is that?" he asked.

The stained guidon had unwrapped itself from the lance pole. Sabin got up on his knees. "Take a good look, Khuyper," he said quietly.

"It isn't—isn't a regulation Army guidon."

Sabin planted his left foot on the ground and tensed himself.

Khuyper paled beneath the dust on his face. "I've seen it before."

"You have."

"Where?"

Sabin stood up. "At the Badwater," he said.

Khuyper stepped back a little. He glanced uncertainly toward the guidon. "Corporal Kostby!" he called out of the side of his mouth.

Sabin shifted a little.

"Corporal Kostby!" Khuyper yelled down the slope.

Sabin's left hooked home to Khuyper's jaw at the same time his right hand reached across to grip the gun wrist. Khuyper staggered back, but he held his grip on the Colt. He snapped a shot just as Sabin drove in, arms outheld, and missed. Sabin butted Khuyper back with a shoulder while he gripped the cursing officer about the waist.

They went down the slope sideways, rolling over and over in a welter of dust and loose stones. Khuyper lost his Colt. He clawed at Sabin's holstered sidearm. Sabin kneed him in the guts. They broke apart.

Khuyper wiped the blood from his mouth. He bent his shoulders a little and went into a slight crouch. His eyes narrowed as Sabin circled to his right. Then the officer charged. Sabin met the attack with a left that straightened Khuyper out. He felt the jolt of the blow and then crossed with a right which sprawled Khuyper sideways, staggering for balance. He didn't make it. Down he went, blood dripping from his nose and mouth to stain the yellow dust.

Sabin rubbed big hands on his thighs. "Get up, sir," he said. "I'm not through yet."

Khuyper groaned a little. He got on his hands and knees. Then he moved with surprising swiftness, ripping a double-barreled derringer from inside his shell jacket. It puffed flame and smoke, sending a slug inches above Sabin's head. Sabin jumped sideways, closed in, kicked the derringer away from the yelling officer, and then went down heavily as his foot turned on a stone.

Khuyper was on him like a cat. His strong fingers dug into Sabin's throat. Sabin hammered at Khuyper's ribs but the officer hung on like grim death. The sky whirled. Sabin saw nothing but the two icy blue eyes fixed with the fascination of death for Sabin Shay. Sabin got a knee up into Khuyper's crotch and drove it up in desperate strength. The grip weakened. Again and again Sabin kneed the cursing man until Khuyper released his hold and rolled away, clutching his groin. Sabin righted himself, laboring painfully to draw breath.

Khuyper pawed for the derringer in the dusty grass. Sabin staggered toward him and kicked savagely again and again until Khuyper was down, his chest rising and falling in his rage and fatigue. Sabin gripped him by the back of his sweat-soaked jacket and jerked hard. Khuyper lurched to his feet. He threw up his arms as Sabin smashed blow after blow at his face until once again he was on his back staring up into the face of the man he had sworn to kill.

"Get up," Sabin said. "You wanted to know what guidon that was. I'll tell you. That's the guidon of Shay's Independent Frontier Company."

Khuyper heaved himself up on his feet. He closed with Sabin. His knee came up into Sabin's groin. He jerked Sabin's Colt from its holster and cocked it. Sabin smashed the Colt upward with his left forearm and sank a right deep into Khuyper's belly. The Colt roared inches from his head, half-blinding him. Then he tore the weapon away from Khuyper. He cast it aside. Khuyper turned to run. Sabin gripped his shoulder and spun him about. Then he really went to work. He cut the mouth and smashed the fine nose. Teeth broke beneath his battering fists. Khuyper turned to run again. Sabin reached down for the Colt but something held him from shooting.

Khuyper sprinted up the draw. Then the lone horseman blocked his way. A slim Cheyenne with a drawn bow. Khuyper screamed once. The shaft struck him in the forehead and jutted there, quivering as if it were alive and striving to burrow deeper. Sabin jumped for the horse he had left ground-reined fifty feet away, with his Sharps slung to the saddle.

The Cheyenne leaped his paint horse across the dead officer, nocking another broadhead arrow to his bowstring as he did so. Sabin snapped a shot from his Colt. The Cheyenne drew back the bowstring.

A shot cracked flatly from the lip of the draw. The Cheyenne slid from his racing mount and hit the ground fifty feet from Sabin. Sabin stopped and looked up. Manfred Schmidt sat his horse, with a smoking carbine in his big hands.

"Thanks," Sabin said.

Schmidt slid his mount down the slope. He nodded at Khuyper. "Deadt?"

"Yes."

The blue eyes held Sabin's. "I did nodt see anything else," he said quietly.

Sabin flicked blood from his abraded hands. "You know damned well who killed him, Schmidt."

"Yes. Howell iss back. The poys are gedding restless."

Sabin swung up on his horse and spurred it along the draw. Schmidt followed him.

CHAPTER TWENTY-SIX

Cobb Howell squatted in the shade of his lathered horse. He inspected Sabin curiously as he slid from his horse. "Yuh been fightin' them hostiles alone?" he asked.

"I met an old friend of ours. Captain Khuyper."

Every man stood up and reached for carbine or pistol. Sabin shook his head. "He's dead. Forget about him. We've got work to do."

Howell stood up. "They's two places I found," he said. "Look here." He went down on one knee and traced a map in the dust with his forefinger. "They's two ridges north of here. Runnin' east-west generally. South of the ridges is where the waggins is penned. The hostiles is massing in the valley between the ridges. Howsomever, at this end of the valley they're in, they's a place where brush grows thick over a low ridge that cuts acrost the valley. They's a place there yuh kin ride plumb into the valley where the waggins is and them hostiles cain't see yuh."

"A score of men," Kinston Forbes said.

"Ain't no use lookin' back for help," Warner Giddings said.

Sabin frowned thoughtfully. "You said there were *two* places, Cobb?"

"I did. West of the valley where the hostiles is, a man kin ride south without bein' seen. Could come in from the west down on them waggins easy enough. Might be two-three hunnerd yards from a hiding place. A long ride if'n yore bein' shot at, which is quite likely."

Sabin wet his lips. He had but a handful of men to cast on the scales of chance. They could be used just once, and that rightly, and it was up to him to choose the time and place. He had no one to lean back on; no one to consult.

The firing grew heavier over the lip of the draw. "The wagons were getting it hot and heavy, sir," Denny O'Brien called down.

"Any signs of the hostiles massing?"

"There's a lot of dust behind that north ridge."

Sabin mulled it over. "There's no use trying to make it sound as though we hold the bull by the horns," he told his men.

"What do you want us to do?" Kester asked.

"Time's awastin'," Corby said.

Sabin looked at Warner Giddings. "How's your wind?"

"Fine, suh."

"Can you work behind the Sioux and come out west of the wagons where that low ridge is?"

"*Alone*, suh?"

Sabin nodded.

Giddings' Adam's apple bobbed in his thin throat. "Yes, Cap'n Shay."

"*Bueno*. Cut north of here. Then west. Come down behind that far ridge. Watch the hostiles. When you see them top their ridge to come down on those wagons I want you to show up on that ridge and blow hell out of that trumpet. Blow the Charge or any damned thing else. But keep blowing."

"What—what do I do then, suh?"

Sabin smiled. "That will be up to you. You'll see what I mean when the time comes. *Vamonos!*"

The minutes ticked past while little Warner Giddings

rode north and then west through a country thick with Sioux.

Sabin guided his small command through the thick brush. Manfred Schmidt silently led his horse along behind the Texans. It was as Howell had said. They were in the same valley as the Sioux, for they could hear the noise of the warriors on the far side of the mass of rocks and brush which shielded them from the hostiles. Bitter dust drifted over them as hundreds of unshod hoofs churned it up.

"Wonder how the kid is?" Howell ventured.

"He's outa *this* anyways," Forbes said.

Sabin and Kester worked their way up the ridge to observe the warriors. "There's sure a slew of them," Sabin said. "Odds of ten to one, Charlie."

"Usual Texican odds," Kester boasted hollowly.

The warriors were forming on the slopes now. Sioux, Cheyenne and Arapahoe. They knew it would be a good day for them. The firing from the wagons had weakened. Wakan Tanka was smiling on the Sioux. Maheo had brought good fortune to the Cheyenne. There would be Thunder Music in the Arapahoe camp. The feathered and painted horsemen lined up under their different sub-chiefs and veteran warriors of many coups. Sabin's eyes narrowed as he saw the thick-bodied chief ride along the line of braves. There was no mistaking Standing Bear. Sabin focused his glasses on the chief while Kester shaded the lens to prevent light reflection.

Standing Bear swam hazily into view. His war bonnet rippled in the wind. He was ready for war. Lance, rifle, bow and quiver, pipe-ax, revolving pistol and scalping knife. He halted his spotted gray and began to speak, exhorting his men. Sabin wanted to try a long shot but he knew better. The time had not come.

"They're getting ready. He's talking it up," Kester said in a strained voice.

Sabin cased the glasses. "Have the horses led up below

the crest of the ridge. And for God's sake, Charlie, don't let any man be seen!"

The first sergeant slid down the ridge.

Sabin watched Standing Bear flourish his lance and ride up to the top of the ridge. There he drew rein and proudly sat his gray. The warriors massed on the ridge, a splendid, barbaric body of the finest light cavalry in the world.

Sabin went down to his horse and led him to the company rendezvous. Down in the valley the wagons stood in their defensive square. The tilts flapped in the strong wind. The wind ruffled the beard of the dead man who lay beyond the wagons.

"I hope he made it," Sabin said, looking at the ridge to the west. There was no sign of life on it.

Standing Bear kneed his horse away from his warriors and started slowly down the ridge toward the wagons.

"Now," Sabin said. "Now, Giddings—*now!*"

The warriors were following their leader. Their left flank was no more than two hundred yards from the waiting Texans.

"For God's sake," Kester husked. "Where are you, Giddings?"

The answer came as the kid showed up on the ridge.

The sun glinted from his polished trumpet as he flourished it and placed it to his lips. The warriors were at a trot now, bunching a little for the hell-for-leather charge which would take them clean through the wagon square. Then Giddings lipped into the brazen, thrilling notes of The Charge. The wind picked up the call and carried it across the valley.

Standing Bear turned his horse toward the ridge where the kid sat his bay. Behind the chief, the warriors were urging on their horses, presenting their broad flank to Sabin's men.

"Now," Sabin said.

"Sabers?" Kester asked.

"Hell no. That's Yankee stuff. Pistols."

"There's a hell of a lot of 'em down there," someone said behind Sabin.

"Just pick a redskinned sonofabitch and charge," Cobb Howell said.

Sabin did not look back. He drew his pistol and sank the steel into his bay. The big horse lifted easily into a run down the rough slope. A warrior saw them and screamed to his mates. But it was too late for a defense. These weren't the usual clumsy, slow-riding Mila Hanska, but a different breed of foemen.

Then the Texans roared into the soft unprotected flank, pistols snapping at ten and five feet, smashing flesh and bone with hot lead. Warriors and ponies went down in a bone-breaking tangle.

Sabin went through it in a wild haze of smoke and noise, dropping two warriors. The Texans struck the milling warriors like a flash flood, spilling the bucks down the slope like tenpins. The warriors milled on the slippery grass, some of them trying to get back up the ridge, others trying to get down into the valley. Some of them hammered on toward the wagons. A volley ripped into the hostiles from the wagons, driving them back. But it was a pitifully weak defense.

Three of Sabin's men had fallen in the spume of smoke and dust. Sabin drew up and slid from his saddle. "Prepare to fight on foot!" he roared above the din. "Dismount! Horse-holders in!"

The horses were led off as Standing Bear rallied some of his toughest warriors for a charge. The Texans lined the lip of a shallow hollow, thrusting their carbines forward. Somewhere beyond the ridge the notes of the trumpet soared again. Warner Giddings was putting spit into his work.

Standing Bear lifted his men into the charge with his roaring bull voice. Fifty yards from the hollow Sabin's command to fire pulled the snapper on the warriors. The massed slugs ripped the heart out of the charge. The second volley caught them trying to break away from a tangle of downed men and horses. The third volley drove into their naked greasy backs and bled them still more.

Then the warriors broke for the east side of the valley, screaming in wild frustration. The new grass was covered with writhing men and thrashing horses, while strange red growths, glistening and bright, showed on the green of the grass.

Sabin wiped his face. "Reload carbines and pistols! Kester! Get in any of our wounded!"

"What about the wounded Indians, sir?"

"You know what to do."

Kester came back to Sabin leading a stray horse. "Si Webster and Jimmy Hunter are dead," he said. "Denny O'Brien is far gone, sir."

Sabin saw a trooper binding Jerry LaValle's shoulder. One more wounded.

Manfred Schmidt looked up. "By Godt that wass fighdting! Now I know why thiss damdt war hass gone on four years yedt. Your men fighdt like berserkers."

Sabin slid his Colt into his holster. The warriors were rallying a quarter of a mile across the valley.

"Mount!" he said.

"They're licked," Corby said.

"In a hog's butt," Kester said. "This is only the beginning, sonny."

Sabin set the steel to his bay, watching the warriors out of the corner of his eye. They started forward. Standing Bear had taken a shellacking, but he was far from whipped. Sabin's bay stretched out. Chase Corby raced alongside. The guidon snapped in the wind. "They're gaining," he said.

"Thanks!" Sabin yelled. "I didn't know!"

The war cries came up from the diaphragm and shot through the mouth. Hundreds of unshod hoofs made the ground shake. Then there was a scattered ripple of fire from the hostiles. Slugs chewed into the Texans and their mounts. They sliced through the wagons' tilts and sang piercingly from wagon iron.

The Texans hung low over their horses' necks and fired across their bodies, emptying the big Colts. The fire slowed the charge and then broke it. The hostiles swept past at one hundred feet, racing to the north, as the Texans leaped their horses over the wagon tongues into the center of the defensive square.

The enclosure was a hell of bucking horses and mules. A man thrashed on the ground, digging clawed fingers into the dirt, while blood flowed from his smashed face. Men jumped away from the hoofs of rearing, excited horses.

Sabin slid from the saddle. About half a dozen men out of the score or more who had left Fort Bowen were still on their feet. Sabin looked about. Then he saw her. She scrambled over the tailgate of a wagon and ran toward him, dropping a long-barreled rifle to the ground. He scooped her up, drawing her face close to his.

"Kathy," he said. "Kathy."

"Who's in charge heah? Dammit! You men theah! Who's in charge, I say?"

Sabin put Katherine down and turned to confront the flushed imperious face of Colonel Clay Bascomb.

"I am," he said.

Bascomb drew himself up. "Where is your officer?"

Chase Corby spat at Bascomb's feet. "Yuh heard him," he said.

Kester saluted Sabin. "They're forming on the slope," he said.

Sabin kneed his lathered bay past Bascomb and looked across the valley. The warriors were stripping down, throwing aside all unnecessary gear and clothing. This time they meant to make damned sure they finished it.

"Heah they come!" Jerry LaValle yelled.

The charge wasn't meant to end in a collision, however. The warriors came on as though shot from a gigantic bow, only to part and race past the wagons, hanging on the far side of their horses. Rifles belched like the ripping of heavy cloth and then the hostiles were gone again, leaving bloody wreckage behind them.

Cobb Howell wiped the sweat from his face. "I hope thet little bastard Giddings got plumb away," he said.

Sabin looked at Charlie Kester. "What do you think?"

Kester fingered a bloody slash on his left cheek. "We either fight from the wagons or make a break for it."

"I don't like a defensive fight."

"There aren't enough of us left for a good killing, sir."

Cobb Howell stood up in his stirrups to eye the enemy. "Hellsfire! Our boys will charge hell with a cornstalk!"

"I ain't about to stay here," Chase Corby said.

"We're damned if we do and damned if we don't," Kester said.

Clay Bascomb had seen his bright new world crumble and dissolve at the edges. By God, he had always made his way in the battle of life and he wasn't licked now. "You, suh!" he snapped at Sabin. "Get those men down into the wagons. I'll take command heah."

Sabin examined him as though he had just discovered a new breed of lice. "Where's Marianne?" he asked.

Bascomb flushed. Katherine Williams pointed at the dusty Dearborn. Sabin walked over to the sumptuous vehicle and jerked open the door. He jumped sideways as a pistol poked through the doorway. It crashed, driving flame and smoke past Sabin's face. Then the pale face of Stacy Bascomb appeared. Sabin jerked the heavy pistol from the shaking hand. He pulled Stacy from the carriage. Then he peered into the carriage. She lay on the cushions with an arm across her face.

"Marianne," he said.

She did not move.

"Marianne!"

She slowly removed her arm. He looked into a face he hardly recognized. Liquor and fear had changed her into someone else. "It's Sabin Shay," she said. Then she laughed.

Sabin turned to Stacy. The young handsome face was

ravaged with fear. Stacy shakily touched his left cheek. "She's been that way ever since the Sioux attacked," he said.

Sabin gripped Stacy by the shoulder. "Get her out of there. Slap some sense into her."

Clay Bascomb pushed his way through the silent men. "I assigned my son to guard his sister," he said.

Sabin measured him coldly. "We're going to fight our way through the Sioux," he said. "It will be rough enough without anything else hindering us. She'll have to ride with the rest of us—or stay here and wait for them."

Clay Bascomb tried to stare down the big man facing him but it was no use. "Stacy, son," he said, "do what you can. Her mare is still unwounded. She can ride. She'll *have* to ride."

Stacy swallowed audibly. He looked from one to the other of the hard Texas faces and groaned. He climbed into the carriage.

"They're massing on the ridge," Charlie Kester said quietly.

Sabin walked to the wagons. "Where's your powder stores?" he asked Bascomb.

"In those two wagons. Protected by sheet iron. My own idea, suh."

"Brilliant," Sabin said dryly. He studied the terrain. He had noticed that the hostile charges had all converged upon the center wagons in the line. The sloping ground had funneled them that way. He looked behind him. Smoke was smoldering from a wagon in which a fire had been put out. "Fan up that Smoke," he said.

"You loco?" Howell said.

"Damn it, I want more smoke from that wagon! Plenty of it. A smudge!"

Some of the men fanned the blaze into life. They threw grass on it. Smoke began to drift about the square, making everything indistinct. Across the valley, the warriors pointed and whooped in delight.

"Now what?" Kester asked.

Sabin flapped the wreathing smoke away from his head. "Get the horses at the south end of the wagon square," he said. "Strip those horses down to saddles only. Have every man cut down his gear to his weapons. Everyone here must ride. If there aren't enough horses they can double up."

"You mean to pull out then?"

"Like the devil beating tanbark."

"They'll rip us to pieces out there!" yelled a teamster.

Sabin shook his head. "My men will go last. The rest of you will escort the women." He looked over his shoulder. The hostiles were still on the slope listening to the harangues of their chiefs. There wasn't much time. He walked to the powder wagons and reached in for a keg. He smashed in the head and dumped some of it on the flooring of the wagon and then ran a thick trail of it to the other wagon. He dumped the remaining powder over the tailgate. Sweat oiled his body and dripped from his face.

Everybody moved swiftly, without talking. The men of the wagon train led their mounts to the south side. A wagon was manhandled from the line. The drifting smoke hung like a pall over the square.

Kathy stood by a clean-limbed claybank. A trooper took her rifle from her and handed her a big Remington. Sabin walked to her and gazed down into the smudged oval face. "There are six rounds in that handgun," he said. "Use five on the Indians."

"I know what to do with the sixth," she said.

He bent and kissed her. "You won't need it," he said. "We'll get you out of this, Kathy."

"And what of you?"

"Every Texas trooper is issued nine lives along with his equipment. You worry about yourself."

She watched him walk away through the smoke. The butt of the big Remington sixgun was slippery with cold sweat. Suddenly, for no reason, she spoke aloud. "I've got nine lives too, Sabin Shay," she said. "I'm from Missouri."

Sabin gripped Todd Shafter by an arm. "Shafter," he said,

"you talk a lot and you were a troublemaker back on the Pease. But you've got guts."

"Thanks," Shafter said sourly.

"Go with the women. If they get cut off, you know what to do. But damn it, man, wait until the last minute. I know how you can shoot a handgun."

Shafter nodded. "I was aimin' to do it anyways," he said heavily. "I had to do it to one sister back home when the Lipans burned the old ranch. They got the other one—" Stacy Bascomb had helped his sister from the Dearborn. She swayed in his shaky grasp. He led her to her mare. She stood there resting her head against the horse. Clay Bascomb looked toward the hostiles. "It won't be long now," he said, almost as if he were thinking of something else. The old man seemed to have all the guts in the family.

The smoke had thickened as the wind had died away. The warriors sat their lathered mounts, waiting. The chiefs had stopped talking. Sabin took a lucifer-block from his pocket and walked close to the powder wagons. He glanced back over his shoulder. They were all ready.

Then the warriors kneed their paint ponies into a walk, coming down the ridge. The pace picked up, faster and faster. Sabin wet dry lips.

"Get ready!" he called.

The warriors lifted into a trot. "H'gun! H'gun! H'gun!" they shouted. This charge would finish the fight.

"Move out beyond the wagons!" Sabin ordered.

He could hear the hurried movements behind him. The hostiles were a hundred yards away. Sabin broke a match from the block and dropped the block into the first wagon. Seconds ticked past before he lit the match and touched off the block. It flashed into life, hissing angrily as the powder caught hold. Sabin turned and ran for his life.

Racing across the smoke-filled interior of the square, he saw Marianne Bascomb break away from Stacy. He made no effort to catch her. She slid from her mare and ran through the smoke, back to her once shiny Dearborn. Sabin yelled. She scrambled into the carriage.

Sabin looked at the wagons. Smoke drifted from them. The hostiles were no more than fifty feet away when a shattering crash broke from the first wagon. The big wagon folded outward like a house of cards. A wheel sailed upward as though shot from a sling. Then the powder kegs in the second wagon let go. Sabin staggered as the blast of air drove him toward his bay. He was up in the saddle when he saw the heavy wheel smash into the Dearborn. Then he raked the bay from head to rump with his spurs and shot out of the smoke as though the powder explosion itself were propelling him.

Behind him the front ranks of the hostiles had been laid flat as though by a giant scythe. Screaming, powder-burned warriors shielded their heads from the stamping hoofs of maddened ponies. Fire raced across the trampled grass. It licked up the tilts and bows of the other wagons, forming a blazing square of vehicles.

Sabin reached his racing men. "Hellsfire!" yelled Cobb Howell. "Yuh shore do things in a big way, Cap'n Shay!"

"We aren't out of the fire yet!"

There was tough fiber in the warriors of Standing Bear. A group of them had circled the flaming wagons. Now they cut in on the handful of Texans who rode between them and the civilians. The screaming warriors bunched for the smash-through. Sabin was alongside Chase Corby. He arm-signaled. The Texans turned to follow the guidon. There was a crash as Texan met warrior. The shock of horse against horse stopped forward movement and the fight broke in a circling quadrille of death. Jonas Gilpin disappeared in the smoke with an arrow jutting from an eye. Jerry LaValle got his death stroke from a pipe-ax. The fight whirled across the flats, a wild kaleidoscope of feathers, greasy bodies, flashing weapons and dusty blue uniforms.

Sabin smashed the face of a buck with a shot from his Colt. Two more went down beneath him. Then he was beyond the fight with an ax slash across his left shoulder. He saw Chase Corby go down with a slug in his belly. A squat buck raced in and snatched the guidon, shrieking in triumph as he raised it. It was Standing Bear.

Sabin closed in behind the chief. Something warned Standing Bear. He turned, couching the lance pole of the guidon and driving his pony toward Sabin. Sabin thrust out a hand to grasp the pole. Their horses met chest on, dumping both men down on the trampled grass as the fight tore past them and shredded down a slope.

Standing Bear hung onto the guidon. Sabin smashed at him with the barrel of his pistol. Then the chief recognized him. He let go of the pole and whipped out a knife. Sabin gripped the knife wrist and forced the arm up. The warrior's fingers probed for Sabin's eyes. He dropped the Colt and rammed his right fist home into the lean belly of Standing Bear. As Standing Bear doubled over, Sabin gripped him by the throat. They stood there in Graeco-Roman tableau, straining against each other. Then Standing Bear dropped the knife and twisted sideways for a hipthrow. Sabin hooked his left arm about the corded throat and drew the greasy head close. He put the pressure on until he felt the burly chief weaken. Standing Bear sagged to the ground, pawing for his knife. Sabin threw him aside, let him snatch up the knife, and then kicked him in the face.

Sabin picked up his Colt and fired from five-foot range. Standing Bear doubled over and lay still.

Sabin looked about. The warriors were kicking up dust to the west. A handful of Texans were left. Manfred Schmidt rode toward Sabin and saluted him with a reddened blade. "Vat are your orders?" he asked.

"Got none," Sabin said.

"It wass a goodt fighdt."

"I'm sick of killing."

Cobb Howell spat. "There ain't enough of us Texans left for a good killin'" he said.

Charlie Kester slid from his horse. "The old colonel is

dead," he said. "Stacy is gone. Took off over the hill. You want us to get him?"

Sabin shook his head.

"The girl is safe," Kester said.

Sabin wiped his face. He handed the guidon to Howell and walked up the slope to her. Katherine ran to meet him. She placed her head against his chest and clung to him as though she'd never let him go again.

CHAPTER TWENTY-SEVEN

S am Nelson's wagon train was ready to roll west. The long common grave on the slope had been dug and filled with the bodies of the dead. The emigrants and the soldiers were gathering for the service. A trooper squatted patiently at his key beside the silent telegraph line. Sabin stood beside Katherine Williams looking down at the shrouded bodies of his men, wondering what had happened to little Warner Giddings. The poor kid had vanished into the hills as though spirited from earth.

"Get on with the service," Sabin told Blalock Lott.

The ageless Biblical words cut across the fresh wind and then there was silence. Blalock crumbled earth into the grave.

And then, suddenly, the telegrapher gave a shout. The people turned to stare at him. His key was clacking briskly. He yelled and stood up, cupping his hands about his mouth.

"Lee surrendered at Appomattox Courthouse six days ago! The war is over!"

There was an emptiness in Sabin Shay. Todd Shatter simply walked away down the hill. He had lost two brothers at Perryville.

"It is the will of Almighty God," said Blalock Lott.

Sabin caught the guidon as the wind blew over the staff.

He ripped the tattered guidon free from the staff and dropped it into the grave. His men were down there, together as they had been since the days on the Pease.

Lieutenant Degnan hurried down the slope to the telegrapher. He checked the message he had received. Then he came up the slope again. He said, "Shay, my orders are to escort the emigrant train to Utah."

"Why tell me, sir?"

Degnan grinned. "This may sound silly, but I'd like to have you and your men come along."

"Well I'll be damned," Sabin said, and remembered to smile back at Degnan. "I'll see how the men feel about it, sir."

The grave was filled. The wagons rolled west. Cobb Howell whistled Sweet Evalina as he cantered past Sabin to take up his position as lead scout. The small escort of troopers had spread out to cover the wagon flanks. In the dust you couldn't tell a Yankee from a Galvanized Yankee.

Sabin squinted through the dust. A familiar figure was driving a wagon at the head of the column. Sabin spurred forward and drew his bay to a walk beside the wagon. He stepped from the bay and sat down beside her, taking the reins from her brown hands. She smiled and leaned against him. Somewhere a prairie lark bugled down the fresh wind.

"It's all over," Sabin said.

"Yes," Kathy Williams said. Dreamily she added, "I've asked Blalock Lott if he can still perform the marriage ceremony."

"He can," Sabin assured her. "I asked him twenty minutes before you did."

TAKE A LOOK AT JUDAS GUN AND HANGIN' PARDS

Two Full Length Western Novels

BLOODTHIRSTY GUNSLINGERS GET THEIR REVENGE IN THIS CLASSIC WESTERN DOUBLE.

Judas Gun

The prison at Yuma couldn't hold him... The blistering desert couldn't kill him... The county's toughest guns couldn't stop him - as he hunted down his brother's killers.

Hangin' Pards

It sure seemed that Holt Deaver had just about the worst luck of anyone in the West. At the age of twenty-five he was dead broke and on the run. He had shot one man in Chloride and had killed two others in less than a week.

So when an old, whiskery, murdering no-good offered Holt ten thousand bucks to side him, it looked like a good thing. It was at least a chance for the best of everything if the gamble paid off—horses, food, liquor and women. It also meant a partnership with a wanted outlaw and a self-conviction for Holt.

But the thought of that last chance drove Holt on. Little did he reckon that even if the old rascal kept his word, it wouldn't do much good with six other bloodthirsty gunslingers on his trail.

"The joy of reading Shirreffs' work is in his mastery of pacing and his tough, gritty prose." – **James Reasoner, author of Outlaw Ranger**

COMING FEBRUARY 2022

ABOUT THE AUTHOR

Gordon D. Shirreffs published more than 80 western novels, 20 of them juvenile books, and John Wayne bought his book title, Rio Bravo, during the 1950s for a motion picture, which Shirreffs said constituted *"the most money I ever earned for two words."* Four of his novels were adapted to motion pictures, and he wrote a Playhouse 90 and the Boots and Saddles TV series pilot in 1957.

A former pulp magazine writer, he survived the transition to western novels without undue trauma, earning the admiration of his peers along the way. The novelist saw life a bit cynically from the edge of his funny bone and described himself as looking like a slightly parboiled owl. Despite his multifarious quips, he was dead serious about the writing profession.

Gordon D. Shirreffs was the 1995 recipient of the Owen Wister Award, given by the Western Writers of America for "a living individual who has made an outstanding contribution to the American West."

He passed in 1996.

Printed in the USA
CPSIA information can be obtained
at www.ICGtesting.com
LVHW030152041223
765612LV00021B/752

9 781639 770687